A
Recursive
Nature

A
Recursive
Nature

Denise Conca

Jouissance is the driving elan of queer sex culture, and yet it is precisely that element of queer sex which still cannot be locked up in an industry, sold as a commodity or scheduled at some mass commercialized ritual. While each element of the sex industry attempts to resolve some fundamental lack and to integrate one's desires into a coherent subjective experience, jouissance is specifically that element of sexual desire which makes such a union impossible. Jouissance is the unnameable desire that one hopelessly attempts to summarize before giving one's body to another: "I want to be negated."

—baedan "joural of queer nihilism"

When a subject is highly controversial—and any question about sex is that—one cannot hope to tell the truth. One can only show how one came to hold whatever opinion one does hold. One can only give one's audience the chance of drawing their own conclusions as they observe the limitations, the prejudices, the idiosyncrasies of the speaker.

—*Virginia Woolf,* "A Room of One's Own"

PART ONE

September 16, 2016:

Dear Bobby:

Expressing myself freely is impossible when the result is so much regret: typing for the pleasure of pleasure.

Let this letter start where the last letter ended: at the moment of regret.

I'm trying to do something here. I have an idea I've been trying to express, trying to convey experience, an experience. Even now, it's what I'm doing: trying.

September 29, 2016:

Dear Bobby:

This letter has stayed in the typewriter, on the platen roll, for the past two weeks. I've wanted to get back to this, these ideas, the experience of the letter to you, over & over. It's been near impossible. This week I am in Oakland, at a house-sit, taken to get more space and to try and spread out a bit, the papers and files and folders, all of which, well, a portion of which, I've carried here with me, the idea lingering that I can't go forward without the return of the past, which I only want removed anyway but on this trip, the thought occurred this morning or late last night: maybe I could try this type of thing, a cat-sit or house-sit and not bring all the books and previous letters with me, just a typewriter and some typing paper and just, as they say, pick up where I left off.

Which is how this letter begins: at the moment of regret and failure. The previous letter's ending with regret is, of course, partially the end of the letter, the actual physical object and the nature of writing: "I'm trying to express something but at the bottom of the page there's only regret at what I wasn't able to. It was through this experience finally actually arrived at and explicitly stated: express myself freely is impossible when the result is so much regret" that I understood what I've always been left with after typing & sending a letter: regret and remorse.

Of course, the actual act of typing is usually quite joyful and at many points, through many lines I do actually forget myself and feel great freedom. This is nothing new, it's what everyone craves: artists, writers, cashiers, everyone, and everyone tries what there is in this world to get out of this world. I am among the very fortunate who achieved this with a drink. And I'd still be drinking if alcohol was still providing that, still producing that effect, that out of this worldness. I mean, I'm among the doubly fortunate, those who drank the way I did and those who've been availed of the more than sufficient substitute for alcohol, which believe it or not, is the steps of alcoholics anonymous. The result is freedom from care, boredom and worry.

Of course, I want to get to the sexy part of this letter, because there is one. Which I will just jump right into telling you without trying to give some kind of an intro to or put caveats on before I even begin.

Last night I had a date. This is somewhat new situation (in a different era I would be using the word 'paramour') and she's been out of town for six weeks. We fucked a few times before she left. Over these six weeks then, I've watched my excitement build, build higher, go a little faster and at a higher vibration until I made myself sick with it, with every thought, every fantasy, every memory and imagined memory, every idea I had about her and me had me sick, and then sick and depressed. Basically, hating myself and my ruinous nature. I mean, seriously, it doesn't take much to really have me at the gate: what other people might call infatuation or a crush has me wanting to die.

So, she's back. I won't bore you with the obsessions I've had waiting for her to get back. I'll just get right to last night: we met at a little park near the lake in Oakland and when it was getting too windy and cold, we walked down Alice Street (which is an unusual street and maybe I'll write more later about why) and after a few blocks, she pulled and pushed and led me against the wall of the Oakland Hotel (or Hotel Oakland).

At this point I notice I'm rushing through trying to tell you something. I too want to get to the good part and I have fear I don't have the patience to do it: to use language, it's easy to fall for the trap that I'm trying to express an idea. Trying is failing, language fails. What I want is to convey an experience, now.

Ok, so yeah, yeah, yeah: now is impossible to describe because it exists outside of language, it exists outside of our brains, even, so any attempt to try and express it is an inherent failure. This is similar to the explosion of gratitude in the twelfth step: we try to carry the message but by trying we fail and then, leaving the meeting we plunge into regret and remorse for having even said anything at all in public, let alone that we are grateful to be sober... I mean, who is grateful to be sober??

Of course, I'd rather write about sex, but that requires the finest touch, and an ease and great ability. I'll stick to typing, typewriter on my lap, excruciating typos galore and endless distractions of the physical realm, even changing the paper, rolling in new sheets and with carbon in-between.

Part of what must be explained about this new affair is that I was experiencing it mostly in my brain. Of course, this was why the weeks were particularly painful and obsessional. But my hope was that if I didn't jack off thinking about her, or if I didn't massage certain ideas and fantasies, I could somehow manage my desire and not be at the effect of wanting. I mean, to be honest, there isn't much difference between wanting and waiting, at least not in the brain. In the brain it's all restless, irritable and discontent, sad, lonely and depressed (let me remind you, things are actually going quire well for me and I'm laughing as I type this). Ok, so I'm telling this part because all of that repression and diversion only resulted in resentment and the sick depression; a disembodiment to manage desire.

She pushed me against the wall of the hotel. It's at 14th and Alice, this special street in Oakland. It's dark and there's some pushing and pulling. She's wearing my denim jacket around her shoulders like a cape. I have on my denim vest (of course) and it takes a minute, maybe more, for me to respond to her physical introduction.

October 1, 2016:
Dear Bobby:

Obviously, days later. Since in my folders and stacks of papers and letters there are at least two other letters written to you ("Dear Bobby") that have remained unsent, it feels important to finish this one before I leave this house-sit over here in Oakland. The risk of packing everything up to return to SF, papers back in folders, folders back in boxes, etc., that this letter, these pages will somehow be forgotten for a few days or weeks and then just seem irrelevant or unrelated to the subject being dealt with.

I feel kind of stiff and tight against the wall. I think she's trying to kiss me or something. My brain was still firing quickly and my body still deadened which is a drag for being sexual. I mean I wanted the opposite: brain shut off and body going crazy. She and I were kind of pushing and pulling each other against the wall, resisting and accepting. Here's where it gets good: she is standing in front of me, my back is to the wall, and I lift her shirt to expose her belly and her bra—she has great tits—her pants are tight, she's wearing a scarf, my jacket like a cape and her belly is catching the light from passing cars and overhead lamps. Maybe we're laughing by now. There is still the push, the pull as I hold her arm's length away so I can look at her. She is meanwhile trying to come in closer to me, to kiss me and also to maybe kind of protect herself because when I say I want to look at her, I'm talking about the kind of look that is wolfish, and a look that says to a woman, "I'm going to consume you," that kind. (I'm noticing I'm fearful to write about that predator dangerous energy I find really exciting; that I actually get extremely turned on by when I perceive women are scared by my desire of them. I have fear this is our culture of misogyny, our rape culture and fear that my participation as a butch, as a woman is abhorrent) and so, after looking at her tits, her bare belly, and then with my hands on her shoulders, looking her in the eyes and smiling, it's a bit wolfish. But in that moment, in the moment of the smile, the disarming, so to speak, I flip her around and push her against the wall.

Of course, my desire has completely embodied me and not only am I very turned on but I'm feeling confident and strong in my body. I push her back against the wall and put my forearm across her neck with my hand on her shoulder for leverage. I'm still smiling, still looking at her in the eyes. I hold her there while I lift her bra so her breasts are bared now too and I step back from holding her and just stand in front of her looking and smiling. She's smiling too, excited, being desired. It's amazing.

And of course, this being outside, engaging in public lesbian sex, we are actually both in danger. We are standing on a street corner in downtown Oakland having sex.

Then we're kissing and I was allowing her to pull me close arms around each other, hips pressed on hips. I put my hand on her throat then, kissing her hard, open mouthed, fiercely, and put my hand down between us. I was holding my hand in a circle, my pinkie side against myself and then thumb and forefinger against her. She kind of pushed my hand away, said something about a bladder infection and wanting to be ready for friday (part of our talking at the park was making a date to go to the beach on friday, perhaps over the bridge, if it was warm and sunny enough?) I gripped her tighter and put my fist back between us. I said, "I'm not going to move my hand at all, I want you to open your pussy." Amazingly, she did and in a second was yelling a lot. Now, even though my fist was between us, I wasn't pressing or moving it really at all, just kind of concentrating. Or not, just feeling it and letting myself go as well. She's yelling in that moaning sex way, wild, and then over her voice, I hear myself, quite loud saying: Sit down on it. Sit down on it. Sit down on it.

The blaze or the flash, or wow, whatever, was intense. It surprised me in that way that that kind of energy play can have: the aspect of "is this really happening? Or am I imagining feeling something that isn't?" But then it was what I was left with that night and the next day: the image of this flash of light like a crystal glowing from within, kind of held in my had, but actually, or maybe, between us.

And I mention a crystal because it wasn't just light or energy; it feels like a physical object (even in the memory) that's materialized, been produced or conjured, or something. And of course, this is why I've wanted to tell you this, to get to this good part: the crystal. The somehow experience of this kind of energy (which I do want to set it apart as queer: very sexy, dangerous, non-penetrative) and a flash of light seem to produce a physical object that I am actually holding in my fist, the base of it against my clit through the seam and buttoned-fly of my jeans and the tip extending beyond my fingers to fuck her. I've been a lesbian for a while, and if this isn't what it's about, I don't know what is.

And of course, here we are again at the bottom of the page and this letter is also ending where it began, all the trying, all the wanting to convey, the did I say enough, the did I say too much. But also, when this queer object—messy, mistakes, typos, typewritten love sent description of sex magick, tactile and hand-held—is held by you, I'm grateful.

January 2, 2017:
Dear Bobby:

I don't even know who I am writing this for; I don't know if anyone cares about this anymore. It feels important to record our culture. This morning this little typewriter when I opened its case already had paper and carbon rolled onto the platen. The desk is cleared off except for the corner, which is a pile of crystals and a carved wooden bear with a fish in her mouth.

As always, it's hard to start here again, at the desk, at the typewriter, on the page, writing. Sometimes it's easier to think it's just typing ("the return of the typist") but I do want to tell a story here, there is something that needs to be expressed. This story will end. Let me start then where this story ends: I'm crying and sobbing, fucking myself with a dick saying over and over please please please.

In the beginning, I'll be honest, I was grandiose. I actually showed up for the first date with a list of things I wanted and wanted to do with her. Plus, I wanted to swim with her in the ocean. It's basically about a date, this story, and it starts over and over and over again, going back and forth through a life time. I mean, I do like typing and the excitement felt, little machine on my lap body tingling, the roughness and distraction of the beginning: fear I won't be able to do this, fear I can't do this.

Which to actually be honest, is exactly where this all begins, not with the grandiosity of a list of actions brought to a date but a list of fears I must surrender on the actual first date.

It's in San Francisco on july 1. It's the week between gay pride and july 3 that is always hot in the city, summer hot. Not sunny and breezy like the rest of the summer but hot like New York: sweating hot. After work and a meeting, I stop at home to change my shirt and grab a light weight jacket. I'm taking bart to Oakland and leaving my bike at home. It's 5pm and the platform is crowded. I've walked along Market Street from my apartment to the bart station. I'm talking on the phone as I walk. My friend Leah is in LA where it's really hot, scary hot.

January 5, 2017:
Dear Bobby:

I've been trying to start this for a few days, except for the short above-ness there seems to be a little progress. As always, I appreciate your patience with all the mistakes, false starts and typos that mark this page as queer. I've changed machines. The big selectric needs to be serviced, the motor is working but the cartridge isn't moving on the rail. This ribbon is brand new and so new in fact, it's splashing ink with every strike of the keys. This is the electric olympia portable. I brought it to New Mexico in 2015.

Part of the difficulty (have I mentioned this already?) is where to start. I mean, that's always the problem, the where is the beginning and the how far back to go.

And so, this story starts on july 1. This is the anniversary of the day Canela and I first saw each other at the store. You and I were cashiering. In the produce section I saw this bearded femme buying avocados. Her thighs were very furry too, she was wearing a short dress and knee-high boots. Her thighs were really shown off. It was the first few days after gay pride and since I'd never seen her before, in fact it had been a while since I'd seen a bearded femme, I thought she must live rurally, like maybe she's in town for the gay pride events.

I'd been out dancing the night of the gay pride, sunday, just after the parade. It was still light out about 6pm but the fog was rolling in making it uncomfortable to stand outside on line to get into the dance party. I didn't go to the parade this year, I'd gone camping with my ex-girlfriend and her kid in Sonoma. I had an idea we could get back together, or at least fuck on this little weekend trip. We'd been broken up for a year at this point, but we were seeing each other once a week, the day she had her kid, tuesday afternoons.

I mean, I really didn't want to start back this far but here it is. I'm standing outside a gay dance party on gay pride sunday. I'm with my other ex-girlfriend from 2002 and LA and I'm telling her about the camping trip. She said, "you know what, you got to stop seeing this person, stop seeing her and stop seeing her kid." And I said I know, but I think this time was the last time for real. I think I'm finally over her. She said with eyebrows raised, "really?" But I knew it this time. And except for getting the $100 she owed me for that trip and the groceries I bought, I never did see her again. I'd been hung up on her for four years, with all of its off-again, on-again, back and forth violent fights. It was one of those relationships when it's over, I'm left thinking I don't even want to be with anyone else, let alone don't feel attracted to anyone else. So, I said to my other ex, this time it's over. I'm finally over her.

Like I say I didn't want to go back this far. I still don't but it's obviously what's needed. I mean I want to continue to try and control this whole story but the only way to enjoy any of it is to give over to all of it. So now, later, is another attempt at that giving over.

2010: me and Mandi break up. I don't want to break up even though I basically can't stand her, don't like her or her life, anything she does and certainly don't like fucking her. I like her kid and have a lot of unresolved wreckage about my dad leaving me and my brothers with a depressed, angry, violent mother and so I feel guilty about leaving this kid. We finally break up, on Valentine's Day, but I continue to see Mandi and her kid once a week on tuesdays after school and for dinner for the next year and a half. Every week as I leave, I'm so sad and every week I think I can't go back, it's too painful. I don't want to be with Mandi but I keep thinking if I can prove myself, or be good enough or somehow do some thing, she'll want to get back together with me. I was newly sober too; my sexuality was all confused and I had no idea of what I wanted or wanted to do. Fucking her was a drag though, and I didn't want her touching me, or what I wanted, was for her to figure out how to do it right. Every week I'd leave and go to a meeting of aa and then the rest of the week I'd do the steps of aa taking my personal inventory, putting my fears and resentments on paper (I'm resentful at Mandi because I have fear she is a terrible mother) and putting my fears on paper even when there was no resentments attached to them: (fear I don't want to see them next week, fear I should cancel); this was happening every week for a year, every week I'm writing the same thing over and over for seven days and then on the following tuesday I'm finding myself texting or responding to a text from Mandi, asking her if she wants anything from the store when I come over today.

The actual time together, with the kid especially, was always so fun and so sweet and so full of love and loving and laughter. It was the amends with my dad and with myself as the kid who was left and with myself as the one who wants to leave the mother and with this power greater than myself that has me sober, clearing away what I think is happening to actually experience what is happy joyous freedom, even though I don't think so.

2011: We take the last camping trip—me, Mandi and the kid. I buy a cheap plastic kite at a grocery store in Santa Rosa and the little thing flies like I've never seen a kite fly: so high and like it jumps up from my hand of its own accord and takes off, soaring higher and higher. Every time we fly it over the course of the weekend, every time, this kite just flies high. Mandi braids my hair and though we snuggle in the tent there's nothing even sweet about it. She feels wooden with my arm around her and not relaxed and I have compassion for her and her wound-upped-ness, her protected-ness, and her complicated child custody situation, which has her with me, who she seems to basically hate, on a trip with her just so she doesn't have to be alone with her kid.

We get back from the little camping trip on sunday afternoon and I can't wait to get out of the car. Thankfully, I'd made plans to meet my other ex-girlfriend, Pristine, at a gay dance party around the corner from my house. We stand outside in the coming-in fog, rolling over the twin peaks with the pink triangle laid up on it, still in our short sleeve shirts and trying to look hot. "You should stop seeing her," Pristine said, "really. It's been over a year since you broke up. You gotta stop seeing her. And the kid too. I know you love the kid, but you gotta stop seeing them". This was the last time, I said. And it was. I knew it.

In 1986, (I mean, if this is what is being written then this is what is being written) I was still obsessed with my first girlfriend from high school. The summer we graduated, we laid in the dunes at Jones Beach. We were drunk and it was sunny and the dunes blocked the wind and I said to her this is amazing, let's stay here, like this, forever. I was so happy. I was so drunk. She turned to me and said, "I'm going to college." I knew I'd made a terrible mistake, but I couldn't quit her. I worked at the vitamin factory in our town and every day I came home, wrote her a letter and waited for the mail to come: did she write to me? I'd drive in my VW bug, smoking cigarettes, listening to the radio out to Jones Beach along the causeway, up and down the Meadowbrook Parkway and then over to the Wantagh, sometimes out to Long Beach, alone.

We saw each other during her breaks from school. She'd come home and we'd get together, get drunk and fuck. I don't remember the fucking actually, I was so drunk. I don't actually remember her touching me. Or me touching her for that matter. I remember waking up one morning on her brother's waterbed in the basement, hungover, but laughing. I mean, at 19, alcohol was still working.

But all I could think about was her. I didn't quite understand the nature of obsessive-minded alcoholism. I thought this was what love was: painful, yearning, pining, terrifying desire. I waited for her to write. Once we talked on the phone she said she'd mailed me a long letter but I never got it. She got a boyfriend but when she came back before school started the following year, we got together at my dad's house. My dad and his family were on a trip and she and I drank everything in the house. We laid on the living room floor, smoking cigarettes, listening to records and I was asking her over and over: don't you want to be with me? Don't you? We went upstairs later into one of the bedrooms and I actually went down on her. That's what we called it then, going down on a woman. She came in my mouth and I was so unexperienced, I barely understood what had happened. I felt good though. And then got a wart on the inside of my lip from her genital warts that I burned it off with lit matches until it didn't come back.

The next day I went with my best friend to the mall, roosevelt field, as we drove I told her I'd spent the day and night with Laureen. Oh no, my friend said, really, you've got to stop seeing her. My obsession was such that it was all I talked about for a year, at least. I'm sure my friend was tired of hearing about whether or not I heard from Laureen, and repeating endlessly what she said a month ago, what I was thinking about her. Oh no, she said as we took the Meadowbrook north to the Northern State, please, you've got to stop seeing her. It's over, I said. I swear, this time, it's over, I can feel it. The obsession had stopped. That's when the wart came, but that was actually so much less unpleasant than the persistent obsessive painful yearning.

So, when in 2011, I said to Pristine, it's over, I knew it then too. Yeah, it's over. Like the switch had been thrown back and I was free. I didn't see them, Mandi and her kid that tuesday because of the custody arrangement and the summer schedule and then it was friday. I was actually seeing another woman who lived in my building at this point. It was initially a hot situation. I was so depressed, and couldn't extricate myself from the situation because we lived in the same building and it was so easy when a person is so lonely to just go down a flight of stairs and eat dinner together and then lay on her bed.

Friday, I go to work. It's july 1st. The bearded femme is shopping and you ring her up at the register behind mine. She and I look at each other and I said to her I like your look and she said I like yours. I was wearing a pair of trousers and a pair of adidas. It was amazing and it continues when I put an ad on craigslist

This is just at the tail end of people using craigslist to find missed connections and at Rainbow this was quite popular for customers to put up a missed connection for cashiers or other workers or customers. As one cashier said, I mean, it's not really a missed connection because you know where I work. But I mention this incident for two reasons: one upon seeing this bearded femme I was attracted to her and it was proof to me that I was over Mandi. For the year that we'd been broken up, I couldn't even manufacture an attraction for any other woman at all (except for my downstairs neighbor) and then here I was actually feeling excited about another woman. It was over with Mandi and here was the proof. The date was july 1.

January 6, 2017:
Dear Bobby:

When Canela and I were first together she told me the story of her and her ex-wife's breakup. They'd been together a while, married and working together and happily ever after. They went to a show some place and her wife won the raffle grand prize: an olivia lesbian cruise. Canela scoffed and so the ex-wife took her best friend. In exchange, Canela decided to go to Michigan. At Michigan, Canela had an affair and even though the arrangement was what happens at Michigan, stays at Michigan, she continued the affair when she got back to San Francisco. Canela and the affair stayed in touch and were emailing, calling and texting. The affair lived in Florida and wanted to come out to see Canela and so they made a plan to do that. No problem except that the only weekend the affair could come was the anniversary of Canela and her wife's wedding. Canela said well, I want to see the affair and maybe we can celebrate our anniversary a couple of days earlier. When Canela told me the story she said, that was the beginning of the end for us.

Well, I righteously blasted Canela. What did you expect, I said. I mean, you go ahead and get married and then basically dishonor the whole relationship. I'll tell you what, I said, if it was me and you said to me that you wanted to be on a date with another woman on our wedding anniversary, I'd say it was over too.

So, Canela and I meet on july 1. Five years later an opportunity arises and I want to go on a date with another woman, july 1. I made all kinds of excuses, but even from the beginning this slap in the face of my righteousness wasn't lost on me. And even now typing about it has me fearful that I've done the same thing and basically put a nail in the coffin for us, that by conjuring it even will cause the ending.

This isn't a story of what I've done. What I want isn't this. At the beach, walking across the sand, I'm looking for the other side. This doesn't even make any sense. We've driven and parked up above. There's steep stairs down to the water's edge. At the end of the day, walking back up I'll be out of breath, the stairs are that steep. On the way down the stairs I'm carrying a box of groceries in my bag on my back like a pack. She's carrying blankets. I also have a blanket, wool with flowers on it. Hers is a moving blanket, the quilted kind that movers use.

This is the third time we've been together. The first night we met at a bookstore in downtown Oakland. It was hot this night, even in SF, but I wasn't prepared for how hot it was in Oakland. I was wearing a denim vest and carrying a second jacket. It felt like a mistake, like having too much. The train across the Bay was crowded. It was a friday night, summer, still light out and I was perspiring profusely on the platform and on the train.

It was hot but I was also very anxious about going to meet this woman. I actually didn't really know her. I'd had a few exchanges at the register. I work as a cashier at a grocery store.

I'm bored as shit with this story already and I haven't even started it yet. I wonder how I've gonna write a book when I'm so sick of typing already. I have some idea I'm gonna impress a woman by writing a book and I can barely even be interested in anything for longer than a few days. I've been trying to figure out how to do this all week, longer even. Yesterday I hit a groove with this and today when I tried to pick back up where I left off, I haven't been able to, I've been so distracted with my fears. My fears of not being good enough. Fear I don't have any idea of what I'm even doing. Fear I'm not even into this after all. Fear I can't write the book.

I talked today to Canela who's in LA so I can have some space to try and write. Our goddam apartment is so small, a studio and while on the phone with her I cleaned the stove and vacuumed the house, watered plants. I want to be writing about the affair I had last year, a highly structured arrangement enacted in elaborate scenarios of dominance and submission. Instead I'm literally sick to my stomach—well, literally sick to my guts, trying to write this has me feeling eviscerated, the colitis has flared and I'm taking steroids.

The lover has left for ten weeks in Indonesia, at least, and at the last minute it was decided we would be in touch while she's gone. I have fear I'm living to hear from her. I have fear I use women as a distraction. Which is actually the least of it. I have fear I pursue women to hate them. I have fear I pursue women to drop them. The fears seem endless. My experience is that they are actually finite, 100 forms of fear. If I can just type this one page today I'll at least feel like I did something. I have fear I should just be taking my inventory. But it's like, if I don't have anything to show for this week, I have fear I'm letting people down. I have fear I'm waiting to hear from Bonarh. I have fear when I do actually hear from her, it's only completely frustrating and unsatisfying.

Trying to get something from a person, including my self, is a complete drag. Actually, it's like a death sentence.

But I keep looking at my device to see if she's sent an email. At this point, there's not even a little boost getting anything from her. I have fear she's actually patronizing me. I have fear she's using me as a transitional object. I have fear I've already expressed too much to her. I have fear I need to back off. I have fear I need to focus on this project. I have fear I can't.

January 7, 2017:
Dear Bobby,

Today is the final day of a week of writing. All week I've spent trying to figure out how to tell the story of the past six months, where to begin. Actually, I began it over and over again all week, now, saturday night, 6:30pm. I drank a lot of coffee all day and into the evening, I'm full and tight with caffeine, bordering on anxiety. I want to start this enough once and for all. Which even here, in this letter, I'm noticing how good I want to sound, how good I want this to read to you, smooth and easy. I want to look good with this whole thing. Or at least sound good with it.

I'm trying to impress you.

This has been nearly impossible, this writing this week, because every time I sat down to type, I'd try and start from the beginning which actually every time I sit down, was going further and further back, into the past. It was like a time warp where I'd start with the date 'july 1st' and then rather than the story unfolding the way my notes are written, building with the usual narrative structure of day after dayness, instead, the story goes backward. Late in the week, I finally just accepted what was happening and let it go. I was back to june 1985 when I finally stopped that day, uncomfortable, I think, at the way things were going.

This is the part about wanting to look good. I want to look like I got this. I want to look like I'm doing something, if not something good, well, at least I'm doing something. I want this story to look that way too, which isn't even close to true. And is actually the whole point of the story to begin with: I'm not doing this and trying to write it as if I am is making me sick.

So late in the day late one day this week, I was back in the dunes at Jones Beach in 1985 with my first girlfriend, my high school sweetheart. We were drinking. I was drunk. Alcohol was still working, as they say, though it's not long after this that I'll be hospitalized for alcoholism. Laying in the dunes, in the early windy cool days of summer on Long Island, just having graduated high school, I thought: this is great. No school, now I can drink the way I want. I turned to her, lying next to me and said, "Let's stay here forever." I was so happy. She turns to me and said "I'm going to college." I knew immediately, even with alcohol's promise, that I'd made a big mistake.

Instead, I got a job at the vitamin factory in our town—counting vitamins and putting them into the plastic and glass jars, labelling them with a mechanical labeler that always jammed, gluing sticky labels to themselves and choking the feeder. When the machines were off, it was for me to clean them. I was terrified that the not-noise in the factory would have the owners, a husband and wife who fought violently and incessantly, come and see why the machines weren't running and then join together and direct their wrath toward me, telling me I was wasting labels or time or that I was stupid.

I believed them. I mean, it was obvious. I was here in our town, working, not at college like everyone else I knew except for the kids who were too stupid to go to college.

Every day after work I went home to check the mail to see if she'd written me a letter. On my lunch break at the factory I'd write her and run to the post office to mail it that day. Then I'd drive my car up and down the Meadowbrook Parkway out to Jones Beach. Most of the parking lots were closed now for the season so I'd drive out, circle the old water tower, a grand tall brick deco spire, and circle back up the Wantagh Parkway or out along the causeway to Long Beach and come up along Long Beach Road, through Island Park, smoking cigarettes and listening to the car radio and cassettes; Pat Beneath, the Pretenders, Billy Joel.

It was fall now, a hurricane knocked a bunch of trees down on Merrick Road and the vitamin factory ("open to the public") was closed while the power lines and fallen tree branches were cleaned up. I was out of the hospital, already in and out, and perhaps this starts the period of the next 20 years which will fall into another chapter called 'trying not to drink'. Most of my time during this period will be spent this way: trying not to drink. Days off, work closed, evenings, weekends, most of the time is spent trying not to drink. I wasn't successful.

I get some idea here of trying to keep it up and not go down that long sad road right now. I mean, without too much explanation of the ins and outs of alcoholism, this period of time 'trying not to drink' actually means 25 years of more or less insanely drunk. And without going into too much of that right now, for an alcoholic, drunk means 'blotting out the consciousness'. So even if I'd like to take a moment to regale you with stories of outrageousness and wild times, there's not much to remember from a black out, no matter what everyone tells you the next day. And aside from a few early highlights, garden variety alcoholism manifests mostly as being intensely sick from alcohol and not being able to stop drinking it. No guns, no cops, no wild drug scores, no nothing but sick-ass miserable depression.

You can understand why I might not want to come here, to this part of the story. I got to feel good, now, and even just kind of circling around that alcoholic obsession feels bad. I mean the great fact for me is that a power has entered my life. This is the part where they say a 'power greater than myself', but the greatest fact for me is that I don't exist. My life is a tragedy, nothing but self-delusion of 100 forms, which is why I want to tell this other story of being sober, which isn't even a story of me being sober. Like I'll try and explain throughout this, I don't exist. My ideas of myself are over. This is an attempt to bear witness to this power that has me sober and alive, despite myself.

This story starts at the beach.

San Francisco beaches have taken me 25 years to get used to, coming from Long Island with its miles of soft sandy gentle dunes, wide soft expanses of the finest, softest sun-warmed sandy beaches. Out here, with wet rocky sticky sand that doesn't brush off your feet even when they are dry is a drag. The wind and summer days that are foggy and cold make swimming difficult but worse is bringing a blanket to spread out for a picnic and then sit huddled under the blanket wrapped around your shoulders as the cold spray of the Pacific blows. There's no sun shining and even though you've brought a bathing suit you can't swim; it's too cold. And now there's too many tourists coming down the newly remade stairways that go from the parking lot at the barracks or along the Lincoln Boulevard in the Presidio, wearing their fisherman wharf hoodies in pastel colors. I don't want to strip down in front of them not even to run in just for a quick ritual dip in the mother, dipping in my head and dropping so my shoulders and heart are in the cold water. I don't want the tourists to watch me run naked to the waters' edge, a body they don't understand doing something they don't understand.

Yet I find myself here, at the beach. I'm on a date. I'm with a woman, ah, none of this sounds right, a glitch begins to happen here, at this point of walking down to the sand from her car, parked on Lincoln Boulevard. I got the groceries from the best market in the world. Is the box of amazing cheeses and crackers, 100% chocolate bars, and other treats not being carried by me in a bag on my back? Did I not give her directions from the grocery store across town to this location? Do I not work at this grocery store not only as a cashier but as a worker/owner? Did I not come up with this plan for us today? Am I not trying to impress her? Am I not facing even as all of this occurs, not my skillful proficiency, experience with women, fuck even my 30 years of bringing women to the beach but instead my self-centered fears that I can't do this? Am I not thinking, nay, ruminating: I have fear this is a mistake?

The glitch is I want to look better than this, I want to be smooth and easy and I want this story to flow from the beginnings of this descent to the water's edge with her and the picnic and the blanket and after we swim and return to the blanket and lay drying off in the hot summer sun, I lean in and kiss her gently, at first the pull back, the way I do, look at her and smile and lean in and kiss her again but this time grabbing her face in my hands and holding her while I kiss her again on the lips with my mouth slightly open, the gentleness of these kisses matched by the force with which I hold her face tightly.

I don't want to be thinking about myself, my self-centered fears and that me being here is a mistake.

January 10, 2017:
Dear Bobby:

After finally hitting a beginning I'm trying to continue from here.

I'm standing on the side of the cliff overlooking the Golden Gate, the bridge in the background and the heavy fog-covered foliage is bright with color from so much rain and wet after the years of the drought. The stairs down to the beach are newly labelled and land-scaped and maintained. This used to be wild and rough and the way down to the gay end of the bay. Now, it's listed online with a caution: 'this is often a clothing optional beach.' The wind is blowing the fog like a blanket up to meet us, standing by the back of her car. I've got a box of lunch and snacks in a box I put in the bag on my back. I've brought a blanket and she has one too, rolled up with a tie around it into a bundle, not folded. She doesn't drink coffee so I brought medicinal strength maté in a jar.

Has the coldness registered yet? Perhaps as I've gotten out of the car and put my sweater and jacket over my shoulder. I'm not even sure what she's wearing. I'm pausing here, at the car, up on the cliff, not descending because I'm fearful. I want to be honest about this moment. I mean, of course I'm conflicted here because I want everything to be just flowing smoothly at this point. I especially don't want to be standing here, stuck, disappointed. It's not a hot sunny day with blue skies.

I've made a lot of preparations for this moment. And I'm even here grandiosely, with a list of what I want from this moment. I've actually come grandiosely with a list that is written, such that when we arrive on the sand—cold damp wet dark sand—and spread out blankets, I will pull this list from my bag on the paper its written on and read it to her:

What I want from a situation:

1. Not unloving: the double negative is my fearful couching of desire
2. Unromantic: it's not about building intimacy for us but love and sex to bless the world
3. Sacred: enacted with a ritual consciousness; not profane
4. I want to be fucked: more on this later
5. I want to be uncomfortable: also, more on this later, though even from this beginning I am quite uncomfortable.

I've been out with her two other times. I met her at the register in the grocery store where I work. I met her on a camping trip for a friends' birthday at the Russian River. I later saw her at the register. I asked her out. She was at register one, the express lane, and I was at register two. The store was busy and when I saw her over there, not at my register, I took it personally. I gave her a look that was intended to mean, "You went to another line? I've been chatting you up for months and now you're at another line?" It was more of a scowl that said, "What the fuck?" she shrugged with a smile and said, "Your line was so long…" So, I called over and said, "Listen, do you want to go out? Like a movie or something?" She said yeah and then left. I had to ask my girlfriend for her number at home that night.

Now, at this point, I'm trying to control this whole situation. I don't want to sound like a cocky motherfucker but it's why I enjoy cashiering: women lined up waiting to interact with me and I'm in charge. The interactions are so pleasant and smiley and short: "Hey, how are you? Thank you so much." It's actually better if I don't ever see them again because basically that's my game right there: "Thank you very much." There isn't much more after that. Not only am I not a player, let's be honest, I'm a choker.

We walk down the stairs. The sky is low and heavy and grey. She's smiling a lot as we walk toward the wall of rocks and she actually is telling me how excited she's been all week about today, this trip to the beach. She says: "All week I've been thinking about today. On tuesday,

I was like 'only tuesday? When is thursday?" Now it's thursday. She's kind of so excited she's run a bit ahead of me on the beach and is turning to look over her shoulder as she tells me she was trying to decide which underwear to wear, what I might like and all week thinking about different pairs until finally she just decided, "no panties at all."

January 13, 2017:
Dear Bobby:

It's funny that I'm hanging up on the cliff, staying here for so long and not wanting to begin the descent, the going down.

The next day after this beach date with her, I sent her an email, like a little post-poem, and it described the long walk down to the ocean's edge, the water, and then something about desire, specifically lesbian desire (I'm distracted now because of course I'm looking for a copy of this and can't find it, so many stacks of letters and papers and notes and notebooks and thinking I'm organizing this all and invariably when I try and reference something I can't find it). But it's this moment of beginning that I want to frame, even though things didn't really get started until october (this is july, or not even, because I went to NYC in july and didn't offer to pick her up when she was there too, her flight coming in late on a thursday; there's some summer flight from SFO that comes in to JFK close to midnight and I had a fantasy about borrowing my brother's car, going out to JFK, picking her up and bringing her back to his house and then next morning waking early and driving out along Woodhaven Boulevard to Cross Bay Boulevard out to Riis Beach where we could swim. I wanted, from the beginning to swim with this woman in the ocean, so most of my ideas about what to do with her and where to go involve some attempts at getting to the water's edge. This beach trip finally was in august).

I want to lay out certain ideas here; there are certain elements I want to convey here. It seems important to try and build the structure that I want to hang this whole narrative on. I mean I've never actually done any of this; so much of it is just happening as it's happening.

We are walking across the beach. It's cold and foggy and she's just expressed to me how excited she's been about this trip to the beach with me. I'm actually quite surprised not only by her desire but her ability to so freely express it. I mean for me this kind of excitement quickly builds to all-consuming obsession so I've been going crazy for a week already. I'm just hoping to get through this date without looking too crazy. For me that always means playing it real close, definitely not laying the cards on the table, trying to be a little cool. It doesn't play well, though, mostly because I don't have the poker face required and I got no game. I fall for every single woman.

So, her saying something like, "I'm into this" from the beginning, as we walk, kind of throws me, knocks me off guard a bit and also provides a great freedom for me. I mean, not to mention, it's pretty flattering. Or feels that way. She says she's not wearing any under-wear. I got the groceries and a list of what I want as we sit down, spread the blankets, her moving blanket and my wool blanket (from the free box at the store). I kind of lay back and she sits up excited, next to me and partially on my lap.

Along the cold beach, there is a wall of rocks. This separates, at low tide, the beach and the infamous gay beach. There is also a stretch of beach between. Each section has its own staircase down to the sand. Sometimes, due to the tides you can cross over and sometimes no. This was one of the no times but as we turned around to get our bearings we saw two things. One, a naked old fag wearing only a cock ring parading back and forth on the beach and on the rocks. Two, a small size crevasse, almost like a cave, back at the base of the cliff as it rises up, like an arch-way, a crawl space, tiny little protected area. Here it is, I say and begin to lay the blankets across the floor here, putting my bag wedged up a bit to lay my head as I recline. She doesn't drink coffee so I've brought a jar full of medicinal strength maté, which we begin to sip.

She's smiling and kind of sitting on my lap, riding my knee and thigh between her legs. Wow, I'm thinking. "Should we stay here?" She asks.

(I'm going to NYC on thursday to work on this project. Canela and our partner are back from L.A., where they were last week, and the small apartment feels really small with the three of us in here again. I'm at the effect of time/space constraints, fears, and wanting to just keep this going—the typing, the trying, the laying this out and mainly the practice—until I get to NYC. As always, I'm so grateful for your generosity.)

January 23, 2017:
Dear Bobby:

It's monday in New York, at my brother's. Got here thursday, typed friday, went up to Poughkeepsie for the other brother's birthday, stayed overnight and in the morning went to the diner for breakfast (The Acropolis) and then me and the brother went to a storage unit his friend has with a giant 300lb heavy oak table, we took off the 4x4 inch heavy legs and still could barely lift the top of the table, even just into the back of his car. I kept saying, "C'mon, on 3, lift this motherfucker" drove down then back to NYC with the table sticking out the back of the open back door of his little car and then "how we gonna get this thing up into the house" there's a lot of discussion and finally then the plan "C'mon, let's just lift this motherfucker and get it up the stairs." Seriously, it's 600lbs. Or, at least that's what he said and he isn't as hyperbolic as me at all. Got it up and in and then legs on but how to turn it over, with the legs on. I mean, how much does this weigh? And again, discussion and finally, "Let's just lift this fucker up and turn it over." Set up everything on it then last night: two typewriters plus this one which I bought while I was here on saturday: IBM selectric II. I mean, this machine is a dream, for real. Might even be nicer than the one I have in SF. So smooth and so nice and so strong.

January 24, 2017:
Dear Bobby:

Now, of course I didn't come to NYC to tell you about driving to Kingston to a storage unit to get a table or carrying it up the stairs or whatever. I have an idea of what story I'm trying to convey: "this is the story I'm going to tell" and yet actually getting to the point of sitting in front of a working typewriter requires all power and then if I'm asking for knowledge of that power and when I get it, I want it to be different than what it is, which isn't my will.

My will is the story of this amazing affair I had from july to december. The story I want to tell is actually amazing: completely sexy and wild and with complete abandon. I have a structure too, on which to hang this narrative, and anyway, I got this whole idea of the whole thing. I want to write to you about this affair I've been having but I got a bunch of ideas of how I should do it, namely I'm committed to beginning at the beginning.

This is probably not the best idea. The rules that I have for myself invariably doubly defeat their purpose; i.e., 'do not put on a clean shirt unless you've washed your neck' usually has me unwashed, wearing the same shirt day after day. And I've mentioned to you the back and forthedness of the story thus far, having me land up on Jones Beach in 1985 before I can even get going at all but I thought I'd gotten that out of my system before I got here to NYC. I thought I'd found a groove while still in SF and had finally gotten going but even then, I was stuck at the Presidio next to her car putting a blanket into a bag to carry down to the beach for a number of days, caught in the wind and fog on the cliff above the Golden Gate where the bridge wasn't even visible on this day.

Of course, I thought "I got this. Now, I got this." I mean, I usually think this and I am quite susceptible to falling for this line of reasoning. I never remember how absolutely unreasonable this kind of thinking is. So, I put a typewriter in its thick double-walled plastic case, wrapped it in bubble wrap and packed it in a big banana box and with a big giant suitcase-- maté, coffee, raw walnuts, papers, books, and a few clothes is 50lbs--checked them both at the curb at SFO and carried on a little rolling suitcase. My thought was I'm gonna need a machine that I'm familiar with, that I know is working and ready to go once I get to NYC. I'm thinking, I got this. I'll get to NYC and my brother will pick me up from the airport and I'll bring everything to his house and the next morning I'll open the box, pull out the typewriter, plug it in and put in some paper and then ready to go. I don't want to spend a lot of time shopping around on craigslist for a good working, already cleaned machine. I mean, emailing back and forth and going out to the person's house and finding out the machine they're selling hasn't been plugged in for five years. Or ten years. Or I mean, let's be honest, at this point, 16 years or 25 years, isn't conceivable.

But that first morning, there's no table or desk for me to put the typewriter I brought with me, no place for me to set up. In fact, it actually feels like there isn't a place for me here, at my brother's, at all. Not only no desk but also no place for me to sleep. And also, no place except for the middle of the living room floor for my box and two suitcases, which is fine but then that means we can't actually really walk around at all without tripping or at least being annoyed, which I was.

I had a lot of ideas about this trip here and what I wanted to do and what I didn't want to do. One thing I didn't want was to come and clean my brother's house enough for me to feel comfortable here. I didn't want to have to try and convince him that the office chairs made of microfiber while they might be comfortable were terrible and so ugly it hurt me to look at them, let alone look at four of them! And I didn't want to be driving all around NYC, Jersey, Upstate or going out to Long Island trying to find a working, cleaned and serviced selectric for me to use while I'm here. I mean, just getting set up and having it take three or four days, I have fear I'll be spending too much time getting ready and that by the time I'm typing it'll be time to pack up.

So last friday, the next day, I got my brother to get rid of some stuff. I sold two chairs on craigslist, took a load to the thrift store and carried a little desk up from downstairs. I set the typewriter I brought up on the little desk and actually was able to type that night on it. It went well, I thought and I was glad that everything had already started.

Plus, meantime I found a real good-looking typewriter on craigslist. Even though that was exactly what I didn't want to do, there I am doing it. I told the lady who posted I'd come saturday morning. She was out in Bayside. My brother's in Woodside. No problem. Drive over in the morning, take the expressway and after there's a morning meeting over there I can go to before we go up to the other brother's birthday dinner in Poughkeepsie.

I find her place, near the North Shore Diner on Northern Boulevard and Francis Lewis Boulevard. Turn right on 45th she said, "I'm the seventh house." The typewriter was in the back seat of her car and I carried it into the foyer of the house, plugged it in and it was like a dream; I think I've mentioned earlier in here. So smooth, so strong, the whole thing felt so good and easy to type on. I fell in love at first sight. I gave her $120. She'd listed it at $150, said her uncle used to work cleaning them but then he got cancer. I thought, of course, him leaning over the top of the machine and breathing in all those solvents, it might've been safer if he just straight up drank the stuff. Although, RIP. The typewriter she had was very, very clean. It looked great and was in a blue steel case, very good looking. So, I said, "Listen, how about a hunge? She balked and I said alright, $120 then and just handed her the money like, this is it, no negotiation. I put it in the brother's car and drove over to the meeting.

I don't even think I tried it at all on saturday. We were just trying to get out the house and, on the road, up to Kingston to look at the dining table in the storage unit. So, I put the new selectric on a low bench and we left. On the way I told my brother about the lady, her uncle, selectric taking 75% of the entire typewriter market through the 60s and 70s and how I blasted off in the meeting, surprising myself and feeling so good.

So, upon our return to his place in Queens, I've described the lifting and carrying of this enormous table and setting it up and how really great it looks here in his apartment, replacing a tiny glass topped chrome pedestal cafe table with four office chairs made of microfiber around it. This new table looks magnificent and we hung a big painting on the wall behind the table and I got all the papers and folders and files and books and typewriters and covered the table. I was like, ok, I'm ready to go, I want to hit this flow.

Basically, forget everything I've said until now. The moment I want is the moment I consider the linchpin (basis, entire theme, anchor, keystone, spring) of the entire story. I'll pick when we're on the beach. We're in a little crevasse but it has a full roof above us, craggy rock, and beneath us, wet sand packed hard. We crawl toward the back, the rocky shore prevents us at this deep low angle from seeing the ocean, except when an especially large wave comes crashing and the spray shoots in the air. I've laid and spread the blankets, hers and mine, on the hard sand and I'm laying now in the cave on my back.

So, let's begin. Even the writing now requires an invocation. Obviously, I can't do this. Trying is only making it worse. I'm committed to beginning at the beginning, but to be honest, I don't even know where that is in this story. So, I'll begin with the naturalist fag who is wearing a leather cock ring and parading back and forth over the rocks and the sand like an old billy goat. He is like a screen for us, inside the little cave, under the roof of rocks, his parading back and forth prevents us from being seen by being seen himself so much. There are a bunch of tourists down here on the beach and the tide is so high us queers can't get to our beach from this side. Everyone is all together, in the splash and spray of the ocean.

January 25 2017:
Dear Bobby:

She sees the naturalist and so do I. I'm excited. All the tourists down here, standing on the rocks, watching the container ships pass under the bridge, red span now appearing and disappearing, pointing in their souvenir sweatshirts out across the gate to where Marin is, invisible, have me wishing for the mid-week trips to Baker Beach of 25 years ago when the beach was empty during the day, during the week, just you and your date and some cruising fags who say hello as they pass. The naturalist harkens back to the time of then and I use the opportunity to tell her about Madmen by Samuel Delany. He writes about having public gay sex. In one scene he is sucking a guy who lives on the street on a park bench in the middle of the day. Delany writes that he knees in front of a guy who lives on the street and in the park and is so dirty and smelly and that the guy takes his dick out while drinking the cans of beer Delany has bought for him and that Delany then kneels in front of him, on the path in front of the bench and takes the guys dirty dick in his mouth, sucks him off and then the guy pisses in his mouth. Now, I love this story but the reason I mention it to her is the part where Delany says: "Most people are baseball fans. Most people walk into a public park and see a bunch of guys playing baseball and that's it. Then, there are those of us who see everything else."

Once the blankets are spread and I've laid back, I mean, why not, arms behind my head. She is quickly up on my lap, straddling my one knee, her hands are on my chest and she asks, "Is this ok?"

This is the moment akin to the breaking of the suit in the game of hearts, no heart can be played until the suit is broken, and when, in my experience, a butch is with a femme, as they begin the get to know each other, sexually, the femme will touch the butch's chest and ask 'is this ok?' This is the game changer, so to speak, when she does this, it begins to set the tone for our further experiences. I'm excited because she's begun this so soon. (In contrast, one of my last lovers, five years in and she finally touched my chest and said, "Is this ok?" and by that time, I was so resentful at the whole thing having taken so long, that she'd waited for 5 years to ask to touch me, I was like stone and said, 'yeah, no, don't bother').

So, the suit is broken. She has her hands palms flat across my breasts, straddling my knee and thigh between her thighs which are thick and I can feel their strength, tightening and relaxing and tight again as she kind of chats, leaning slightly forward looking at me, touching me.

I've spoke of the preparations I've made to be here with her, the procuring of provisions, the food, the blanket, she doesn't drink coffee so I've made maté in ritual strength, medicinal. I've talked to my girlfriend about meeting this other woman and we've, like lesbians do, discussed it at length. I've also made a list of what I consider to be not criteria but perhaps certain specifications in a situation that may develop.

The primary situation with my girlfriend, whom I'll call Canela for this story, is so compelling that anything else has to be quite select.

I'd been with this woman, shall I call her Bonarh, on a date and we went before a movie to the UC campus, just at the edge, near the entrance on Central Street. Just a bit up the path there, before it winds around to slowly climb up through the campus there is a grove of eucalyptus trees. I've always been frightened by these trees' non-native invasion but this night, early summer and early evening on a date, early on, I'm struck by their beauty. This small grove of them is in a ring and rather than massively taking over all the ground, they have stayed almost like a redwood ring, small, contained circle. It's as if I'm encountering these trees for the first time, like when I was young and still always taken with their incredible smell. I'm so drawn to them that I tell Bonarh let's lay there and I pick a spot in the center, just slightly off to the side, in the middle of this tree ring. The fact that I'm so drawn to this area alone speaks to the feeling of magick but as we lay (she brought a blanket on her bike) on the earth, looking up at the tree canopies like constellations, tree branches and leaves above blowing in the light wind, and suddenly everything is pink. The blowing leaves above twinkle like bright tiny red stars and the strips of eucalyptus bark, long and hanging, also dancing in the warmth, pinken. In fact, all around but especially these towering trees have taken the glow of the setting sun: the golden hour and all around in this grove everything is aflame. It has to be now, I think.

I've been trying to figure out all night how and when to kiss her because I want to, I've wanted to kiss her but as usual, I'm thinking too much about how and when. In this moment of magick though, I forgot myself enough to roll over, off my back. Bonarh is on her back next to me, she's also been laying looking up. I put my arm across her and lean in and kiss her.

There is something about the way I've put my arm across her chest, or her upper belly that sparks between us, almost more than the kiss which seems almost anti-climactic at this point in the story. Is this the beginning, I wonder again. Here at this moment under a setting sun, sky deepening and darkening and air cooling. I've taken off my shirt. I'm wearing an a-shirt and a v-neck t-shirt and I've pressed my upper body against hers now. My thigh is pressed against her thigh and I'm using the leverage of this pressing to hold her against the ground with my belly and chest. I hold her face in my hands as I kiss her. And, as I say, what excites is not finally this kiss, though, later when we stand from the blanket I'll find myself, feel myself, my pussy, very wet. The excitement comes from this holding, restraint, pressing down on her. As we kiss, it's easy, and by this, I mean, I'm not really forcing something with my mouth. Surely you can imagine the first kiss with a new lover, the exploration of energies and exchange. I'm allowing that to happen and I'm allowing myself to experience what's happening, just feeling it and not forcing it. It feels good.

I'm also not climbing on top of her completely. I'm interested in her and in doing something different than I've been doing most of my life. This seems a tall order. I'm so habituated to acting and reacting the same way to everything, which I have to admit, usually isn't very good. I'm impatient. I hate waiting and I'm always thinking, "I'm getting fucked over so there's gonna be a fight". It's insane to live like this. It's alcoholism and it's a drag. It centers in the brain; this kind of thinking that 'I gotta fight', and 'fuck everyone!'. It's being manufactured by a brain that's hard wired to drink. To be diverted from this drink is a seeming miracle, one I'm grateful to bear witness to on a daily basis. But let me not get lost here. This is the point of the list of specifications I was interested in pursuing rather than it being a list of dating requirements or how the other person had to be, it was more a list of ways that I wanted to experience myself differently.

January 27, 2017:
Dear Bobby:

I was also thinking I was getting too old for all this but by this I mean all of it, everything, cashiering, trying to write, living in San Francisco as a middle aged (I mean, as I was approaching 50, I was hoping I was already way past the middle, I'm thinking this better be near the end of all of it; even another 30 is gonna be too much and too long) obviously butch dyke, just living in San Francisco through the boom economy that leaves most of us behind, bearing witness to neighbors living in tents on the street, watching friends have children in their 40s, dating, being in an open relationship: all of it. Basically, being alive. I'm thinking all the time: I'm too old for all this being alive.

This is where the list comes in. Now, I've written a bit about the list already but at this point I want to explicate clearly its purpose. I'm down all the time, can't find interest or excitement in anything, not even a hot girlfriend who'll hop up on me at any moment to suck me off. No books, no films, no friends, no food, no yoga, no hot yoga: nothing holds or incites interest. I'm depressed. I'm barely even jacking off. At the lowest point, not even a fantasy of jumping off the bridge can be sustained or rubbed into something like relief. Meaning not even the thought of well, if I feel this bad tomorrow I can kill myself, not even that holds any interest. I'd been sober for about seven years at this point, and to be honest I was getting a daily reprieve from things being so bad I'd want to kill myself. Taking an inventory and doing the meditation really was taking the edge off, providing stress relief and freedom from resentment and worry. It's just that not having a reason to kill myself didn't actually give me a reason to live.

I wanted to feel as good, better actually, then I did when I was drinking or else what was the point of being sober. I mean, how can an alcoholic live sober if they don't have a more than sufficient substitute. I didn't get sober because I wanted to be a good person or a person who had a job and relationships. I got sober because alcohol stopped giving me any relief, in fact, every time I drank at the end, I was very sick.

Something's got to happen, I thought and I thought that meant I had to do something. Like get a better job or a better apartment, or for fuck sake, write something. The more I tried any of that, the more humbled I got, because any ideas I had didn't make me actually feel good, not to mention the fact that I never had any power to actually pursue any of them. Or if I was able somehow to muster a non-existent will trying to pull something off in this world, I'd so exhaust myself I'd be in bed for days, recovering. Now this is difficult to convey, the sickness of an alcoholic when they are sober and then even more difficult to convey the actual abandon to a power greater than oneself, especially so if one doesn't believe in that power. How to bear witness to a god one doesn't believe exists. And yet, even that non-belief, even the expression of non-belief in this power, expressed by a sober alcoholic, bears witness.

And so does this typed page, bear witness.

I've explained that I have a whole structure through which I want to explain what happened. And like every story, it's the same: what it was like, what happened and what it's like now. And right now, it's pretty great. It's like a heroine's journey, down and further down and then deeper, and then the return and sharing the experience with others.

What's needed in the beginning is the first part and the list is part of those preparations. It turns out that the procuring of typewriters is as well. I mentioned the food and the blankets, and securing this place here to relate this whole thing to you.

In the trees at the golden hour, I'm leaning over and kissing her. It's the beginning so I'm not forcing anything. I'm trying to not force my will on this situation but to let it unfold and reveal what it will be in itself.

She asks me a few questions like the nature of the open relationship with Canela and what's allowed and that type of thing. She also says she has some ideas about what she wants in a situation or relationship or sexually. I've some ideas too but that aren't fully formed and I notice when I think about 'what I want' it's basically just the opposite of what I'm doing now, so it feels false, just like the same assertion of my will except from the other side, two sides of the same coin and I want something new. I'm craving something new. A new idea to interest me enough to get excited. Me thinking, "oh, I want to try the opposite of what I'm doing over in this other situation," is still coming from my brain.

In another situation, I'm going over to a lover's house in Oakland. Michelle's just broken up her 10-year marriage and wants to get back in the game and get her sexy back on. We get together once a week and I fuck her. She's got the sexy for sure and fucking her is so great. I feel so fortunate to have met her here and to be the one who's in the right place at the right time: I'm getting all she's giving.

January 30, 2017:
Dear Bobby:

But meanwhile what's also happening here is that I'm allowing myself to get fucked. That was the difference. And it was good. And it was in this situation, with this woman, where the dick energy really developed. I've variously described this energy as a crystal or beam of light or as a palpable manifestation of some fierce sex magick or whatever. And in our queer time of an engendered era, there is an idea that it's all phallus and all cunt: the phallus is the dick and the cult and the tongue and the hands and fingers and feet and that the cunt is the cunt and the dick with urethra and the ass and the mouth and every pore on the skin can be penetrated and that people all have phalluses and all have cunts. But when pussy is still used specifically to separate some people from others to assign privilege to some over others, to express misogyny and the resultant violences that occur as a result of this hatred, I thought like some other women, I want to claim my cunt as the beautiful source of pleasure it is, as a woman. To actually have my own experience with my own cunt as a site of pleasure. And that, in this moment of ours, in this era we share, as my female body ages I want to claim it: female. Woman. Butch. Lesbian. And that the compensatory behaviors that are actually based in resentments, are my own fears of not being good enough. Not strong enough, not butch enough, not feminine enough: a self-will in collision with itself is never satisfied.

But when you have the kind of fantastical phallus that can fuck a woman across the room without even touching her, just by looking at her (of course the eye has always been the consuming penetrator organ) it's hard to undo that kind of a habit. There's great feeling of competence and ability that comes from years of practice and this is one of the benefits of actually being an aging butch: the continued experience of being female in a female body fucking women. I've been extremely fortunate in this regard. And without sounding cocky, so to speak, about any of it, in many spiritual traditions the belief that our entire existence is false and that the only reality is god, well, then why should a fantastical phallus be any more or less real as a beam of light or imagined crystal or just a good, good feeling, and overall feeling of goodness prevailing, and when a good feeling is happening I have fear about trying to switch that up. So, if I'm fucking her, for many years it's been this way, and when she reaches for me, I brush her hand away. It's easy to think in this case the dick is the source of pleasure.

Bonarh has to piss and there is a discussion of this: will she piss in her pants beneath me? Will she leave the cave? Hold it in? I haven't written enough here, not can I relate everything that happened, transpired or was invented with memory, even by now. It's not necessary I know, but I'm unsure of what I want to convey exactly: my confusion? My feelings of being less than? What I want to relate is this:

Bonarh is sitting up and I'm reclined below, slipping my hand into her corduroy's waistband and my flattened palm up under her shirts between her breast and then to the base of her neck and pulled myself up to kiss her. She opens her mouth to receive me. I get up from beneath her and come at her from behind. Her pants, open, are at her thighs and her ass is halfway out of her pants. From there, I come behind her and grab her around her thick middle. She's on her knees, facing away from me, at the mouth of the small cave, I'm behind her, slipping my hand now in her pants and she's wet with a hard, hard clit. I'm rubbing it and then I lean back and unbutton my shirt, take it off and toss it on the blanket in the cave. Then, I think, fuck it and pull the t-shirts over my head too. Now, I'm topless and it's all exciting. Her shirt I pull up and as I lean forward, my bare breasts and belly are against her bared back. I put my arms around her waist again and lean forward deeply, pulling myself into her and telling her as I push her forward, "stay up. Don't fall forward. Stay up and take me like this." My jeans are against her ass. I'm pushing with my hips and pulling her with my arms as we kneel in the sand. There's a man nearby on the rocks watching but harmlessly.

I slip my hand down the front of her pants, then pull out and unbutton and unzip the front of her pants and pull them further, her pants down past her ass, and I grab her clit with my hand, I grab her clit in my hand and as I do I say, "I want this. This is what I want."

And so, finally, we can begin.

Now, even when I'm writing this, I'm distracted. I finally hit a groove when Canela's home. She wants attention. I spanked and hit her in the kitchen, then turning her around in front of me. "Kiss me," I say, telling her to turn back around again. I'm in the chair and she stands in front of me, and telling her again, "Turn around now and kiss me." I get so hot so fast, taking my time, slapping her ass and warming her up, pacing each slap of my hand that I have to take off my shirt and sat there in an a-shirt. Earlier, it was face-slapping. Even earlier, her sucking me off and I came in her mouth and rubbed myself on her face. That was the start of the day. The end is her jacking herself off in the bed next to me, silently.

All throughout the day, the intrusions and distractions, the thoughts and actions and trying to write, remembering, conjuring, imagining, hoping and jacking myself off with all of it. I want to write the part now about Bonarh fucking me suddenly.

I was on my back with my pants off. I don't remember the lead up to it and in fact, much later, when she's fucking again in the fall, I'll ask her, "Bonarh, how did my pants come off? How was I completely naked on the beach in the cave with a guy watching you fuck me from the rocks above, as you fuck me?" So, already with socks and shoes off, already topless and now, caving in the cave under the blanket, and she's fucking me. Strong, deep, hard, all the clichés even have me feeling so good, so surprised and even now, I run my hand up and down, across my body, my belly, breasts while she fucks me, like a cave in the cave and how to describe this feeling of being so filled up with her, her fingers deep and twisting and digging. She's looking at me the whole time, it seems even when my head is thrown back and I'm seeing the low roof of arch, carved rock roof-like, an arch and as I'm letting go, yelling, crying, laughing and coming and then again, pulling myself to come again with her inside me, the blanket over us, her sitting between my legs and hand on my chest while I cry and come and the blanket with tiny holes of being quilted spread like a star filled sky over our heads and consultations are mentioned.

This everythingness now inside me: the sand, the fog, the spraying salt water, blankets, her hand, her eyes on me, a cave, star-filled existence, fucking, slapping, not unloving, lesbianism exalted, experienced, exclaimed and called forth, answered, brought forth to bless and rule the world, I come again.

Oh, Bonarh, I like the way you fuck. It's good. Earlier, when I'm touching her she's saying my name over and over and then asks is that even your name? Do you even want to hear your name? No, I answer, this is the name I took to protect myself for where I was going down to. It's surprising to me, her question, but always my answer because it comes so easily. Later, while fucking me, I'm jacking off, yelling, laughing, she has another question: "What gets you off? What really gets you off?"

Desire is caught in my throat and I'm ashamed I don't know the answer. I begin to spin out, fearful that there isn't anything that really turns me on. The thoughts are the usual 'fear that I'm not good enough' and the question lingers and asks again and again. I'm somewhat confused, because what I've relied on is the idea that what gets me off is getting women off; what gets me off is turning women on. But for myself, as an actual physical body, not just as an idea of some kind of fantastical phallicism or narcissistic exercise, I'm not sure how or even if I liked to be touched. I'm saying this as a question obviously, since I'm describing loving how I felt when Bonarh fucked me, though I hesitate and don't write 'loving how Bonarh fucked me'.

Either way, what I try and tell myself or don't, is it's the experience while it's happening, while she's fucking me that feels good. Of course, the re-thinking about all of it has me doubting myself. But let me say this, without a doubt, this kind of excitement feels very good. Bonarh fucking me in the cave: I'm touching myself and running my hands up and down my body, over my belly and my breasts and then I'm jacking myself off while she fucks me and I come hard and maybe immediately continue into the second one which has me yelling again and then the third which is me crying, sobbing a tremendous release and laughing hard I'm so surprised. She pissed once and I wonder if that was how I got my pants down, her pissing. I had my hand in a fist between us, and I'm rubbing her cunt while she pissed. And then, I'm soaked, the blanket well and stuck with sand.

Let's return to the cave, the converging actually of two caves and colliding of a low arch. It's here, now that everything has been gathered that this can begin: the blankets, the provisions, the maté in ritual strength, and the request prepared which becomes the invocation of desire.

As I said in the golden hour in the grove, even me thinking, "oh, I want to try the opposite of what I've been doing over in this other situation," is me asserting my will or my ego; trying to pull something off. I want something new. So, I started a list, and actual list on paper, putting my desires and attractions into words. One idea

I wrote was the idea of wanting the sex to be sacred, as opposed to romantic or profane. 'Sacred' refers to collective representations or actions that are set apart; that which transcends the everyday life; the rituals which acknowledge the transcending of the mundane. Yeah, magick. Also, not romantic, meaning not for an idea of 'us' but for all; the escalation being increasing transcendence, not necessarily increasing intimacy for us, though, of course, opening to love (I'm not unloving) just not the love of romance but a spiritual love. This of course now seems quite a tall order, perhaps not even possible. I wrote myself a note that said, "not unloving, transcends; not personally transformative (do I or her need to change?) but explicative for us each and both: i.e., what is being created when the focus isn't on creating an 'us'?

Of course, all of this relates to the second idea which is that I'd like to push myself to be uncomfortable, to push past what I'm comfortable doing or performing. This means I had the idea of how to be with women ('I know how to be with femmes') and how to be comfortable, finally in the way I fuck or how I feel confident that way. I'm the kind of butch who loves to fuck women. And I've been at it a minute now. But I'm ready to push myself, to experience perhaps being uncomfortable during sex, to actually have the experience that I don't know what's going to happen next, what I'm going to do and then, as a result, what she'll do. I've relied on this for a while and I'm curious what else is available for me.

I wanted to transform the dick energy.

She's up on my lap, hands on my chest in the crevasse on the blankets. I've come with a lot of ideas and she's met me. Well? I ask and Bonarh begins: "It's not really ideas," she says. "They are more like desires" and her own list is stated. I pull a pen and paper from my pocket, having to hoist her weight up as I lift my hips to reach in the front pocket of my levis and as she speaks I take notes. "First of all, listening and sensitivity. But also, I exist. I am a person. These are the base lines," she says, and then quickly follows with, "I want to please you. I'm into submission. In every way, from being a hole to service." This she says so directly, so seemingly easily that I am quite surprised. I'm almost speechless. A lot of women have said a lot of things to me but this is so very clearly stated. I say to her, "Your directness and clarity are exciting." We make out. She's still up on my hips and to kiss her I pull her head a bit closer and lift my shoulders to meet her mouth. There's an exchange about her not bending all the way down and she stays up. I flip her over then and I'm on top. I'm actually fearful at this point, surprised and fearful but I take my turn. What I want: sacred not romantic. I like having sex outside. And I want to be uncomfortable, pushed past a comfort I feel fucking women.

It has been hard for me to claim the idea or label of being 'dominant' and I don't identify as a top, but my lovers relate to me this way and the dynamic between us is that way. And as I was stating, I wondered if when I was thinking what I wanted, if everything was just the opposite of what I was doing, isn't that the same thing basically, and if I wanted to get fucked, which I did, though it didn't actually make the stated list, did that mean I wanted to be submissive. I didn't think so, but I couldn't imagine something other than this. So, this was already a surprise, or unexpected; another opportunity presented for me to refine an aspect of my sexuality I'm uncomfortable claiming or enacting.

January 31, 2017:
Dear Bobby:
Even as we leave the beach that day, walking up the new stairs which makes it easy, I'm starting to feel sadness about this being over. This is just how I am. I go up fast and come down fast and hard, rapid cycling. She dropped me off in front of the store where I'd left my bike and we had a moment there. I'm fearful I'm gonna look needy, or worse, tear up as we part. I mean, I'm that over-reactively sensitive. It's one thing to cry when you're getting fucked, that's hot, or can be, but crying because the date is over? Please, butch, please. So, I try to rein it in a bit, kind of pull myself together, get a little hard. But as we stop at the curb in front of the store, she turns to me and says she's turned on by me or is into this or something. Again, it's her directness that is so alluring. I say, "You are very sweet, Bonarh. It's very appealing." And, she is. There is a sweetness to her directness

and it catches me off guard. All of it has me so heady, so feeling unlike myself. I'm so glad for it all.

The type of person I am, I got to feel unlike myself. I got a major personality problem: my own. I mean, yelling, screaming, cursing, crying and that's just at the register with customers. I got to be rid of any ideas I have of myself. Part of the problem is any idea I have of myself: anything I think is fraudulent. Writer, top, butch. What I do is drink. I'm a recovered alcoholic and anything else is what this power is doing.

Hearing Bonarh say her desire was to please me, either be a hole or of service has me excited, even now, through my body. Even with my doubt: did I hear her right? Do I think I know what she means? And then I remember my own stupid list of explications and I feel a little sick... But remorse and regret and questioning remembered manufactured images aside, without a doubt, this kind of excitement feels very good and the rest, the persistent fears and resentments are simply the re-sending. I feel so good actually that I'm actually able to listen to Bob Seger and get romantic about my funeral.

It's this kind of good feeling, rajasic energy that's providing a vibrational, productive passion that I'm craving. I want to blow out everything that's old and stuck and I want to get on it, fast. This new feeling and excitement foster enough action and activity that what can be asked is what do I want.

Bonarh texts me and asks to see me. To say I'm excited is an understatement. I can feel my heart pounding in my chest. I have a 45-minute dinner break. "Come and meet me in the store," I tell her. She's got the car in front on Folsom and I hop in. Ok, let's go, do a u-turn and let's go back down Folsom.

I listen to her. On the drive two blocks over to Enterprise Street, she is saying she usually has a lot to say but not now. I touch the curls of her hair at the nape of her neck. We park the car and the sun is strong through the windshield. I close my eyes and put my head back against the seat and spread my arms across the back of the driver's seat. I let my legs fall open and just rest. I smile. It feels good, with images of her and sex in my imagination, and the sun on my face.

She says she's been writing and reading, or re-reading. I forget

which. I tell her about hearing her on thursday: did she say she wanted to please me? No, perhaps at this point, she'd already mentioned
wanting to give me pleasure. We were sitting up in the front seat, she
was turned and like 3/4 facing me, slightly reclined on the passenger
side. She was sharing her concerns about the time constraint. The
seeming constraints, I said. She said that there was only enough time
for one thing to happen. She talked about pleasure, giving me pleasure, I put my left arm across her chest and shoulders and pushed
her back in the seat and then reached across her with my right hand
to the recline lever next to the seat, pulled it and pushed the seat flat.
Then I snuggled up next to her.

"Pleasure? I thought you said 'please me,' that you wanted to
please me." She said no, pleasure. "What is the difference," I asked.
Well, she said, 'pleasing' sounds like a little puppy, sitting, waiting. I
forget what she said 'pleasure' was, so stuck did I get with that image.
I put my face close to hers and started to unbutton her shirt and said
one of the things I kept coming up against in the past few days was
the idea of her pleasing me. "I want to please you" and how when I
heard it and thought about it, it felt discordant in my body and imagination but that now, in the car, with the sun getting low and heavy
through the wind- shield, the idea of her wanting to give me pleasure
felt very familiar and I knew what to do with it: resist it. And then
almost immediately as I expressed this, I felt the high-speed vibrational energy and excitement slow to a level that felt comfortable and
familiar; resistance and defiance, ah. Oh, yes, I thought, I'll fuck her.

Unbuttoning her shirt now, her laying back, I'm describing
my week since the beach: high vibration. High production. A lot
of re-reading and not much fantasy about what could happen but
a revisiting of what did happen. As the excitement builds, faster,
seemingly, I have been slowing everything down and repeating everything from that day, scene by scene. I'm whispering, talking close
to her face and unbuttoning her shirt, slipping my hand inside. Her
belly. Her bra. Perhaps her hips, still clothed.

What happened in that cave? I ask her. I keep wondering how I
wound up naked, caving in a crevice, getting fucked. How did that
happen? I'm getting hot now, thinking of how she responded while

I was asking her this: squirming on the seat and listening but also trying to answer my questions. I took off my shirt. I said, "I was behind you, you were facing into the low roof cave and your pants were pulled down. I was touching you and had your clit in my fingers. I was getting so hot I took off my shirt: unbuttoned my shirt and took it off then looking at your ass bare, exposed, I thought oh fuck it and pulled my t-shirts over my head and tossed them to the side, in the cave with the button-down shirt. Then, I leaned forward and that's when you felt my belly on your back."

By now, her shirt was open to her navel, actually just above. She's wearing a black lace bra and a black undershirt; the kind women can call a camisole. The shirt is old and faded and very soft and with a small sexy, sexy tear between her breasts. I sat up a bit in the car and said, "Yes. I want to see those gorgeous tits again." Actually, they are quite spectacular: round, firm, amazing size, perfectly shaped and thick nipples. Perhaps the most beautiful breasts I've had the pleasure of contacting. I say to her yes, this is what I wanted, to see these gorgeous tits again. She's revealed them, pulling them out from the bra and pulling her shirt down from her shoulders, my hand is rubbing her cunt through her pants. How did I land up naked on the beach under a blanket in a cave? How did that happen? I ask her again.

I'm on top of her now. I'm looking at her, her eyes, her tits, her belly with the small tattoo near her hip. I realize she's wearing a pantsuit, not a blouse tucked into slacks. Hmmm, the waist is tight at her thick, strong middle. I like this pantsuit, I say, "but you're not allowed to wear it anymore." I slide my arm into the suit so the back of my hand and wrist and forearm rest on her cunt.

I'm begging the narrative to hold me now as I start to get distracted. I'm wanting, even now, as my desire builds to leave the page, the car, the inside of her pantsuit. I'm so close, at this point, of entering her, actually putting my fingers in her cunt and so close to fucking her.

I'm touching myself now, pulling on my nipples and sliding my hand down my own pants. I'm not wanting to leave this excitement and I fear once I come, I'll be getting up from here. I'm using my left hand and fingers to spread my lips and press my clit. I'm not wet, or only slightly so but I am excited and could easily come.

This isn't going to work, I say, as I slide my arm down the front of her pantsuit. I shift myself on the passenger seat so I'm coming at her from higher, not between her legs. The back of my hand reaches her clit and cunt. I turn my arm around so she's in the palm of my hand and we kiss. She looks happy, sexy. Tell me you want to please me, I say, and she does. Tell me you want to please me, that you want to give me pleasure.

I start to quickly touch myself here, thinking of Bonarh's breasts and then of her left breast with the tiny mole, red, raised on the side and how this imperfection is the place where I can land, feeling solace in my completely imperfect body, my female bodied failure, and I immediately begin to flesh out the narrative that's been underlying this one, the narrative that's been developing concurrently as I've been re-telling this one which is Bonarh on her back in her bed, hands behind her head, nipple clamps, harness and dick thrown on the bed beside her. "Put all your energy through the dick, no, not through it; instead, like your cunt is a sleeve, enveloping the dick so that your cunt is fucking me."

February 2, 2017:
Dear Bobby:

"Put all your energy through the dick," I say. "No, not through it. Like your cunt is a sleeve enveloping the dick so that your cunt is fucking me." I come quickly with my left breast in my hand holding my nipple tight and I'm surprised actually how good my breast feels from this position on my back: full, round, satisfying. I come a second time and then a third, pulling myself, standing now, remembering and imagining and feeling good, pushing my thighs hard next to the desk, tossing my head back, pausing to remove my glasses, toss them on the bed and come hard again. I feel good, caught in the music and the various narratives spinning, and unreeling, overlaying, repeating, reviewing, recreating.

Yesterday, getting back to my register directly from her car, getting out of her car on Folsom Street at the produce door, I say, "we still have a lot to do together". Her bra, shirt, and pantsuit are disheveled, her breasts are actually bare. Her pussy is on my hands, face, and, walking across the store, I put my hands to my face and inhale. I'm wet. The store is busy though and I have to jump on immediately, just start ringing up groceries with heart pounding, head spinning. Lightness fills me; I'm completely distracted and full. The customers appreciate how good I'm feeling because I'm reflecting it all to them: smiling, flirting, spreading the love and good feeling; balancing friendliness with accuracy, counting back change when they pay cash.

Very quickly this turns to a feeling of disappointment, a feeling of not quite good enough, a feeling of well, people don't have anything and a feeling of predictability. This is the other side, I think, of feeling comfortable, confident and defiant to pleasure or the idea of being pleasured or pleased. I actually feel myself, as I go on with the shift, getting heavier, eating some cheese, bread and crackers. Washing up and pissing, finally on a break, telling myself: "I told you so." This seems obvious as of course corresponding to the line, "fear they all just want me to fuck them." I mean, even in the front seat of the car, I'm thinking, "Oh, yeah, pleasure, please me?" The way that this feels comfortable is to resist it." Mostly, this translates as, "better not let her touch me."

But the fear they all just want me to fuck them persists. And I do. And I did.

My arm twisted, her cunt in my palm, slipping fingers in, it's not enough. She takes off the pantsuit, pulls it off her shoulders, down to her waist, shaking and lifting her hips and ass to pull it past to her thighs and when I try to climb between her legs from the seat I've fallen back into frustration and then to watch her I am amazed again at how much Bonarh is willing to give, how much she wants this. In fact, when I do actually get there, my fingers fucking her, squatting somehow on the driver's seat, above her between the steering wheel and her body nearly bare, belly, breasts, thighs, now too, Bonarh says, "Yes, Cashier. I need this. I need this." Does she catch herself then, because next she says, "I want this, oh, I want this."

When I'm fucking her, I want to say here: finally, when I'm finally fucking her, not just because of the length of this narrative but also because even though the experience itself is so short, seemingly contained—65 minutes from store pick-up to store drop off—I've already been at the effect of the desire from waiting. And so, the plunging in, the diving in, the pulling myself into her, the pulling of Bonarh to me (my hand rests on her throat) and then yes, the pushing into this open wanting. She is remarkably nearly hairless. Again, let me say when her breast, belly, and thighs are bared, they are particularly so because of their hairlessness.

I'm breathing hard now and must get up and go to work. I'm wanting to stay in this dream world, the slipping story of her car, my bed, this page, and not be standing in a black shirt and tight levis with scuffed combat boots. I'm wanting to be in an a-shirt on her hips, in her bed, dreaming, imagining, fantasizing. And when I take a break, there's an email from her, sent apparently while I'm jacking off at home and echoing everything I'm doing, thinking, and writing. I send a small pic of these pages. And getting back to the register ten minutes later, reading and re-reading her notes to me, my heart is pounding and I'm breathing so hard I'm almost panting, like a wolf, wanting and wet and maybe mouth drooling, scaring customers, perhaps, with my growling and predatory desires building. The rest of the afternoon passes quickly, and then an extraordinary meditation and back to the register, slightly still in the ether, drinking strong maté left-over from yesterday and then another bottle from the cooler shelf. Then upstairs in the lounge, longing, yearning and re-reading the wolfish animal-like text I sent she responds. And now, rushing through the rest of what I want to express.

As I exited the store at 5:45pm, out onto Folsom ahead on the sidewalk, she is standing in the sun, not leaning against the building but standing close and as I come up to her, she is surprised by my hello. "Were you not expecting me?" I cheekily say and she says no, I wasn't expecting you to come this way, I had oriented myself toward the other door." But what I liked was her waiting for me, ready for me.

In the car, before we fuck, while there is tentative touching still and I'm questioning her about her experience the past few days, she shares an image she describes as a fantasy about my shirt. My shirt? One I've worn? Or…? "Yes," she says. "One I've seen you wear." Later, while I fuck her, I ask about the shirt, fucking my shirt? She laughs and says no, like biting it, something like an animal. Thinking I'll savor and re-read the email she sent later or whenever and even with the first text I started to go down with fear I expressed too much, fear I'm stupid, fear she's not into me and fear she thinks I'm stupid. Then, and also now, my wrists are sore and painful. Too much fast-paced cashiering? Yoga? No, parked on Enterprise.

Through the night, I'm woken with excitement and desire, and now, the first time I've sat down today, I'm wasted. I can't even think about writing. Mostly, I'm wasted in my brain and thinking actually of turning my attention away from this excitement for the next ten days or so, though I'm fearful of the results: will she feel this and leave herself? Even now, I don't feel like I can get back to that excitement, physically and then I think, oh, just a little more, one more visit to the bed in her room with my dick and harness, telling her to take her clothes off. And this leads back to one more visit to the front seat of her car, parked on Enterprise with the seat pushed back, the driver's seat is reclined almost flat. Comcast vans are lining up on this alley, at the gate, at the dead end coming back at the end of the days' work. While I'm fucking Bonarh, a butch getting off of work is leaving the yard where the trucks park. She walks by and as she passes, I look up and give her a sweet, broad, cocky smile and she smiles back.

February 7, 2017:
Dear Bobby,

Soon after this time on Enterprise, Bonarh goes north to Portland for six weeks. Canela and I take a trip to Mexico, to the beach.

On the flight to Mexico, we are seated in separate rows and attempts to sit together are thwarted by stewardesses and stewards: those rows are extra rows, you can't sit in extra rows if you didn't pay extra. And other passengers are traveling in couples and also don't want to sit separate from their companions. I read magazines and watch Canela's hair above the seat and the back of her head around the side, not the aisle. Leaving the house in the morning, I have much less trip anxiety than ever before—I slept well, everything was packed the night before, everything cleaned in the apartment, we

48

have plenty of time getting to the bart and to the airport —but still I'm barely able to concentrate or distract myself from near constant thoughts of so many women. Going into meditation after finishing the first magazine it is a seemingly continuous series of images: Michelle, T, Bonarh, Jacey, Canela, very stimulating and the entire flight I've been aware of my clit in my jeans and my nipples pressed against my shirt due to the buttoning of my corduroy levi jacket.

I adopted an attitude of compliance at the TSA going through security. Go through the scanner? Sure, no problem. Take out the toiletries? Sure. Hold my pants up above my waist, No problem. Hold the wallet in my hand above my head? Sure. Empty all my pockets? Take off my shoes? Jewelry? Belt? Yes. Yes. Yes. Without the rushing or running late, fear I will miss my plane, I don't even ask to opt out. No problem, wait in line like everyone else, no special considerations needed. Hands held with wallet above head in socks in the scanner. Everything removed and still the screen shows a highlighted area near my groin. "Well, I'm wearing button fly levis," I try to explain, which obviously corresponds directly to the image on the screen. TSA agent says she will have to pat me down. I say, sure, no problem. And again, lift shirt so she can slide her fingers along the waistband of my jeans. I hold the pants up higher on my waist, above my hips. My belt is off so of course my pants are falling. She puts gloved fingers inside the waist band of the pants, front and back, pats down the inseam and puts special attention on the actual button fly: rubbing back and forth, up and down, while I stand with arms raised. As she rubs across my breasts with the back of her hand she asks, "Do you have any sensitive areas?" She then swabs my hands, front and back, palm and back of hand and says, "Ok, now I will check your wallet." I say sure sure sure through this whole thing. Canela is already on the other side with shoes back on and tied, waiting with a fearful look. TSA takes wallet, leaf's through the cash, pulls out cards and ID while scanner checks swab, reads my ID and reluctantly as I've passed the scan and swab test, passes wallet back to me and says "please go through the scanner again". I step in again, sure no problem, complete compliance, no problem.

The area is highlighted again as I step from the scanner and TSA says, "stand here a moment, please". "Do you think it could be the button-fly on my jeans?" I ask. "Can that be it?" TSA says, "Are they men's pants?" With an air of compliance, I answer honestly: "Yes, men's 501 levis." "Well, that's the problem," she says. "You're wearing men's pants."

We arrive that evening on a small island off of Cancun. It feels like a transition to being away, to being on vacation. Our room is nice though, with very cold a/c and right on the beach. It has a little kitchen, bathroom and a comfortable bed. We put our suitcases on the kitchen table and Canela starts to settle in a bit. I immediately put on the dick and tell Canela to take off her pants. We get on the bed. I lube up just the tip of the dick and then run it up and down her clit. Then, just kind of fucking her clit between her lips. Then playing with her cunt with the tip of it, putting it in just a little and pulling back out, then pushing all the way in. We are looking at each other and smiling, then I'm looking at the dick hanging off my hips and at her cunt. It's been a while since she sat on the dick up on my hips and I got off, hard. She took the harness off me and washed the dick and we lay on the bed together.

When we got up, it was sunset and I stripped and convinced her to do the same and we went out into the water under a full moon and swam, naked.

February 10, 2017:
Dear Bobby:

After we are down in Mexico for a few days, I begin to feel my self, my physical body begin to relax. It's hot here in august, humid and the water is warm too, which laying and floating in this salty warmth adds to the overall feeling of physical ease and relaxation. Even waking with back pain and leg pain—the usual— is soon alleviated by the moist heat. There is a three-legged cat who lives where we are staying and I say to Canela, "I don't want to fall in love with a cat while we are here." Canela said, "How you not gonna do that?"

We drank coffee out on the patio in the morning before it got too hot. Canela got up to go inside the little cabana and I followed her in. I folded my towel into a small mat and took off her shirt and told her to kneel down in front of me. I took off my undersuit and stopped in front of her and told her to suck me off. It felt amazing, her mouth open, her head thrown back, neck bent completely back and my entire pussy inside her, her tongue working to get me off. We laid on the bed after and fell back asleep and when we woke again we put on our bathing suits, went down to the water and swam a bit. Then sitting reading in the shade, another swim and then do the afternoon steps. Then we dressed and took a taxi to the north end for dinner and an aa meeting for me.

The directions to the aa online were very precise and clear: "across through the door on the left side, down the hall, up the stairs in the back, across the roof to the door that has a large aa sign on the door." Plus, when we pulled up in the taxi, the building was green and white and was painted mural-style, covering the entire front façade in English and Spanish the days and times of all the meetings.

After situating ourselves to the meeting location, we walked around the malecon and found a place to eat. I had fish. So, did Canela. It was grilled with very delicious green salsa that is local here. During dinner we were talking about our sex life, our polyamory and then, with two iced coffees and the salsa sweat, I'm feeling so good I offer to talk about my sexuality and how I've been experiencing it. Of course, any feeling good so often borders on mania and then a plunging regret of having said too much, narcissistically, unintentionally saying something hurtful or opening a can of worms. Anyway, at the table I said to Canela, "I want to express myself to you as a friend. I don't want you to have a big overreaction, taking what I say personally and then it being all about you instead of about me, trying to express myself." I mean, I'll be honest, I'm selfish.

She replied, rightly, "Yeah, sure, I hear your request and I want very much to hear your experience. But my reaction is unmanageable, as you know, and not personal to you." I was already getting fearful and fear I was going to sound cocky. I also had fear I wanted to keep a level of discretion. This is the part of the open relationship I find a challenge: how to express to Canela my experience without divulging actual acts or specific dynamics or even specific words exchanged; how to keep intimacies intimate.

After dinner, Canela paid and we walked a bit in the north end, through the few blocks of tourist mall-style shops and t-shirts and hats and souvenirs and restaurants advertising, on sandwich boards in front, 'mexican style' drinks, but we're in Mexico, what else would they be. Then the big hotels on the northern most point, at the water's edge. These are thankfully much smaller than the big hotels we passed in Cancun. Here, the beach is wider and sandier than near where we are staying, and here, there is also less seaweed. It is raked on the beach and in the water and then piled in tall piles in various places on the sand. The water itself is very shallow and there is a roped-off area for hotel guests to stand in. The water is that shallow, thigh deep. This area is full of people as we walk by, people standing or sitting in the water so it's shoulder high. Some had drinks in their hands. It was close to 6pm now and the beach, the wide sand, the swath, still was full of people laying on their towels or on chaises. Most of these people had devices in their hands, staring at the screens while the sun set Canela and I walked out, looked around then turned around to walk back to the street.

By now it was tense between us. As an example, I tried to use the situation with Michelle. I said I was butch with her. There wasn't a lot of overt dominance being enacted between us. Canela said, "Butch. Top. Dominant. It's all relative."

February 13, 2017
Dear Bobby:

We are too abnormally strained to pursue any interest which only adds to self-pity and uselessness. The only use for pity and uselessness is for a drink.

What I want is to be more creative to enact other ways of expression that aren't replicated with Canela and I. That's what I'm trying to express right now, I said, actually right now. I'm highly caffeinated and sweating. We were still talking, we are still talking but by now, I'm getting fucked up. I am fucked up.

I want to be intimate with Canela but I don't know how, I think. At the same time, I want to protect the intimacies I'm building with other women, wanting to protect not just their desires but my own as well. This may be different for fags and dykes. Partially, there is still shame in desire for me.

As we walked, I said I was exploring ways of performing my desire. The conversation was getting rushed as we began to walk quickly and cross streets to avoid taxis, mopeds and strolling tourists. I was fearful still: am I saying too much, but I'm wanting to give a lot.

Canela got excited hearing that I was exploring my desires and expressed again the idea of her topping me, of there being more of a switch dynamic between us. I stopped on the street, as we crossed in front of the ferry landing and taxi stand, and said again this is not something I am interested in at all.

Mostly, as we were now at the aa clubhouse and I'm about to go in the door on the left-hand side, up the stairs in the back to the roof and then cross the roof to the little door marked 'aa', I felt the limitations of language. As Canela said while walking, "actually, butch, top, bottom, dominant, serving, none of these actually imply a proscribed behavior. I mean," she continued, "none of them mean 'the one who gets fucked.'" I said yes, that's what I'm excited about.

I'm going to leave out the next part of this story which involves a long-held, deep-seated resentment which ends basically, with the line: "what kind of people would bring a child into this unfair world?" and had me by the age of five wanting to kill myself even without an understanding of what that meant.

What I will briefly divert to however, is this story of sitting on the patio in Mexico the next day, in the morning before it's too hot. A small terrier has come, barking from the vacation rental house next to our cabana. This dog growls at me from the edge of the patio and edges closer followed by his person—a young woman in yoga pants, tattoos, speaking Spanish to the dog, chasing the dog, who is skirting her every move—she comes all the way onto the patio to get the dog and she carries it back to the other side of the cement wall between us. The wall prevents their large infinity pool from being seen from our side. The dog returns moments later, without her, quietly, comes directly to me and my feet and still quiet, lets me pet the soft fur behind its head.

There is another lone woman beachside, praying. Her hands and arms are spread wide as if in offering or receiving, standing still. She makes no notice of the little dog, who has run over near her now. When I look again, her hands are together over her chest.

Canela made a scrambled egg for the three-legged cat who is walking around, surprisingly well as it's the back leg that's missing. It seems to have only a limp when it jumps onto the chaise lounge. The cat sniffed the plate of eggs and disappeared and hasn't been seen since.

Meanwhile, the iguanas appeared and quickly smelling the eggs, ran over and started eating. The smallest one was first but soon a bigger was approaching and bullying the smaller one and then overtaking the plate. The iguanas move quite quickly and the speed at which they came to the scrambled eggs was quite startling. I, of course, was fearful they would come onto the patio and walk across my feet which are bare.

The plate was soon empty but they iguanas boldened: clapping, waving towels, tossing books toward them, standing up with a folding chair brandished in their direction: nothing startled them enough to run away. Now I was really frightened. I bent slightly to pick up the empty plate, would they charge? Though of course, they are of no threat, the voraciousness of watching them charge each other, the speed and hissing-like sound and then the rapid consumption of the eggs was disconcerting, coupled with their now unwillingness to back down. I took the plate into our room. As I turned, one or both of the iguanas came and ate up the pieces that had fallen off the plate. Their mouths were egg-covered as they ate.

February 14, 2017:
Dear Bobby:

(Just got the selectric back from Queens Typewriter.)

When those pieces were gone, the iguanas came and sniffed and stayed close to the edge of the patio, expectantly. I brought a pitcher of water outside and poured it on the spot to wash away the scent of eggs, but the smallest one just came then and drank the water pooled on the rocks where I poured.

I said people are a destructive force. Even our best intentions go awry, dangerously interventive: we fuck everything up, ecologically. Iguanas eating scrambled eggs from a plate? After dinner, we bought a can of cat food at the small mercado.

There's a breeze now just beginning and the iguanas are waking. After swimming we laid on the beach under the shade structure. We talked about our sexual dynamics and relationship and all of the complexities involved, all of the complications involved in dominance, submission, service, etc. We discussed the difficulties in arriving at these places and the questions and fears each of us faces. Is it misogynist to dehumanize? Is it anti-feminist to accept service? I have fear I am just using her. It's difficult now to write the questions because they seem simplified here and as we discussed them there was not only the ethical and mental challenge but the physical ache of difficulty.

This is related to the conversation with Bonarh on the way from the beach when talking about cocksucking and thinking of two men there: the idea of worship, prayer, service, submission, etc., but when it's male/female the undercurrent of these concepts and acts is also the misogyny of "I'm going to choke you with my dick" and I said the trap of course is the attempt to police one's own desires. I want, as a woman, as a dominant woman, to at least consider my desires in terms of where there occurs an anti-woman, woman-hating, misogyny. When an entire culture is founded in patriarchal oppression, how can a sexual desire of dominance and submission that doesn't contain the idea of killing women be developed? This part is queer desire.

Canela and I feel good, very good actually, at the end of this conversation, like there has been some resolution. I don't feel at the effect of the inventor, that I've felt since we've been here the past two nights: fear I'm a selfish lover, fear I'm cocky and arrogant, fear I use women. All of this written now actually bears witness to the action of the steps: putting the fears on paper reveals them to be false and reveals their unreality mostly by how silly and obviously powerless they are. So, these too now seem so stupid but while at the effect of them it's quite painful. I don't want to be the kind of person I think I am. I want to be a loving, generous, pleasure-providing, woman-loving butch playing with power, not a careless, selfish, cocky, domineering asshole. There is so much relief in our conversation that Canela falls asleep.

When we wake from that nap under the fan in the sweating hot room, I call Canela, naked, to the side of the bed: "Come here." I'm in underwear and an a-shirt, laying still on the bed. I spit on my thumb and begin to caress her clit. This is the way she likes it, I think, and she asks to lift up her leg onto the bed. I say yes, still stroking. She begins to pull her lips apart and asks, "Can I?" I say no and actually push her lips closed and grab her clit from beneath, tight between my thumb and fingers. Her face changes and soon she is completely pulling away and saying, "If all you ever do is tease, it's not enough. You want to use the dog metaphor? Sometimes you give a dog a treat just because you love it, not as a reward for anything. I have fear you never want to give me pleasure, that it's always just about your pleasure. And if your pleasure is always about denying me, it's very hard." She said she had the feeling of being pleased with her other lover and I said I was glad she did. On the bed then I just listened mostly but I felt kind of like a jerk, completely. I said I was willing to try something new and when I said it's not really a part of our dynamic, I tried not to sound defensive. I said I was glad she had the power to express herself.

She had pulled away by now and said she didn't want to have sex now that she'd already gotten turned off, or something. She did lay in my arms, though

February 16, 2017:
Dear Bobby:

I'm just continuing to address these to you to keep myself honest; I have fear if I'm 'just writing' I won't and will get lazy and begin to believe all my fears: fear this is stupid, fear this is boring, fear this is a complete waste of my time, fear this is a complete waste of your time, etc.

We see what we believe and everything we believe is a mistake. The belief that destroys everybody is that the world lives outside our head. We hate the world; we hate ourselves. We found a way to kill ourselves and the world we hate. Force obsessive aggressive fight or flight but no human power. How do you flee a believe system? The 12 steps.

It's hot the next day too. Getting up after meditation in the afternoon we drink terrifyingly strong cold brew iced coffee on the patio which still has a bit of shade. I'm soon sweating, profusely. Canela too and in fact, she needs to go inside, "It's too hot," and she turns on the a/c in the room and makes some late lunch (eggs, cheese, guacamole, chips, bread) to eat. I'm really high: two iced coffees in this heat in the afternoon—online says the heat index is "feels like 110°," and even after eating I feel dizzy and good. We lay on the bed reading, but I can barely concentrate.

Soon, I'm re-doing the scene from yesterday evening: laying on the bed and calling Canela over, spitting on my thumb and rubbing her clit and shaved velvet lips. The same but better. Lifting her leg and spreading her lips, we look at each other and laugh. Soon, she's dripping wet, soaking the bed and I'm saying I want her to feel good.

Canela comes and I get up and push her on the bed on her back and fuck her. Easy the way she wants it, not the way I want it and soon I'm reaching for lube. I'm pushing in deep and then pushing in my fist. I feel so good. She says she feels good, too.

February 17, 2017
Dear Bobby:

The root of our troubles is fear, self-delusion. If I believe in any of it, I'm at the effect of all of it. The delusion that I have a life and I'm living it is my problem. We're getting what we're getting because we're seeing what we believe.

Of course, the fisting is the highlight of the day. It feels a bit rushed—over here. Last night Canela said it's been productive to have the luxury of so much space and freedom to talk in depth about our sex life, to have sex and actually get to the difficult fearful parts and express those too. The space to just swim all day. And of course, to write like this.

So much of what I experience as pleasure occurs in my brain which is why when Canela spoke of teasing her being physically hard for her I understood because, yes, that is a big part of my pleasure, pushing women to a point of difficulty physically. In the car last week with Bonarh and exploration of the difference between her wanting to please me and her wanting to provide me with pleasure. It is a subtle or profound difference. I said ok then. I was uncomfortable with the idea of her pleasing me but when she said provide pleasure I could feel my body immediately relax, the pounding, beating, frenetic pulse of excitement slowed and I said yes, I know how to approach pleasure: resist it. At least in my body, like if she were to touch me, or try to touch me. I turned then and fucked her which was hot and exciting.

After I felt oh this was somewhat predictable, meaning mostly that I performed predictably: sex means I fuck the women. Also, I was experiencing the let-down back at work, busy shift, somewhat ejected from a precious, sacred cove into the marketplace, hungry, tired, wasted from the surge of adrenaline, of anticipation, quite suddenly. It wasn't until I was writing about the whole thing, and also even more so reading her ideas about our experience that I was able to fully experience the pleasure. The pleasure of the text, so to speak.

I mean, I don't think it comes as a surprise if I say I have difficulty feeling physical pleasure. Or that my relationship to physical pleasure is at best, conflicted.

This night I have a dream. It was difficult to fall asleep, so much coffee all day, I laid for 45 minutes then finally an inventory was taken and I must have dropped off right after that. I don't remember. I was craving coffee right up to the end, as I fell asleep, but this morning, it feels hard to drink, though I need it more. I dreamt of going into the city with my dead dad Dennis and my ex, Pristine. In dreams it's always hard to tell if Dennis is dead or alive. We're going to NYC and stopping along the way at White Castle. Pristine is hungry and orders grilled chicken though we are on our way to lunch. I'm surprised that White Castle even has grilled chicken. She's too hungry to wait. The restaurant is crowded and, on the counter, a previous customer has left a box of donuts. Dennis is talking to two of the women also waiting for their order: Queens matrons. He's kind of crying, "I didn't know my mother before she died and now I won't know my daughter." He's pointing at me as he says it and it has the dream quality of also meaning "my daughter won't know me before I die." I'm opening the box of donuts, helping myself to what looks like chocolate coconut, asking Pristine to split one with me. She's disdainful, she hates sharing food but another customer at the White Castle grabs the other half from me. I'm eating the donut as I wake and they aren't very good, disappointing, like the double chocolate paleo donut at our store. This is the second disappointing cake dream since we've been here.

I'm fearful to write about last night going to bed with Canela. Earlier, as we lay reading I told her, "Don't tempt me with your ass. I'm too wasted to slap it." I was too full with an entire days' activities already. A bit later, as I come back from a piss, she's on the bed on her knees pulling her pants down, wagging her tail. I slap her, a bunch, and she's laughing. She likes it. With each series of slaps, she's leaning forward, out of reach from the where I stand on the side of the bed, her hips pressing to the mattress, laughing. "Get back up here," I say, as she wags from side to side and looks back over her shoulder at me. Slap-slap and again the same. I'm telling her to spread her legs, "isn't that what you like?" I ask, "to spread your legs?" "Oh, yes," she says, "Can I spread my legs?" I slap her pussy, her ass, which is reddening with my palm prints. I grab her labia and pull her toward me. I pull my underwear down and pull my own lips apart and push my clit against her asshole. She's laughing, shaking her ass. She says, "I love you fucking me but I never laugh the way I do when you're slapping me." I'm still at the effect of the cocky butch image that's being created here. The portrayal of this character as myself when actually I am quite fearful: how I look, how I sound, how I perform.

I can't just do something that I think I should do. That's humbling.

When it's cooler the next day staying here on the beach seems like it could be possible to stay another few days. There's less flies in the breeze. Overall though, I am filled with the fear I'm stupid, fear I'm worthless, fear I'm a failure, etc. I have so many ideas about trying to impress Bonarh, how I'll do it, what I'll do or say when I get back to San Francisco, the letter I'll try and write and send.

Actually, I fear I have nothing to actually express or communicate. I mean, who wants to hear, "I am completely filled with anxiety when I think of you" or, "I'm already fearful I've ruined this before it has started" or, "I've already grown bored playing and re-playing my same old ideas over and over", or", I have fear I'll want you more that you'll ever be able to give".

This is what the big book is describing when it says, 'as a result of the steps, especially as a result of meditation, we are in much less danger of excitement'. This is what excitement looks like for an alcoholic: over-reactive self-centeredness that leads to such a level of desperation: "oh, yeah, not even this." Now, how to express that to another person, and why exactly. This kind of darkness, this kind of love isn't very appealing. "Oh, yeah, no person, not even you, can relieve this alcoholism.

February 28, 2017:
Dear Bobby:

No human power can relieve my alcoholism. Self-knowledge avails nothing because it's self-delusion. I haven't turned good; god is doing for me what I can't do for myself. It's a joke to think I've done any of this, ever.

This seemed to be one of the difficulties with Michelle. She continually wanted her love to be enough to relieve this condition. She was always saying, "but I love you. My love is real." And no doubt it was, but her kind of perverse psychology, which to be fair is just actually what human love is, consisted of the idea that the reason she was feeling bad was because I wouldn't or couldn't accept her love. I have to base my experience on the spiritual axiom that if I'm feeling bad it's because there is no satisfaction in another person, place or thing. When Michelle and I went to Copenhagen, it was the middle of northern European winter, january and cold and grey and dark. We lay in bed for the first three days we were there jet lagged and falling asleep at 3 o'clock in the afternoon, no matter how much coffee we drank. Of course, we tried to talk about what was wrong, to process and find out if something was actually wrong, were we having problems? We were both tired and irritable and I didn't want to leave the house. Michelle was unable to express anything except "I'm feeling bad because you're feeling bad" and then the strange dangerous twist of thinking that would have her push me in front of a bus so she could relieve me of my depression. As if it weren't her resentments that had her feeling bad. Even with the oppressive grey skies, sleepless nights in an uncomfortable bed, jet lag and her crying jags, she kept saying over and over, "I mean, I'm just so happy to be here with you." She actually seemed quite miserable and was asking me over and over, "what's wrong?" Everyone knows when it gets to that point between two people, it's probably over already.

It takes all power for me to awaken to my resentment; a complete psychic change to realize, oh, I'm resentful. And not a better than thou kind of attitude, just pure gratitude for the knowledge that no one is doing anything to me; it's fear and resentment.

After the trip to Mexico, Canela and I return to San Francisco. The economic disparity is stressful and palpable. On my short bike ride to work, five blocks if I use the bike lane and don't cut through the back way the wrong way on one-way streets, the sidewalks, gutters and even the middle of the streets are disgustingly dirty. And by dirty, I mean not just litter and trash and papers, but dead rats, human feces, entire contents of rooms in apartments, suitcases with zippers busted open contents flailing on the ground. There is also a surprising number of lamps: desk lamps, standing lamps, night lights and bedside table lamps. People are living in tents amid the stench of urine. Bicycles, shopping carts, laundry carts, baby carriages and hand trucks form the base of some of these homesteads, wild on the street under the freeway overpass, along the alley behind my apartment and in the city college parking lot across the street. A few blocks further afield in any direction is a repeat of these cities within the city.

I'm glad for my rent-controlled apartment, of course and for its poorly lit bathroom because I don't quite see myself aging. The stress is taking a toll though. I drive over the bridge to my lover's after taking my belt to the ass of Canela. We had a brief overlap at home after her camping trip in the van with her best friend and I've just come home from work. I'm so happy to see her and she leans forward on the back of the desk chair and I use my belt and finish her off with my flat hands. We go fast and high and she says, "I wish you could beat me all night". I'm off then myself in the van to Oakland and I'm imaging as I listen to the radio—not a device hooked up to the radio but listening to actual radio stations as I've done since I've been driving, changing stations every minute or so—I'm driving through the cornfields of Indiana.

March 3, 2017:

Dear Bobby:

Farms that stink with petrol chemical fertilizer and pesticides, hazy humid blurry thick air as I drive to Indianapolis Airport from Fort Wayne, not over the Bay Bridge between San Francisco and Oakland and I'm feeling young, taking off my shirt and driving in an a-shirt with my middle-aged breasts grown larger and soft belly falling over the waist of my levis. The music has me nostalgic, strong, beautiful and a lover.

Goddamit, if I can just write.

In between songs, the news of a gay dance club being the scene of the latest mass shooting our sacred space has been violated.

I have fear I should be trying to finesse this whole thing a little. At least try and make it sound good or something. But the truth is most of this story is about how bad I feel. I mean, goddamit, I've never felt good. That's alcoholism. The only reason a person has to drink to oblivion is because they feel so fucking bad sober. I can't manufacture a good feeling and I can't write a good story. My story makes me sick, literally. But no money and ill health is god's provision and has me receiving the spiritual help that I crave.

I want this whole thing to be about this amazing sex magick that's occurred but it actually doesn't mean a thing if it's not a story where I'm literally being lifted off my death bed on a daily basis. Just to get to the store to cashier I need an entire psychic change; a spiritual experience. Thank god for the steps which are a shortcut to that spirit, diverting me from a drink, a drunken miserable life.

Of course, though getting back to the register is a drag, not even the grandest of god doing overrides the idea that what I want is to be outside sitting writing in the sun somewhere instead of standing at the register sleepily wanting to be somewhere else. I'm thinking about writing to Bonarh most of the time, even though I don't want that It's yearning and uncomfortable. I am by nature overreactive but this surprises even me. Where is this excitement coming from? She's not actually here. All of this is being manufactured in my brain. What normies call a crush feels oppressively like a crushing juggernaut, and I'm beneath it.

Even being touched sexually, getting fucked doesn't provide relief. When Michelle reaches for my cunt after I've fucked her, my first thought isn't oh, yeah good. I'm thinking well, let's get this over with. She pushed into me. I grab my clit and start jacking off. The other night with her I tried a twist and while she fucked me and I jacked off I was looking at her and saying, "I hate this. I hate this part," over and over until I came. I mean, I came hard but it's conflicted.

And maybe that's what's required for sexual pleasure; complexity and ambivalence. And the fact is, that I am actually getting off, that I am coming, so according to experts there isn't a problem, physically or psychologically, but combined with my dislike of being loved, my dislike of being touched seemingly begins to add to something.

And while the thoughts of Bonarh begin to be consuming, I'm not convinced that is an actual obsession. Mostly I'm full of comparisons and the wanting to be acknowledged and appreciated by her, approved of, yeah, I want her approval. I mean, I'm trying to get to the good part here, but there seems still a lot to go through.

Meanwhile, from Portland, Bonarh is writing me a letter.

She's riding her bike around Portland and while she is, she gets a text from me. What did I say? I wanted to fuck her. She rides her bike to a park, gets off and locks it up, begins to hike up the hill there. It's late afternoon, the last golden hours, she says, and she finds a fantastic spot dappled in the sun hanging, by a tree on the side of this hill so she could watch the sun shifting. She's just off the path but at this hour the park is less populated, only the guy who is a level above her in his own bunch of bushes with a hammock set up is around. She's had to clear away a bunch of vines with serious thorns, she writes, before she can sit down, off the path, somewhat hidden though in an urban park we're not exactly talking about wilderness.

Before she sits down, or is it immediately after, she's pulled down her pants and underwear, below her ass and lips so she could touch herself as she reads. Or was it the reading that elicited it, she writes.

Nevertheless, her pants and underwear were down by the end and even though what I'd written had her laughing, it was hot, she said. Mostly what was hot was the buildup of waiting. The waiting for the page and the waiting of me not giving it to her right away. It's allowed her to imagine in that place of waiting a lot of doing and being done. "And being undone by you," she writes.

She sits in the fading sun, moving locations, and as she starts to slide her fingers over her cunt and clit, spitting and sucking on her other hand's fingers before she reaches around to slide into her ass, she notices how the right hand feels so much more, or is it that she feels more being touched with her right hand. At some point during this, she's flooded with the same pre-cum we had together when I was over her, leaning on my hand, balanced above her and fucking/ not fucking her and she's building and getting wetter. Every once in a while, a person would pass on the path, within earshot, but she continued, doggedly and so damn slowly until she sped up and then she would breathe and return back.

Then, imagining my mouth at her ear, my mouth scraping actually her ear, the light was on her face and chest, she noticed the thorny vine was back and at the place where her ass met her fingers, almost at her cunt. She didn't stop she said because she loved the way it hurt and that, the hurt and the thought, is what finally took her over the edge and as she came she was pissing. So much of the time she had to piss and then there it was, going back in the earth by the roots of this blessed vine.

Then she sat for a while and took it in. The park was quiet and the sun was ablaze setting for real now, above and then through the trees, a soft glaze and she thought of all the good things she was thinking and feeling and then just breathing.

The next morning before work I'm lying in bed, trying to write. I'm trying to find some excitement in something and finally lose interest and set aside pen and paper and re-read her letter. I hate myself for my boredom but I push on anyway. I want to get off before work and I still have to get dressed and make some breakfast so I push myself. I lift my shirt and think of the nipple clamps in the bedside table drawer, imagining bringing them when I go to see Bonarh and taking them out, putting them on her and then laying her on her back and laying on my back on top of her, feeling the clamps and her nipples on my back and skin. I'm too lazy to get up and get them now, the awkward angle of reaching into the drawer from where I lay. Instead, I rub my torso with my left hand. I'm judging myself, my body, my sexual response—which seems less than excited. I have fear I should be better.

I look over at the bookshelf from where I lay: Macho Sluts, Leathersex, Oakgrove, but I'm even lazier to get up out of bed to get up for one of those either. I was to spend an hour now reading after writing and then a swim. I don't want to go to work. The books call out: Lispector, Drummer, Delany, Kristeva, and I do come, hard, crying out hard and loud and looking back at the shelf, nipple between finger and thumb, touching myself slightly differently than I normally do and I come again, quickly, calling out this time, "Please." Then I jump up to get ready for work and my date tonight with T, packing the straight jacket and an empty folder to carry the recent letter with me to work in my bag.

As I'm about to leave the apartment, finally as ready for work as I'll be with breakfast and some lunch in my bag with the straight jacket and the letter from Bonarh and the copy of the letter I sent to her. I hated myself after sending it, filled with remorse like I'd said too much and too stupidly. But now as I'm bringing my bike out the door a text comes and it's a pic of the letter, received and on her bed. I stop now and re-read it to myself in a low whisper. How does it sound? My feeling isn't one of despair this time but familiarity. The idea of holding my desire and letting her express herself excites me. The thought that has been with me for the month: what gives me pleasure?

It's hot outside, too hot. I'm thinking about everything too much and as usual, working is a relief. The real relief doesn't come until the next day though when I break down crying at the meeting. I mean, really broke down with it, bent over, open mouth, body wracked with sobs and and ideas of the 'I am.' It, the self-will, kills us. I was so glad for the release and the audible expression of miserable existence and humiliation. My tightly held, restrained ideas of myself and what I'm gonna do, need an explosion of power to wrench them loose. And despite myself and the ideas of who and how I am, they are being released and removed: I need to be free of the idea that I'm a writer; that I'm a lesbian; that I'm a dominant lover. I'm a garden variety alcoholic and to get right down to that, bodily and mentally different. No comparison.

I woke up this morning and immediately thought: I don't want to be thinking about Bonarh. I'm confused and resentful. She's left a voice mail saying she's on the east coast with her lover there and I'm thinking and wondering does that person fuck her as well? I'm cleaning the bathtub and thinking of my own situations: with Canela, with a vanilla lover, the straight jacket and typing with T and I'm re-reading Bonarh's letter and mine.

March 9, 2017:
Dear Bobby:

Bonarh returns to Oakland; Cashier and Bonarh set the terms of their arrangement; the project begins in earnest.

This moment begins at the Autumnal Equinox, the beginning of a new season, the day and night are of approximately equal duration all over the planet.

The night before, Bonarh calls to tell me she's back, closer now, she says. I, of course, want it all to start right now, as we are talking, I want her to come to where I'm staying on retreat in Oakland for a week.

I've been sitting out in the yard, drinking coffee with cats in the sun and waiting for Bonarh. It is at this point, this week that I've allowed myself this waiting. It feels a bit dangerous, though: the waiting is wanting and for me, wanting is wanting a drink, eventually. So, I've allowed myself small doses of this desire to build and build and get a little higher until I was sick with all of my ideas. I rode my bicycle around Oakland, the flat streets that are tree lined and cleaner than in SF, going to the swimming pool, it's a reprieve. The weather has changed too, so every day is hot and sunny, very hot and sunny.

On the phone, I want to tell Bonarh to come to where I'm staying, now. In our brief conversation though, it becomes clear that she needs to meet first, like before we fuck. She wants to check a few things out.

We actually don't know each other at all, save for a few letters sent and so we set a time to meet tomorrow: in Oakland near the lake at 19th and Alice. There is a large tree, canopy spread over head. And rolling up on my bike, she looks up at me, she's looking at me as I approach and she's smiling. I lay my bike in the grass and perhaps lean in to kiss her, but this is unclear. Perhaps I sit next to her, my back against the tree trunk as well and when I do and then look up myself, I'm facing now downtown Oakland and the skyline of that city, tall buildings, street lights, parking lots and traffic signals and above it all the sun is beginning to set, the sky glowing red in west behind us in the trees, the grass of the little park and the lake. It's already dark it seems, and my view of this direction is like that of looking in a forest, thought a small one. What I'm trying to describe here is the contrast of this spot where Bonarh and I sat and the rest of the world: light fading busy traffic and populated. We are alone in the park as it darkens and then, as the sun is set, it gets colder now the way it does in the bay, not like NYC where night brings warm, dark air and that's what's so great about summer there.

So Bonarh asks her questions. But soon it's too cold to continue sitting under the tree; we must move. Getting up, I give her my denim jacket which she wears around her shoulders like a cape. I have on my denim vest and I lock my bike at the parking meter along the parks' edge. Now, if all this sounds familiar, it's because I wrote to you about this in october, the days following this and so forgive my repetition here. We walk along Alice Street, a quiet street that leads from the lake to the downtown Oakland through the back way.

What's special, though, isn't the street, it isn't the city or location. What begins to happen here is the queer sex magick. I'm not actually even aware of it until later. During this, especially during this walk down Alice, I'm thinking of a million other things, most of which I don't remember and those of which I do I won't relate here, for fear of my constantly repeating myself. Instead, let me pick up from the moment that Bonarh pushes me against the wall of the building on the corner of 14th and Alice. There is a stretch of sidewalk that is tree-lined, and across the street a parking lot on the three other corners. Along the side of the building on Alice. It is darker, quieter since the front entrance is on 14th. As Bonarh does this, pulls me, pushes me against the building, I'm brought out of my rumination and to the street.

What begins here is the description of it all: my back to the building, Bonarh is leaning in to kiss me. It takes a minute for my body to catch up to what's happening. Turning then to her, turning to face her, she's smiling. It's in the pushing and pulling that I'm starting to get excited, that I'm kind of re-waking up, getting up. And when I smile back at her, it's a long leer: sidelong look showing salaciousness, malicious predatory desire. I put my arm up against her shoulder and hold her that way: an arm's length away while I look at her

I lift her shirt at this point.

Her belly, then bare, catches the light from the headlights of passing cars, and then I lift it a little higher and now her tits, in a bra, are shown as well. Bonarh is patient here and allows me to look at her like this, bared belly and bra'd breasts. Then she does try to come in a bit closer, to lean in and kiss me again. I look her from her body to her face and catch her eyes with mine and in that moment, there is a slip in her attention and I flip her around so she is now against the wall, her back up against the wall and immediately I put my hand on her throat. I put my hands on her shoulders. I press into her, hips against hips. I lean back to look at her again, lifting her bra so her breasts are bared too.

Now, we are standing against a building in downtown Oakland, out on a street corner, streetlights and passing cars illuminating our activity: two dykes engaged in public lesbian sex and the reminder in all the excitement of light and not light, shown and not shown, visible and invisible, outside public, the actual danger we are both in, the risks of these desires.

I do lose myself in this, thankfully. Then I'm reaching down between us, our hips pressed together, our bodies pressed together, leaning pushing into the building on Alice, I reach down between us with my hand in a fist and place my fist between us in the way I do, hand curled in a fist, the pinky side held against myself, the front of my button fly levis, and the other side fingers curled in a circle against her, thumb and index finger in a circle. She starts to push my hand away and I say stand still and don't move. I hold this fist still and I tell her I'm not going to move at all, you be still. I gripped her throat tighter.

March 16, 2017:
Dear Bobby:
Then with my hand on her throat, my hand curled into a hollow fist pressing between us, holding a place or a space between us, I lean back and look at her again. I'm smiling, a slightly wolfish, predatory smile looking in her eyes. She meets me here and I lean in again, not so much to kiss as to breathe the same breath as her, our open mouths now pressed in exchange, inspiration. Don't move, I say, stand still. I'm not moving at all, just holding my hand in a circle, open mouth, speaking and breathing into her open mouth and feeling it all: the building heat and excitement and beginning of the slipping into another realm, not the street in downtown Oakland, but as if through to another place.

"I want you to not move, stand still and open your pussy," I say, and amazingly, she does. Bonarh is moaning and yelling in that kind of sex way, wild and then over her voice, I hear mine, quite loud and I say, "Sit down on it. Sit down on it. Sit down on it."

The blaze or the flash or the light or whatever happened, was intense, and palpable. It surprised me in the way that this kind of experience does: the aspect of is this really happening or am I imagining feeling something that isn't? But what I am left with then, that night, and now is this: the image of this flash of light like a crystal glowing from within, held in my hand, between us; a crystallization, not just of light or energy but as though an actual physical object is materialized, been produced or conjured. This is the good part: the crystal. The somehow experience of this kind of energy, queer, very sexy, non-penetrative, dangerous and the flash of light and I'm holding a physical object in my fist, in the space the hollowed open fingers circled. The base of this against my clit through the seam and button-fly of my jeans and the tip extending beyond my fingers to fuck her.

This is the manifestation of my cockiness. Oh my god, it feels so good, this place of magick and power and it is with this objectification in the moment, this emphasis of production, literally, and sense experience that we transcend.

It is the revealing of this phallus, so to speak, that once it is experienced, there is the realization that it isn't actually necessary, nor actually wanted at this time. I don't want to be relying on this kind of dick energy and this is what I want to transform, my reliance on riding and running this however beautiful, practiced and good feeling it is. As a butch, what I've been working is with my hands. I'm thinking of my cunt.

A human brain is going to methodically deconstruct an experience of all power.

People believe what's in their heads. People who say they understand an infinite all power are talking about their own ideas.

I'm not impressed with myself. I am asking to be rid of myself.

The next day, I'm riding my bike back from a morning meeting. I'd woke too early, before 5am and just did the steps: took an inventory, meditated, then laid back down and slept again till the alarm. Then jumped up, made coffee and rode my bike over to swim. Then rode to the meeting on Howe Street in Oakland. When I got there, it was a half hour of meditation. I got there are minute or so late, sat down and the meeting was very quiet. There was even a sign on the door that said: 'Quiet. Meditation in progress.' The door slipped from my hand as I tried to close it gently.

But when I sat down, I was like, I can't sit through another half hour of meditation! I just meditated and then I swam! I need to blast this off! So, I sat for a couple of minutes. After trying to come into the room so quietly, I then got up to leave. Outside, I checked the aa schedule again, maybe there was another meeting happening close by that I could go to. But no, only the 8:15 at the central office, that was like a half an hour from now. So, better go back in to this meeting. So, back inside the building then back to the room, back opening the door as quietly as possible and of course the door slipping from my hand a second time and slamming shut as I try to sit as quietly as possible. And then sitting down a second time, I realize, no, it's true, I actually can't sit here for 20 minutes. So, after another minute or so, I get up again and leave the meeting, the quiet meditation meeting, a second time, pulling the door quietly behind me. I ride home fast on the bike across the flat streets of Oakland and get home and eat an egg and some meat and hang up my wet bathing suit and turn around and head back out to the central office for the 8:15 meeting there.

Arriving there is no better! There are only 4 or 5 guys in there, and as usual it's so dirty linoleum, pine-sol smelling down and out aa. One guy said he was a dope fiend and I thought, "fear this meeting is a mistake, fear I'm trying to prove something, fear this is the wrong meeting," with no mind of the fact that I already left another meeting thinking it was the wrong meeting. But the steps worked. I took my inventory and we read from the book and I laughed.

March 18, 2017:
Dear Bobby:

Lack of power is everyone's dilemma.

The reason we're suicidal is that we think with a chronic progressive disease it shouldn't be so hard to be sober.

It's not people, it's my reliance on them.

Reality is spiritual so what's the matter is false.

After spending a bunch of weeks through august and then into september both trying to fan slowly a gentle flame of desire and interest and at the same time trying to squelch an overreaction of crush and lust, alternating between waiting and wanting and warning, writing and receiving letters and wondering, Bonarh and I met in Oakland. As the sun sets over the city scape in the west I turn and face the park where we sit. It's already dark on this side, looking east over the lake with strings of lights marking the popular path. She and I are under a tree, backs against the base, sitting side by side. My bike lays on its side in front of us in the grass.

She's asking me about the various other women I'm seeing and I list them off, somewhat casually. And then of course, there's Canela.

But I explain our agreement, which is perhaps hard to understand, I say, because we don't have any agreement and no rules.

After a few more questions, Bonarh climbs up on my leg, straddling my thigh and sits facing me, on my lap. I feel stiff. Rigid. What's the matter? I'm feeling or not feeling really. It's here at this moment that we begin to notice how cold it is now that the sky is darkened. The streetlights are on around the lake and around this small annex of the park, though not near where we are, under the large oak. Looking up above us, the canopy is like a dark veil or ceiling painted black. I take off my jacket and put it around her shoulders as we get up, pick up my bike and c'mon let's go, let's walk a bit.

Alice Street is quiet, leading from the park here to downtown Oakland. The lights from the apartments we pass are all glowing yellow in the windows and this adds to the good feeling. She's got on my jacket and is talking about something. I don't think I'm even listening. I'm wearing my denim vest, of course. As we near 14th Street, we pause for the light to change and then we cross. The three corners are parking lots, with trees, and the fourth a building we are passing now. The entrance is on 14th and as we walk along Alice we step into the shadow of both the building and the tree at the curb and it's in this spot she makes her move. She pulls me and then pushes me against the wall of this building. My back to the wall now, so to speak, I'm almost frozen, stuck here. She leans in and kisses me. And then again, leans in and kisses me. Passing cars throw their headlights across us for a moment, light and then again, shadow and the yellow ness of Alice Street.

Reawakening from repressing desire means embodiment and inspiration. It is perhaps her breath that starts me, more than her touch which I barely feel in this state anyway. Her open mouth over mine, her panting breathing into me and out, yes, a resuscitation, reanimation of my self. It's in the pushing and pulling then I get excited.

As she's leaning in, wait, I look at her, fiendishly, wolfishly.

May 1, 2017:

Dear Bobby:

Perhaps let this be an interlude; perhaps let this letter mark the intermission or pause.

A couple weeks ago, things are a bit tense with my lover and me. I think we had a misunderstanding upon parting the day before, which was a real hot sunny day in Oakland on Piedmont Ave. There is there Chinese food, a vintage clothing store, and also a cafe for coffee. They used to serve Double Rainbow ice cream here and I'd get It's a Goody often, when newly sober. The iced coffee is amazing.

I almost didn't leave Oakland that day, turning the pickup truck I'm driving while my friend is in NYC, around and around, u-turn after u-turn, trying to decide if I should go back to SF across the bridge to a meeting or stay in Oakland with my lover, enjoying the day. I had one thought and that was "later" and I hurried over the bridge then. The thought of later being so terrifying, I sped across the city and up the hill to get out of time altogether.

Then the next day, thursday, she calls to clear things up. I start yelling on the phone at her about what, I don't remember, and then again, look at the clock and realize I got to get to the meeting. "Just come over and meet me," I say to her, though I hadn't planned on spending the day with her. I wanted to get something done that day. I'm late, and again trying to speed across the city, on Fell Street from Franklin out to 7th and Irving but I don't realize it's 4/20 and the traffic is so bad I'm almost crying as I drive. First, the day not going how I thought and planned, and now, late for a one-hour meeting, stuck in traffic and hating myself. A friend texts and says she's going to the 12:05 meeting around the corner from my house and I've only gone three blocks as it is, trying to get to the 11:50am so I turn around, park the truck on Gough and go to a meeting where I find, as we read from the big book that I am crying tears of gratitude, then just as quickly, racing out the door and back home to meet her.

I'm thinking we'll go out to Golden Gate Park, lay in the grass out there but the traffic is still so bad, maybe worse now and I'm actually past the tears and going crazy. She's driving, thankfully, so I tell her, turn off of Fell Street and we'll try to bypass this mess. We are out at Cole Street and there is a cafe on the corner of Cole and Hayes. "Double park. Let me out. I'm going to run in." Now, I knew I needed to meditate even before I left the house, but I was so driven by the idea of working it out with her that I said 'fuck it, I'll meditate later' and tried to override it with more coffee.

The cafe people told me it's 4/20 and that's why there's traffic, especially going out to Golden Gate Park and then everything made sense. Except why their coffee was so bad as to be undrinkable and also the fact that I asked if they had maté and the lady said yes, tea, right and I said yes and then I asked how about some soy milk with the maté and she said yes, maté latté? And I said sure, if that's what you want to call it...my iced coffee terrible and made with regular ice not coffee ice cubes like on Piedmont Avenue and the latté was just that: a latté made with expresso and milk.

Back in the car, I'm more pissed and hateful, can barely drink the coffee, tastes terrible, isn't working. She doesn't drink coffee, so won't drink the latté. I hate everything. We gotta get to another park, fuck the Golden Gate Park, especially on 4/20 and unmeditated, I can't be in that much smoke and weed. And now that it's in my consciousness, of course, every car we're passing and is passing us is loaded with four or five people and completely hot-boxed and driving real stupid. I look on the device for another patch of green and find a place in Pacific Heights: Alta Plaza. I give directions while she drives and then I tell her how to drive too: "Turn right at the next corner, be careful of that car turning left, can you go a little faster, make this light, please..."

Then at the park. I haven't mentioned that it is a sunny day but very windy. I think the wind, combined with still not having med-itated, is contributing to my terrible angry and irritated mood. We park the car at the curb of the park, I dump out the coffee, ice and latté in the gutter and actually throw the cups right behind, out of the car onto the sidewalk. I think at this point; it occurs to me at this point, maybe meditate now in the car but I got a lot of ideas about wanting to look good, look like I got this and not look like I 'need' to meditate, 'I enjoy the spiritual effects' I guess is how I want to look instead of 'basically my fucking life depends on a twice daily meditation practice'. So, again, I think 'oh, later'.

May 2, 2017:
Dear Bobby:

It's maybe two now. The park, on the side we've arrived, is very steep. We're on the north side. We can see the Golden Gate Bridge and the gate itself, even from miles away and from this elevation, the water looks so inviting. But as I say, turning to face the park, it's very steep. We grab some blankets from the trunk of her car and enter the park. I have fear I've already ruined the day, what with my near constant complaining and irritations. The grass here is green but to sit on it means sitting on a slope so we cross the park, go up to the top.

Up on top it is cement and there is a fenced playground for children and some sort of park building and what looks like a boot camp type group of people, all in exercise or yoga pants and sneakers, men and women, doing some movements in unison. It looks terrible. Crossing here, through their group, we get to the other side of the park. It's worse somehow, steeper or windy-er, and also completely open and exposed. There are some trees here, but under the trees it is just dirt and it is too windy to be out of the sun.

Plus, she isn't wearing a shirt, just a purple bra and she is saying she is going back to her early 90's bi-dyke roots (Now, perhaps you can understand my attraction, despite the non-coffee drinking) with some short shorts and boots, though in the 90's longer cut-off shorts were more popular. I don't mind this update.

The other side is as unappealing as the first side. Along the paved pathway a man and woman pass us. She asks is there a better park around? We wanna make out. At this point, just a moment before this, she's pulled me to her, put her arm around me or something and it's helped me settle, I have to admit. The two say well maybe Lafayette Park and they point vaguely east or something. "Will it be less windy?" They don't know.

Also, at this point there enters an exposition of class: 'those two'? I ask, "What are they doing in the park in the middle of the day in the middle of the week? Don't they work?"

Earlier in the week or the day before I'd said to her while my hand was fucking her cunt: "This is what lesbians do: they fuck each other in the middle of the day in the middle of the week; if they have jobs,

75

it's part-time and flexible, and one of them is actually on disability. This is the gay office. We are holding the space even in these times of social, racial, and economic injustices being legislated: every time we fuck, the world is blessed." I love feeling so good fucking that I'm grandiosely praying and that is the gay role, the office of gay love and sex and everything else, for everyone. She comes then, spraying from head to belly and thighs.

"Maybe they have the kind of jobs that they work on their computers from home for an hour and have the rest of the day free." I scowl. We begin back to the car, this has been a bust, this place, let's get the fuck out of here. She tells me then, kind of just making conversation, that she went to an ivy league college. "Why are you telling me this?" I ask. "It's something about being more vulnerable with you," she says. I'm so pissed I say, "being vulnerable means being present in the moment, not some story from the past."

Walking back to the car, her arm is round me. This is something I normally don't allow. She's also kissed me a few times, kind of pulling me close and actually really kissing me. This is something else I usually don't allow. But as we arrive back to the side that is now the other side, we get within spitting distance of her car, parked at the curb. I won't make it, I think to myself, getting in the car and driving someplace else, fuck it. We'll stay here. I chose a somewhat flat area, it's grassy, very grassy and full of mown grass pieces in clumps all over. This area is like most of Dolores Park: just a somewhat sloped field, very exposed but the park on this side does seem somewhat empty: the exercisers are at the top, the children too are in the play area which is fenced up there. On a bench, another couple are sitting close and kissing and hugging. Another couple are above us, standing on the slope higher up, smoking weed. They finish and walk across the park as I am finally relenting; I'm spreading out the blanket she's carried from the car, pulling off my boots and finally collapsing basically onto my back, I put my hand over my eyes to block the sun and look up at her.

She's smiling and that's nice. We quickly do a re-do of the day before, a misunderstanding. We clear it all up. Laying down the wind's not bothering me much. She's sitting up on the blanket next to me.

I pull my hat down over my eyes; the sun is so bright. And then I'm up on my knees and rolling her over, pulling her shorts down and spanking her.

May 3, 2017:
Dear Bobby:

I start out slow and easy. I want her to be able to take a lot, so at first, it's just gentle slaps, alternating sides, slapping each cheek and pinkening her. Her shorts, worn without underwear, are at the bottom of her ass, right at the top of her thighs, framing her body and presenting herself for me. I'm getting excited though and glad for this release after so much stress of the day and getting to the park and just being alive, Quickly, I'm really hitting her and she's making noise. The park, the wind, the sun, the blanket, and her ass in front of me: that's it. A little faster and I'm laughing and feeling good and her ass, red now, looks amazing.

Then I dive my face into her ass, and I mean, deep: tongue fucking her and rimming her, fucking in there with my whole face, tasting smelling licking. She's backed up on her knees now to meet me, pushing back into me as I'm pushing and diving into her and I'm reaching around and grabbing her clit at I tongue her ass and then pull down further her shorts, take them all the way off and cover her with the sarong she's brought. Then diving in again, pushing my thumb in her ass and fucking her.

Then more: there's shit there so I stick in my two fingers to pull it out but it's messy. She says she'll shit here, so I pull out, pull shitty fingers out, wipe them on the grass. She squats next to the blanket with the sarong now wrapped around her like a little tent with her head and shoulders out. "This is the first time", she says, "I've ever sat and shit in a park next to my lover who's just fucked my ass in public. I feel so good, I'm feeling so good." I say, "You know just what to say to me."

And all of a sudden, she says oh no. I look behind me and two cops are crossing the park and coming right toward us. I reach over and put on my shirt. I've been in just an a-shirt. She stays seated, wrapped in the sarong.

"Do you know why we are here?" the cops ask. They ask for ID from both of us. I say I don't know as I pull out my wallet and stand up to hand him my driver's license. "Please sit back down," he says. She doesn't have her wallet or purse, "It's in the car," she says. "You don't know why we are here?" cop asks again. I say no, I mean, well, we were fooling around here. "Yeah," he says, "but a little more than that, it sounds like, huh? I mean, she's not wearing any pants."

At this point, she says, she's pushed the pile of shit beneath her to the side and she's using her feet under the sarong to pull pieces of grass over to cover it.

The cop says someone has complained and I immediately wonder if it was the white-haired white couple, man and woman who were walking their dog past us a way away while I was on her back with my thumb in her ass. At one point, I looked over and saw the two of them and their big dog on the paved path at the entrance to the park talking with a younger white woman who was with two small children. Did the white man and woman point at us? Or tilt their head toward us? Something seemed in retrospect to catch my attention enough that I told her beneath me to shush. This is something I usually don't do as I find her deep loud moans and screams so exciting and inciting and disturbing. Beneath me she said, "Huh?" and I said take it easy or something like that. And then dove back in: fingers, mouth, hands, ass, and cunt and clit and shit.

We are sitting while the cops ask questions. We are sitting apart while the cops ask us questions, separately. I've had to put on my glasses because the cops asked me to read the address on my license. "Is this correct?" I know it is but I'm so fearful I say hold on and reach for my glasses on the blanket to read my own ID. "Yes, that's correct." Then, the cops call in our IDs. Running them, they call it, I look over at her and smile and wink, quickly. The cops are saying this is a misdemeanor. Someone has complained they said. The one cop is talking on his radio. The other is closer to her and is saying, yeah, it's a misdemeanor but unlike other misdemeanors, like open container, where you can just pay a fine, this one is Penal Code 314.

The cops are both young asian men. The first one at first looked like a dyke as they first walked up, but then I realized oh, a dyke from the 90's, really short hair and butch and super sexy. Then, closer, the bullet proof vest looks like she/he is binding maybe like a transman. The other cop reads only as bio-male and why is that I wonder, sitting on the blanket, not wanting to look at either of them too closely, not wanting to seem anything but compliant and easy going which is something that I have to work at quite strenuously. Both of them are quite young and I realize from my position here, early 20's, I'd guess.

May10, 2017:
Dear Bobby:
    And before I can even finish the story at Alta Plaza...
    Last week my lover and I drive up to Shasta for a few days. We stay in the town in a motel to do an FMT procedure. Basically, this is transplanting her shit to my ass and colon via enema to treat my ongoing ulcerative colitis. More on that later I'm sure. We come back to SF on saturday evening and then on sunday try and figure out how she will get the shit to me from Oakland where she lives. She comes by my place in the late afternoon and produces a sample and while she does, I look at the PFA movie schedule. 'The Holy Mountain' by Jodorowsky is showing at 7. It's 6:25! The film description reads: "The thief defecates into a container. The excrement is transformed into gold by the alchemist..." I yell to her in the bathroom, squatting over a plastic small bucket, "Hurry up, we gotta go see this!" and then hurriedly driving across the bridge—thankfully, sunday evening no traffic—and across Berkeley to the theater, drop her off in front with my wallet. "Buy our tickets with my membership card and the cash. I'll park and meet you inside the lobby."

June 20, 2017:
Dear Bobby:
    So much time has passed, or so much has happened is the preferable way to state this. And in this time, what they call "life on life's terms," what else. So, sadness, sickness, betrayals, breakups. Also,

movies, meetings, masturbation, and moving furniture, eating meat. I go to extremes; reading, writing, not writing. As always, just getting the paper, this page, back into the machine today is a success.

In between the story at Alta Vista and the bare beginning above of the BAM parking lot, which is actually the bank parking lot next to BAM in Berkeley—there is the moment on 17th Street near Mission on may 1. Thrift Town is closed now, permanently citing 'rising costs' in the city. Of course. The auto glass store on 17th Street ('Twin Brothers') is still here though and this is where I meet my lover. Her car window was smashed, parked the previous friday out behind my building. We'd been out to Fremont that day, getting a security screen for her hatchback and also a second key. There was an amazing donut shop on the way and we also did some thrifting and then on the way back, swung through SF to see my cat friend before going back to Oakland for the night. The window was smashed in the hour we were upstairs and I pathologically blamed myself.

Monday afternoon, then, she is working in SF and then going to get her window done. I send her a link to twin brothers shop and tell her I'll meet her there. I ride over on my bike, putting typing aside. She was standing outside on the sidewalk when I pulled up. I said to her, "Hello, troublemaker," and locked my bike to the parking meter and we walked around a few blocks in the Mission, up to Valencia, into Community Thrift for a moment but it's crowded—the first monday of the month being the big sale day and now it must be 5pm or later—across Valencia to 18th and then back to Mission and passing the closed Thrift Town ('R.I.P' - I cried the day and week or so before when I pulled up to shop and saw it gated and the signs in the window and I wasn't the only one; others stood with me in disbelief: if Thrift town is gone...? They came for the Volvo repair shop, the art supply store, the shoe service on 16th Street, who was there when they came for the Thrift?) and the two of us strolling, dropping into the donut shop on Mission where I bought the old-fashioned cake variety, both glazed and unglazed, almost daily in the fall of 1994 while housesitting on 18th and going to new college around the corner. This time, now, the donuts didn't look good, perhaps sickly sweet or something. Then back along 17th street to the chain link fence next to Twin Brother Auto Glass (which this is the second time at least I've written a story about an auto glass store—see 1996's 'On Levan Glass') and we stop our stroll.

Against the fence then, I lean, my left arm bent at the elbow and my body at an 'A' angle there, held up and cool. She puts her arm around me and it feels good. Actually, I'm surprised I notice this, this feeling good from being touched and I realize it is that and not something I'm think about. It is here then that I'm able to begin. As she is coming closer, and we are talking, I'm trying to explain everything to her: yesterday, the day before, last week, the day after tomorrow, and I'm wrapping and weaving days and events into a confusing blanket of time and unreality that I suddenly throw over us both. She's now against the fence, leaning with her back against the fence.

June 21, 2017:
Dear Bobby:

She's leaning with her back against the chain-link now. I turn, like a quarter turn, and now I'm next to her perpendicularly and I'm leaning against the fence, leaning on my hand and my arm is outstretched. I look at her sideways kind of with my head cocked.

In the car window smashing event of the week before a bag was taken from her back seat. This is less noticed by her, who usually carries three or four various canvas bags plus her purse, each with one or two items inside: a shirt, an extra sweater, some boots, a book, but as we got to the car that night, evening, my neighbor in my building on a floor below me leaned out his window to yell to us: "I saw them break your window! I took a photo of it happening from up here!" He then threw out the into the photos printed out and sure enough, there were two people, a man and a woman, clearly breaking the window. Next pic: leaning into the car through this broken window. Last pic: pulling out the canvas bag that was on the back seat. When she looked at the pictures, she said, "Oh no, my boots. They were in that bag".

This was a pair of boots she'd had for 17 years which coincidentally she'd shown me the week before as a pair she'd wouldn't wear when we went out. The soles were ripped and worn down completely and the zipper on the side was ripped. Also, at least one shoe repairman'd said it'd cost more to fix them than they are worth. (Please excuse the stating of the very obvious in this aside that this is what late stage capitalism looks like).

I have to admit, after seeing the boots, I wasn't that sad to almost literally see them go. And though the bag had some sentimental value, she told me she used it to carry an object I gave her in the fall, it hadn't been used for that in a while and actually also had a zipper that need to be replaced.

Having just had a zipper replaced on a vintage leather bomber jacket I can attest to the difficulty of this task: no one would even try it, not my tailor ("the leather is too thick"); not the shoe repair guy I brought it to ("I don't have the zipper"); plus I couldn't find the zipper anywhere to buy to bring to any of these places, only on-line and only sold in bulk. Even the hipster boutique of handmade leather goods on Gough couldn't or wouldn't do it. He sent me to a shop out in the avenues. I finally had it done in Queens, NYC.

It was over the weekend then, that she told me the other item that she was missing after the break-in was the gold chain she got in Indonesia when she was there in the winter. This, I have to admit, was actually sad. The chain was quite beautiful, heavy gold links with an S-shaped clasp that was weighty without being masculine and long and quite nice Since I grew up on Long Island, I do feel I have some level of finesse regarding gold chains, meaning, I know a good chain. This one obviously cost many hundreds of dollars.

This was mainly where my feeling of guilt and remorse lay, in the stolen chain and the fact that unlike the window, or even the boots that could not be replaced, or at least not so easily, and though it is quite insane, I could not help the thoughts which plagued me all friday evening into saturday and then sunday, that if only I'd done something different, the window would not have been broken, maybe. Not have gotten the donut in Fremont? Not came back to feed my cat? Not have enjoyed myself with her the way that I have been?

At the fence then, her neck is bare, no necklace. Standing with her there, with her leaning on the fence, me standing and leaning next to her, the blanket of time-confusion and unreality thrown up above us, like a canopy high, I begin to tell her about the benefits to the necklaces loss. "Well, first of all I say, "The loss of the necklace leaves you neck bare." And it is here, I continue, "that I can now take the belt from the loops of my levis and slip the belt around your neck. I haven't wanted to with the chain there, the smooth leather with the thick chain and an entanglement between them, but now, your neck is available to my belt."

It's about 5:30 in the afternoon now, she'll be the last customer at the glass place. The rush hour of the Mission looks mostly like a long line of cars crossing town on 17th Street, stopping at the Capp Street stop sign and then waiting for the light on Mission. There is a line of cars parked at the curb on both sides of the street here, unlike on 18th where there is a tow-away zone for rush hour: curb parking prohibited. There are bicyclists and pedestrians.

It is here then, with my belt going around her neck imaginatively that I lean into her. She spreads her arms wide and loops her fingers through the chain-link just above her head. I lean into her and speak very quietly in her ear while holding my fist—as though the belt end is wrapped around it—against her neck. The belt has become like a handle in this respect, less like a collar. I lean in close to her ear and whisper, "I want everyone to see what we are doing."

June 23, 2017:
Dear Bobby:
"I want everyone to see what we are doing."
I say this because after Alta Vista and the incident there, we are wondering can we still have sex in public and how. She begins with the idea that maybe we can practice invisibility. No, I say, I want everyone to see what we are doing. My fist is close to her neck, like my knuckles and pressed against the side of her throat and my face is close to hers. It's as though my body is light and I'm pivoting myself on my fist rather than my feet and I swing myself around to face her and then I press my whole body against the front of hers, against the fence. Our hips then are locked, or at least held together tightly.

"What I want to do is open your shirt," I say. "I want to unbutton your shirt so your belly is bared for everyone who is passing and in their commute." When I talk to her like this we both get very excited. "And once your belly is bared, your shirt open, I'll have you lift your arms just a bit higher on the fence so that your breasts are also bared, the shirt, open, just hanging off your shoulders. Open shirt, arms extended, fingers through the fence links and the belt around your neck." I'm kind of chanting this over and over, alternately close to her face, by her ear and then leaning back and kind of dancing in front of her. We're starting to slip in now to the place this can happen.

I'm talking about what happened at Alta Vista through this all as well. I'm talking about how I pulled her shorts off in the park, how she was lying face down on the blanket we'd brought to spread in the grass and how windy it was on that sunny day. "I got my mouth on your ass; I dove into your ass with my face. I was eating your ass and pulling you onto me. I had my tongue buried in your ass."

Thankfully, all that ass stimulation had her having to shit, to get off the blanket and squat in the grass and shit over there while I lay on my back, smiling, soaring, in an a-shirt with my arms behind my head like a pillow, watching her because it was in this moment while she's wrapped in a sarong, squatting and narrating "I've never done this before: shat in public while my lover watched," and me saying, "You know just what to say to a dyke," that the cops walked up.

She saw them first and said, "Uh-oh," and I turned and saw them crossing the grass from the park's main entrance, not walking on the path. I get up from the blanket and put on my shirt. I'm buttoning it as they approach. I'm actually quite fearful and thinking I have no idea how to handle this situation. I don't look behind me at her but I am trying to stand between them and her. But there are two cops and they split up upon reaching our blanket. One stands at least a few feet from me and gestures for me to stay where I am. How is this conveyed so clearly so quickly, I don't know. The other cop goes behind me and stands near her. She is still squatting. Cop tells me to sit down. The first cop asks me for my ID. I reach in the front pocket of my jeans and pull out my wallet and then open it and hand him the license. He looks at it and calls me by the name on the card and asks is this my current address. I'm so fearful and confused I say, "Uh, let me put on my glasses."

This is the point that I think to myself, oh, they must see we are middle-aged women; that however we were read across the park, up close it is apparent we are two middle-aged dykes.

The cop asks after I look at my license and hand it back to him for me to sit back down on the blanket. I mean, he doesn't ask, he tells me to "sit down." I'm sitting then, looking up at him while he's on his radio, strapped to his shoulder calling in my name and license number, running it, is what he says.

The other cop is talking to her, asking for her license or ID. She says it's in her car, which is parked right at the curb. She offers to get it, but cop says no, just for her to give him her name. He has a small pad and pen and he's writing down what she says but then there is confusion and she has to spell and re-spell her name again and again and then tell him her birthdate. While all this goes on, both cops talking at once and spelling names out loud, I look over to her and our eyes meet and I wink at her. I'm not a winker in general, but I'm not usually in this type of situation, either. I want to show her connection and protection and love. She smiles.

Cop asks me, "You know why we're here, right?" and I say as stupidly as I can, "No." "No idea?" he asks and I say, "Well, I mean, we were making out." "Yeah," he says, "It wasn't just making out." I don't admit to getting her up on her knees after pulling my tongue out of her ass and leaning her shoulders forward so her chest is against the ground, hips raised and then lubing my thumb with my mouth and fucking her ass like that till she screamed.

June 24, 2017:
Dear Bobby:

I don't tell him how happy I felt to take her this way, so easily and so deeply. I don't tell him how turned on I am fucking her like this, in public, purposefully disruptive. I need the tumultuous state that comes as a result of queer intentional recreational outdoor sacred sex. I'm too depressed otherwise.

And in fact this day at Alta Vista is an especially depressed day what with mostly everyone in the city rushing out in their cars to Golden Gate Park for a big smoke-out at the end of april, all the pervasive marijuana smoke in passing cars and even on the sidewalks has me feeling down and suppressed. I mean, god bless everyone who doesn't have that kind of reaction—depressed suppression and lack of conscious contact—from smoking weed, I think everyone should get as much relief in this world as is possible.

When we've arrived at the park it's probably close to 2pm or later. We'd finally gotten to the park, after being in traffic and pulling to the curb at the park first thing I'm thinking as I dump out the coffees I bought on the way over is, 'I gotta meditate' but I'm too vain and fearful of how I will look, saying after we've just been together on a date for an hour: I need to do something else. So, I push on. I think, maybe later, though 2pm or 2:30 is the sweet spot for meditation in the afternoon. But as soon as we are out of the car then, walking up the grassy steep hill that is this park, in the bright sunny wind, I'm so irritable and discontent, all I'm doing is complaining anyway. It would actually be a service to her to not be pushing through, tired and thirsty; to actually have taken the meditation in the car and be a bit more clear headed.

I'm spending so much time with this moment in the park because I'm trying to get to the bottom of what happened, to really parse every line and ask what did we do wrong? Unmeditated? Too blatant? Too arrogant? Too explicit? Not enough of the intention set? Not enough protection conjured? Wrong place? Wrong time? But also, because I'm hoping that by somehow understanding this day in the park, by placing all the factors of race, gender, age, class, side by side something can be understood about the politics of these and the politics of public space and surveillance.

As a middle-aged white dyke who has mostly ridden a bicycle, not driven a car, I've had blessedly few interactions with cops. This is the first time I've been asked for my license when I wasn't in a motor vehicle, in fact, and I will admit, I was quite frightened, wink to her aside. Later, I'll write about how when this occurs another time, she and I will exclaim, "Oh no, not again!", quickly apologize and say we are leaving this area immediately. But this first time feels so frightening: to be woken up from the asleepedness of privilege.

And in fact, other than telling us to sit down and stay seated which feels like a show of their force, the cops actually don't treat us bad. Neither touches either one of us, neither makes any comments about us, our appearances, and in fact, the one tells us quite kindly what the consequences could possibly be for us, if in fact we were having sex in the park. For one, he says, "This is a misdemeanor. But unlike other misdemeanors, such as 'open container', where you would just pay a fine and be done with it, this is Penal Code 314: 'Indecent exposure' which means possible jail time and $1,000 fine just for the first offense. "Second offense," cop says, "is a felony." But worst of all: any conviction subjects us to lifetime registration required as a sex offender. Cop goes on to say, "We received a complaint today. Someone called it in. Now, we didn't see anything and we'd have to find and identify the complainant but, in this case, daytime, middle of a public park with kids nearby…"

On crowded rush hour 17th Street a couple weeks later, I'm trying to repair the rend the incident with the cops created. I'll be honest, having this type of outside, public sex is very important to me. Disrupting, using the chaotic powers of ritualized sex, prevents stagnation and keeps true creativity and flexibility possible. This is what Judy Grahn describes in Another Mother Tongue, the first gay book I ever read. So, with my lover against the fence, my fist against her throat, my hips pressed to hers I tell her, "I'm gonna unbutton your shirt so it falls open and bares your breasts and belly. I'm gonna pull the dick out of my pants and rub it up on your stomach." Standing up together this energy feels so good like this, like easy to run the energy between us. For a moment while we're there like this, standing against the fence, my lover looks away from my eyes to the movement of a pedestrian walking past and I call her back to me, to us.

June 25, 2017:
Dear Bobby:

I have the imaginary belt wrapped in my fist with it around her neck, buckled. I pull on the end a bit to get her attention back to me, to us, to what we are doing. "Hey," I say, "You think these people see any of this, of what we're doing here against this fence?"

She wants to know if we are casting a spell of invisibility and I say no, not invisible, those people don't exist. This complicates my desire to have everyone see what we are doing together; I want the people to see me dominating her, to see me with a beautiful woman. I want everyone to see who is with me.

My face is close to hers and I say, "Do you need this belt pulled tighter?" She says she doesn't need it. "I like it," she says, "I want it." That's what has remained with me.

So, after trying to understand what would be needed to continue doing exactly what I want to do wherever I am, my lover and I go to Berkeley to a movie. Next to the museum is a bank parking lot which can be used after hours for general parking. Now that the on-street parking across the street next to campus has changed to a bus stop, I was somewhat worried about getting to the movie on time so I dropped her off at the front entrance with some cash and my membership card to get the member-price tickets. I sped away and then remembered the parking lot and swung in there and sped around and found a spot in the far-left corner. I jumped out the truck and ran inside to meet her in the lobby. "C'mon," I said, and with my hand on the small of her back, led her through the museum to the back stairs up to the theater.

After the film, we go down to the basement to piss, then back up the red stairs and through the lobby, this time at a stroll. I'm smiling as we saunter past all the people standing chatting in the crowded lobby and my lover is looking at me and she's smiling too. Outside, through the heavy glass doors, there is another clump of people chatting but standing there, right on the other side of the exit. I comment about this, righteously, but we laugh and my hand goes to her back again as I guide her to the truck.

Earlier in the afternoon, she'd come by my place unexpectedly.

She'd sent a series of texts which my little computer didn't receive and so, I didn't respond. But I got the one that said, "I'm in the city can I come by?" I was laying on the couch with the cat, reading, so I said sure and hurried to straighten the place up. She came up then and came in and I offered her a glass of water (she doesn't drink coffee) and when I handed it to her, she took the glass, drank and handed it back. There's something slightly off about our interaction, though I still don't know about missing her texts. There seems some confusion between us.

It's from here that I take the glass, half-empty now back from her, turn, re-fill it at the sink and turn back to her. I smile at her and she smiles and reaches out for the glass and I throw the water in her face. She's surprised and there from here begins a long discussion. "Do we not have an agreement that you will only eat or drink what I put in your mouth when we are together?" "Yes, Cashier." "Then this water thrown at you should be expected." "Yes, Cashier." (And although this is not exactly what happened, I'm trying to actually make it not sound so much like a scene of the hard top bordering on being an abusive asshole. I'm also trying to cut some corners with this part of the story)

She comes up. In the kitchen, I offer her a glass of water and she drinks it herself, then she comments on it and I say what will happen. She says, "You'll throw water in my face," and I say, "Yes, I will." I turn back to the sink, re-fill the glass and turn back to her. We are looking at each other, smiling at this point and after a moment, I throw the water in her face. Does this sound better, if she knows what's going to happen before it does? "This is our agreement, is it not?" "Yes, Cashier," she says.

Her clothes are wet so I say take them off and I'll dry them in the oven. She's surprised. She seems angry though her admitting this takes close to an hour. In the meantime, there is a lot of diversion and attention to the clothes in the oven, checking them often and keeping the setting very low, and also a lot of diversion in terms of talking about the whole thing thus far. I finally get her to say she's surprised and upset. She also keeps saying she's confused.

We've been engaged at this point for a week in a project of taking her shit, putting it in a plastic bag, adding water so it gets to the consistency of a thick soup and then putting it in an enema bottle and inserting it up my ass: fecal matter transplant. This is with hopes in rebuilding the micro biome in my colon for relief of the colitis.

June 26, 2017:
Dear Bobby:
    This is why we are at this movie in the first place. My lover is in the bathroom, trying to shit an afternoon shit in a bucket for the FMT preparation. I'm in the living room (actually, in my 395 sq. ft. apartment. This is a couch, not an actual room), laying on the couch reading the PFA movie schedule. The Holy Mountain is playing and the description includes, "the alchemist asks the thief if he wants gold and then the thief defecates in a bowl and eats it" and I yelled to her in the bathroom squatting and pissing on the rug, "Hurry up! We have to go to this movie!" She comes out then saying she thinks she's too stressed to shit here and now but her clothes are dry and I throw them to her and say let's go.
    I've been so sick with the colitis and then with the flu that I've mostly laid in bed for two weeks in april and even after the flu then I'm on steroids for the inflamed colon. The steroids work for the inflammation but the side effects are severe, including some angry mania. Even though the water throwing incident was completely within our arrangement, on further thought I'm left wondering if, in fact, it's just me trying to prove myself in my somewhat weakened state, or even an overreaction from the medication.

June 28, 2017:
Dear Bobby:
    We drive to PFA quickly across the bridge. I'm fearful there will be a lot of traffic on a sunday afternoon but not this time and so I speed but carefully and then through the tunnel and over the other side, which always has less traffic than the other side, and onto 80 up to the University Avenue exit. We are making great time and listening, maybe, to the radio as we drive. As we get onto University,

I say, "Oh, this will be the hard part now," meaning crossing town on the one, usually crowded, throughway but even then, we sail along.

I'm asking her over and over, "How did you feel then, in the kitchen?" and she either doesn't understand the question or is too rattled by all of it or confused, as she's said, to answer directly until we reach San Pablo. At the light, I say, "The look on your face when I threw the water was very exciting, a real turn-on. It was more than a look of surprise." She said, "I was mad." I said, "Yeah, more than surprise, mad." "Yeah, I was so mad." "Thank you for getting to that," I said. "It's hard for me to say I'm mad." I said, "I know. That's why I appreciate you expressing it." "Yeah," she says again, "I was mad."

She asks, "Why did you wait to throw the water?" I said, "I'm not meting out discipline. You're not a dog being trained, nor a child being reprimanded. I'm not punishing you, this is simply our arrangement." We arrive at the theater and I drop her off with cash and my membership card. "Get us tickets. I'll meet you inside."

After the film, we are strolling up Center Street to the bank parking lot. Across the street is the bike racks where I fucked her in the fall but we don't mention this. My hand is on the small of her back, leading her to the truck in the far corner of the lot. It's past evening now and dark and the truck is also in a shadow thrown by the wall of the bank. She finally sees the truck but as we approach I lead her to the driver's side, not the passenger's. Her surprise at this is palpable in her body; I feel in her back the surprise of not going where she expected. The driver's side is darker, more in the shadow and actually not visible in the headlights of other cars as they come and go through the lot. I lean her against the door of the truck.

It seems private over here. Basically, I start to fuck her right away, holding her feet, and therefore legs, together with my own feet. She's wearing her new pink bra, pink net shirt, pink cashmere cardigan, cotton drawstring pants in a reptilian print, with a brown felt hat and cotton serape-style scarf. I'm wearing vintage Florsheim loafers, grey 501s, brown tooled leather belt, brown plaid flannel wool shirt, top button buttoned, denim vest, with a regulation baseball cap that I've altered so it reads, 'Lesbian' instead of 'St. Louis'.

I'm pulling a shaft from my cunt to hers, holding it in two hands and then leaning forward on this energy beam to push into her. I'm fucking her like that for a while, both of us dressed completely, slight variations on this and then repeating to her, "Surprised, upset, oh yeah, mad." I'm asking her about being uncomfortable in the wet clothes and reminding her of the morning we went out to the Albany Bulb as the sun was coming up. "Remember how fearful you were that you were going to be cold out there?" She says yes. "Was it worth it?" Yes.

Even just from this fucking, and I say just only to explain that all we are doing is riding a shaft of light between us, she starts to come, over and over.

July 1, 2017:
Dear Bobby:

Even just from this fucking, and I say just only to explain that all we are doing is riding a shaft of light between us, she starts to come, over and over. This starts to sound like the Penthouse forum letters I read in my parent's porn stash but her pants are soaked again. I untie the drawstring, reach into the waistband and fuck her right out, fingers in, thumb on her clit. Now, she's really coming, wet, and soaking, and she's yelling. If I'm sounding cocky it's not my intention.

I'm standing at the side of the truck, my weight against her, pushing with my hips or pulling back to look at her, her face, her open mouth; all of me then in my hand between us. Her thrown back head, yelling and then she looks at me. It's that that I want. This is what I want. And what we're doing; what we're doing together with this light and shaft and energy and it feels like magick.

We kiss a bit. I retie her pants and we smile together. The dark sky, standing in the shadows, the parking lot has been emptying as we've been here in a timelessness that creates spacelessness. We stand again then against the truck for a moment and then it's over. We walk around the back of the truck to the other side and I unlock the door, open it and hold out my hand as she goes inside, then close the door as she's in. When I do and turn around, cops are filling the parking lot.

A cop calls to me as I've turned from her in the passenger seat. "Excuse me, Sir," or something like that and when I turn to face him, he sees and I show him I'm a woman. And he's surprised. "Oh," he maybe even said. There's three cars lined up in the lot, I saw them racing in as I turned from the truck. They pulled up silently but lights are flaring and flashing atop the cars. All the cops are out now, standing in the lot and looking at me. It all happens so fast that there's a cop behind me already at the passenger door, opening it or asking her to open it, I'm not sure. I try to look over my shoulder at what's happening but the lights, now flashlights, and the cop in front of me is keeping me from seeing her.

By now, of course, I know what's happened, though the show of force here and the stealthful arrival has thrown me off. The cop asks me something, I don't know what, but I'm answering, "We were making out." "Making out?" he said. "We'll, we've just been dating a short time, and you know how things can get…" Behind me a female cop is crossing from near the other male cop and the truck where my lover is still sitting. This cop stands then with another female cop and when I see them both, the one looks at me and raises her eyebrows and smiles. The other cop asks for my ID, phone number, and says someone called in and reported a rape. "That hasn't happened here, has it?" he said and kind of laughed. Or did he? It's actually over quickly, faster than the first time at the park and quickly, I am back in the truck next to my lover. I start the truck, put it in gear and shake my head, looking at her.

The cops all get in their cars and drive away. I put my arm across the trucks' bench seat and look over my shoulder to back out of the parking spot so we too can get out of here. As soon as I do though, I realize how fucked up I am. I put the truck back into neutral and turn off the engine and look at her. I'm completely demoralized. I ask her what she needs, is she ok. She says she feels ashamed and is trying not to feel the shame that she is too loud, that that's the problem: she's too loud and too much. I say I'm asking myself, "What are you thinking? Why are you doing this?" I have fear I'm not protecting her and fear I should be protecting her. Also, fear this is wrong. Even though my intentions are good, I'm a producer of confusion. I feel terrible actually.

I ask her what she thinks is happening. I mean, I'm acting now like I don't know but my intentions are actually to be disruptive, as I've stated many times throughout this whole story here.

On the drive back across town to her house she tells me all the exciting parts like as a reclamation between us which now I can't even remember all the details, so full of fearful remorse and regret I was, but I drove on MLK slow and easy, stopping at yellow lights even, not speeding but being real steady.

July 3, 2017:
Dear Bobby:

I drive my lover home and drop her off in front of her house. I double park the truck, get out and walk around to open the door for her, walk her to the sidewalk in front of her house. The hazards are flashing on the dark street. We kiss good night and as I'm about to leave her I take her hand, push it down the front of my pants and growl hoarsely, "Fuck me." She pushes her fingers in my cunt and I hold her shoulders and smile, rocking my hips to meet her. It's quick, I'm wet and then back in the truck to drive over the bridge to San Francisco.

At this point, in the truck, alone, driving now quite fast, racing all the big SUVs and Prius' and Subaru's' in my own brain, attempting to best everyone out there on the bridge, I'm stuck. I'm at that point I'm at now, which is almost wordless trying to make sense of what's happened. Over and over, I'm asking myself what are you doing? And not having an answer. What am I doing? I mean, what am I doing with my life? Yeah, what?

I'm actually sickened to think about most of this; sick with guilt and shame and remorse. Abnormally strained with abnormal fear. And as I'm exiting the Treasure Island tunnel, onto the broad expanse of the old bridge with the city in view, I realize I'm insanely driven, to a drink. It's like I'm racing to it.

I take a solemn oath, I will not have sex in public until I can figure this whole thing out, figure out how to be safe, to protect us, use a spell or some sex magick or something, but I feel too bad right now to do this again, sick, as I've said, with the absolute unmanageability and remorse I'm feeling. Too much guilt and shame, including the shame of my vanity in front of my lover, fear I look bad, fear I look like a chump, contritely bowing my head to the cops as I say, "No, I had no idea…", playing stupid for their entertainment, middle- aged butch dyke, what are you? you think you're a man? Can't even see her own ID without glasses on, grey hair and yeah, when the glasses are on in a properly lit bathroom mirror, lined face and aging skin, thankfully I can't see how I look for real, I can't look like this, fucking 50? For fuck's sake. I mean, this is the same thing I've thought since I was 5 and that is I have be dead, only now, with a lifetime of mistakes and mistaken beliefs, I'll tell you, it's that much more mesmerizing that I got to get the fuck out of here, no more fucking in public, no public sex, no dominating her on the street, no forcing her into anything, not in cafés, or thrift stores, nothing, until I can figure out how to do this.

July 4, 2017:
Dear Bobby:

A month later we are in Nevada City. A lover's friend has got a vacation rental for her birthday and I went up for 36 hours, for a little out of townness for a bit. We drive up in a lot of traffic the back way because we were in the east bay, 24 to 680 to 80 at some point and even on a thursday, it's a lot of people driving all the time every-where. Nevada City. Arrive in evening and eat dinner and take a hot tub and go to bed and then in the morning, heat water for coffee in a microwave oven next to the bed on the night table and then do the steps. For breakfast there is chicken livers and eggs and butter and crackers. The people are socializing then over coffee and their own food and in the living room. I read a book and write on a couch.

Suddenly, it's 11:30 and I jump up, check the little device for where there is the nooner and say to my lover: "Wanna drive me to Grass Valley or lend me your car?" She drives and as we are on the way, she says can she come into the meeting with me? I say sure. She says then, "I hope there is someone in the meeting who does the steps." I say there will be. Me. I'll be the person in the meeting who does the steps. "No," she says, "I mean another person." I don't tell her that there are only about 100 men and women who do the steps daily.

Instead, I tell her there are, oh, about only 250 people worldwide, doing the daily steps.

Mapping and re-mapping from our location, u-turning and turning around, then we are at the aa clubhouse in Grass Valley, just as the meeting is starting. The steps being read and the preamble and traditions. Then a reading, and even without some of their coffee, I'm feeling good. I move to a chair closer to the front of the room and settle in. Aaah. And as one guy shares, I'm really feeling good and think ok, this might be as good as I'll feel in here so might as well and I raised my hand right as he finished and I shared. As I shared I was laughing and relating to the reading and I looked over at another guy in there and he was also laughing and smiling and nodding his head. And when our eyes met, it was so much reflection, I just kept going. Finally, I said, "Goddamn it! I'm fucking grateful to be sober." And he jumped in right behind me and shared too. And as he shared, he was talking about doing the steps daily! It was amazing and I laughed while he shared. I mean, I need it, the belly shaking vibrations of laughter, not just an intellectual smirking. It was great and after the meeting, he and I ran up to each other and kind of hugged and I said who showed you the steps while he was saying you're from SF, you know Tom?

Then, leaving the meeting floating or flying through the air and back into the car, it's immediately like, "I'm hungry and thirsty" and so snack-lunch while I break the meeting down repeatedly saying how amazing it is to be at a meeting and have the surprise of a fellow being in there. Drinking water, too. I'm sure by now I'm ready for coffee. So, onto the little device, mapping and re-mapping and texting with the lover's friends about where they are: Nevada City. We'll meet at the crystal store.

Have you ever been to the little store there in N.C.? With the floor covered in stones and the space is tiny so it's really powerful feeling, so packed and jammed in, crystals on all the shelves and even just three people makes it totally crowded and the store's proprietor sits on a low stool behind two shelves in the back and just asks, "Any questions?"

Having just been to Shasta twice and in all the places there, plus in general 2017 has been a year thus far on intense crystals, being in this small space had me quickly overwhelmed so I waited outside on the bench and when my lover came out, said let's get some water and then I'll meditate. The N.C. downtown is just a few blocks long and maybe just two or three side streets so we set off then. Around the corner is a small corner store but as I began to go in, I immediately saw the place was basically a liquor store with display cases and also stacks in the middle of the sales floor of cases and cases and I said you know what, let's go someplace else. I felt already altered by being too thirsty and also from the crystals. We walk down the street. Almost every little store in this town has crystals on display in their front windows and I commented on this as we walked along.

We reached the end of the long street not having found another store except one off the main street that only sold the water owned by coca-cola, so we didn't buy that water there. I was getting irritated by now, walking even a few blocks with so much stimulation and no meditation and I was ranting righteously about everything in this town and also about doing the steps, how grateful I was to have something to do, to do whatever the fuck I wanted, and then when I'd done it, to have a way to clear away all the guilt and remorse I felt about doing it. Across the street as we rounded the corner was a small café which was closed. "Fuck this place," I said, and as we walked back up the next street a 50-year old Buick Wildcat GS crawls around the corner and slowly drives by like it's floating on air. "Wow," I said, "That car is so beautiful. I get hard just to see it pass." With this, I grabbed the crotch of my 501's in my fist.

My lover then drops to her knees and puts her mouth on my fist and looks up at me from there. We are in the middle of the sidewalk on a street in Nevada City. I put my other hand behind her head and pull her in deeper while opening her mouth with the fingers of my right hand, fucking her throat. It's like this for a second, or maybe less, me looking into her eyes and smiling when a cop car comes from literally out of nowhere and is suddenly on the curb right behind us. I didn't see him drive up, just that he was there, in the cop car with his sunglasses on saying to us, "This is unacceptable. This is not acceptable."

She quickly turned and says, "We're about to leave town."

PART TWO

July 18, 2017:

Dear Bobby:

In the fall I'm at a house sit in Oakland. My friends have asked me not to have any of the women over, please don't have sex here. I'm studying No Future and re-reading, as always, Coming to Power. I don't want to start off with the no-sex prohibition but I have fear its kept me jammed up from starting this part: in which Bonarh returns to Oakland; Cashier and Bonarh set the terms of their arrangement; the project begins in earnest.

This moment begins at the Autumnal Equinox, the beginning of a new season, the day and night are of approximately the same length all over the planet. An overall feeling of goodness prevails. I wake early in the morning and ride my bicycle on the flat streets of Oakland, swim, go to an early meeting. The weather is like fall, sunny warm, not hot. I can sit in the little backyard of the housesit with my shirt off in the sun, reading and writing, interacting with cats who take turns sitting on my lap on a chaise.

It's the day after the walk on Alice Street. How did we leave it as we rode our bikes from the park back across Oakland? Today, I'm riding home at 9:30am. I send Bonarh a message on the device: "at what point today will you come by for me to fuck you. No talking, nothing else." And then because I've plunged so quickly after sending, a minute later: "You'll need about 20 minutes."

July 25, 2017:

Dear Bobby:

She responds quickly, catching her breath, she says and is noon good for me?

I'm sitting with my shirt off and wearing shorts in the little back-yard in Oakland. It's sunny and hot in this small sheltered space behind the house and with a cup of coffee and a notebook and pen and paper and reading and writing, cats taking turns sitting on my lap and glaring at each other, my schedule is somewhat flexible. So, yes. 101 Echo is sent, it's in the back so I'll meet you in the front and when I go out the front door to meet her then, a moment early, the cat for whom I'm responsible and who is not allowed out under any circumstances, in fact, runs out.

This cat is quite large, with long, long, grey fur, like a giant coon cat and quickly he disappears. I'm not familiar with the neighborhood nor with this cat's habits. His people describe him as defiant, even with them, and so when I'm standing out in front of the building calling his name, I'm not surprised he doesn't answer. And just as quickly as this cat ran out the door, I'm thinking of myself: fear I will look bad if she arrives and I'm having to spent the 20 minutes not fucking her but looking for a cat. And of course, what if I don't find him? That's not merely an inconvenience but an actual situation of having to explain: "ah, yeah, I lost your cat."

A man and a young boy are walking up the street on the sidewalk. I've gone back in the apartment, made sure the other door was shut so the other cat didn't also go out and then got my device and keys and went back out front. I ask the man and boy, "Did you happen to see…?" "Yes!" they say, a large cat was over in front of that place, and a few doors down the street there are some bushes. The cat was walking down the sidewalk, they say. I hurry and actually don't call the cats' name. Instead, I walk quickly and search all the spaces I think I'd be if I was this cat. Suddenly, there he is, sitting like a loaf of bread and quite content it seems, or certainly not agitated. He squints his eyes as I approach and I squint back but quickly reach down and lift him. He is quite large and quite heavy. I walk back quickly to the apartment, juggling cat and keys at the front door, cat beginning to squirm in my arms and then, tossing him inside, brushing off the front of my levis- and t-shirt, return to the front to meet Bonarh. I'm surprised when I look at the time: this entire incident has taken only a few minutes.

Bonarh is walking up the hill to the apartment as I reach the sidewalk, so I stand watching her. She's smiling, seeing me there. As she reaches me, I grab her arm and lead her inside, saying only, "Come on." We walk through the front room of the apartment down the hall and past the kitchen to the back bedroom. I don't have to repeat my instructions which were no talking, and I like this. I place her at the end of the bed, facing the bed, and I stand behind her. I put my arms around her from behind and squeeze her tightly, a bearish hug, like a tight bondage. I put my face against the back of her head and smell deeply, her hair and skin. Bending my knees then, still with her in the tight hold, I lift her and hold her off the ground, pulling her to my chest and against my thighs.

July 26, 2017:
Dear Bobby:
    I'm not impressed with myself, I'm asking to be rid of myself. This is where this starts then, with an idea of remorse before I even begin. Chasing a cat, drinking coffee, leading women to a bedroom. Laid out like that, it seems it's a good run, so far.
    I'm holding her off the ground, lifting her with my thighs and holding her tightly with my arms wrapped around her chest. My mouth is near her ear and holding her like this, I'm telling her about the night before, the walk on Alice Street. "There was a blaze of light between us," I said, "and then this opening."

July 27, 2017:
Dear Bobby,
    Now, even in this letter, I'm acting like I even now can understand what happened, what was going on even then at the beginning with this crystal light.
    In fact, this is what all of this is about, putting a series of events, seemingly connected into a narrative to make sense of all of it. This is what people do, what people have always done. It is the self-will asserting itself to be right. And my life depends on me not being right about any story I have, especially about anything I may or may not have done. I have to be right with god which sounds instead of humbling humility like grandiose delusion. And it's why the story of being at 101 Echo actually seems more plausible. The idea of me getting behind Bonarh and lifting her off her feet, sweeping her up in my arms and telling her, "Suddenly, between us, there was a flash, like a blaze of light, an opening."
    Quite quickly, when the opening occurred we went in. Like an entrance to an ancient cave or a door in a room in a dream, the moment evidences a rend in the fabric of existence: the journey begins.
    I lay Bonarh then on the bed, her knees bent and feet stay on the

floor and I stand then between her knees, above her on the bed, and just look at her. In the laying her there, her shirt lifts, have I already loosened her pants? She's laying in bra and panties on the bed. She's not saying anything while I'm repeating the story from the day before, already grooved into a habit, "…a flash of light, from within but between us…" and this incantation takes over and guides us today.

As this repetition builds, my hand is held, like a fist, in front of the button fly of my levis. My fingers are curled into a circle and while I look at her, she's watching my hand, which isn't moving, just being held still.

During this part there is a second story being told and that's the story of the girls in my high school who got fucked like this by the guys at the keg parties when parents weren't home. "This is how the girls in my high school got fucked, laying on a bed on their backs in a bra and panties by the guys who told them to shut up, to not say anything, to just be quiet." I begin at this point to fuck her from where I'm standing. I'm looking at her there, on the bed and almost all of my energy and focus is in my fist.

The searching and researching to get the experience: can it happen again or was the night before just some idea I was left with after the fact, some fantasy of sexual experience. Did what I think happen happen, or did I just think it happened. If it's real, then let's do it again. Of course, I'm not saying anything like this to Bonarh, I'm talking about her bra and panties now, her shirt pulled up, her pants pulled down and me standing over her watching her laying still and quiet on the bed. My fist is still, not moving, and while I'm watching her watching my fist, she begins to move, slowly, and at first not quite rhythmically, just squirming and the energy begins to flow through her body. There's deeper turn on and still she's not looking at me directly.

We stay riding like this for a moment, another moment, and then I throw myself on the bed next to her, laying side by side. My face then is against her ear again and now I'm jacking myself off. I slip my fist into my levis. I put my left arm across her belly and hold her there like that and as we build a little bit higher, I'm telling her to open up for me, to open her pussy for me to fuck her. Still in bra and panties, me still with levis and t-shirt on, we fuck like this and as she opens, I feel my chest open in a way I wasn't expecting. My chest opened and suddenly I'm crying, lying next to her while I jack off and she holds herself open to me.

August 2, 2017:

Dear Bobby:

In that moment, me telling her to open her pussy, her cunt, not just her hips, in that moment, that breath, that blaze happens again. My chest opens, expands and I cry a bit, almost come but I'm swept away and into it. I'm existing in a place that barely exists, exploiting a realm that barely exists.

As part two, begins I'm wanting the narrative to take over, I'm wanting the authorial voice that is asserting itself to fade away, and as the characters start to experience a transcendence through the sexual enactments, so too we as the reader can slip in and slip away. All of us, Cashier,Bonarh, writer and reader, can forget ourselves in a good feeling. What is required for that? I want to experience this as I'm typing, the ease and flow of a story spun out without using the miserable recreation of memory. Who knows what happened yesterday? The brain is trained to modify experience and store it as memory anyway; right now, I'm writing fiction. The making of history is a willful act of memory; the act of creation a fine line of self/not self.

I'm swept away and into this moment where we lay for only that long before I'm jumping up off the bed, buttoning my fly and pulling Bonarh up off the bed as well, pulling her shirt back over her breasts and belly, pulling up her pants from below her hips, hurrying her out of the house so I can finish the letter I'm writing to you.

August 5 2017:

Dear Bobby:

I'm trying too hard and that night I sleep terribly, waking many times full of dread and anxiety, self-hate. In the morning, the inventory I ask to have removed is mostly the lines: fear I'm not being honest; fear I'm not being fair to Canela; fear I'm not being fair to Bonarh. Like most mornings, I want to feel better than I do. Then

I meditate and go to a meeting, riding my bike across town in the early morning.

Bonarh arrives on time this morning. She knocks on the front door and I let her in, leading her through the front office to the back of the house and into the kitchen. I kiss her hello, briefly but intentionally. I'm nervous, slightly nervous to begin. What do I think I'm doing, I wonder. A month of fearful consuming obsession and now she's here. I've prepared lunch for us. I'm really trying to pull something off, or prove something, or something. As usual, what I want is not to be thinking about everything so much. I want to just get into it with her and then take off, flying.

Canela had suggested I start this whole thing by clipping Bonarh's nails, and so, with Bonarh here finally, I get the nail clippers and sit on the couch, my knees apart, legs spread and tell Bonarh to sit there, between my thighs. From behind her then reaching around her, I clip the nails on her fingers. I do a terrible job and make a lot of jokes about being a beauty school drop-out. I'm squeezing her with my thighs as I do this very rough and ragged cutting. As I do her right hand, leaning forward and looking over her shoulder to see her hands positioned over our laps, my mouth is near her ear. I ask her, "Do you want to do this easy or hard?" She says, "Hard," even though she doesn't know what that means. "I trust you," she said.

"Ok," I said. "Easy is where we chat most of the day, driving up to Point Reyes or Limatour Beach, and then it starts when we spread a blanket on the sand and we are having sex. Hard is we start now. Do you want to change your answer?" I ask. "No," she says. She trusts me. Now.

I unbuckle my belt and pull it from the loops of my levis. I put the belt around her neck, pull the end through the buckle and then notched it. I'd imagined her undressing and so I got up from behind her on the couch and told her to undress. She stood in front of me. I sat back down on the couch and watched and directed what to take off first and then next. No, now your shirt, now your pants. She undressed and kept on the belt, her necklace, and the t-shirt she'd worn under her shirt. She wasn't wearing a bra.

We'd planned to go out to the beach today, perhaps over the

bridge to Black Sands. I was fearful about staying at the house but then went for it. The bed is in the other room. I tell her to go lay on it. I undress then. I put the dick and harness on the bed, nipple clamps alongside. I tell her to put the dick on. She does. She's on her back now. I loosen the belt and re-notch it. I lift her shirt and put the clamps on her nipples. "It's my first time wearing these, just so you know," she tells me. I ask her if she likes to fuck with a dick and she answers: "Yeah, I love it."

I lay on my back on her belly. This is one of my favorite positions for fucking. Then, there is a lot of energy play: "Close your pussy. Pull it up your cunt. Push it up my ass. Hold your hand here and pull it through my clit." I'm directing and leading, pushing and pulling where I want the energy to go, how I want to use the energy to fuck me. On top of her like this, her on her back on the bed, me on my back on her belly, I want this flow channeled between us so I'm riding her hips with the dick between my legs. My head rests next to hers, nestled on her shoulder as I give my commands.

At one point, she's talking about how she's holding back, that she's really strong and that she's not fully giving everything. Something like that. I rolled off her and sat up next to her. I said, "Number one, this is normal, a normal part of submitting: some people cry, some get angry, some try to push back and resist and some do a lot of intellectualizing. That's what's happening now. Number two," I said, "I'm stronger than you. Whatever you bring, I can take it. Don't hold anything back. You don't have to with me." I swung back around and sat on her hips, facing her and grabbing the belt around her neck like a collar in my fist. I slapped her face repeatedly and quickly. "Do you understand me?" I asked. "Yes," she said. "Then fuck me now."

She rolled out from under me then and began to position herself above me, grabbing the dick hanging on her hips in her hand. "No, not like that," I said. She puts her hand in my cunt, fucking me hard and deep. I was laying back and letting her fuck me. I felt her strength and desire; I didn't have the fear I should hurry up or get it over with, or that she wasn't that into fucking me or doing it because she felt like she should. Enough inventory has been removed, or some of it anyway. It was hard to come though, hard to catch it, the climax. I do enjoy her though, her rhythm and pumping me. Then, I grabbed the belt again, catching the long tail of it and wrapping it in my hand, pulling her closer to me. I told her to close her pussy now and to open her mouth and then as she did I did come. I patted my shoulder and said, "Lay your head here," and pulled her head to my chest. "Let your body go onto me." Her hand was still inside and we laid like that.

After a while I asked her what do you need? "Nothing," she said. "What do you want to express?" She started talking, saying she liked this. I talked about the energy play, how much I like it, the building of a flow, through my own body and between us. I like feeling in my cunt excitement and pulling it up through my body and into my hand to be delivered to her clit. I want to circuit this so she can push it back to me, grabbing my nipples, or kissing me with her mouth open.

Soon, my stomach is growling, gurgling. I'm hungry. I get up, get maté, chips, cheese. We eat in the bed. "Is it tiring to run the show?" she asks. I laugh and read to her from the big book, explaining anonymity, explaining going to meetings, and explaining having to surrender all my ideas: "I'm a producer of confusion, not harmony. I'm like the actor trying to run the whole show. If only all the players would do as I say," I say, "the show would be great! Life would be wonderful! But what usually happens is that the show doesn't come off very well. My basic trouble is that I am a victim of the delusion that I can wrest satisfaction and happiness out of this world if only I manage well."

Now, this kind of talk excites me tremendously. I have the book in my hand, the little book from my bag, and I'm opening to various pages from the first 164, quoting and laughing. This is my experience. I explain to her my ideas, including this: "I'm gonna go to aa and look good. I'm gonna share some tremendous spiritual experience and I'm gonna correct what everyone else in the meeting has shared. I'm gonna punish everyone…" It all has to go. I have to surrender all my ideas, especially the ideas that I think are good. I have to have an experience of something other than myself, an experience of power. I said to her, "Of course I had a lot of ideas about today even: you get here, we get in the car. Go to the beach. Here's what's going to happen. Here's what you're going to do, me thinking my plans about what you'll do are real, is too dangerous for me."

At some point, we are back in the living room. I heated up some of the maté and we shared a cup. I was wearing my net shirt. She was wearing the dick, nipple clamps, belt around her neck and her necklace. I was asking her about her desire for submission. It was difficult for her to answer, she was conceptualizing and being quite vague. I was kind of laying on the couch now, her next to me sitting up but very close. I took off her necklace. She's in her head, talking about I really don't even know what. I want her back in her body, I want to feel her physically.

August 6, 2017:
Dear Bobby:

Her body is quite solid and thick, strong. This is what I want: to feel her physical desire, to feel her desire for me and my body. It's difficult, it seems, for her to articulate what she wants but the dick hangs from her hips and she is kneeling over me where I lay on the couch. Soon, we're fucking;Bonarh is fucking me with my dick. I've stopped talking, stopped asking her all the questions I've been asking her and for a moment, I'm not directing her every move. I want her inside, I've wanted her inside me like this, from above, fucking me with the dick I've used fucking women for 25 years. This is what I've been thinking about since the beach in the cave there: Bonarh fucking me with my dick.

I'm getting into this, too. I'm lifting my hips and getting up on it. Bonarh was into it, too. I could tell by the way she was looking at me, watching me take the dick in my cunt, reaching for more. She said, "Lift your hips," to me and she was starting to put pillows underneath me. I said we need some lube. She said, "I have some in my car." She pulled her pants on over the dick and tucked it in as she zipped up, and then pulled her sweater over her head and tucked the belt into the collar and ran out.

When she came back in she took her clothes back off. She jumped on the couch and said, "C'mon," patting the spot I had been laying on, "Lay back down over here."

I grabbed the belt in my hand, pulled her to me and slapped her face repeatedly, hard. I said, "It's hard to fuck a woman with a dick from the bottom. It's hard not to get cocky when you're wearing a dick." And then I really started in on her. She was crying. It was great. I was slapping her face, I'd pulled her to her feet with the belt in my fist like a handle almost, and we were now standing in the little room face to face. I'm taller than Bonarh so I was using the belt to hold her up;Bonarh had to stand on her toes to meet me where I wanted her: very close to me as I began to talk loudly and in her face. No more husky whispers in her ear; I'm talking quite loud as she cries with each time I slap her face. I'm slapping her face, alternating sides at a fast pace.

As I slap her and she cries I tell her this is an honest release and to let out as much as she is able. "This is what you're here for," I say, "this is why you came over. Not to hop on top of me. You came because you're into submission." I ask her, "Right?" and through her tears, she nods yes. At this point, I started fucking her, alternating a slap on her face held still with the belt in my hand with a reach down and behind the dick and harness to slip into her wet pussy with two fingers. Or maybe that was later. I took the dick off of her at a certain point, stripped her all the way down. "Are you punishing me?" she asked. "No, I'm stripping you down. Spread your legs." Then I'm slapping her pussy, hard. Before this, I bit her tits. She said, "Please don't mark me so they can see it at work." I said, "Oh, do you have some image to maintain?" or something like that. I bit her again, hard. Mostly, I'm holding the belt in my hand the whole time and pulling her repeatedly close to my face. "You are crying because your lover is slapping your face. This is what you wanted." By the third time she was crying, she was smiling, too. I said, "Yeah, this is an honest release and you like it."

The first couple of times she cried she was fearful. She was saying she was afraid of losing control. She said she was fearful I wouldn't like it. I said, "Look at me. I'm smiling. I like you crying,Bonarh." I slapped her pussy a lot, telling her to keep her feet spread, her legs open. I was asking her all sorts of questions about being fucked, about her idea that she had a bladder infection, that she shouldn't be fucking, I asked her about the last times she's been fucked, to tell me about them. While I'm asking, I'm fucking her, slapping her pussy and still holding the belt, tightly buckled around her neck in my hand and she is confused and it's hard for her to answer anything, hard for her to express herself, especially as I'm getting going, faster with the questions and physical attentions. Finally, I said to her, the reason I'm asking is because you described a recent experience of being disembodied during sex. The way we are having sex, it's dangerous if you can't be present, dangerous if you are armoring or whatever. I said, "This is life and death for me. If you get hurt, whatever, you'll heal. If I hurt you, I can't take it."

At a certain point through this, slapping her face, I said as she cried, "I'll give you something to cry about," and I felt her get fucked up or slightly disassociate and I immediately said come back here, or, stay here and called her back and held her. Then I gave her the last sips of the reheated maté, told her to catch her breath and began again with the belt in my fist, slapping her face and pussy while I fucked her.

August 7, 2017:
Dear Bobby:
    A natural break came at some point and then sitting behind her with my arms and legs wrapped around her on the floor and rolling onto my back, pulling Bonarh on top of me I said, "We'll make a transition soon, we'll get up and eat and dress and I'll take the belt off your neck," and we did.
    By the time we were getting out of the house and I as getting dropped off at bart, it was two or three in the afternoon. My truck was parked there so I jumped in and drove across the bridge and then in cross-town traffic up Ninth to Larkin, cross on Grove to Van Ness and it's very frustrating with all the traffic. Plus, everyone is on their devices as they drive. From the higher perspective of the truck I can look right in and see everyone driving by, looking down.
    I went to a meeting and laughed a lot, and shared I was grateful to be sober.

On the way home, I was stopping to have dinner with Canela at our apartment. I parked the truck in the lot and as I walked across the lot and then up Brady past the hair salon I suddenly had the thought: I want Canela to fuck me. I'd texted her earlier as I got in the truck and said it can work out if you're still available for dinner. I brought steaks.

Upstairs in the apartment I took a piss, fed the cats and got a dick from the drawer. I had a snack of crackers and butter and almond butter. I was very hungry. Then I thought, 'oh, maybe we shouldn't fuck. Maybe we should just eat dinner.' I put away the dick. Then, I noticed the magick wand next to the bed. I tried it. I mean, it must be about 30 years since I used a vibrator. And I don't think I've ever actually come using one. If I did, it isn't something I remember. I think Bella from New Jersey had one when we lived together in Long Island. But I seriously barely have any memories of us even having sex together, let alone anything specific. And mostly what I remember is her not fucking me.

I was waitressing at a family restaurant in the town I grew up in. I don't know what exactly a family restaurant is but this one was owned by a family in our town, the Puccios. The dad, John, was the boss. It was his dad's restaurant before he died and the dad loved it, John Sr. He was very social and personable and liked everyone, so they said. John Jr. hated the business, hated serving people, and hated that all the customers called him Jackie because they remembered him as a little kid. But he was at the restaurant every night, chewing Tums. The food at this place was delicious. The specialty was the veal parmigiana but we who worked there could have the chicken with spaghetti marinara and it was just as good. Plus, the servings were like for two people so we could order a dinner while we were working and then take it home and have dinner for the nights we didn't work. Plus, they made pizzas, extremely thin crust pizza like a cracker or a matzo.

The three sons worked in the kitchen except for the youngest smart one who went to college instead, and just bussed tables on school breaks. The two older sons also hated the restaurant and John the 3rdwho made the pizzas actually smoked right over the dough while he rolled it out thin. We were all out of high school and just working in our town, and every night going out after work to the bars in Freeport. One night at the Harbor Inn, there was another lesbian there. She worked at some other restaurant or was there with her brother and I was with the people from my restaurant. Somehow, we all sat at the same table and then she and I went to the bathroom at the same time and grabbed each other, started kissing and then I went down on her, which is what we called licking pussy and eating a women's cunt.

She stood against the wall of the bathroom with her pants pulled down and we got into it, wild. This was mostly the kind of sex I was having at this time in my life, just out of high school and somewhat closeted. The sex then was somewhat furtive. A lot of bathroom sex with women at parties, a lot of drunk sex, a lot of blacked out sex. I actually thought a reason I drank so much was because I wasn't comfortable with my sexuality. I didn't understand alcoholism; I didn't understand the reason I was drinking the way I did—to oblivion—was because I'm an alcoholic. This woman and I fooled around for a while and then came back out to the table and made a lot of jokes about 'meet me in the ladies' room' but actually we were worried that the rest of the table knew what we were doing.

I was living at this time in Long Beach with Bella. She was from a rich family in New Jersey and also had rich cousins in the rich town next to my home town. She was older than me, maybe 21, and she still sucked her thumb. She didn't really work except when one of her cousins called in sick to the rich uncles' company where they all worked. Bella had a mental illness which didn't bother me. Mostly she watched soap operas and ate sandwiches from the near-by deli. Her favorite was turkey and swiss with mustard and mayo. What bothered me was that she never bought me a sandwich or even asked me if I wanted one when she was going out to get one. I mean, we lived together but she told her family and the uncle and cousins that we were just roommates. There was a second bedroom in the front of the basement apartment with an extra bed in there. I worked at night, leaving to drive up to the restaurant at around 2 in the afternoon. I mostly just read books and drank coffee all day. I didn't eat because 1). Bella didn't buy me a sandwich and 2). I could have something like soup or a salad when I got to the restaurant. If the boss John wasn't there sometimes one of the brothers would make the waitresses a plate of spaghetti meatballs to eat while we rolled the silverware and set the tables.

Bella was home most days like I said. Sometimes she took classes but mostly she just watched teevee and sucked her thumb. I was in the bedroom, reading, drinking coffee and jacking off. I tried to get her to come back there with me, tried to entice her, but I didn't really know what to do. I think even for me there's just so many times a person can be turned down for sex before they stop asking. All of this makes sense except for why I stayed with her or even, why after she threw all my stuff out onto the sidewalk when we had a fight, telling me to get out and not come back, I begged her to take me back.

This was a pattern for a while.

The only other time I could have used a vibrator was in Chicago, living with Liz. By this point, I was a drunk, drinking daily, even when I didn't want to drink. The whole Liz story is a bit complicated for this story, so I will save the details of who she was and how we met for later but she was a hoarder and a collector and very, very messy. Against my better judgment I let her move into my apartment but mostly because my dad was living with me in Chicago and I didn't know how to get him out, how to ask him to leave, so I finally said to him one day sitting with him at the well-lit day time bar around the corner from the house (which is why I think he moved to Chicago in the first place, because of a description of this bar I had written to him about. He liked the idea of being able to walk to a bar because he was living rurally in Lake Charles, LA). We were watching Wheel of Fortune on the teevee above the bar and I said, "Hey listen, Liz and I want to live together…" He didn't say anything but this wasn't unusual for him at this point at all, so I lit a cigarette and said then, "I can help you find an apartment in the neighborhood." It was actually excruciating, getting out these two lines to him and I had to be so drunk to do it, tell him in this sideways way to move out.

Liz moved in september. She had so many books and papers and cats I gave her the back half of the apartment to use as an office and any time anything of hers started to encroach in the front half, like a stack of mail, or some books, or photocopies, or her purse and backpack, I'd take it all and put it in the room in the back and close the door.

Liz had a huge box of sex toys. I'll be honest: this was my main attraction to her. Dozens of dildos, in every size and shape and color and in latex, plastic, and silicone. Also harnesses, mostly very feminine harnesses brightly colored and accented with lace or something. Most of the stuff she had was very low quality. I found out her favorite place to buy anything sex related was some xxx bookstore on Clark Street in Chicago. She and I went there once together, like on a date. The place was fluorescently lit and the shelves were full of video tape boxes wrapped in saran wrap. And then all the toys. Plus, Liz had tons of vibrators. Most of these weren't working, maybe no batteries or had gotten wet or something spilled on them but a few still turned on and Liz loved them. Or at least she seemed to like them. Most of our sex consisted of putting a porn tape in the VCR and jacking off together on the couch, her with the vibrator, me wearing a dick in a harness and both of us smoking cigarettes. I always thought about our relationship as like the brothers living without their parents in The Outsiders.

When Canela came home I was vibrating myself with the wand. I was laying on our bed and still had on my pants and jacket. "Fuck me, huh?" I said to her and she smiled and said, "Yeah, let me go wash my hands." I made her a snack of crackers and butter too and got back on my back on the bed. No romance, no foreplay, just let's do this. I got the wand back on me and on my clit and cunt and told I her I never used one of these. She was fucking me intensely and the soles of my feet were burning! We were smiling and fucking and even though I didn't come like this, it felt so good to be with her.

August 8, 2017:

Dear Bobby:

It's during this time, after high school, living on Long Island, working at the restaurant, that I was trying not to drink. I'd already been hospitalized once for alcoholism. I even went to a meeting of aa in Long Beach where I was living. This wasn't my first encounter with aa. I must have already gone in high school. But going to aa as a teenager is a complete drag. For one, when you get there, everyone says how lucky you are to have gotten to aa so young. Lucky that alcohol is already not working so much so that at 16 or 17 I'm coming to aa? You call that lucky?

There was a women's meeting in a church basement around the corner from my apartment in Long Beach. It was in the morning so I could go before I went to work at the restaurant. I was terrified walking in. I mean, maybe I didn't even walk in the first few times. And of course, this was before the internet and the idea of just looking up stuff like aa meeting locations from the privacy of a hand held device didn't even exist. It wasn't even in our consciousness. Finding a meeting of alcoholics anonymous required finding the hotline phone number, like calling information and asking them to look up the number or looking in the yellow pages at your parent's house. Then calling the hotline and them telling you where the next meeting was or the one the next night. Then you could ask them to send you, by mail, the complete schedule of aa and it would come to your house in an unmarked envelope.

It was helpful to have a schedule. Then, days before work could be spent smoking cigarettes, drinking coffee and staring at the listed times and locations of the various meetings. Then, maybe on my way to work, I'd drive down one of the streets where there was a community center or a church or temple and see if I could find where the meeting would be held on friday or next tuesday. A few days of this after an especially bad hangover—most of the time trying not to drink meant not drinking for a couple days, getting a few days together and then drinking again, every brief recovery followed by worse relapses. So, I'd look at the aa schedule for a few days, hungover and sick, can't even eat not even the left-over spaghetti and meatballs, smoking, coffee, and then after work that night, going out and drinking to a blackout. The next morning I'd throw the schedule away, saying to myself as I did, well, this shit doesn't work.

That's the problem with righteous know-it-all alcoholism; the complete lack of power that is endogenous to the condition.

I did finally make it to the women's meeting in the church basement in Long Beach. I went down the stairs, fearful, sweating and actually having no idea what to expect. To be honest, some of the meetings I went to in high school, I went drunk, so I have no idea what happened, just a vague memory of a bunch of people in a basement. And this was the same, a group of women all downstairs with a bunch of long tables arranged in a square around the room. Now, I don't remember much about this meeting either, except that I sat down and all of us were smoking. I mean, smoking a lot of cigarettes, and also drinking coffee. At this point in my life, late teens, early twenties, it wasn't uncommon for me to have 5 or 6 cups of coffee before noon. And I'm sure I had close to that many before this meeting. And then I sat down and had another couple of cups. And then I started to hear what was being shared.

It was amazing, all these women talking about how much they loved to drink. I mean, finally, I'd met women who drank the way I did or at least they said they did, but it seemed like they did. I never had any friends or other girls in high school who wanted to drink with me, especially not if they did drink with me once or occasionally twice. They'd never usually talk to me again, let alone drink with me. I was too violent, too mean, too entirely unpredictable and downright scary. I'd often get drunk and threaten to kill myself. Or to fight anyone who came around. I'd have to be dragged, literally, home. I'd actually punch women who were around me. And guys. I was astonishingly crude and unmanageably hostile and antagonistic. It was actually dangerous to be around me, especially in a car, where I'd probably try and grab the steering wheel as we drove, swerving our car into oncoming traffic or the center divider.

But it was these women, female alkies, who I understood. I was laughing and feeling really good with all the tales of their mayhem and wreckage: ruined relationships, crashed cars, lost jobs, spending the day laying on the couch drinking to oblivion. It was amazing. I felt like I found my people, finally. Of course, all this coffee and cigarettes had me spending most of the meeting in the toilet stall, but the parts I heard had me feeling really good. At one point, I was coming out of the bathroom and one of the women was standing there. She smiled at me and asked me a couple of questions, I forget what but whatever I answered she kind of nodded. Maybe she asked if I was sober and I said yeah, obviously, I mean, I'm not drunk right now. She hugged me before I went back into the meeting and when she did she said, "You're not eating much, are you?" I didn't want to get into the whole story about chicken parm and leftover pizza and bringing meals home from work, so I said I was ok. As we turned away from each other she said, "You know you never have to drink again."

That was basically the last time I went to the meeting. I wasn't there to not drink. I mean, I wasn't even legal yet to buy booze legally. I wasn't sure what aa was, but I thought I knew what alcoholism was: a drinking problem, and if could just learn to drink like a normal person, then I could drink the way I wanted, which was all the time and to oblivion. Honestly, I didn't want to get drunk, so drunk, every time I drank. Sometimes I just wanted to take the edge off and have a good time, couple drinks like everyone else after work. Blacking out and humiliating myself, actually hurting myself and being so sick wasn't what I was going for. But never drink again? I laughed when she said that and grabbed my pack of smokes and left the meeting.

I was living alone in a studio apartment in Long Beach. This was right before Bella and I moved in together at the other end of Long Beach. I bought a sleeper sofa, brand new, and my brother helped me pick it up and move it to the apartment. I had a small mattress and box spring that I got from someplace before that, so sleeping on the pull-out couch was an improvement. Next to the bed I had a cardboard box with a bedside lamp on it.

Moving into this place, my first place out of my mother's house, was huge. A big step for me. Bella actually had the apartment before me and then she moved into a little house that her uncle owned and she let me take the lease over on this place. It was right across the street from the beach but I was already so sick with alcoholic depression I couldn't even make it across the street, not even to walk on the beach or even on the boardwalk, though occasionally I'd ride my bike on the boardwalk to go over to Bella's on the other side of town. It was hard for me to go out in public alone because I had fear people would look at me. This is the grandiosity of the self-hating alcoholic.

When I moved out my mother said, "Everything you have, I own, so you can't take anything." I wasn't 21 yet but I was 19 or 20. I left her house with a couple of books and some clothes. My grandmother came to the apartment once and brought me a few plates and a pan and pot. Not that I was cooking. I don't ever remember even going shopping. Though, I must have bought coffee somewhere. I had a Mr. Coffee drip coffee maker. My dad gave me an old bureau, quite beautiful but it had been painted over. I spent a week or so with interest applying paint remover and smoking cigarettes while the powerful chemical solvents melted the paint and then scraping the curled crumpled wet pieces off. I was so high and it was so satisfying.

I didn't have a teevee; this was something I was actually quite proud of, though where I had a consciousness about no teevee being a good thing, I have no idea. I knew though that part of the freedom of getting out of the house I grew up in, out from under my mother, included the freedom of no teevee. I had an understanding of the regime it was supporting and creating. The people I worked with came over one night after work and then the next time they came, they said they had a housewarming gift for me: they all had chipped in and bought me a very large teevee set. I hated it but at least it meant Bella would sometimes come over to stay up late watching the shows after the news all night, sucking her thumb in the blue light, sitting up in the couch bed, facing the teevee.

I had only started masturbating at about age 19, so basically everything was changing really fast for me. Let me say at this point, that I sucked my thumb until I was 13. Perhaps that was the affinity I felt for Bella. I was a late bloomer for sure. But once I started I tried to make up for lost time. The days in the apartment were mostly spent just jacking off. It seemed everything finally made sense to me.

August 17, 2017:

Dear Bobby:

I was basically spending every day, all day, before work at the restaurant, jacking off in my Long Beach apartment. It was right across the street from the beach but I was too fearful and full of alcoholic depression to even go over there. Even during the spring, before the start of the actual summer season when during the week it didn't cost anything to go over and go on the sand, I stayed away.

I went to the library often, still using the one in my hometown where I had a card. I looked up 'lesbianism' in the card catalog. I found books by Jane Rule and checked out probably all of them, read them and returned them, went back for more and then started at the beginning again. I didn't really understand what she was writing about, everything was very coded. I'd read Another Mother Tongue the year before while still living at my mother's house, keeping the book in a drawer when I wasn't actually reading it. I didn't think my mother'd be mad, necessarily, if she knew I was gay, I just suspected she'd ask a lot of questions that I didn't have answers for. When she did find out, she was actually mad, but that's also another story.

But even after reading that book lesbianism still seemed this underground, secret culture and even though I understood I was lesbian. I couldn't figure out how to access this underground. Mostly, I was too fearful to talk to anyone. When I read in books about these women seeing each other at cafes or at college or even on a street in their downtown and then going up and talking to them, it seemed impossible. I'd never be able to talk to a woman like that, let alone talk to a woman about being gay like that. Plus, my town was a suburb. It didn't have a cafe or a downtown. I was one of the few people who took a bus places and I never saw any other women who might be like me on the bus. Or at the library.

There still seemed a lot I was missing, like I was still outside. Jane Rule books were engaging enough but even they didn't have any sex in them. Or if there was sex it was so subtly described I read paragraphs over and over trying to figure out what happened, if anything had happened at all. I was desperately wanting more explicitness but I had no idea how to find it.

Most days, I'd wake up and make a pot of coffee and then drink it in bed, reading, doing crossword puzzles and smoking cigarettes. I can't imagine what else I was doing except jacking off. Especially after drinking so much coffee and smoking so many cigarettes, all the stimulation had me feeling good. And even though I didn't have much experience with women, I had had some sexual experiences with women, mostly drunk, mostly blacked out, mostly me forcing myself on friends or friends of friends, I did have one very specific fantasy I used daily.

The apartment had windows that covered the front wall, very wide windows that if there wasn't another apartment across the small courtyard and another building across the street would provide a view of the ocean. The windows had big slat aluminum venetian blinds. I kept them open since I was inside most of the time. It meant though, that my neighbors in the apartment complex when walking by could see into my unit. I didn't want to get up and close them before jacking off though, so I usually just rolled out of bed and onto the floor, laying there in the space between the mattress and the wall.

I imagined that I had a small red sports car, like a Fiat Spider, and that I was racing this car on an empty parkway, driving really fast. Suddenly, in the rear-view mirror lights are flashing and I hear a siren: a cop. I pull over. The cop gets out of the car and comes over to the driver's side of my car. This cop is big, with a tight uniform and mirrored sunglasses. The cop asks for my license and insurance. I'm a little defiant and smart-mouthed and answer like, "Or what?" Cop says get out of the car. Did I mention I'm wearing a tight miniskirt with my levis denim jacket, sleeves rolled up? I get out of the car and cop grabs my arm, twists it behind my back and pushes me forward onto the front of the car. The car is hot from me speeding around and leaning over it is uncomfortable but when cop leans onto my back, actually pushing me onto the hood of the car, the heat burning through my jacket onto my belly and tits, feels good. The cops' hand is on my back between my shoulder blades holding me down. I'm trying to keep my face off the hood of the car. The cop lets me up though and I stand but I feel how close behind me cop is: very. "Put your hands on the car," cop says and over the wheels the side of the hood is cool enough to stand like this. Cop though kicks my feet back behind me, pulling me backward from behind so I'm leaning forward, bent over the side of the car. All this has happened so fast I don't have time to say anything.

Standing leaning like this, cop's feet are between mine, spread apart, that's how close cop is to me and cop has night stick which I feel in cop's hand which is again on my back, holding me with pressure, and stick is across my back and shoulders. Suddenly, cops' gloved hand is under my skirt, pushing my underwear to the side and sliding right into my pussy. I'm that wet and open. I take one, then two thick leather-gloved fingers easily and quite quickly. I'm pushing my hips back against cop trying for more, wanting more.

I'm furiously jacking on my clit on the floor of my apartment, coming hard and going again and again as if I'm making up for lost time, body straining and reaching and stretching into this idea of being fucked bent over like this. I turn around after coming and look at the cop who has taken off sun glasses and is unbuttoning uniform shirt, and, of course, I see now, it is a female cop who had me like this. And though I use and re-use this story over and over again, this part, the surprising reveal is always my favorite, seeing her face and breasts bared.

I do this most of the day and usually right up until the time I have to leave to get to work on time so that I am jumping up, jumping into the shower and though the owner, John of the restaurant, has repeatedly asked me, told me to wash my uniform for work, I usually don't so that after the shower I'm picking up black chinos and red t-shirt from a pile on the floor and pulling them on. Why wash them, I figure, since even when I do wash them in hot water and soap they still smell like pizza and chicken parm and the salad dressing stains never come out. Plus, I worked last night, how could I find time to do a load of laundry before work today.

Now, during this time Bella and I are girlfriends, though mostly closeted to our families and friends. Later, when we live together, I move into her place which she rents from her uncle. There are two bedrooms and we say we are doing it to save money. During the day when we live together I actually do lay in the second bedroom a lot.

I'm there mostly jacking off and since Bella is in the living room watching soap operas, I don't want her to hear me coming again and again. At this point I don't know how to entice her to come with me into the bedroom. And trying to come on to her while she's watching teevee and sucking her thumb hasn't had positive results either.

I actually don't have a language even for sex, at this point. When Bella and I are having sex one of us usually goes down on the other one. That's what we called it. And usually at a certain point, while I was going down on her, Bella would say "go inside me." Of course, this meant to fuck her but we never used that language. I certainly didn't have any way to describe my fantasy even though I went over and over it. It wasn't a story I told myself, it was outside of language, the cop fucking me with gloved hand wasn't described to myself, I just let the images tell the narrative that brought me to climax: mirrored glasses, night stick, my short skirt, the hood of the car, gloved hand, thick fingers, gloved hand, gloved hand.

August 18, 2017:
Dear Bobby:

And this remains, a series of images that tell a story without words bringing me to climax. Even now I don't read porn as much as go over the same stories again and again, dog-eared pages in pulp paperbacks. I know most of the stories by heart, almost word-for-word, but it is the images connoted and conjured that I've formed in association with the words on the page that have me excited. As I read, holding the book with one hand, or laying the book with cracked spine open on the bed while I stand next to it, looking at the page, the first sentence of a paragraph and then my eyes closing and my head falling back and saying to myself, "Oh yes, here is the part where she climbs up on her father's lap…" and then, it is not the words but the image of her short skirt which she's wearing, pantiless, that has me coming, repeatedly.

The day after we were at 101 Echo, I called Bonarh. "How are you?" I tell her to come meet me today. She's available at 5:30pm. "Is that ok, Cashier?" Yes. I spend the day doing laundry, packing to leave the housesit, finishing the letter I'd begun to you there. I finished the letter at 4:45 and raced I'd with swimsuit to the pool but on saturdays the pool closes at 5 and not 5:30 and so I fucked up again. Ride and buy carbon paper and paper from Creative Reuse instead and then bike back to Echo.

Bonarh comes up at 5:30 or 5:45 and I grab a couple of things and we go out the front door. We begin walking around the neighborhood, up to the end of Echo where it meets Rose and then to Kingston, Lake and Linda, weaving back and forth through the streets. The sky is beginning to orange a bit, the intense blue and sun of the day fading. As we walk, all the cats are out, crouched in their late afternoon poses, under cars parked in driveways, up on porches,along side houses.

As we walk, I ask her how she feels after yesterday. Bonarh is excited; I can feel her energy is up. She says she feels great, full of love. I take out a piece of paper as we walk and take notes: love, sense of love and generosity;surrender; trust; pleasure; sensation; the feeling as if she's been taken on a ride; attended to. She has questions for me, too. "How," she asks, "are you able to compose something like that? It must," she continues, "require a lot of work." And then, "What do you get from a scene like that?" This is where she gives the list as her answer. I write everything down. And then I encourage her, "When I ask you to tell me everything, I want to know everything. Not a censored version of how you think you should look. This isn't a job interview."

Then it all comes, all her fears as well: how she will look in public, fear she's not good enough, "fear I'm not worthy of this attention, fear I didn't perform well, fear I didn't take enough, fear I'm not fierce enough, fear I'm not a good enough femme ("I want to be cool," she adds), fear I disappointed you." The subject/object pronouns get tricky here, because even as I type to describe her fears, I'm completely related. These are the fears of the self-will, my own fears, the fears that I wrote that morning myself as I did the steps.

August 19, 2017:
Dear Bobby:

When she said the fear about not being able to take enough, I laughed and said, "Hilarious! That's the classic submissive fear!" We were still walking through the streets up behind Piedmont Avenue. I said, "Ok, I'll answer your questions," and I read the list back to her: love, surrender, taken on a ride, generosity, trust, pleasure. She looked at me with question and I said this is what I get from that kind of scene. She cocked her head again and I said, "The same; I want to surrender to this kind of experience as well."

We continued walking. She said she didn't want to tell me what not to do, what her boundaries were because she has fear that's what I'll do first.

Yeah, I laughed, you're right. But then I explained, she could tell me these things or not, it's what she's bringing and what she wants uncovered. "It's what's charged," she said. Yeah. Then I said, "Listen, there are tons of people who will get together with you like this and negotiate, respect boundaries and offer safe words. That's not me. What we did together was amazing. It doesn't necessarily mean it could be or should be repeated."

I said earlier to her that the reason I want to surrender to this kind of scene is my own insane cockiness, my arrogance and of course, my defiance. I said this is why I'd do exactly what you'd said you don't want: not because I'm an asshole but because I'm an alcoholic and completely defiant.

Bonarh is still whirling from the day before and now from this walk as well. It's hot between us, even this walk and talk. The explicitness of our desire, of each of our desire expressed is what has everything feeling so charged and excited. We aren't even touching as we walk, though I am walking very close to her, slightly behind her left shoulder, kind of using my body, but the energy from my body, to push her along or guide her. I'm purposely not touching her physically because I don't want the discharge of energy that can occur with touch. I want it to build higher. And I'm straining with desire.

"The kind of scene I want with you is the kind where we both take off." How is all this done, she asks. She feels attended to and she wonders how do I remember her words and what she's said? "I don't remember everything you say," I said, "I'm constantly working the narrative and repeating that back to you. In that case," I ask, "what are you going to withhold from me?"

The only thing she says, is that she doesn't want to be dominated in public. I say, laughing, "Of course." She says, "I'm fearful to even say it. I have fear as soon as I say it you will slap my face right here." Yes, I say.

I stop walking and look at her. I face her on the sidewalk and say, "This isn't a game for me. I'm not wanting to just do something because you say don't, though I am driven to do that. I need to surrender for this to be good for me too. I don't just get off doing what you don't want. My desire is more complex than that. I get off on fucking women, for one. I also enjoy being in a d/s dynamic with women. But what I want is for your submission to be difficult, challenging and not me forcing you. I'm not a sadist."

"And furthermore," I said, "plenty of people will be more than willing to play any number of games with you: to do what you want, or say you don't want or to listen to your intense descriptions of the way you want to submit or be dominated or whatever. That's not me. I bring it all and expect to be met. I give a lot and want the same: a lot."

Bonarh is kind of almost speechless by now; I still haven't kissed her or touched her, though we've been walking close to an hour. She's looking at me and I say, "take a few days and see if this is attractive to you, if this if what I'm offering is something you want to pursue." And then we separate having come back around to Echo Street as the evening is darkening.

The next day or so, is that all that passes?, I can't make any other plans with anyone else. This is so uncomfortable because I have fear I'm waiting to hear from Bonarh. I don't even want to write that here. It's like all the good feeling and satisfaction of yesterday just has me wanting more, instead of feeling satisfied. I've already had a lot of thoughts about 'next time we are together...' and I have fear if it's not soon that we are together next time, I'll lose interest.

When we were walking on saturday, I read her the letter I had just finished that afternoon, kind of like "here it is: everything. All my work, everything I've been working with recently." I have fear it didn't mean anything to her, fear I overwhelmed her, fear I came on too strong, fear I chased her away. I am resentful at myself because I have fear these are the same fears as last week, which in the end boiled down to fear I am inadequate.

August 23, 2017:
Dear Bobby:
(I'm out in the West Hamptons; never been here before, at a cousin's retreat and I'm back on the little Olympia electric portable; selectric has the correction capacity, not this one. My apologies ahead of time for the typos and mistakes, leaving here tonight or tomorrow morning and trying to keep at this, keep this little streak going)
By now, I'm tired, bored with myself. I have a slight headache and feel like I could fall asleep. This is an obsessive brain driven by fears, self-delusions. If I don't get fucked up though I don't have an inventory to take. Without the primary purpose of the steps, what life?
The next day Canela is sleeping in. I got up at 6, did the steps, drank coffee and fed the cats. At 7:30, I go in and wake her. I need to leave at 8:30 to go to a meeting.
She's sleeping on her back, the way she does when she's alone in the full-size bed and there's plenty of room for her to spread out. Her eye mask is still on, arms above her head. I put my hand on her wrists, bend and kiss her deeply while reaching down to her pussy with my other hand. She rouses a bit, opens her mouth and starts to wake. I pull off my underwear and climb up on her, ass on her chest, cunt in her mouth. She still has on the sleep mask. I still have my hands on her wrists, pinning her. It's so hot, especially as she starts to suck me hard, pulling her head and mouth back and forth on my clit and then is pulling it up from her belly. I lean back, put my hands on her hips, arch my back and lean down on my ass, pushing her chest deeper to the mattress. When her hands are free, she looks at me and I'm looking at her smiling. It feels so good.
I dropped my bicycle at the shop for a tune-up and then walked to work: down 12thto cross at South Van Ness, Otis and Mission

and then pick up 12thon the other side, across from the gas station, passing the storage unit place and the people encamped on the sidewalk there. Across the street is another, larger encampment, usually with dogs as well. Reaching Folsom, there is a flyer on the light post for a party on sunday night at the Eagle and I thought about putting a double belt around Bonarh's neck and pulling the belt through her legs over her cunt and thought where it would be buckled together and how when suddenly I remembered the thick leather harness, full body and putting it on her—she's a bit broader than me and I imagine it fitting better; I'm for sure too small now—and I got extremely excited. It feels good coming to work, smiling and all I want to do is jack off in the bathroom.

Since there are only two bathrooms for 100-150 workers at any time, this is a practice I rarely indulge in, maybe only late nights but then at that point why not just go home and go at it in the privacy of one's own bathroom. Usually, there is a wait to get in the bathroom and then a line behind me so no-go as far as jacking off to orgasm in there.

But I do admit to going into the bathroom and jacking off for two or three minutes, standing by the sink, levis fly open, hand down my pants, inside my underwear and rubbing my clit to extreme excitation and then washing my hands and exiting the bathroom, not having come but feeling good enough to do a shift on the register, smiling.

That's what happened this day then, arriving at the store a few minutes early before counting a drawer, I slip into the bathroom, no line, and unbutton my levis, hang my bag on the hook, lock the door and grab myself in hand. My clit is hard and in a moment I'm wet. I lift my shirt a bit, holding it up with my left hand while right hand rubs and jacks off and then quickly, as I get close to coming, I take a deep breath in and out and sigh and stop. Button jeans, wash hands and go count-in a drawer. Most of the shift though, I spend thinking about Bonarh. She came to the store the night before to tell me she thought about what I offered her, an arrangement, and that she was interested in pursuing it. I was on a break from the register and missed her. She sent a note instead, a pic of her handwritten note, sent digitally, "Cashier, magick I'm into this. I'm into you. I want to get deeper in, so, yes".

August 28, 2017:
Dear Bobby:

At this point I'm obsessed. Or maybe I already was. Canela was noticing my distraction a month before. I admitted it at first, saying yes, I'm thinking about Bonarh even when I don't want to be but then as it gets more pervasive, the all-consuming thoughts of Bonarh even when I'm with Canela, I try to down play it. I'm actually trying to be honest with Canela, trying to be present with her and not try to hide anything from her. But I also have a strong desire to protect her and not cause her harm and I have fear telling a woman that I'm with that I can't stop thinking about another woman is hurtful. I try mostly to down play it and manage my feelings. Meanwhile, I constantly want to kill myself. But this is nothing new and doesn't actually seem like I can rely on this as a symptom or indicator that I should change my behavior.

Not to mention the fact of what's happening in San Francisco at this time with the art supply store closing and tent cities along the way to work and then sprouting up behind the store and on the other side of the street and really everywhere. The sporting goods store has also closed and so for a while there is a large encampment of people living along the back of that building. On-line and then with customers there begins to be a discussion of what to do with the homeless, who are called as such and not even as those people, which is dishonest enough in itself, denying the fact that for 99% of us, there is the element of that could be me living out in a tent threat, though the customers, who are loyal shoppers, but as evictions increase, and more and more rental units are being turned into vacation or air bnb short-term rentals, and more and more of the diversity of our customer base decreases and who is left are property owners, I notice I have much less in common with these white liberals, who present themselves as well-meaning, but are actually talking to me at the register about 'rounding up these people' kind of talk. I mean, even just hearing this is so stressful and for a sensitive person like myself, already so close to the edge, already living on the edge, this alone makes me want to die.

Let alone what I seem to be doing. Most of which I'm completely blind to, as they say, blindly pursuing at any cost what I want. My experience is closer to something like I'm being driven rather than that I'm doing this, pursuing this other woman, Bonarh, so relentlessly. But also, because I'm actually being met there, in that pursuit or obsession by Bonarh. After the day at Echo, there was a question Bonarh asked which was, "What should I call you?" and I said it depended on what she wanted. Did she want to be sweet, have a sweet arrangement where she's calling me Cashier? Or only use my last name, calling me King. I ask her is that the kind of submission you want to show me? Or how about if you aren't even to use my name at all? Anyway, I say, what I want from you is for you to ask to come for my pleasure. I say, "before you come I want you to ask me if you can come, for my pleasure".

This works quite well at Echo, Bonarh, while I'm fucking her, rubbing her clit, asks to come for my pleasure. I stop rubbing and ask her, holding her clit in my hand, "Is this for me? For my pleasure? Or because you think you need my permission to come?" She shakes her head in confusion. "Is this because you want to come, Bonarh?" She says yes, Cashier, I want to come. And I hold her there and explain again, "This is for my pleasure, Bonarh. You said when we started this, what you wanted was to please me. Is that still what you want?" Yes, she pants. "I want then for you to ask me, "Cashier, can I come for your pleasure?" and as Bonarh begins to ask I begin to grab her clit again and pull and rub her, jacking her off and saying to her "this is what I want. I want this." And she comes in my hand.

Over the next days then, after hearing from her via digital pic sent or handwritten note saying yes, Bonarh begins to call when she wants to come for my pleasure. At first, she is completely unsure of what I mean by this and she is calling as though asking for permission to come.

August 29, 2017:
Dear Bobby:
And I will throw the question back to her, "Do you want to please me,Bonarh?" This place of tension is where we will ride for months,- Bonarh requiring a kind of training in what is my pleasure, what pleases me which she has difficulty discerning from her own plea- sure: if what she wants is to please me and I'm saying what pleases me is her coming for my pleasure, it becomes easy to see her confu- sion develop. Or where it would develop. And actually, this is what pleases me the most: Bonarh's confusion. I get very excited when she isn't sure what to do or what I want; when she has to surrender into the not knowing space and let something new take over. And so, this is where Bonarh begins to call to ask if she can come for my pleasure.

We never make a specific agreement about what or how she will do this, and this collaborating together, as she calls and usually leaves a message for me,as my response to her either by text or calling her back and leaving her a message, becomes quite engaging. Deeply so. This is when I begin to be obsessed. And since calls are coming from Bonarh at all hours, day and nightly, I'm feeling met here in this place of surrendering into not knowing, of giving over my own ideas of what I want and what I will do for that.

At first her requests are quite specific, such as her stating that she would like to come that night before she goes to sleep, or at the very latest, sometime in the morning when she wakes up, before she gets ready to go out for the day. I laugh when I hear that one, that request. "Because," I say when I call back and leave a message for her, "you're asking to come for my pleasure and not your convenience, unless I'm misunderstanding what you're asking for."

Now, at this point, though I've never said "you can't come unless you ask for my permission." it is the way Bonarh often seems to be interpreting our agreement. The second time she calls she's clearly self-conscious in her request. She's kind of laughing as she asks me if she can come for my pleasure, to please me and as she's laughing she's saying, "You know, I don't know if I can do this all the time in my life but here goes: Cashier King, can I come for your pleasure?" and she laughs. When I call her back, I say I find her difficulty in asking an extreme turn on. "Yes,Bonarh, go ahead and come for my pleasure. But that is actually the arrangement: to please me. So, when you've come, send me what you're thinking when you've finished."

Canela is pissed and I'd say rightly so but justifying any resentment is slippery. She wants to know why Bonarh is calling all the time. Am I saying enough?

How to do this? Any of this. Which has already been done by Kate Millet and I'm comparing myself to her. She's blending politics and the personal even while she's denying doing it, plus pulling off non-monogamous bisexual relationships and life. Her high-drama, self-absorption,capturing the grief,longing, obsessive desire leading to her exquisite moments of flying: Fumio, Celia, Magda not even Claire yet, every line poignant and painstakingly so, "in order not to err, one does nothing... and the fear begins. Can't trust this". For me, meanwhile, every line has me wanting to die; with every line, I have to kill myself.

If this is to you, it has to be good, or good enough. If there isn't you then I won't do this. I won't tell this story that seems to need to be told or at least documented; a lesbian archive. Again: the making of history is a willful act of memory. I want this moment to be a part of history, not forgotten, even if it means exposing my mistakes, my shameful, selfish, self-centeredness. Even if I have to look bad.

Re-re-reading Flying, the third time through in as many years, I'm hanging on Kate's every line. Every line has me handwriting, copying sentences from her book into my note book, like a high school girl reading the Bell Jar. How can, how is it that Flying isn't taught in high schools?Even the edition now, with Millet's own brief introduction, explaining what it is she's doing, documenting, she says, and says the importance of this new life.

Printing in 1990, the first since 1974 when it first came out and though this is like a dream for me: laying with my lover on a couch in L.A., during a heatwave down here for a cat-sit and the use of an apartment and studio for which to write to you everything that happened last year. There is a hot breeze with the windows open, temperatures in the mid to high 90's and Bonarh is reading Flying to me while I take notes in a notebook on my lap. Millet's a vitanuova, american english, surely captured more deeply than Kerouac's, or at least, offering a version for us, for gays and lesbians, for women artists, for those of us with outrageous notions of how to live and love. Before AIDS, before the 80's and the Reagan era that actually hasn't ended but has only worsened to an unending era of empire as a way of life, to this moment of now, of a sociopath in the white house and the end that is in sight is the actual end of it all, Kate is writing about loving women, her coming out nationally as a lesbian, being questioned in the media: "Well, are you?" and the "taste of sun on my warm arm, salty, good" and "go down dream mouth tongue singing on her center tasting knowing her essence" and flying.

"What am I doing" is my constant refrain, every moment not completely occupied with errands, chores or the steps is a constant berating of myself. "What are you doing?" is among the kindest since what it all eventually leads to is "You have to kill yourself, this is useless, stupid and self-indulgent." I'm comparing myself to Kate Millet and I'm coming up short. How did she do it?

Canela at this point is already angry. Her weekly situation with Lee has basically ended at this point. After their romantic getaway to Paris on a plane, flying together and going through TSA, no problem, Canela came home bored, a bit, or at least wanting not to be seeing anyone else. I already was what with Michelle and T, and then asking for her friend's phone number—we'd made out at the dyke march a lot—and a couple days later giving me Mary's number, Canela started yelling.

This was maybe only the second time I'd ever heard Canela yell like this, full voiced and actually screaming: "What!?" she said. "You must be kidding me! Mary was drunk at the dyke march!" and I went plummeting down as if I'd fallen in a hole. Drunk? I was kissing her, and I mean kissing her, tongue in her mouth, making out, faces close, smiling while I looked at her, breathing in her breath, probably, and it was booze I was after? I chased Mary all day, all over Dolores Park, and every time I found her, we kissed some more. I seriously thought I must be super into her but then Canela tells me she was drunk and I have the terrifying realization: I was pursuing a drink and that close to it, for the last time when I kissed her as we left the park, I pulled Mary close and she had a flask of whiskey in her hand. At this point, even before Bonarh, Canela was already thinking the whole polyamory wasn't working. She wanted simple non-monogamy, not falling in love with other people and not having full-on, full-time other relationships. Casual flings, hookups, and fun flirtations is what she wanted.

Next weekend though, she's going with Lee to New York City to see a 24-hour performance in a church.

August 30, 2017:
Dear Bobby:

September 1, 2017:
Dear Bobby:
On october 7, we had a date. On october 7, Bonarh and I had a date. Bonarh had called and offered me various times that she was available but I said no, not an hour or two here or there. I want the whole day. I want you to make yourself available to me for the whole day. She said friday and I said, "OK, be ready at six am."

Canela is pissed and I'd say rightly so, but justifying any resentment is slippery. "You made the date for what time?" she said. It meant I'd be getting up at 4:30am to drink coffee and do the steps including meditate and then leaving at 5:30 to get over the bridge and to Oakland by six.

We talked about the whole thing, Canela and I, and she expressed her jealousy too, not just being upset about having to wake up so early, not even get up with me, but be awoken and then try and fall back asleep. Plus, she was going to NYC that day with her lover, Lee, to see a 24-hour performance, kind of a whirlwind trip, coast to coast. I don't know if I justified my idea about 6am with that in mind. I don't even know if I had that in mind, so selfishly thinking of myself I was. But then after the talking and expressing ourselves Canela said, "I thought of how you can start your date on friday. Shave Bonarh's pussy." I got turned on, really, deeply. "Wow," I said, "you're really kinky, Canela. Really a freak."

When I get to Bonarh's house in Oakland that morning, it was still dark. As I pulled up in front of her house, I saw a light on in the upstairs window. I knocked gently on the door and she came down and got me. Then we went upstairs to her room. I sat on a low stool next to the bed and she lay down, kind of sprawled across her bed. She had on a shirt and skirt.

I'd brought a copy of the emails she sent me over the summer and I pulled them from my bag and tossed them up near her head. She opened the folder, saw the emails and then recognized them as her own and blushed. "Read them to me," I said. She took out the first one and started reading. It was quite sexy, especially the line where she says "I will do anything for sex." I was still on the stool next to the bed while she read; she was laying on her back and I sat watching her. She finished the first page and I said, "Go on," and she began the next one. In this second one she was describing meeting me and wearing underwear and a skirt, of not wearing underwear and making it real easy for me. I liked this one and she read it and I remembered it. I smiled and started to get turned on; listening to her read her own words that were intended to be read by me on a screen. Instead, I'm watching her lay on her back, exposed even with the clothes on and beginning a bit to squirm.

I still was wearing a button-down shirt, long-sleeve blue chambray, levis and denim vest with fake sheepskin lining, engineer boots. I'd taken off my wool fedora when I arrived in her room and also the denim jacket I'd worn over the denim vest. I stood now, standing next to the bed on which she lay and unbuttoned the wrists, the cuffs of my shirt and began to roll up my sleeves. She read on. When my sleeves were rolled up my forearms, I took off my vest. I stood watching her then with arms folded across my chest. The email she's reading describes how she would indeed crawl across the floor for me, to meet me.

Walking to the end of the bed, I kneel on it and lay between her legs, lifting her skirt slowly. I begin, no, actually I dive right into her pussy, still covered with her panties, pushing my mouth and tongue against the material and pushing my tongue into her cunt covered with the cotton. I bite her clit like this, through the thin fabric, and she moans. "Roll over," I quickly say, "and keep reading." She's on her belly now and I reach up and quickly pull her underwear off, pushing the skirt up over her ass and hips. Now, I'm on my belly too, laying on the bed from my waist up, legs still in levis and feet still in boots kind of hanging off the edge of the mattress. I'm propped up on my elbows, face very close but not touching the middle of her thighs. I'm now watching her ass and cunt, both of which seem to feel my eyes on them, both opening and closing as if they are breathing of their own accord.

By now, propped up on her own arms, holding folder of papers, faced away from me but certainly able to feel my breath on her cunt and thighs, Bonarh takes a deep breath; her breathing has become heavier with shoulders shaking a bit on inhalation. She is reading the part in which she describes holding her thighs together so tightly that it makes access for me difficult, would I like that?

My face goes immediately into her ass, pushing my nose and mouth and then tongue into her hole, licking and fucking her while my hands spread her cheeks. She's moving now, shifting her hips side to side. I want to get in deeper so push against her with my elbows as leverage, holding open ass to get deeper in her ass and holding her firmly to the bed while I do; she's trying to lift her hips to meet me but I'm not allowing this. I push in harder, opening my mouth wider, wanting more of me inside her.

Of course, she's wet now. And her cunt is wide open and I push my tongue here, too, alternating ass and cunt with my mouth, still holding her tightly against the mattress. I don't want her able to grind her clit nor to buck her hips. I want her only open to receive me and want to begin to convey to her, give her an understanding of the difference between my pleasure and hers; me fucking Bonarh like this has me quite hot and I'm getting off. My pace is speeding up now. I'm going faster with my tongue, deeper and between holes, sucking and spitting into her and licking and really pushing my mouth into her ass, then my nose in her ass while my mouth is at her cunt and breathing breathing biting and licking. Bonarh is moaning face down into the pillow and when I lift my head up, pull out of her I say, "keep reading," and she re-reads the part again about keeping her thighs closed tightly so my entering will be made difficult. I put my thumb in my mouth, wet it and then slide it into her ass, fucking her slowly while my mouth sucks at her cunt, I'm purposely avoiding her clit and now just keeping my tongue at the opening of her pussy, circling around while I fuck her ass, letting all the weight of my upper torso and belly fall on her fully, pinning her now as I grind through my levis, my clit on the bed. When she feels this fucking, Bonarh comes, face down in the pillow, a muffled yell while I continue in the back for my pleasure, still fucking and sucking, pushing into and against the mattress, my groans going directly inside her.

I pull my thumb out slowly body now collapsed on her, then stick my thumb in my mouth again, kind of sucking myself now. Her smell is on my hand and covering my face. I roll off and let her up. She too rolls over, slowly, then turns fully to look at me and she smiles. "You taste good," I say. She smiles dreamily then, kind of closing her eyes and laughing. She goes to the kitchen and gets us water.

When she comes back into her room, the sun has been up a bit by now and Bonarh turns off the lamp on the small bedside table. In the daylight, I can see how thin her t-shirt is: her tits are so clearly visible, it's like she's not wearing a shirt at all. She says she couldn't decide whether to wear a bra or not and asked a friend: "Should I wear a bra or no bra," and the friend said, "Do you want her to see your tits or to take off your bra?" I said, "I think you made the right choice; your tits look amazing."

We ate breakfast after this, her sitting on my lap at her table in the kitchen while I fed her steak and eggs.

September 2, 2017:
Dear Bobby:
One of the reasons we met at six am was because she had a class to teach right in the middle of the day, so after we ate, we separated with plans to meet back up at 1pm.

I contacted a couple of women and said I was going to a meeting at the Rockridge fellowship (which isn't actually in Rockridge: the Rockridge fellowship lost their lease on their meeting place which was in Rockridge and had to move to the Mandana House off Piedmont Avenue in Oakland just up the street from Kaiser on Broadway. Mandana always already had meetings there and also other things like therapists could rent offices maybe, but either way it's now just know as Rockridge) did they want to meet me? One of them said immediately: "Yes! So needed! I've been laying here in bed awake for four hours and can't get up!" The other said she was at work but then by the time the meeting started she too slipped in and later said "I told work 'something suddenly came up" so I could leave and get to this meeting." We all shared and it was like a bottle being passed around; just more and more power and gratitude being expressed and by the end we were all laughing and feeling really good.

I was grateful to be reminded of the primary purpose which is to stay sober and try and carry the message, help other alcoholics to achieve sobriety. Which I mention only because like most people I'm thinking I've got to do something in this world. I can fool myself and think and think, "Oh, money, property, and prestige… I'm not that into that pursuit." But when it's stated instead as "sex, security and society," I know I am driven to try and pull that shit off. The ease and comfort of the aa meeting and the remainder of the primary purpose lets me off the hook: "Oh yeah, I'm not doing any of this. I couldn't."

Which after the meeting I went into the truck and sat and took inventory mostly about my fear that I can't pull off this date with Bonarh and then meditated. Since I was up since 4:30 and already had quite a big day, I was completely ready. Oakland was hot, really hot and inside the truck I was perspiring like I was in a sauna, sweat just dripping off my head and face but my meditation was great and when I came out, I drank a little water, turned on the radio, and drove back over to Bonarh's house. I parked in front, across the street and took a few more lines including fear these steps won't work.

I knocked again on her door and she came down, dressed again in a skirt and thin t-shirt with no bra. I asked, "are you ready?" She looked a bit surprised. "Uh, oh, should I bring some food for us?" "Are you hungry now?" No. "Then let's go." She goes back upstairs, gets keys and puts on shoes while I wait in front of her house.

Bonarh was able to get the keys to a large rehearsal space just a few blocks from her house and we walked over there. I had my heavy leather bag full and carried on my back. We walked over to the space silently and not touching at all but walking very close, her right shoulder and side slightly in front of me. I'm leading her from behind with the energy from my body. Once or twice I reached my hand over and touched the hairs at the nape of her neck.

The afternoon now is hot and I've taken off my long-sleeved shirt. It's in the bag I'm carrying with two dicks, two harnesses, a jar of maté brewed as to be medicinal strength, the folder of Bonarh's writing to me, two of my own journals and a bag of toiletries. I'm wearing a white net shirt with the denim vest over it, arms exposed, my hat, levis, and the engineer boots with thick wool socks. I'm glad for the weight and heat of the boots on my feet; the heaviness helps keep me out of my head which is ruminating and churning with thoughts and fears that I can't do this, even though I don't know what this is.

When we arrive at the studio, Bonarh unlocks the rolling gate and the padlocked rolling door, slid them open while I stood and watched. Inside was the studio was cool and less bright. It felt a relief to be out of the sun and also into this quiet, large, open space. I put down my bag and unpacked a bit: took out water, maté, the canvass bag with the harness inside. I took off my hat and vest, folded the vest and set the hat on top. Bonarh unrolls some blankets and a mat and makes a pallet: "It's like a little bed," she says and smiles. "Now lay down," I say and she does.

I pull nipple clamps from the front pocket of my levis, the dick and harness she wore last time from my bag and toss both on the blanket pile. What with the heat of the day, the early morning rising, the heady excitement of listening to her read while I fucked her this morning plus the power of the meeting and the blast off meditation, I feel altered, high. I lay next to her and hold her in my arms, kind of tightly. Even with everything, I'm still at this moment, just as we are about to begin, fearful I will be a disappointment. My head is near spinning and my heart is pounding. I asked her, "are you ready?" "Yeah," she said, "Yes."

I unbuckled my belt, pulled it through the loops of my jeans and put it around her neck. "At first, it goes on very tight, remember?"

She's standing now in a t-shirt and bra, belt around her neck. I pick up the dick and harness she wore last week. She looks expectant at this moment. I stand up and begin to unbutton my levis, holding her eyes with mine. I'm wearing leather suspenders and the button of my levis is open, pants hanging then just off my hips. Her eyes drop as I thread the harness through my legs, pulling the straps through and inside my underwear, holding the harness as I push the dick through the hole and cockring. She watches as I buckle the harness onto my hips, make adjustments on each side. When it's on, when I'm strapped in, I take the dick in my hand and feel its heft in my palm and look at her again, calling her back to look at me, my face and look eye to eye again.

I button the bottom button under the dick, my underwear is also pulled down under the dick, and I make a few more adjustments: levis on hips, suspenders on shoulders and then grab the dick in my fist. Yes, this is the look I imagined as I grab the belt by the long hanging end in my other hand with the thick leather cuff on my wrist, dick hard and stiff. I spit in the palm of my hand and stroke the dick, leaving it wet.

"I want to suck your cock," she says. I slap her face. "We're not here for your desire, Bonarh, nor for you to do what you think will please me." "Yes," she says, "I understand."

I tell her to take off her shirt. She lifts it over her head and as the shirt gets caught on the belt around her neck, I use the opportunity to grab her wrist above her head and to kiss her mouth through the thin cotton when the shirt covers her face. She's caught and held like that, standing in just her bra with her face covered. Her mouth is open though and I push my tongue against the cotton and into her mouth.

I'm repeating the story she told me this morning about her friend saying do you want her to see your tits or take off your bra? As I pull the shirt the rest of the way over her head and pull out her arms. I'm lifting the bra then over her tits and they fall out of the cups; I pull on her nipples, asking her "did you tell your friend I won't take your bra off? That I'll just pull it up and out of my way?" I grab her nipples between my fingers tighter and repeat to her again: "Do you want her to see your tits or take off your bra?" She's moaning now as I pull and squeeze harder, her mouth open. "Which did you want, Bonarh? What did you tell your friend you wanted?" Her tits are full and round and marked by yellowing bruises from the bites I made last week. I'm holding her away from me as I pull and squeeze; the pain has her wanting to fall forward, wanting to come closer to relieve the pulling. I ask her again: "What did you say you wanted?"

September 3, 2017:
Dear Bobby:
"Here's your harness," I say, pulling the heavy leather full body harness from the canvas bag, shaking it out to untangle it. The buckles and snaps are clicking and clacking as I do. I lay it out first on the blanket pile. Her eyes are wide. The straps of leather are thick and heavy pieces. I begin to put her into it, over her head, pulling her arms through and then taking it off and putting it on again; it was backward. Buckling Bonarh in and then pulling the strap between her legs from behind and snapping it through the cockring: the effect is incredible. The straps go over her shoulders and around her diaphragm, across her ribs, around her middle and meet in a large ring in the center both front and back; solar plexus and between shoulder blades on her back and then the thick long piece that spreads her legs and snaps in front in another ring circling her clit.

"Stand for me by the wall," I say, "show me how it fits." The effect is incredible; the leather has transformed her, and even more than simply a dick and harness, this full body device has made her ready for sex. We've drunk the maté by now, sharing the jar back and forth and I'm beginning to feel the effects; I'm really starting to fly. Seeing her in the leather, posing, turning for me on my command, bending over on my command is thrilling, and I could stand like this for hours, arms crossed across my chest, thick fat dick hard and sticking out of my pants, pressing on my clit and watching her follow my directions.

She needs to piss, though and I say go ahead but that this is the last break she will have. Yes, she understands. While she's in the bathroom, I stand and stroke the dick in my pants, squeezing the shaft so the head gets full. When she comes out she retakes her place on the wall. I've slapped her a bunch already but now she looks like she's crying. Her bottom lip is pouting. She says, "I forgot to tell you something earlier when you asked me if I was ready." "What is it?" "I forgot to bring us water to drink." "Are you thirsty?" I ask. "No, but…" I slapped her face again.

The wall is covered with a curtain which I pull back. "Turn around. Look at yourself," I say, "You're wearing a harness with a belt around your neck. Do you think you're in charge of this scene? Do you think you need to manage this scene?" "No," she says, "no I don't."

"What else?" I ask, "What else is bothering you and keeping you from being here?"

September 5, 2017:
Dear Bobby:

"Well," she says, "I said we could be in this space until 6 but I have rehearsal at 6:30pm and I'm going to need to transition," She started crying. I slapped her face again. "Very good, what else?" She said she couldn't think of anything. I slapped her some more, asking, "You sure?" "No, nothing," she said.

I said, "Good. This is what I want. It's what your brain is ruminating on." "Yes," she said, "It is." "This is good. The slapping has kind of shook you up, loosened the clamp your brain has on these ideas."

Her eyes are full of tears and she's pouting her lower lip. I grab the end of the belt and wrap it in my fist and pull her very close to me. I like her like this, softened and ready, or more ready for what I want, for what I want to do. What I want is to be flying, transcending body and my own brain's ideas of the here and later, into now where nothing—food, water, time—don't exist and both of us are on a ride of feeling good. I want to forget myself and everything I think I should be doing or saying.

"Ok, so you forgot water. You didn't manage time well and what else? Oh, you took a piss, so that's taken care of." I'm holding her face close to mine and I'm slapping it with short fast slaps, delivered not hard but in quick succession. "Your brain is telling you shit." I turn her around, "take a look at yourself. You're wearing my harness with my belt around your neck. Do you think you're in charge of this? Do

142

you think you're managing this?" "No, I don't." "You're not. That's not why you're here."

I lead her to the middle of the studio. I take the belt off of her neck. "Stand away from me. I'm going to hit you with this belt." Doubling the belt in my hand, I take it first to her ass, hard. Red flares up immediately. "Have you ever been hit with a belt, Bonarh?" "Yes," she said. "2002, with a group of people I was having sex with." 'Add it to the list: forgot the water. Fucked up the time. Waited for 15 years to get hit with a belt." I begin to swing the belt wider so the strap of it lands a bit softer in a steadier rhythm, back and forth across her ass, each stroke leaving a red stripe on each side. "Hold still," I say, and take the belt to her shoulders which are broad, maybe more so with the leather straps of the harness.

I pull a chair from the side of the large space and place it in front of her. "Bend over, lean over the chair." Bonarh does, places her hands on the back of the chair and leans forward, her tits hanging down. "Spread your feet apart, widen your stance." I'm stroking the dick on my hips as I order her and she's looking back at me over her shoulder. "Yes," I say, "very good." I lift the belt again and swing at her ass, lightly and quickly so her hips swing side to side in the repeated pattern of the strikes. "Stick it out," and Bonarh leans even further over the chair, pushing her ass toward me. Her cheeks spread and the wide leather of the harness rides deeper inside, splitting her ass in half.

September 6, 2017:
Dear Bobby:
"How do you think you look now?" I ask her. She's leaned forward and pushing her ass toward me to meet the belt. I've undoubled the belt and now I'm letting it fly across her ass. I want to see her lose control. When I pause I walk around to the front of her. I lift her chin and look at her face. Her eyes are full of tears but they haven't started falling yet; she hasn't quite let go yet. "You gonna try and hold it together?" I ask, "Let's see what you can do then."

I walk back around behind her and tell her to stand up straight, just rest her hands on the back of the chair, don't lean forward, I say.

I begin again with the belt doubled over in my fist, to slowly hit her starting at her shoulders, crossing her shoulder blades, down across her ass and to the tops of her thighs. I'm going slow but steady and hard, back and forth and as I'm hitting her, I'm telling her how much I like how she looks, how much I like the way she's taking it. "Lean over again, please," I say, "Stick your ass out for me again." I stand in close and she can feel my breath on her back, my jeans, the crotch of my jeans is brushing her now reddened ass, that's how close I'm standing and I begin to gently pet and caress her ass cheeks. Each side is warm, almost hot to the touch. "Oh, c'mon, lean all the way over for me," and I grab her hips in my hands and pull her back into the dick on my hips, not entering her but so she feels me there, dick between her legs and my hips pushing into her from behind.

"How do you feel?" I ask her, holding her tightly like this and she is shaking against me and says, "I feel so good." "Let me give you a little more then," and I step back, and let the belt fly across her ass now full-on, actually just beating her with the belt. "Please stand still," I say, and she is past moaning and into yelling now, her ass swinging is as much to try and avoid the belt as to greet each stroke. "I want you to take a little more for me, Bonarh, give me just a little more."

Bonarh begins now to cry, quite deeply sobbing. I stop the belt and pull it through the loop of my levis so the long end hangs down along my leg. I take Bonarh's arm and hold her up from the chair and I sit down, then guiding her to my lap. I hold her in my arms and she cries like this, heavily against my shoulder, while I pet her hair and head and croon to her.

September 16, 2017:
Dear Bobby:
I'm sorry to begin almost every letter this way but as soon as I think 'oh, ok, I got this finally, I finally see what's happening and how to do this' I take a break for a couple days and then wonder what am I trying to prove. What? That I can fuck a woman the way she wants? That I've done something good? I mean of course my belief is having sex blesses everyone everywhere but even for me that's pretty grandiose. I'm hoping to find a higher good with this, or at least in

the telling of it. Shall I live a life of perpetual desire, attempting to funnel energy to a spiritual life or shall I just say fuck it and let god manage a spiritual life: attempting to live honestly is difficult, near impossible enough.

September 18, 2017:
Dear Bobby:
   And what's honest for me is pursuing this situation full on. Friends and family begin to be concerned; I hate myself actually and hate my ideas of sexual obsession. It's not that the desire—to control and dominate women sexually, to push and pull them past what they think are their own limits, to strike and beat and bind women while I bring them repeatedly to orgasm, to have women crying and shaking and moaning and begging, "please don't stop" as I fuck them, again and again, pushing, pulling and guiding with my hand and fist—is pathological, rather, it is the obsessive nature of my passionate compulsion. It's like I'm powerless to resist this all-consuming, excessive drive. It borders on inescapable torment. The only idea I have is to let it run its course, to wind it out, full-tilt, hell bent for leather. I do the steps as rigorously as ever, relying on this power to keep me sober, for every alcoholic knows behind every obsession lies the great obsession.

September 20, 2017:
Dear Bobby:
   Before I began to hit her with the belt after I strapped the harness on her, I put my dick on my hips in my own harness. I stood in the center of the room. Bonarh was to the side. It was like I was performing the action of putting on the phallus while actually putting on the phallus. It was hot. My dick is so beautiful, thick and long with the most beautiful tip, like a thick full tulip bud as the crown and a heavy long vein running the length of the underside.
   I got this dick in 1992 at Good Vibes on Valencia Street. I lived at Valencia and 22nd above the ravioli shop Lucca's on the corner. There used to be a bus that went on Valencia out to City College and then to State—the 26—and my window was above the bus stop. I was 25

then and I'd never used a dick before. I don't know if I'd even seen one, but—no, now I'm remembering, I had a girlfriend in the early 90's and we went to Good Vibes a lot together; all the dykes in the Mission did. On saturday afternoons the stroll was along Valencia: Muddy Waters near 16th, Community Thrift then Amelia's Bar at Sycamore, New College on either side of the street between 18th and 19th, Women's Craft West and the bookstore, Old Wives' Tales. For you, I will mention El Buen Sabor, which was on the corner of 18th and still is and the KFC which was on the corner of Hill Street which is no longer there. We'd drink mochas at Muddy's and smoke cigarettes til the afternoon, stop at Community Thrift and then go over to Good Vibes. It was great for cruising and seeing friends, women from the neighborhood or from the thursday night club run by Junkyard, Zanne, and Fresh at Paula's Clubhouse on 16th and Albion. We mostly just saw each other walking around the Mission, which sounds so romantic, but before all the devices and online stuff, that was how we did. Plus, a lot of just happy coincidences, seeing a woman dancing on thursday and then the next week seeing her riding a bicycle on Valencia and both of us stopping and chatting, "Where you going? What are you doing?" and exchanging phone numbers that were for an actual telephone in your apartment that was shared by me and my roommates and a good roommate was a person who paid rent on time but a great roommate took phone messages, actually wrote down phone messages and told me when a woman called and what she said.

September 21, 2017:
Dear Bobby:

My girlfriend and I never did buy a dick all those times we went there; I don't know if I should have taken it as a sign or what. But in 1992, a mutual friend introduced me and Josephine. The friend was just getting a new girlfriend and figured she'd be spending all her time with her so she introduced us, me and Josephine, so we could have each other when she wasn't around.

Josephine was amazing with thick, thick red hair always perfectly cut and she spoke with her hands. She told me stories about her ex-girlfriend cutting her hair in the salon where she worked when it was closed and I'd never heard anything like what she said. She was butch but we didn't really talk about things like that, it was just on the cusp of becoming the biggest topic in SF after AIDS. But femmes flocked to her! She taught me everything, which I needed a lot of help. And she was kind, really kind and gentle, that kind of butch, a very gentle butch who was so beautiful and powerful and handsome, everywhere I went all the women would finally talk to me to say, "Where's your friend Josephine?" I didn't care I was so proud that they knew I was her friend and so dopily naive that I didn't even know how, or even that I could, try and play it my way.

Josephine told me about using a dick to fuck a woman. I mean at this point, we called them dildoes unashamedly. I finally asked her to tell me everything, to show me, something. We went to Good Vibes ourselves, stopping first to drink coffee at Muddy's. Josephine always got a treat with her coffee, like a little cookie, or a small pastry like she was a European or something, eating it very slowly with sips of black coffee. I'd get the biggest cookie they had and scarf the whole thing down in two or three bites and then feel sick to my stomach. Seriously, I had a lot to learn.

When we got to the store, Josephine said look around. "Which one do you like?" I had no idea or I was fearful, I mean how to choose? Josephine was patient though. She began to pick up various models and sizes and explain to me what the good part of each one was. "This one has a nice easy curve," she said, "the weight of this one might be too heavy for the harness." We also called dicks 'strap-ons' really referring to the harness and dick but I think it was also the influence of that lesbian feminist idea about not wanting to mimic men combined with the lesbian feminist reclamation of enjoying our sexuality. Josephine showed me harnesses and which could be used for packing, though I thought I'm a long way from that!

At the time I didn't have a girlfriend and I kept trying to think of some imaginary woman who I'd be with and what she would like, how big should I get it and this kind of thing, personalizing the age-old question, what do women want? Realistic? Representational? Big balls? No balls, just a base? Thick shaft? Long and thin? Josephine explained them all to me, holding each one in her hands and then she said again, "Which one do you like?" and she explained to me what it meant for a butch to have a dick, to fuck a woman with a dick, and that the owning and liking of a dick, the wearing of a dick and liking it, is what pleases the women.

Bonarh seems pleased. I put on the dick. It's beautiful. It's heft, it's shape, and best of all, it's removable. I stand in the center of the large space. Bonarh watches. With suspenders holding up my levis which are unbuttoned at the fly to let the dick hang out and off my hips, I'm stroking the beautiful dick in my fist. This performing phallus, this real, not real masturbatory action, the pulling and jacking off of real/not real turns object into subject, desired and desiring, somehow all the more interesting because it is between the female gays.

She's staring at me. I'm turned on. "Come over here," and she stands in front of me. She's watched me as I pulled the harness through my legs, inside my levis and buckled the straps at my side. I'm spitting into my palm and then stroking the dick, leaving it wet. "I want to suck your dick," she says, and I slap her face. "You said what you wanted was to please me. Are you guessing what you think will please me, or are you telling me your desires, what you want, Bonarh?" I grab her hand and pull it toward me, taking her fingers to the edge of my cunt, which is very wet. I hold her wrist and the dick in my fist, in one hand with her fingers there under the dick. "This might be the only contact you have with this dick all day."

September 23, 2017:
Dear Bobby:

"You like this?" I asked Bonarh. "You like how this feels? You better enjoy it because this might be the only time you touch this dick all day."

She's on my lap crying now after I beat her with my belt. Suspenders hold up my levis which are unbuttoned. The fly hangs open with this beautiful dick sticking out. I croon to her and pet her head while she cries, holding her. She's naked except for the thick strapped leather harness I put her in. As she calms down and stops crying, I begin to slowly rock her back and forth, gently, and subtly I'm rubbing the tip of the dick against the wide harness strap between her legs.

"Stand up, please and I'll give you the final blows from the belt." I pull her over to the far wall of the large room and stand her against it. I stand facing her; the belt, again pulled from the loop on my dungarees, is in my hand and hanging to the floor, inert and still. I look her in the eyes and ask, "Ready?" She shakes her head. I lift my eyebrows and I tilt my head and she immediately understands how to respond to my unspoken question. "Yes, I'm ready," she says.

I double the belt and begin, never taking my eyes from hers as I swing in wide and across her belly and then back and forth building a rhythm. Her skin reddens and red lines appear horizontally across, giving a much more literal meaning to wash board stomach; she's striped. The next hits are to her chest, above her breasts. Here the marks left are not so perfect. The straps of the harness are still the most prominent feature. It is the contact of the belt in my hand and the leather she's wearing and her exposed skin that I'm finding exciting. Facing me like this, Bonarh sees every stroke, every swing of the belt coming. I'm holding her eyes and I'm smiling. I'm wet from using the belt on her like this, hard and harshly and forcing her to watch my enjoyment.

Soon she's crying again. Without stopping my rhythm of beating her I say, "Tell me your fears," and she lets out, through the tears a litany: "fear I'm ugly, fear I don't have enough money or the right clothes, fear my tits are different sizes, fear I should be better, that I don't get fucked right, that I'm too new for this, that I'm still in incubation," she says. I'm actually laughing outright. Now I really feel good. The expression of these self-centered fears is an expression of power and that's what I'm actually craving and getting. I'm laughing and hitting her with the belt and she's crying and I say, "Incubation is over, Bonarh. You were born when you said to me, 'I want to please you'." "Fear I can't take it," she says. "You are," I reply, "you're taking it."

Bonarh is wearing the heavy leather harness. Earlier, explaining to her what this harness meant, and this particular harness' provenance. "You are in service to me in this harness. The weight will remind you of your submission and the restrictions on your movements will remind of this as well." Buckling her into this, snapping the straps, I put my two fingers through the cock ring in front. Her hard thick clit is there and ready and I jack her through the cock ring. "I want this. This is what I want." The metal of the ring rubs the skin on my fingers raw but grabbing her and pulling her with the shoulder strap in my left hand while I push onto her clit with my right has her coming and moaning quickly.

It's through this cock ring that I pull a smaller dick. This dick is shorter than my beautiful dick, shorter and thicker and bigger balls. This little dick, which is actually not so little, is good for packing: soft enough to curl into levis but sturdy enough to fuck on the fly with. The wide base of the big balls also feels good against a clit when it's worn, constantly pressing and stimulating. This short fat black dick with the wide head rides most of the day on Bonarh's clit, held by the cock ring and the strap that bisects her belly. Without the hip straps for control, she'd be hard pressed to actually fuck with this dick but that's not what I'm expecting. I want to see her submission as well as experience it; to see her with a hard-on she can't fuck with and that I won't let her touch either, is exquisite.

Bonarh takes the final round of being hit with the belt as I laugh and she cries. "These will be the last ones," I say and she's now crying yes yes yes while I'm telling her, "You're beautiful, beautiful, tough." I drop the belt to the floor. She says thank you.

September 24, 2017:
Dear Bobby:
In the next moment, I'm down on my knees in front of Bonarh. She's surprised by this move and really doesn't know what to do. I tell her: "Stand still." I put my hands on her hips and push her back against the wall. I've shifted to squatting so I can use more force from my thighs. From this position then I push with all my weight into her and hold her there, against the wall. I look up and catch her eyes again, open my mouth and take my own dick in my mouth.

Back on the beach those pages ago I wrote about wanting to transform the dick energy on which I relied for so much of my sexual expression, my sexual experience. While it was enjoyable, I was fearful the habituation was perhaps limiting my own awareness of who and how I was and am. Was my proficiency in one area perhaps even a compensatory behavior designed to protect me from literally experiencing something else. Well, I couldn't know until I tried to do something different. This was the idea I had anyway, embarking on this situation with Bonarh, to not rely on my own dick energy; to not rely on my experience of sex being that I fucked women with a dick. I had no idea what it would look like though.

I took the dick in my mouth. I took my dick in my mouth. Bonarh stood still where I held her against the wall, the dick hanging from her pelvis. With the harness and this short thick dick and her full round tits, her skin pinked from being hit with the belt, she looks sexy. Hot. I'm before her, holding her, pushing her, kneeling squatting and leaning into her, wearing levis and black engineer boots, a white net tank-top and leather suspenders with a black dick off my hips. I'm pulling the dick deep into my mouth, fiercely, taking all of this not so little dick in. I'm looking up at Bonarh as I do this, giving her a dick-sucking smile as I do, mouth full and eyes open.

She's almost lost, nearly gone over the edge, finding it hard to keep her eyes on mine, lids nearly closing in a reverie. I'm pulling harder and then leaning completely on the dick, I take it down my throat. My lips now are on her belly, I'm kissing the leather straps of the harness. I begin to gag, to choke and that thick viscous saliva from deep in the throat begins to flood my mouth and I slide back, pulling the dick out of my mouth, pulling my mouth off this dick and take the whole thing again, back of my mouth, into my throat and begin a rhythm of fucking her with my mouth. Now it's hard for my eyes to stay open.

Sucking her off like this, is liberating. Expansive. I'm sucking and fucking and choking and gagging and I've hit a rhythm. I'm crying as well, tears streaming down my face and the thick saliva fills my mouth. Bonarh is moaning too, not quite crying now, but the idea of being sucked like this, taken like this; the idea of being used like this is clearly thrilling her also. I lean back and let the dick fall out of my mouth and close my lips and spit fully onto her belly. A mouthful of dick-sucking spit hits her and she cries out. And then again: lean onto the dick to the back of my throat, gag and choke and through my tears, lean back, look up at beautiful Bonarh and release a mouthful on her. Her chest, her tits, her belly and yes, her face soon are dripping with the spit-come from my throat and I'm flying watching her barely able to contain herself.

I haven't let her touch me, haven't let her put her hands on my head or even to thrust her hips. "Stand still, Bonarh." I'm getting off on this, sucking a dick to assert my will and desire; Bonarh's submission proved by her act of surrendering to my desire. My head is spinning and as such, I'm going faster, sucking harder, taking her deeper into my throat and choking more as well, gagging and holding her to the wall as I press deeper onto the dick, holding her there, tears and spit come reflexively and my response: unleash on Bonarh again.

She's soaked. Hair, face, eyes, thighs: wet. I reach down between my legs and grab my dick and hold it and Bonarh cries out. "Oh, please! Can I come? Cashier? Please?" And releasing my dick, putting my hands back onto her hips, pushing her again and myself, taking the dick and her, deep again, I nod my head yes and now it's Bonarh's turn to unleash a torrent and she screams, beyond crying out and her hips shake spasmodically and she comes for my pleasure in my mouth.

September 25, 2017:
Dear Bobby:

At the end of this scene in the large studio, I'm packing up everything to go. I take off my dick, put on my shirt, I pull the not so little dick from the cock ring on the harness she's still wearing, put the belt back through the loops of my levis and button them up. She's watching me as I do, gathering and placing the books and papers back into my leather bag. Bonarh is barefoot, just wearing the harness.

"Can I keep it on?" she asks. And I say yes, but that means you'll be wearing it. She says she understands and I tell her to get dressed. When her shirt is on, I pet her face gently and smile, "Thank you, Bonarh, for all of your generosity." I'm very pleased. She folds up her blankets, rolls them into a bundle and puts them under her arm to carry home. I ask her if there is anything she wants to say or if she has any questions. She says no, not right now. "I feel so good," she says. "I don't think I can think of anything." "We'll separate outside, on the sidewalk." She says ok. "Meet me on monday on my break at 5:45pm to show me the bruises, please. Wear a skirt that I can pull up to see the marks I've left." I lean in, kiss her, gently and lightly and then we walk to the door. We hug a final time and then part. I walk away as she's locking up the gate.

When monday comes, I'm hot with anticipation, my head's swirling still days later with remembered ideas and my body still feels the experience in my muscles and sore jaw, raw throat. I'm on my break at work and I step away from the register. Bonarh is outside in front of the store and she breaks into a smile when she sees me approach. She points to her car parked at the curb. "No, let's walk."

Across from the store's front entrance is the intersection of the streets 13th and Isis and it's here we walk to, under the overpass crossing in the middle of all the rush hour traffic quite dangerously. On the other side, along Isis are some old warehouses but mostly new condos. Either way it's not well lit and not a street with even much foot traffic. It's here we stop in the shadows. I turn to face Bonarh and she stops and I push her against the garage of a building with bordered up front windows and a construction permit stapled to the plywood. The builders are long gone for the day. We find the right spot to stand to be out of the range of the automatic motion detector light switch and we are obscured further by the energy I put out around us: a delicate blend of public space being used for private events—isn't this what the share economy has exploited as well?

I lift the skirt Bonarh has worn to please me. Believe it or not, I'm surprised to see the harness on her, wide strap between her legs. I put my hand on her shoulders to lean into her deeper and feel there too the straps under my palms. I smile. "I like the way my harness feels on your body, Bonarh." And I grab the shoulder straps and harshly pull her mouth to mine. In the surprise of this pulling by the straps, the almost lifting her, Bonarh's mouth opens so she is ready when our mouths meet to receive my tongue deeply.

And then the display. "Please turn around, Bonarh" and I lift the skirt over her ass and pet her skin with my fingers across the bruises. Her ass is red still, and around the side of her hips is where the bruising has come up the most: purple lines on both sides. "These are

153

beautiful," I tell her. She says yes, almost proudly. "I've spent so much time looking at them over the past few days. I've wanted so much for you to see them." "Yes," I say, "they show your submission." And yes, the physical evidence of her submission is exciting all over again. Just brushing my fingers over the lines, the marks, the spots the color and slightly raised skin is turning me on and pulling me back into that place of surrender, the place both of us can take off from.

"Do you want to see the front?" and I say yes turn around. She does and I lift her shirt on the street here to above her breasts. The harness frames each tit and meets at her solar plexus in a large ring from which another strap on each side surrounds her middle under her breasts, on her rib cage. The magick of the intersection, and the potency of this crossing: 13th and Isis, is explicated further when time is removed, of leather as an amulet, specifically a conjuring amulet "the fetish to which a certain erotic drive attaches itself and through which a certain erotic desire commands its visible incar-nation" (Fritscher, Drummer) has always occurred in this location.

My head spins as I turn Bonarh slightly to catch the streetlight on her chest: incredible. She's covered with bruises from the whip-ping I gave her with belt and these marks, when I step back to really take them in and to trigger the electric light flooding our creation now have me back in the ritual again of surrender and being surrendered.

September 27, 2017:
Dear Bobby:

The people who live on the street behind my building have been fighting this morning. This isn't unusual. In fact, it seems like it's days like today—hot and sunny early in the morning—that seem to have everyone's tempers aflame. I think I recognize the voices, that I've heard these two specifically fighting before. It's a couple and I'm not sure if they live on the street in one of the tents or sleep in the hotel next door and have the sidewalk, like many of my neighbors, as an outdoor living room, with chairs and everything else except for privacy. I can never actually hear what the two people are yelling, but it's the tone that I recognize, the tone of a fight that comes from intimacy, the most painful kind of fight because it always seems to be the same fight and in fact the words that did reach my open window are both of them saying basically that: "you always say that" or "I told you this would be the last time." The frustration of all of it, the same fight with the same person saying the same thing being fought in public is perhaps what I relate to.

This morning though it gets violent and other people out in the back start yelling as well, taking sides, yelling 'stop it' or 'leave 'em alone!' The fight and yelling on all sides escalates for a while. The day, even at 9am, is hot already; there was a fire yesterday in the Oakland hills and residents had to be evacuated. I'm trying to ignore the yelling, all the yelling and then the car horn honking that seems to also be involved somehow. I turn the volume up on the music I'm listening to and try to drown out the sounds from outside, from the street below.

But it's too much and for too long. Between songs I still hear this couple fighting: "It's over! Get your shit away from mine!" "I already told you! I'm leaving! I'm leaving you!" I go over to the window and pull the screen away so I can stick my head out. I don't want to even, I don't want to witness someone else's private fight, and actually what can I do. I hear the car speeding before I see it and then it's on our small block. The cops race up and squeal brakes as they pull to a stop yelling for everyone to sit down. I start to cry immediately. In moments, it's quiet outside. I don't hear anything else.

The next date Bonarh and I have is a sunday evening. I'd worked that morning, my regular sunday morning cashier shift. After work I went home and meditated, then went to a meeting at 4pm. I took the bart to West Oakland then and Bonarh picked me up at 6pm. It had rained most of the day but stopped at that point. I sat on a bench in the passenger pick-up area while I waited for Bonarh. I had on levis, engineer boots, a denim shirt, denim vest, plaid overcoat and leather cap.

Bonarh pulled up at the curb and got out of the car and came to where I sat. I didn't see her until she was in front of me; I was taking inventory as she arrived. She sat immediately on my lap, on my thigh, straddling my thigh, facing me and I pulled her tight. I'd been planning what I'd say when I saw her but now I forgot what it was I was thinking, so I just smiled and kissed her shoulder.

In her car then, we drank the maté I brought in a large glass mason jar: medicinal strength. I asked her as I held the jar to her lips if I had to tell her to swallow when her mouth was full. No, she said, wiping her chin and brushing off the front of her shirt. Then do it, I said, lifting the jar back up to her to drink from.

We drove out along 7th Street to the end, past 880 to where 7th turns into Middle Harbor Road and begins to curve around, back toward the train rails and container ship ports. There's two parks here. Middle Harbor Shoreline Park closed at dusk and had a gate blocking the parking lot, already locked with a padlock. It was beginning to rain. We turned around and went back toward 7th where it continues off Middle Harbor and ends on a spit of land and a little park: Port View. This is a parking lot and a walkway paved along the water with the view of the busy Oakland port. We pull into this parking lot. A few other cars were there, the sun was setting at 6:30pm and with the rain again, the sky was darkening.

We sat then in the car, kind of settling. Bonarh had some questions including about if she wore nail polish, could she still fuck me. I didn't understand and she explained, "I mean, your cunt and the polish, it's not a natural brand. Also," she said, "after last week, everything pales in comparison," and she's not able to conjure the pain when she's masturbating. "Yes," I said, "the brain can't remember pain which is why pain is so useful to get to now."

September 29, 2017:
Dear Bobby:

"Yes, the brain can't remember pain which is why pain is so useful to get to now," I say, "and yes, these experiences are outside of the realm of normal: this is what was offered in the cave on the beach: sacred, transcendent, love."

I ask if she is ready and she says yes. I lean over and pull the lever to lower her seat back then take off my belt and put it tight around her neck. This signifies the beginning. We fool around like that. I'm on top, kind of riding her hips. "Here's that butch lap dance," I say and then, "Let's go," opening the car door and jumping out.

It's past dusk now, 7:15pm or later. There are a few other cars in the lot and it's cold and windy. We walk to the edge of the park which is in this part just a concrete esplanade, like a sidewalk with a fence and benches. At the fence I open my jeans and tell her to fuck me. She is already shivering so I take off my denim shirt and put it on her over her sweater and shirt. I'm now in just my net a-shirt. She's fucking me standing like that. The air is wet off the bay. The ports and the giant cranes are lit up brightly, glowing and twinkling. There are a few other cars and trucks passing by on 7th but not turning into the parking lot.

Looking for this small park area after finding the other park already closed with gate and a sign "Park closes at dusk," we drove past perhaps 75 or 100 semis in line to unload containers they trailed, windshields wet. It's not quite raining. And though there is all this traffic at the port it is eerily isolated and lonely. The people have been replaced by automation for the most part, previous generations of dockworkers and truckers standing at the piers while ships' hulls are unloaded are now a single truck driver in the cab of their trucks, watching small electronic devices and dock workers have been replaced by one person, operating the crane lifting containers directly onto the trailers. These were the venerable teamsters and longshoremen. Now, a drive through this area is like a sci-fi movie: lonely, raining, brightly lit with distorted light, fully automated and a people-less environment.

It's not quite raining but windy and wet and she's fucking me. I jack off while offering encouragement: "Yeah, harder, more, fuck me deeper." I come leaning back with my head thrown back yelling looking at the clouds pass in the night sky overhead. I come twice that way, the second time harder. Bonarh is at my feet, pants pulled down past her ass with her face pushed against my cunt and clit. I pull her up. It's drizzling now, or just more wind or whatever. I lift her shirts, look at the harness, turn her around to face the bay over the railing and grab her clit.

I tell the story again. "I got behind you. I reached into your pants. I felt this clit and I said, 'I want this. This is what I want.'" Jacking her off, fucking her, bending down, squatting behind her and pushing my face into her ass, feeling the strap of the harness with my tongue, wanting to unsnap it, wanting to release her. Fucking, pulling, grabbing. Her back is to me and I reach for the belt, unbuckle it and take it off and hit her ass with it. Repeatedly. More fucking. before reaching fingers through the cock ring to jack her off.

She's facing me now. It's raining, not heavily, and leaning against the rail, her pants pulled down, her shirts pulled up, I strike her belly with the belt, her strong thick mid-section. She cries out, "It hurts." then she's back in position. I strike her thighs. The same from her. With the wet cold air, the leather belt has more of a sting with each swing against her. With her shirt up, I spit on her.

We both face the lot, our backs to the bay, against the railing, under the streetlights in the rain and as I look at her, I'm smiling and she nods her head yes and I swing around and spit on her some more. Kissing throughout this. She's on her knees. At one point she's lying face down on the black-topped path. When she gets up her bare thighs are wet and stuck with gravel and dirt. I pull the belt through a few loops of my levis and stand over her, kneeling before me. She puts her mouth on me, is she fucking me too? I let out a stream of piss and the release is so great I throw my head back again and yell, scream my relief to the sky. In the streetlight, I can see the rain and though my skin is wet, I don't actually feel the rain hitting. I pull her face and head away, bend down and pull my levis and underwear further down as well, past my knees so as not to soak them with piss and push back into Bonarh's mouth and let go again.

While she leaned against the rail earlier she said she wasn't cold anymore. I took my shirt off of her and put it back on myself. I was shivering and when I fucked her and she came, the cuff of the sleeve of my shirt was soaked.

September 30, 2017:

Dear Bobby:

It's raining hard now, large drops that are distractingly felt. I'm shivering even with the shirt on. I pull Bonarh's pants up, button them, but can't work the zipper. "Whose hands can work like this?" We go back to the car. I start it. She's in the driver's seat. I pull a blanket from the back, cover her then tousle her head and hair with it, turn it so the then wet part is over her legs. I pull the heavy quilted moving blanket from the back and cover her with that as well. I turn the heat and the vents on high and get out of the car and drop my pants again to piss in the rain. It's a long full hard stream. Then back in the car, button fly, buckle belt and take off wet shirt, crawl under blankets with her. She's kind of holding me, snuggling me from behind.

When I arrived at West Oakland, I was on a bench, taking inventory. Of course, this is all my inventory, literally. What else do I have? My inventory isn't me, though. It's the story I believe, my story. I didn't see her pull up though I was automatically looking up from the page in my hand just about every time a car pulled into the lot or the passenger pick-up and drop-off section. She got out of the car and approached me. I was fearful, I had wanted to greet her with a smile and a 'hello lover' greeting. In fact, I'd imagined it repeatedly. She called to me as she approached and I barely had time to respond. She was at my side, on me before I could get up and then astride my thigh. This is how she mounted me in the circle of eucalyptus on the UC campus in august: I was kneeling and had taken off my shirt, was in a t-shirt and an a-shirt and kissed her and she excitedly came close and straddled my thigh. Even to write about it now excites me wildly.

From under cover we emerged. It's like a sauna in the car now. She's sitting variously on my lap and in the seat in the harness. I'm setting up shirts and sweaters to dry over the heater and blowing vents. "It's like a tenement," she says. It's really raining now. We're laughing, fucking, crying. The street lights reflected in the drops of water on the tree branches and leaves in the wind are like lights, twinkling, an xmess tree. She's crying. I'm holding her in my lap.

Suddenly it's 8:30. I barely even know what we were talking about but she did start something about how she honors my hard life and what got me here. She thinks she should take care of me, something like that, because of some idea of my hard life. I immediately corrected her and then said, "Actually I'm a corrector; no matter what you say, I'm going to defiantly correct you. But understand, I've had nothing but a blessed life. I didn't have a hard life. I had alcohol. I'm actually one of the most fortunate people in the world to firstly have had alcohol for a spiritual experience and then to have the steps: a more than sufficient substitute for the out of this worldness that alcohol once provided." Then, I push her off of my lap and into the seat and I get into the driver's side and try and blow the condensation off the windshield, rolling down the windows and take off speeding.

I'm speeding out of the parking lot, turning on the headlights, passing through the port, through red lights on rain slicked streets to get to the butcher on Broadway before 9pm. I don't tell her where we are going but just speed and jack her off as I drive one-handed and I'm so high I say to her, "What kind of crazy person lets a suicidal alcoholic drive their car like this?" I'm racing and smelling my hand and fingers and speeding and saying I want this clit and telling her to pull her pants down and turning on MLK to cross Oakland and slowing down for the cops coming the other way and leaning over to put my face, my mouth on her cunt and the light's changing to green and the tires are spinning on the wet street and skidding out at the next intersection, swerving to a stop half way through the intersection and then going through when the lights don't change and fucking her over and over and so happy, so high, so feel so fucking good like flying and she asks, "Cashier, can I come for your pleasure?" It's so so good, going so fast and wild I can cry now feeling it. I was crying then too, flying and crying and fucking her, unsnapping the strap, jacking her off, pulling on her clit and there's the butcher, on the left and I'm like Dean parking cars, I glide this one to the curb easily, smoothly, right in front across the street and hurriedly, it's 8:58pm, turn off the engine, grab my vest from the back seat, tell Bonarh "C'mon, we're here. If you want to come in, get dressed," and I race across the street, pulling on vest over netted undershirt, sniffing, inhaling my fingers and palm, panting, running: it doesn't matter. The butcher has been closed since 8pm anyway.

On the drive over, I'd said to her at a light, "I should have told you to stop talking. I never should have let you start talking. I should have slapped your face and said shut the fuck up."

October 3, 2017:
Dear Bobby:
On the drive over I'd said to her, "I should have told you to shut up. I never should have let you start talking. I should have slapped your face and said shut up." I'm racing to get to the butchers on Broadway before they close. I'm jacking her off, reaching into her pants as I drive one-handed, pulling on her clit, car swerving and skidding in the rain-slicked Oakland streets, I unsnapped the harness strap between her legs and I'm fucking her as I drive, turning to look at her and then at the street ahead, out the windshield peripherally. Leaning over into the passenger seat where she's seat belted in and I'm smiling and wolfishly leering and laughing and feeling good. I'm talking about fucking her while I fuck her and drive and talking about driving and fucking her as I speed through the red lights that aren't changing fast enough for me, crossing Oakland on MLK where there's less traffic and I can make the right on red on 40th and pass the bart station under the freeway and at the light on Telegraph, I can turn fully to her and explain to her again as I grab her clit, "I want this. This is what I want." I can't imagine I'm actually slapping her face, not from the angle of us sitting side by side with me driving: I'm a righty, though the way I'm feeling, so good so sexy so hot and lustful, I wouldn't put it past me to think I didn't slap her with my left hand, maybe just short taps in rapid succession, asking Bonarh over and over, "This is what you want, isn't it?"

She's made it across the street now inside the shop with me, standing at the counter looking at all the meat, wrapped in the darkened case. I'm wearing the denim vest and undershirt, hair is wild and so high and still I'm putting my hand to my face, my fingers to my nose, sniffing deeply inhaling while running from counter with wrapped meats and lights off over to the reach-in cooler with sausages. Bonarh is smiling, happy and laughing and I tell her she's off the hook, that the butcher closed at 8pm. Even if she wasn't talking at the piers we wouldn't've made it over here on time anyway. I buy lamb merguez sausages and we get back in the car.

Now, I'm on top of her. She's back laying on the reclined passenger seat. I am slapping her now, again and again. "You think you should take care of me? This is how you can take care of me, Bonarh. Submit to me when I take my belt off. Let me fuck you whenever I want. And fill me up like this. I'm riding her hips again. I'm saying yeah get in deep. Get deep inside me. I'm saying I don't want to feel like I haven't fucked you that much. She asks to come again for my pleasure. We are yelling and screaming through all this, growling. I get up, stand in the space in front of the passenger seat, head bent and torso crouched over her in the seat. I get up and pull my pants all the way down. I'm fucking Bonarh leaning over her in the seat.

It's confusing here if I'm fucking Bonarh or I'm asking Bonarh to fuck me. I want to sit on her with my pussy wet and open over her clit. I want her to push her clit inside me like that but the front seat and pants down isn't making that possible. I flip over and lay then on my back on her belly. I start directing her: touch me like this and like that and not like that. I'm actually distractedly thinking about the sausages and cooking them in her kitchen and also thinking about shoving a whole sausage into her mouth and would we have privacy to do that in her house, and if we went to her house, would I be able to leave. I'd been thinking about that all week: wanting to stay with her tonight but thinking I shouldn't, thinking I should maintain this as a scene and not let her down. My distractions break our field and soon I feel her distractions, too.

I start the car after she pissed on the street between the two open doors. I reached up and turned off the interior light as she pulled down her pants, more privacy. Then, when she's back in, doors closed, I take off from the curb, speeding again and drive to Piedmont Avenue for burgers but everything is closed. Up and down the block, pulling u-turns to check all the places again but nothing's open at all. I stop the car and we eat some blue cheese, walnuts and a piece of bread I have in my bag, then some chocolate. I'm putting my fingers down her throat, brushing her teeth with my fingers and she's gagging. I don't want any of this to end at all.

After eating, even just that little bit, I finally looked around and saw that I'd parked the car in a bus stop, way out into the street, like a drunk person. On Broadway, after the butcher I switched it and asked her, "What kind of suicidal person lets a crazy alcoholic drive their car like this?" Now, I'm laughing. I re-parked the car, backing it into a spot behind the bus stop against the curb.

She climbed in my lap, put her head on my lap and I pet her, still in the harness. I didn't want to end but I knew I should protect what we have. "Let's talk to fully transition" I said. I was fearful her interest was waning. "Please read me the letter you wrote." She perked up and got it from her bag. She also gave me the letter she wrote to me on her birthday. Then she read it to me while I laid back in the half-reclined driver's seat. I felt so good listening to her, her words and her voice pouring over me like golden light. "Again," I said. She read it three times, I think, while I asked her questions about each line: Who? What? Fears? Stone butch? I alternately had my eyes closed and open and lay writhing in the seat, listening and really basking in the attention she was giving me.

And then finally, I start the car again. It's late and I drive to the bart station and there we kiss goodbye and I hop out, run across the street and run across the plaza at MacArthur, swipe through the turnstile and then up the stairs to the platform, train coming and hop on, grab a seat and then ride through the tunnel back to San Francisco and Civic Center and up the long steep escalator, walking with the mechanized stairs help, to the seemingly empty United Nations Plaza until eyes focus and see neighbors sleeping on cardboard boxes flattened under blankets in the doorway of the café and around the corner at the edge of the theater, an encampment of people and dogs and bicycles with cigarettes and cell phones. I'm grateful to have a bed with Canela asleep to get into and close my eyes and sleep, however fitfully.

The next day Bonarh calls and asks if I have time to talk. I'm writing but put it aside. Why not take the call rather than write, live. We talk for two hours then, going over the night before together. "Did you have a good time last night?" I ask. "Oh, yes. Yes," she says. "Yes, everything was good." "Yes," I said, "we had a good time. We had a good time together."

We talked again about surrender and submission and the harness and Bonarh's wearing it and what happened on Broadway and the brain and unmanageability and we jacked off together and then she talked about going to the woods. I pulled out my calendar and got fearful and then we spent an hour scheduling through december 31. At a certain point she told me she's going for ten weeks to Indonesia. I expressed myself: "Wait? Normies put something on the calendar and wait. Alkies drink." I laughed and so did she. It was actually sweet. I shared a lot of experience: surrender at the gates of insanity and death ("you had fear you were gonna die in the car, last week, at the studio, the time at that house wherever that was"), and how fortunate I am as an alcoholic to be at that place, insanity and death's gate, continually. It requires surrender.

"This will end before you go to Indonesia," I say, "We'll get together that last time in december and you'll take off the harness and I'll take it back. I won't hold you while you're gone, for one, and you'll be able to focus on whatever it is you're doing there while you're there. You won't have the distraction of the harness and the constant submission. For two, what's the weather like there? I can't imagine it could be very comfortable in rainy humidity wearing a leather harness no matter what you're thinking." We end the call with plans to see each other soon.

October 6, 2017:
Dear Bobby:

During this fall Canela's and my friend, Leah, begins staying with us in the apartment here. It's great to have her around. She's also a sober alcoholic doing the steps. I'm grateful for her powerful reflection. In the mornings, we all wake up, I open the curtains and we all begin to take our inventories then meditate together. I pop up out of meditation and make us all coffee and we all chat and talk about our hopes for the day ahead. After, we take turns in the bathroom, get dressed and all go off, perhaps we'll have dinner later. It feels sweet and good and powered up and like a family but let's be honest: the apartment Canela and I have is less than 400 square feet! It's two rooms with a bathroom and a large closet and our friend Leah keeps her large suitcases in the hallway behind the bathroom door. Our two bikes are in the hallway too. And though the kitchen is large enough to eat in at a good-sized table, the three of us in there at one time is quite crowded and mostly, two people, two of us have to be sitting at the table while one person is standing, at the stove cooking or at the sink cleaning up. Canela and I have worked it out over the years so that I can be at the stove while she's at the sink but that leaves out Leah, who wants to help out, or do something, contribute in some way. "Please, just sit down," I say but I also don't want her to do the dishes after dinner. I like the plates washed on both sides and soap used with a sponge and not that she wouldn't or couldn't do that, it's just that I notice not everyone does. And I mean, like I say, I'm glad she's with us, and glad to be able to provide a place for her, but for real, we are all three sleeping in the same room. She's on our couch which is at the foot of our bed, but like literally just a foot or so from the foot of our bed, next to the 8-foot tall cat tree.

Oh, did I mention the two cats who also live here with us? Not that they take up that much space, but their accoutrements sure do. The cat tree with a two-foot by three-foot large base and four shelves stretching to the ceiling and then their litter box in the bathroom next to the bathtub and glasses of water, which while I'm mentioning it, I might as well say that they knock over or at the very least, splash their drinking water all over the carpet or window sill which they've also claimed for themselves, sitting on the wide space overlooking the trees and tents on Brady Street, Mount Diablo in the distance. Not that we could sit on this little area but just the idea that every single space in here is being used, actively, even more than ever the little nightstand next to my side of the bed is towering with stacks of books and papers and notebooks and the same is true for the even smaller table next to Canela's side; now, Leah doesn't really read books but she is on her device constantly and I have fear that the light from this device, especially at night, is disturbing my brain or melatonin or just actually waking me up while I'm sleeping.

Even in the 90's when all my dyke friends lived together or lived in shared housing with lesbian roommates it was never like this: so tight and crowded and even if some german dykes came and crashed for like a week or two, they'd sleep on a couch in the living room and the rest of us each had our own room. It'd be an inconvenience having a houseguest but not like this, not like animals crowded in a cage. And Leah wasn't actually a lesbian, I mean, who is these days anymore? Everyone likes to say queer or even dyke, almost no one I know says lesbian. But she was hooking up with and instant messaging with women on Tinder plus all the guys she was going with. She identified as kinky herself, would accept Canela and I calling her queer, which actually felt good to say that and be included with her like that. Our home group of alcoholics anonymous was mostly straight and white and believe me I had to continue to take my own personal inventory about not fitting in, about the group being closed minded and racist. Leah herself was hapa, but no one else even saw her that way, they just assumed whiteness. I understand this is the way of the world, I mean I, at least yearly, had to explain in my share that, "No, butch doesn't mean I want to be a man; I am a lesbian woman." And I'll tell you how much of my own personal inventory I have to surrender to even be able to say that; to even be able to go back to the meeting and not say, "Fuck everybody! Fucking misogynist racist bullshit! fuck them!" and instead just go drink. To be brought humbly to my own ego-deflation and the reminder of the fact that my life actually depends on this group conscience. I'd look around the room during the meeting and see these people are staying sober with the steps. Now, I'm getting my own experience of lesbian polyamory and staying sober no matter what.

October 7, 2017:
Dear Bobby:
    The three of us are crowded into the apartment and it's tight and there's not a lot of privacy for any of us. I've already been continuing to take my own personal inventory about needing more space to write and read and work on projects. But the good part of it is that there is more reflection of conscious contact with this power and that's what I crave.
    Also, the days no one has to go to work early, we grab our suits and after coffee we all hop in the van and drive out to Baker Beach.

Rush-hour traffic is all going the opposite direction. We are among the most fortunate women alive, in the steps and going out to swim at the beach during the week. Leah is a strong swimmer; she knows how to surf. I'm ok, comfortable in the open water, having grown up on Long Island and spending a lot of time at the beach as a kid. I'm not the strongest swimmer though, and to be honest the waves and current at Baker are often too rough for me. I can get in, partially, dive through a set of waves, but I cannot always get out past the break, especially if I've been tossed a couple times.

For all of my suicidal ideation it's actually amazing to experience the self or body or something fighting to live when under the water. The instinct kicks in I guess, or more likely, what is true is that what my brain tells me is false. A lifetime of hearing the rumination of "I've got to die, I wish I was dead, I've got to kill myself," is just what my brain is encoded with. When I'm caught in a wave, thrown to the bottom of it, dragged out with the current and back flow, I feel myself pushing up and getting just my head above water, enough to breathe a breath before being pulled under again; I'm not allowing myself to simply slip under and drown. Not if I can help it; though I tell Canela and Leah if I die out here swimming, know that I died happy and doing something I enjoyed.

Canela grew up in the desert. She was on the swim team but in a pool and so she gets in, gets wet, dives through and then spends the rest of our trip running back and forth on the sand, running all the way to the end where the beach curves and ends at Sea Cliff with China Beach on the other side. I love watching her run along the shore like this; happy, fast, strong. Sometimes a dog will join her, happily running alongside as she calls it and laughs, playing.

Tuesday morning Leah's phone light wakes me. I'm trying to fall back asleep but I'm already too resentful and hateful. So, I get up and do the steps, fear it's a terrible meditation. I fucked up the coffee yesterday, pouring boiling water over the grounds for the cold brew today and then I didn't want to waste a whole pot so today I just reheated it. It tasted like old, reheated coffee. I took my cup back to bed and continued to take my personal inventory and all the usual suspects appear: Canela, Leah, Bonarh, Michelle. Plus, all of my 'want to die' inventory. Leah is making us second cups of coffee fresh; brown for her, dark roast for me. We meet in the kitchen and I cry a little at the sink: "Ten years sober? Wtf? This 'want to die' life?" Leah says, "We have to go to a meeting." "No," I say, "We have to go swimming." Canela's in Oakland at her lover's so the two of us grab our suits and go out there. I'd never be able to do this alone, no matter how much I wanted to so I'm grateful Leah is here.

The rain and cloud cover this morning make it feel warm, make the air feel warm and the water too but once we are actually standing in our bathing suits at the water's edge, looking at the ocean, grey and rough being met by the grey sky, I say to Leah, "Maybe going to a meeting, sharing and crying 'I'm nearly ten years sober' and the humiliation and necessary ego-deflation would have been easier than this."

The waves are breaking steep and high and far out. I'm tossed and tumbled and thrown back to shore, panting, breathing hard and I try again. Leah is out there, swimming. I wait and wait and try and try and finally get out there only to swim just a bit and have to let the waves push me back in again, body exhausted, dangerously so, it feels like from trying to fight the waves, tossed and tumbled again. We jog to the van, pull off our suits, towel off the sticky sand from under our breasts and on our bellies. The air is still warm and it feels good to be a woman, naked outside, in the city with another woman.

We dress and begin to drive back across the city, high with endorphins and negative ions, salt water absorption and flotation. It is possible to forget oneself out in the ocean and to feel good enough afterwards as to continue the feelings of nothing-ness. We plug in Leah's device, so hated this morning, into the van stereo and play our playlist and feel happy.

October 9, 2017:
Dear Bobby:
On the way back from out at Baker, there's a text from Bonarh. I'm driving so Leah sanely says, "Pull over. I'll drive and you can text." I swing to the curb and we switch. Bonarh says she's in the city and I say I'm at the beach. It's a back and forth a bit. It's impossible,

she says, though she wants me and wants me to slap her face. Of course, I'm reading the texts to Leah as they come in. We are laughing and excited and still in the post glow of the salt and the swim. "Impossible?" Leah says, "Tell her to 'make it possible!'" I text that then and a location: the parking lot behind the mattress store next to my apartment. Bonarh texts one word back: 'ok.'

Leah and I are back at the apartment now, parking the van in our lot behind our building and she goes upstairs to shower. I'm shivering now that I'm out of the van and away from the hot air blown from the vents. My hair is wet too. I zip my jacket and run down Stevenson Street and cross Gough to where I see Bonarh's car parked. I jump in the passenger's seat, reach over and turn the ignition key to start her engine and then turn on the heat and blower in her car. I immediately climb on her. Under her shirt her skin is warm. She's wearing the harness and a brown belt with her red corduroys. Between her thighs the ribbing has rubbed flat and smooth, and the fabric seems like it's about to give completely, leaving what I hope will be a hole for my hand to slip through, I say.

I pull up her shirt and I'm looking at the harness and her breasts. We're both now in the driver's seat. The back is slightly reclined and I tell her to put her hands above her head. I'm kissing her sweetly, kind of, what else? I start the face slapping. Sitting on her lay, facing her, my left hand is on the seat back, propping me up, over her face. I ask her, "You over this situation, Bonarh?" and my right hand is slapping her. With my right hand, I slap her, open-handed, across her face. "Are you bored with this situation?" Is she mumbling or fearful or what? I ask her again about taking care of me. "You think I need taking care of?" I ask, leaning in closer to her face, my breath on her as I hit her with the fast short slaps I like.

"Yeah, I see where I didn't understand," she says. "Where?" I ask. "Well, I see you need to go crazy." "What?" I'm slapping her harder now and sitting on her hips, pinning her with my weight. "You think I'm crazy?" "No, no, I don't." "Well?" "I see that you need to..." "What?" "Ah, I don't know...that you need to go on a ride."

This ride is a quick one. We are in the car behind McCroskey's for about half an hour. I'm on top riding her hips and telling her to push it in deep, "Yeah, this is how I told you to take care of me, Bonarh. Let me fuck you when I want and push it in deep like this." I feel how wet and open I am. She hasn't brushed her teeth this morning and I tell her I like it. "It's very good, Bonarh, not brushing your teeth before you meet your lover in the morning." I push my hand down the front of her corduroys to feel the smooth leather strap through her legs widening her cunt with its thick edges. I grab her clit in my fist and start to pull on it, thick hard knob in her soft, sweet skin. "What do I say when I touch your clit, Bonarh?" She shakes her head, "I don't know." "How many times do I have to repeat myself?" I ask, "Do you have a disability I should know about?" This morning there is a lot of face slapping. She says she doesn't have a good memory. "Ok, we're in the cave..."

"I'll start again: you're on your knees, facing away from me. I'm behind you. I take off my shirt, unbuttoning it and take it off, then take off my undershirts too. I toss them all to the pile of blankets on the sand. When I lean forward my bare breasts are against your back." As I recite this again I'm rubbing and pulling on her clit in the car, my mouth is close to her face. "My bare skin is on your back and I reach around and push my hand down your pants and I feel your swollen clit and what do I say?" I'm pulling and rubbing, looking into her eyes, asking her again, "What do I say?" She's breathing hard, shaking her head, panting. "I want this, this is what I want."

Yes, she says, and asks to come and does, twice while I hold her there, arm across her shoulders, pushing her down, holding her down, then fucking her and she asks again. "I have to go to work," I say, still fucking her. "I have to go get ready for work." She sticks her bottom jaw out like a mad dog underbite and this completely shifts everything. I like this though I'm momentarily confused. "Stick out your jaw like that again," and I fuck her some more. "C'mon, hold it out like that," and she comes again, hard. I like this.

October 10, 2017:
Dear Bobby:
    I like this. I get out of Bonarh's car soon after this and I come up stairs to the apartment. Leah is out of the shower, getting dressed

and then we are making coffee in the kitchen. I'm telling her some highlights of the car and then I pull out the letter I wrote to you on september 29-october 1, 2016. I start to read it to Leah and we drink the coffee. After two paragraphs, we look at each other and say wow. Leah's in her jeans and no shirt, no shoes. I'm in my underwear. I'm laughing and crying and laughing as I read and at the end, so much power has shown up we are flying. "Thank you for the 12th step," she said, "I'm so speechless. It's the most beautiful thing I've ever heard." "It's this power, huh?" I start to talk maniacally and I'm saying all the normies who I've read it to are so kind, I'm grateful. But to get a chance to read it to my fellow, It's amazing. "I was so sad and lonely, took so much inventory then wrote it. It's amazing, right? Obviously, god doing." She cried a little and then when I got in the shower, I heard her sobbing on the couch for a long time. It's a sweet release that blesses both of us.

It's also good to have Leah in our apartment because it means Canela and I can take trips and Leah will stay with the cats. We go to Detroit to meet my brother. Canela and I arrive the night before he gets there and we stay in an air bnb. It's comfortable enough; we pick the room with the bigger bed and two night tables for reading. In the morning, we have coffee in bed then hurried and jumped up to rush Canela to an al-anon meeting north of the city in Bloomfield Hills.

I brought coffee, books to sit in the car with though mostly I am on the device switching back and forth: texts, pics, letters, voice mails all sent from Bonarh. Right now, this is what is holding my imagination, though the excitement doesn't necessarily center in my physical body as a turn-on. It's in my brain more, interest being fired in ideas of possession, dominance, ownership, and Bonarh calling to ask me for permission to come for my pleasure.

Drinking coffee now in the church parking lot, this is the time I've been waiting for; a few minutes alone. No Canela, no racing to get ready for a date, for work, for a meeting, no cats to feed or clean up after, no Leah no Michelle no one else. Finally, being here my brain feels fried from the stress of the week and my arms and hands, too exhausted to even push the pen across the paper. This week and last, I won't even go back over the past year, has been so intense facing the inventory of fear I have to take care of her—who is slipping as a target, it's whoever she who is in front of me at any moment. All of that childhood wreckage, I'm ashamed there is still so much, all of the mother's insane, murderous suicidal overreactions and the resulting nervous system effect on me, the trauma patterning that occurs from that type of stress exposure: 'fear my mother will kill herself, as she is threatening to do.' Growing up, going to school, just wanting to get home and go to sleep, never having an interest in anything and certainly no way to pursue anything. Child too depressed to want to do anything; mother too depressed to encourage any activity. I mean, it's all alcoholism, generations of alcoholism—debilitating, immobility complete lack of power to pursue anything but a drink.

I'd love to have the space to push through all this, to get so frustrated with myself, I put this down and pick up a book to read and then find myself slowing, and slowly touching myself, maybe nipple clips, slow, if I can and not try and get it over with, starting to jack off and allowing myself to arouse myself. Pulling, slowly getting to orgasm and enjoying it and then picking up the book again and writing about it, typing a letter then as well. I want the time alone, for myself, to follow my desires, my body, to come for my pleasure.

We meet my brother at the airport that afternoon, picking him up and going to eat dinner. He wants to move to Detroit, wants us to consider moving there with him, living in a big house with him. Detroit is hard though; cats, dogs, people, buildings abandoned and depressed. I meditated three times. Then when my brother and Canela left to get us breakfast for the morning, I read. I wrote and jacked off looking at the ceiling tiles in the room and the sprinkler on the wall, thinking of something I don't remember.

October 11, 2017:
Dear Bobby:
The next date Bonarh and I have is at 6am. I'm ashamed to admit this since this is basically what Canela asked me not to do: set the alarm early, like about4am so I can make and drink coffee, continue to take my own personal inventory and then meditate before driving over the bridge. It's too early, she says, and then she's up and

disturbed. And to be honest, Canela is over this situation I have with Bonarh. She wants it to end, as soon as possible. I tell her the dates I have planned with Bonarh, the ones she and I have set, and that this whole thing will end in december, before Bonarh leaves for Indonesia.

During this week, Bonarh has called and left a message at 2:30am. She wakes in the harness, which she's by now, pretty much wearing all the time. She's hot hard wanting to come. Her voice is muffled sleepy breathless, sounding like she is literally undercover. I can't even understand exactly what she's saying, but from the tone of her voice I know she's asking to come for my pleasure. I write back a text: "Yes, Bonarh I want you to come for my pleasure, thinking of how good my belt feels around your neck on the looser, second setting I've used, with my fist holding it tight against your throat, and when you write to me about this, for me, I want you to refer specifically to how it feels when I'm unbuckling the belt, pulling it through the loops of my levis and begin to place it around your neck."

Also, during this week, I'm often finding myself lost in the reverie of the night at the West Oakland piers. Before sleep, as I close my eyes, or while sitting in the sun on a break from the register, I allow myself to sink into the memory, into the physical experience of that night: in the rain, Bonarh fucking me from below, my back against the metal fence, lifting my shirt outside, yelling and screaming in the rain, the trucks lined up at the port, her lips on me while I piss in her mouth and on her hair. The belt. The belt. The belt.

My idea that this whole thing has to end when she leaves december 31 has been discussed between Bonarh and I. For one, I have fear I can't wait two months for her. The kind of longing, pining desire, yearning feels like a sickness to me. Too hard and walking the line of a dangerous type of fantasy existence I can't or don't want to tolerate. I'm trying to disguise, or deny this fear with the idea that I know what's best for her: "Well, you are going to Indonesia to have a new experience, a beginning, and when you come back this will be completely different" or something like that. I try explaining this to her, but I have fear I already talk too much, or try to explain too much; fear I need to be more principled.

So, the morning of the date, I set the alarm for 4:30am. I hate myself even as I'm doing it but at this point, it's obvious I've been driven by my obsession; I'm not choosing or doing any of this. I can't and wouldn't. It's too complex, to high-level, requiring a mental engagement and acuity that I honestly don't have. Yeah, maybe I can pull this kind of negotiation off once or twice, thrice, but then I fuck it up or say simply, fuck it. Communication, direct, honest communication isn't my strong suit. I often say the wrong thing, occasionally say something offensive and women tire of me quickly. Whatever is happening in this situation, with both Bonarh, and Canela for that matter, is happening because of this power. It sounds grandiose, but I have to believe that or I'll kill myself with the guilt and remorse.

I try to slip out of the bed with Canela, not turning on the light but going to the kitchen to make coffee, do the steps. I've packed a bag yesterday and put out my clothes for today. But Canela comes to the kitchen, mad. "Make your coffee and go do the steps in the van," she says. Ok, I say, full of a contrite heart. And wondering though where will I take a shit after I drink coffee in the van.

So, I get dressed, pour coffee in a lidded jar, grab packed bag and a plastic container and take everything down to the van in our parking lot. I'm already jacked up, even without the coffee. The excitement about today's date had me feeling like I barely slept. I take as many lines of inventory as I can, squat over the container, shit and put the lid on, gulp the last of the coffee and sit on the back bench in the van and close my eyes. We don't judge our meditation, we take it easy and take it as it comes. But still I'm thinking what seems like the whole time, "Is this even working?" Finally, out of the meditation, I hop into the front driver's seat, first making sure the plastic container of shit is secure and won't tumble while I drive, start the van and turn on the radio and begin to drive to Oakland.

October 16, 2017:
Dear Bobby:
I start the van, turn on the radio and pull out of the parking lot. It's still dark; the sun at this time of year doesn't come up til 7:30am. I'm smiling, glad to be on my way, glad for the relief of this day simply

174

having arrived, so much anticipation and resulting anxiety that's been building as I waited, planned looked at the calendar. It's today finally.

Out of the lot onto Brady Street down to Mission and news radio in between songs says a tractor trailer has rolled over on its side on the bridge. I wonder how it will affect me. But through the spiral curve of the entrance ramp, there is more traffic than I expected at this hour: 5:15am. Cars slowing as I reach the 101s and 80e split and going slowly on that expanse that crosses the city. I'm wondering will I be late, should I send Bonarh a message saying there's a jam up? Up ahead, lights flashing then darkness.

At Fourth Street, the last exit in San Francisco before the bridge, all traffic is being diverted off the freeway. Cop cars with lights blazing and flashing block the freeway and all cars must leave the freeway. Now what, I think. I'm wondering what to do. The exit puts all cars and many trucks onto Bryant Street and I just follow along in the stream of traffic, wondering what to do. Up ahead though is, I remember, the entrance to the bridge that comes from the right side just at the base of the bridge off Bryant between 2nd and Rincon.

Once, trying to cross the bridge on a friday afternoon rush hour on a date trying to get to the PFA Theater in time for a movie I drove all the way down Bryant, trying to avoid traffic on the freeway, thinking I could somehow sneak in and out-smart the daily commuters and tried to enter from this entrance and found myself crawling along even slower than from any other place I could have been as there is like 3 or 4 merges in this short ramp and I was stuck and yelling in the van, "Fuck this!" repeatedly, scaring my date.

The traffic diverted from the bridge is some cars but also a lot of big trucks, tractor-trailers trying to get to the Oakland port before rush hour, loading and unloading containers and getting on their way. At the streetlights on Bryant though, these trucks are cumbersome and starting from a dead stop requires many gear changing maneuvers. I take advantage and pull out but on the right side, sneaking along to pass the trucks and then the left side, crossing the double yellow line and pulling ahead and hurrying. I squeeze in front of a big truck as it begins the steep climb of the entrance ramp at Rincon. There's traffic here too, the rest of us who remembered this entrance.

I'm on the ramp now when there is a siren behind me, horn honking lights flashing and in my rear-view mirror, I see cars trying to pull over to the side of the tight ramp made more tight with the merge here. Sirens, lights, horns and the radio, turned up volume on the scratchy ripped speakers provide mostly a back beat, songs can't even really be deciphered and with everything that's happening, I'm not really listening anyway.

Often in major cities, when an emergency vehicle is racing, with lights and sirens, everyone, as required by law, pulls to the side of the road to let it pass. There is the driver who will use this opportunity to quickly pull in behind the emergency vehicle very close behind and then speed along with the vehicle in front as if being pulled along in the drag.

I'm up on the ramp at the tight spot of the curve. The firetruck is very close behind me. In front of me is a taxi cab. Instead of pulling to the side and letting the truck pass, I lean on my horn and get right up on the taxi. I'm yelling, "C'mon! C'mon! Let's go!" I'm so close behind the cab, I'm almost pushing it as we round the final curve to the bridge and good thing because in the rear-view mirror all the other cars have yielded to the firetruck and now it's right behind me. I still don't pull over and instead let this truck with all its might and force and sirens and lights push me up the ramp and onto the bridge. The truck is pushing me and I'm pushing the cab.

I'm up on the bridge now and the overturned truck is to my left, laying on its side. There are a few cops there and surprisingly there are flares lit. On the radio news I heard that the truck is leaking fuel! The firetruck has turned left behind me though and is just arriving at the accident site. In my rearview mirror though there is nothing else: no other cars come onto the bridge after the firetruck; the entrance is closed now, it must be, and me and the taxi are the last vehicles onto the bridge. In front of us, there's almost nothing either: without the headlights from other vehicles the crossing of the bridge from SF to Oakland is unlit so the roadway is dark. I stay close behind the cab, pushed and pulled as if driven across the bridge to Oakland.

October 18, 2017:

Dear Bobby:

I'm the last car over the bridge before they close it. I've been pushed onto the bridge surface by the emergency vehicle behind me, lights flashing and siren sounding, horn honking as if to tell me 'get the fuck out of the way'. Instead, I let myself be driven up and over and onto the bridge and when I look in the rearview mirror there's nothing behind me. The firetruck has turned back to the overturned truck on its side leaking fuel surrounded by flares and the increasing fading flashing lights. Ahead of me, me still on the cab's tail, the cab's headlights light the dark bridge and me following so close behind with my dimmer headlights and the rest is darkness. Only the Treasure Island tunnel is lit and then to the new side, still no one else behind me.

I take 580 to 24 to 51st Street so I can stop at the Walgreens on Telegraph open 24 hours to buy a toothbrush (rushing out of the house this morning with coffee and packed bag, I forgot to grab the toothbrush). I arrive at Bonarh's at 6:15am and call her to come down. We jump in her car and go to Cole Coffee. It's still dark in Oakland and the few customers at Cole on College seem to be regulars, reading the newspapers. I go to the side door on 63rd—I've never understood the difference between the two sides of the same place—and get a coffee to go. Getting back in Bonarh's car, I've placed the hot coffee on the floor between my feet and as she pulls away from the curb I promptly spill the entire contents on the floor, soaking the carpet. Wait, I yell, but it's too late. Bonarh backs up and I run in again and the woman there seems to understand and refills the cup for free. I'll try again.

We drive to the Albany Bulb. I haven't been in a while, two or three years I think, at least since the last time the community rallied to clean up the bulb and that meant clearing out all the people who were living there in tents and semi-permanent structures they'd constructed of plywood and tarps and other items. It was hard to see how these homes were built because they were so well camouflaged in the overgrown bushes and behind some of the abandoned concrete structures, plus the entire bulb was so wild. I mean, there was a path that cut across the spit of land near the racetrack but it was just that and most of the land was accessed by tiny 'dog paths', single file trails that mostly went under bushes, they had to be basically crawled on, or stooped over walking to pass through them.

But of course, it was worth it: all of the urban art and installations that were out there—graffiti, sculptures, land art. Every curve on the trails brought a new view of the bay and hills and the Berkeley clock tower and the surprises of a huge person-like formation of driftwood and trash. Or something that looked like a ship; from certain vantage points on various hills, this looked as if it were floating on the bay, a pirate sloop headed out toward the gate.

It was always quite scary going to the bulb in that way that wild feral-ness in an urban setting means magick, underground, secret and secreted and clandestine and exciting: the feeling of being in a space where anything can happen. Do you remember when the mighty Buena Vista Park was like this?

At the parking lot, Bonarh and I stand near her car and add layers to what we're wearing. I pull on a pair of rubber pants with suspenders, a t-shirt and my lug sole Redwing boots. Bonarh has on leopard print faux fur leggings and a t-shirt. We hike back through the mostly cleaned out bulb. It looks almost manicured: bushes are trimmed, trees are pruned, the paths are widened and maintained with wood chips! Well, this isn't exactly what I had in mind but let's try and see what we can conjure in this sterile environment.

We walked to the far end, to the concrete slabs that are just about the only remaining reminder that this was once just a landfill. Of course, the cleanup has been presented as a way to ensure safe access for all users of the park. But what about those of us who crave it dangerous, I wonder. At the slabs we are facing Richmond, it's drizzling slightly this morning, wetting us, our hair and the ground. The trail is muddy and puddled. On the concrete, like playing cards that have fallen from a hand, we stand. I strip Bonarh.

I take down her pants, lift off her shirt over her head, have her step out of the pants she's wearing; just the harness now. I'm hitting her ass with my hands. I tell her about Chuck Renslow and Dom Orejudos ('Etienne') and Chicago and IML and the harness she's wearing, and then I'm fucking her. She's crying quickly this morning. She says she's fearful she'll get wet if it rains. "You will," I say, "You will get wet if it rains."

October 19, 2017:
Dear Bobby:
     In the morning, driving in Bonarh's car after I've gotten coffee (which is too hot to drink, especially while in a car) I'm asking her about wearing the harness. Last time I saw her she said she'd told a friend who'd seen a strap under her t-shirt and asked her about it: "What's that?" That it was my harness and that she was basically wearing it all the time. In the car then I ask her, "So, tell me about your experience in my harness."
     She begins describing the feeling of the leather on her skin, the weight of it all and then quite quickly she's fucked up, confused and unsure of what I want to know. "Your experience," I say again. And when she begins again she's speaking metaphorically and as if the harness were a symbol. Soon, because of the early hour, we are out at the parking lot of the bulb, changing clothes and shoes for the damp drizzly day, adding extra layers and socks and boots. I've paused my line of questioning momentarily during this, letting her get settled.
     Then we are on the trail, hiking back to the deeper side of the bulb, easily avoiding puddles on the well-kept trails. I barely recognize the place now in its park-like atmosphere. I begin to question Bonarh again: "What is your experience in my harness?" She's getting angry now, and begins to answer by saying, "Well, like I said…" I stop on the track and face her. We've been walking side by side and now I turn to face her. She stops then and turns to face me and I slap her face. I hold the back of her head in my left hand and hit her with my right. She pouts and tears up. "I'm calling you to me," I say, "This isn't a metaphor." I say, "It is an actual harness. You are wearing it in submission to me." "Yes," she says, "I understand."
     Out on the concrete slabs overlooking the bay and the gate and its bridge in the distance, I get my own bearings in a triangulation of points: here, Baker Beach on the other side and with its view of that bridge, and then that bridge. Yes, here I am. Sky is grey and raining,

the grasses have been cut, the bushes trimmed and the trees pruned and my lover is standing on the edge of a spit of land with me. She's naked but for the leather harness she's wearing that covers her belly, shoulders, splits her cunt with a wide strap and a cock ring which presses on her clit. Richmond is in the distance, Alcatraz, Angel Island.

I tell Bonarh about Chuck Renslow, his businesses in Chicago starting in the 50's when he began taking photos of male models and was making physique pictorials and sending them via US mail, which was what this first business was shut down for: 'transporting or sending pornography through the mail'. He and his lover, Dom Orejudos, lost everything, including the building they operated the studio from. But just as quickly, Renslow, a masculine homosexual, started a gym, Triumph Gymnasium, and all the guys went there in Chicago to work out. This was in the 50's and wasn't like gyms today with steroids and classes. It was serious boxers and weight lifters and guys into men's bodies. Something happened with this place, mainly because of the gayness and that place too was lost. Renslow then started a bar, a motorcycle bar where men who were vets of WWII and into the masculine culture and into biker gangs could hang out.

This was before there was such a thing as leather culture and in fact, this is arguably the beginning of that culture. Or the cultivation of that aesthetic and interest. The bar got shut down by CPD (Chicago police) and Renslow just went on to something else—another bar, another location, another space but always catering to his own interests, and as time goes by, he is more able to express what his interests are: leather, levis, boots, motorcycles and s/m. His bar, The Gold Coast, became a leather bar and then the home of the first International Mr. Leather which then became Chuck's major interest, at least financially. Of course, IML is still going, 40 years later. Renslow basically invented what we think of as modern gay culture, certainly in Chicago, albeit while it was happening in other cities, granted, but Renslow, with the IML event, really blasted leather culture around the world.

Living in Chicago during this event was better than living in SF during the annual Gay Pride because of the knowledge of what

Renslow built this culture from. Plus, the fact that even in 1995, going to a lesbian bar in Calumet City just south of the city of Chicago, though right on the Indiana state line, required parking behind the bar and entering from the back door which was locked and required a knock and then a once over from the small door in the door which the bouncer opened and assessed us: were we dykes is I guess what she was checking. Then she unlocked the big door and let us in and locked the door behind us.

October 21, 2017:
Dear Bobby:

My harness then has a distinguished provenance: the leather culture from which the IML was found. I worked in a thrift store in Chicago, the kind that was started during the AIDS crisis as a way to fund health care and what to do with all the dead fags' stuff.

The store by the time I got there was just amazing. Like an xmess every day. What did you want? Books? Records? Toys? Vintage kitchen items? Items related to Hollywood musicals? Broadway musicals? Sport paraphernalia? Sporting goods? Jock straps? Clothes? Shoes? Bicycles? I even got a car from the thrift store. Of course, as workers, we had first look at all the donations and the first chance to buy anything. There was so much stuff being donated that we got 50% off and could basically buy as much as we wanted. We still filled up the three dumpsters four times a week, there just was so much stuff donated versus sales-floor space. This of course is a whole other story in itself, this era of the thrift store in Chicago and the individual items I got while working there so I won't go into that too much. Let me describe however a certain type of donation which was not uncommon.

This is that of the sex toy/leather category. Occasionally, a duffle bag or canvas sports style bag with zipper and canvas straps or gym bag or footlocker would be dropped off. The front door of the store opened up to a table where people could drop off their donations and then take a tax form for themselves. (Everyone always wrote that their stuff was worth more than it was; in fact, the more garbage they dropped off, the higher they claimed for taxes). These big bags or footlockers would usually be heavy and pulling and lifting them to the sorting area, opening them we would be surprised: often thousands of dollars of gear would be in the bag or box. Harnesses, ropes, cuffs, dildoes, leather shirts, pants, hats and the bar vests. So sexy! Sometimes it'd be a mess, just like a big tangle of all of it. Sometimes it seemed like a long time since this stuff had been used. Sometimes we could tell because the stuff would have tangled and occasionally melted. In one case, the bottle of lube's top had come off and everything was sticky with it and some of the latex items had disintegrated and everything mostly in that had to be thrown away.

Some of the workers there hated to see this kind of donation. Even if they were gay, they were prudish or this just wasn't their thing. It was mine though. I'd dive in and pull out each and every item that was in the bag and hold it up, trying on vests and hats and harnesses over clothes and lining the dicks up on the table. We usually put certain items aside for the appropriate times of year to make a big sale area corresponding: all the trees and decorations for xmess, costumes for the halloween and anything leather for IML in may. So, a lot of this stuff would go into that bin for storage. I tried as much as I could, but so much stuff was just too big for me; muscle pumped fags rarely wore an 'S'. But we didn't, couldn't sell the dicks: "health code" is what our manager said. So, I'd line up the dicks on the sorting table and at the end of the day we'd mostly throw them out. I did get this harness though. And tons of vintage porn mags.

It was extremely rare to get a donation like this from leather dykes. If they got rid of their stuff, they weren't bringing it to the store.

When we came across this type of donation, a full huge set of everything, seemingly, the person had, we workers would wonder what happened. We wondered this when other types of large, complete collections came to the store. Since this was the early 2000's, post AIDS-cocktail, antiretroviral therapy, it was rare that the person had died, or rarer we thought. But was this a result of a breakup? One time a guy came in with a dozen Italian men's suits, high quality, well made, very expensive. And then a few days later another guy came in, went to the suit rack, pulled out a few—we only put a few suits out at a time on the rack—and brought them up to the manager and said these were his. He wasn't the guy who dropped them off but said that, "Ah, there had been a mistake at home" and the suits were "mistakenly" donated. Seemed more like resentfully donated but who was I to say. Did the leather donator have a sudden change of heart? Or lifestyle change? What happened to these men?

Bonarh is standing at the edge of the Albany Bulb wearing just my harness. She looks hot: the straps bare and accentuate her tits, cross her thick middle and the ring in front circles her clit. She's taken off her clothes, I've helped her, pulling her shirt overhead, lifting her feet to pull off her pants and now she stands before me. I'm talking about the harness, situating it in time and place, then and now and pulling together Chicago and San Francisco and now Oakland and Albany and through it all even with my ownership, this is a leather man's story, of what men wear when they have sex of a certain kind.

Even as I'm watching Bonarh, projecting my history, my desire literally manifest by my harness, which she's wearing for my pleasure, her exhibition at my request, nay, my command, has her displayed in public for all to see, what I want is to be seen in this moment: my observation of my desire. I'm performing this moment as well, this wanting my desire to be desired and the tension of this moment, in the rain in the morning as the sun rises without casting much light through the cloud cover, is difficult to experience for the slipperiness of the shifting subject and object which has us become fraudulent imposters, gay deceivers, playing with a narrative of lack, even while telling a story of possession; simply our existence connotes visually ascertainable absence, and our presence and here-ness, described with a narrative of desire and a fetish object for substitution, does not allay the deeper problem: the implication of our nowhere-ness, our nonexistence.

And even in this now very public park, well-traversed by tourist day-hikers and dog walkers, we are alone. It is early morning and we are out on the edge of the bulb on the concrete slabs that remain from the bulb's days as a landfill which are smooth and a bit slick, even in or perhaps because of my lug soles. Bonarh is barefoot. I'm telling her stories while I slap her ass with my hand. She's standing and I stand close to her and begin almost immediately to fuck her.

My left hand holds her shoulder while I fuck with my right. Quickly she's crying: her feet are cold. I stop to grab her socks from the pile where I've placed her clothes and then having her hold my shoulder, I bend down and lift her feet, one by one, brushing the bottom of each off with my handkerchief before putting on her socks. Ok? I ask. She shakes her head yes.

I begin to fuck her standing up and now she stays present with me: no more fears of being cold, fears of feet getting wet, fears she will get sick. Even though it is raining the air is quite warm. I fuck her faster now, harder and then squat in front of her to get at her cunt from underneath, to push in deeper and as I do, Bonarh begins to come, her breathing heavier and her voice louder with moans. Echoes from the surface of the bay, which is still like glass and Bonarh is her loudest. Across the jetty, a person walks past, wearing yellow rain pants and jacket, with a dog.

I pull Bonarh down to me as I lay on the slab and place her on top of me. My hand is between us and I fuck her like this, thumb inside her as I push with my hips from underneath. She comes again, her face next to my ear, yelling. We are still for a moment then and then we pick up all the clothes from the pile and walk to the jetty to swim. The rocks are slippery here and we strip and dive in. The water feels colder than Baker but great and I'm laughing out loud as I swim around.

Watching Bonarh at the water's edge, removing the harness before she jumped in the water, has me filled with a sense of loss and grief, seeing her actual naked body, her beautiful female form unadorned now, invokes the end of this arrangement, her removal of my harness is foreshadowed in this moment, against the grey morning sky as I watch her enter the water and with the few strong strokes is a distance into the bay. I find a firm footing on the rocks and make my dive, the bracing cold water stopping my tears and pounding my heart and blood and I move to stay warm and we talk about Jones Beach, Rockaway and Riis Park on Long Island.

Later, after all this day while eating a meal in her kitchen, Long Island will come up again. It's revealed that she is a jew and this is a surprise to me. She says "I thought you had a fetish for jewish women?"

I do! I exclaim and then try and say something else quickly to cover up what I think must sound shallow and as if that's why I'm attracted to her, though the more I try to explain, the more anti-semitic I sound, so I stop and say yes, growing up on Long Island, it was very obvious that the jewish girls were better than I was and they wouldn't give me the time of day. I mean, growing up catholic on Long Island it didn't take long to realize jews are just better, no matter what my family said. But today, it's like I'm attracted in a new way, like personal.

I'm trying to keep my personal life out of this as much as possible. I want to maintain this arrangement as cleanly as possible: non-romantic, an escalation of sexual expression, not intimacy, not unloving, but as lovers. I have fear talking about my long-standing attraction to jewish women reveals a part of me that should best be kept out of this.

October 24, 2017:
Dear Bobby:

The water is so cold only swimming really can be done, either a crawl stroke or on my back, which I prefer, looking at the sky and waves and the bulb if I lift my head a bit which I do, the water is so cold.

After, we climb out and dress, mostly with wet skin into clothes. Or at least I do. Bonarh pulls on my harness, buckles it and pulls straps into place. I'm watching as I pull on my boots. She then pulls on her boots and we walk to the car in the parking lot, across the bulb and down the path. She's just wearing the harness and her boots. I've even offered to carry her clothes with my items so she is really bare and exposed. She's uncomfortable but walking proudly.

In her car there is some discussion of finding a butcher that's open this early (most open at 11am!) Ok, Market Hall. We drive over. She asked a question about the letter I wrote to you on september 29 and I started to talk about it and then couldn't stop, full of the 12th step experience again, regrettably. By the time we've arrived at the Market Hall, I'm wishing I'd never said anything at all. Even sitting silent and sullen in the passenger seat has to be better than this, I think, though my experience is that I can't live like that either.

At the butcher counter, I order some steaks and while they are being cut I run to the front of the place and grab a coffee. It's too hot to drink and while waiting for it to cool I see rotisserie chickens twirling on their spits. I'm so hungry I can't wait to cook lunch; I get half a chicken and we start to eat it while the butcher is still cutting the steaks. It's terrible: too salty, greasy, but we eat it anyway, standing on the sidewalk and I'm trying to wash it down with the coffee which also isn't very good.

We drive back to her house then. I go inside with her, shit in her bathroom and then go back down to the van. I change my clothes and do the steps: I continue to take my personal inventory and then meditate. When I come out, I make maté and the weather has changed: it's warm and hot and sunny with very still air.

October 27, 2017:
Dear Bobby:

It's hot like summer, still with no wind and quiet but it's fall now. In the east bay, it even smells like fall, like leaves falling and the thickness that comes from them being piled in the street along the curbs in the gutters.

Bonarh and I walk from her house on 45th to Telegraph and cross. We walk the back way which now doesn't exist anymore; a tall condo complex has been built on the spot we walked past to cross Telegraph. We pass the pizzeria on the corner and down the block to the dance studio. Again, Bonarh unlocks the gate then the tall heavy rolling door and then the inside door. Again, the studio inside is dark and cool, especially after the afternoon brightness of outside.

Inside, we begin to set up together. I have my bag and the bags inside the bag. I've brought medicinal strength maté in a jar which I pull out now and we begin to drink it, passing the jar back and forth. I take off my long sleeve shirt, I'm wearing just a net undershirt, levis, black engineer boots. I'm sitting on the edge of the riser platform and Bonarh stands in front of me. I ask her if there's anything she wants to say, has anything come up since this morning, any fears or concerns she want to express, anything she wants to tell me or anything she's thought about. She says, smiling, "I like this, Cashier. I like you."

I quickly respond to her, "This isn't personal. It's part of the dy-namic. It's inherent." She's so green, I have fear I have to protect her. Plus, I want to get myself off the hook. I'm trying to explain that what she's feeling is most probably the result of the intense sexual arrangement we've been in, not as a result of anything that I'm doing or anyone that she thinks I am, anyway that she thinks I am. This is important to me because I'm fearful that she's thinking her deep feelings are as a result of something, someone, that she imagines me to be instead of as the result of the way we're engaged in using sex to experience a feeling of transcendence. I don't want her falling for me. I want to forget about me.

I tell her to go take a piss and then I will and then we will start. She says ok. When I come out of the bathroom, I'm wearing new tight levis 501s, my engineer boots and the net undershirt. I take off my belt, take off her shirt, beat her ass with the belt then.

November 7, 2017:
Dear Bobby:

And then the sex; what we came for, why we are here together. I want this. This is what I want.

My belt is wrapped around my fist, the buckle in my hand and the long loose end too. She started talking about her defensiveness then. I got her to the back wall and I'm hitting her front: her belly, shoulders, above her breasts. Now she's crying again and talking about bedrock, her own deep bedrock layer and saying she was mad, and as I hit her, she was laughing. Me too. I put the belt around her neck and dragged her over to the set-up blankets like a pallet.

I told her I was ready for her to fuck me. She did, using her fin-gers. I stopped before I came. Then a distraction or something and she's cold wearing only the harness, no clothes on. I lift the blanket from under us, one of them, and pull it over us. She says she's kind of stuck, I forget her words exactly. We each piss again and while she does I put on my dick. When she comes out I tell her to lay down again. She's on her back, flat with the thick strap and ring in between her shoulder blades beneath her.

I pull out a bag of clothes pins from my satchel. And slowly begin to apply them to Bonarh's arms and legs. Up and down, inside of her thighs and out, belly breasts neck then labia inner and outer, pulling her lips wide and spread for each, pinching. She's covered with about two dozen pins and I tell her, "Lay still, I don't want any to fall off." I have two clothes pins left, one in each hand and I begin to play with her nipples with each, rubbing each nipple with the wood and opening and closing the pins on her nipples, not quite fully but enough for her to feel it. She's breathing with her mouth open and teeth clenched, sucking in air as I let go of each pin and leave it for a second, two, three on each swollen nipple, thick now, looking at her eyes as I do, holding her there with me in a deep space of sensation and pleasure.

I've pulled her up to a kneeling position during this application and she looks amazing, and by this, I mean her pleasure.

For me, this woman is kneeling in front of me, still, with hands resting on her thighs just above her knees, covered in clothes pins and wearing just my thick strapped leather harness in complete submission, as if I've tied her with ropes or bound her with cuffs and restraints. It's the space we've entered here together that has this exquisite sense of accepting the domination or desire, our desire, each of our individual desire but both wanting to transcend and we are there again. The application of pain, of extended duration, of constant attention, has swept across her face and her look is that of sublime pleasure and this is where my pleasure is: that look on her face pulls me along and out of myself into a divine state of enjoyment.

The clothes pins hang from her pussy, lips pulled and the way she's kneeling, with knees spread wide, the pins are almost touching the blanket. "Lay back down," I say and then I'm fucking her with the dick that hangs from my hips. So sexy, so perverted, I'm able to slide the dick in so slowly and to hold myself up on my fists and knees so as to not knock off a single clothes pin as I enter and slide out of her cunt, in and out. The vision of this alone, black dick from my hips and open button fly entering her wet cunt lined with wooden clothespins is enough to have me soaring, swooning and then fucking her long and hard and sweet.

And then she says, "I'm also kind of green this way. I'm like a virgin. Mostly I've been fucked in the ass." I get fucked up then. I'm surprised by what she's said and I can't even tell why I'm so disturbed but now I am. I say, "I have fear I asked you this on Echo Street, like your sexual history. Or at least a bit about it. And I told you mine, I told you about myself." Part of it is, if she's like a virgin, I'm thinking I should be careful, take extra care when taking her virginity.

I was getting more and more fucked up and then fearful I was being ruinous. I felt caught. The more I tried to explain how fucked up I was and so suddenly, the worse I was making everything. We lay together and I'm starting to sob. How is this happening, I'm thinking but the tears are bringing relief, something is being expressed and it's probably better without words.

"I want you to fuck me again before we leave," I say, "I'll piss and come back." Ok. In the bathroom I don't even want to look in the mirror, just piss and rinse my hands, wipe my tears. Back in with Bonarh, I take off my pants and the dick and then put back on my boots. I lay on the blanket and cry and sob and Bonarh starts licking me, then fucking me and I'm crying sobbing and thinking, 'I had a really hard week' and then as I think it I realize how crazy that is and I start laughing. This happened again and again and again.

November 8, 2017:
Dear Bobby:

This happened again and again and again: I'm crying and sobbing and thinking, 'I had a really hard week' and realizing how ridiculous that is, I'd start laughing. I asked Bonarh, "Are you thinking you're fucking a crazy woman?" "It's not crossed my mind," she said. She fucks me. Again and again and I come over and over. I'm sobbing while she fucks me and I look at her and say it out loud, "I had a really hard week," wondering if hearing it will give it any more validity but no, by the time I've said it again I'm laughing and laughing really hard now. I feel so good, the tears, the release: my body is shaking with vibration from all of it. The last time I'm saying, "a little more, c'mon, give me a little more…" and I come hard, body lifting off the blanket pile on the floor in a spasm. Crying laughing fuck.

I dress while Bonarh waits. I lead her to the mirror on the wall of the dance studio, to show her all the work. The bruises haven't come up yet but her torso belly breasts are stripped with red marks. Deeply. I turn back to my satchel and begin to pack everything I've brought. My hands are shaking; still, the being released by all this. I have a little hard bread and cheese and we eat a bit before leaving to walk back to her place. Out on the street, it's fall fully: grey low sky with a stillness that doesn't disturb the piles of leaves on the sidewalks and in the gutters. I take her arm tightly as we walk the few blocks to her place; leading her and holding her close as we cross Telegraph and pass a few blocks to her house.

At her house, we eat steak cooked rare. I feed her at her kitchen table. Then we had a sweet check in before I left. She liked the clothes pins and the way I fucked her, she said. We'll meet briefly on monday during my shift on my break.

Then I'm in the van, looking on my device for a meeting to go to before I go back over the bridge. As I'm driving, Canela calls. I'm excited and surprised and I answer but soon I realize I'm resentful. Thank god I'm on my way to a meeting of alcoholics anonymous: resentment is the number one offender. It kills more alcoholics than anything else. From it stems all forms of spiritual disease, for we have been not only mentally and physically ill, we have been spiritually sick. Selfishness! Self-centeredness! That, we think, is the root of our troubles. Driven by a hundred forms of fear, self-delusion, self-seeking and self-pity, we step on the toes of others and they retaliate (aa Big Book, pg 62) so our troubles, we think, are basically of our own making. They arise out of ourselves, and the alcoholic is an extreme example of self-will run riot, though (s)he usually doesn't think so.

It's a beautiful night, the air is warm in the way that a cool day without sun but thick cloud cover can retain the reflected heat as the sun begins to set. It wasn't windy. I was feeling good. I wanted to share this good feeling with someone and now here is a call from Canela. Quickly, though I'm resentful. I have fear Canela begrudges me a good feeling. It seems nearly impossible for me to not realize that Canela would not want to hear about how great my date went fucking another woman but unbelievably it's true. I expected Canela to be happy about this fact of me spending the day fucking Bonarh. My lack of sensitivity galls me, now. Then as I drove to the meeting I had a list of seemingly justified resentments based mesmerizingly on what Canela had done to me. Thank god for the steps, to be grooved in the habit of putting my resentments on paper with the lines, 'I am resentful because I have fear....'. Nowhere does it say, 'I am resentful at Canela because of what she did...'and like I say, my life has depended on this simple formula for living. Otherwise, I'm left with some strange mental distortion about why isn't Canela happy for me getting with someone else and since that doesn't make any sense, in that confusion there's a drink.

I make it to the meeting, just as it's started. How it works is being read. The room, the pine sol-smelling, dirty stained linoleum with upholstered chairs also stained and coffee being brewed, is crowded. It's early on a friday evening. I slip in and grab a seat in the back and settle in. It's when I look around the room I realize I'm the only woman here. I feel like I am disturbing their group conscience, like perhaps this is a men's meeting. Did I read the schedule wrong? But I actually feel too bad to leave, to get up and try and find another meeting somewhere else. It's a speaker meeting and the guy who is sharing is an alcoholic and as he starts to share, I feel better. I do the steps, I take my own personal inventory about even being in the meeting, and I'm able to listen to what he's sharing, rather than thinking only of myself. This in itself is a spiritual awakening. I'm relating to what he's sharing and I'm laughing. Thank god.

November 9, 2017:
Dear Bobby:

I'm relating to what the guy is sharing and I'm laughing, thank god. This meeting does something different. Instead of a show of hands for those wanting to share, the speaker just went around the room and called on each person. Well, he called on each man to share because even half way into the meeting, I'm still the only woman there. I sit in the back and have thankfully, blessedly, gotten relief and I'm able to listen to all the shares and when addicts share and I'm disturbed, I continue to take my personal inventory. Finally, it's close to the end of the meeting and I'm the last person who hasn't shared. The guy finally nods to me, or points to me and says, "Yes?" like, "yeah, you" and I introduce myself and then I say I'm so grateful to be in a meeting of alcoholics anonymous and grateful to be sober. I'm fearful this is a men's meeting and that I've disturbed the group conscience but I really needed to hear everything I heard and I'm grateful to have the steps to do in a meeting where I feel like I don't belong because it turns out, I feel the same in almost every single meeting I go to, including my home group and that is like I don't belong.

The next day is saturday and I've been rotated so I'm cashiering on my day off. It's the shift starting at 8:45 which is good because at least then the shift is over early in the day. I get to the store a bit early and call Bonarh. She's talking about her virginity and devotion. She asked me about my actions. I said of course. She said, "What, of course? What?" I said I'm choosing very specific acts so that our roles are clearly delineated and so that she can rest into what is expected of her. "Like we spoke about yesterday: this way you don't have to guess or figure out how to be. With clear delineation you can feel the security in your role."

This branched off into her feelings of devotion. Before we started I tried, fearfully, to deflect her devotion. "This isn't personal," I said. I told her she was green. I have fear I have to protect her, fear I have to take care of her, fear when someone is turned out there is responsibility for them. I have fear I got to get off the hook. Soon, she's crying. "I want to feel devotion and everything else. Trying to protect a person denies them feeling everything." "Yes," I agreed, "everyone is entitled to the dignity of their own experience. I'm trying," I said, "to give you as much information as possible so that your experience can be based on that."

This morning there is more power to express to her, "Your devotion, exultation, transcendence are welcome and also the intended result of very specific acts which are chosen very consciously." Much like those in a monastic life, fasting, praying all night and in the morning, self-flagellation to produce and experience transcendence and devotion to god. It's not a personal action for their own good feeling, though that is achieved, but to bless the world. "I'm not choosing these actions to have you devoted to me: I'm choosing these actions so I don't have to rely on trying to win you over with my charming personality, because I don't have one. I crave my own loss of self."

And then at work, cashiering at the register, incredible sore back and shoulders, arms, thighs, a reminder. Noticing I want to start the day with Bonarh all over again, beginning with the arrival at her house and then driving to get coffee. The Bulb, the water, the folded blankets, sitting on her tiny couch with her head in my lap. Languishing, or wanting to, in the experience; wanting to pull the blanket of it all over me and lay with it all day. The fall-ness in Oakland, Bonarh coming and yelling over the bay at the water's edge, heavy cover of clouds with occasional blueness, suddenly, from the grey, warm air with leaves turning and shadows amidst piercing light.

And then what I'd intended and rehearsed to write was: and then today incredible sadness.

I'm thinking this has got to end. I have to end this in december, before she leaves and the sadness of that idea. But if it's not for personal and is intended as a highly structured arrangement, then what's to wait for? I mean, I have an idea I'm trying to protect her or to do the best thing for her, but let's be honest, I don't think I'm capable of waiting. "Normies mark a date on a calendar and get excited as the date approaches. Alkies drink." And even this date, the end of december, is so stressful and filled with so much fear every time I think about it, the excitement of it all turns to anxiety and then a sick sadness.

November 10, 2017:
Dear Bobby:
The next day, I was reading and writing. I was actually getting back to reading and writing. Through this whole expansion period of the late summer and fall, I hadn't been taking time for myself, what with dating and the relationship with Canela and working. I mean I was barely even taking time to masturbate. So, I pulled Coming to Power off the shelf and read a bit. I started jacking off, rubbing

my clit and thinking about the clothes pins on Bonarh's neck; the way Bonarh held herself so still once they were on and then on her nipples. In my thoughts was the opening and closing, the tight spring being stretched.

This is where I begin in earnest, pushing and rubbing harder, pulling on my own nipple getting wet and then as I open to myself, the deep sadness. I don't want to allow it or follow it. The sadness seems so indulgent, too indulgent. But the situation with Bonarh is where I want my attention, my energy, my focus. Other situations, brought on as a distraction have provided much but now I want the single-mindedness of what is going on with Bonarh. The desire and the desire to completely fall into what's happening. I am more and more convinced that this needs to end before she leaves and a lot of the grief and sadness is about that: her leaving and the fear I can't stand it, won't be able to stand it. I want to say something to her tonight but fear there's not enough time.

The idea that we could continue seems improbable, not to mention impossible. I mean, that I would say to Bonarh, "Find a way to contact me and ask my permission to come for my pleasure while you are in Indonesia." That she would even agree to this seems unlikely, let alone how could this arrangement be maintained over that kind of time/space separation. No, what makes more sense is for me to pull in through the winter and strengthen what has occurred as a result of this expansion period.

I'm on my back on my bed, rubbing my clit steadily, without variation in pressure or speed. I'm touching myself the way one touches oneself, which is the way that one knows and likes, the way one pleasures oneself, by oneself. I'm not trying anything to seduce myself, or to mix it up or to provide any unknown excitement. This isn't my left hand, this isn't a left-handed, unorthodox action, no sinistromanual as if to touch oneself as a stranger, to feel the strangeness of the other as oneself. I want to feel this as one feels their breath, as one feels one's heartbeat, as if I'm simply alive.

The day before Bonarh calls and leaves a voice message: "Cashier, I want to come for your pleasure." I'm excited to even see the notification of a message from Bonarh and even more excited to hear her voice, but this isn't even an actual ask. I text Bonarh in the morning: 'I got your message this morning. It's always good to hear you in that state: waking up so turned on finger touching clit. The wanting to come for my pleasure and the stating of that state but not asking is particularly pleasing, Bonarh.'

I'm not in a rush, just pounding away with a regularity that I have been accustomed to knowing will get me to the climax. I don't have to try and catch or ride or strain or stretch for a chance at maybe perhaps, oh can I get there. This is the pleasure one has in touching oneself. So, I allow myself to let images, forward and back, come through my consciousness in this sure and absoluteness.

Arriving the other day with Bonarh at the studio, her pulling the door closed and locking it from the inside. After we settle, saying to her, "We had a good time together last time we were here." She smiles and agrees. "What did you like from last time, Bonarh?" The first thing she mentions is me on my knees, sucking her off as she wears my dick, gagging choking and then spitting all over her, covering her breasts, belly and face with the thick viscous throat spit. Yes, I say, and I'm glad because this was for me maybe the most amazing surprising part as well.

I'm holding this image but in my body as a feeling, trying to not have it go through my brain as an idea but to keep the felt sense of the dick in my mouth, the release of coughing and pulling back from her hips and the letting go as tongue pushes through lips; the phlegmish saliva. I'm rubbing and holding myself in the place I like: the build without effort, the lifting and certainty of coming orgasm, the relaxation of non-exertion and non-desire, the certainty is that sure there isn't wanting when one touches one self, only satisfaction that comes from the confidence of knowing what one possesses and I'm really feeling good now or is that just feeling now, the being-ness of now that can be without thought or idea just the rubbing pulling non-thinking perfection that one is able to provide for oneself and when I am there there is only that: perfection, sublime pleasure.

November 11, 2017:
Dear Bobby:

I sent Bonarh a text and tell her to meet me on my dinner break while I'm at work ('wait for me at the water cases in the front of the store') and when my relief comes I grab my bag and walk toward her. She waits for me and as I get close enough, I grab her upper arm and lead her out the front door of the store. I've told her to park her car on Folsom and it's just about dark as we get outside; it's fall dark which means not just darker earlier but also seems just darker. I give her directions to Enterprise and we go back there again—the short tiny alley off Folsom behind comcast and the chinese food donut store where I also buy my lottery tickets. It's a dead end but with a surprising amount of traffic due to the comcast parking lot with a gate and all the comcast trucks are returning at the end of the day.

One the way down Folsom I asked Bonarh, "Do you have anything to say? Be quick, because we have a lot to cover in this short time." Bonarh says, "Uhm…no, I don't think so…" and I slapped her face a bunch of times, quickly. She likes it, she says. On Enterprise, parked, she kneels on the driver's seat, kind of facing me, waiting.

She's dancing on friday and has invited me to attend the performance. In the car then, I start to talk about this event on friday. She says we won't actually see each other. I'm surprised, I guess, aren't I going to see you? I am trying to express that this is an unusual situation: to be together in public and what would the protocol be? I'm left unsatisfied as I was fearful of not knowing what I wanted.

Ok, secondly, the end. I say, "You will give back the harness. It will be a very intentional and prepared for act. But this will end. We don't have an open-ended situation. It is bound by very clear parameters and the idea that those can be continued or put on hold is antithetical to our arrangement. She agrees. I say, "I want to state I'm very sad already at the thoughts of loss." I say, "Seeing you without the harness at the water's edge was surprisingly heartbreaking." Bonarh asks, "What about when I come back?" I say, "What about it? Who knows what will even happen tomorrow? You might come back and be like what was I doing? Or maybe we can be friends or you might be like, 'please Cashier, put the belt around my neck again…'" She asks what about our other dates planned in november and december? "Yes," I say, "we will still have those."

At a certain point, Bonarh says about the ending, "I mean, this is all about what you say goes, Cashier, like your word has set this up." I immediately correct her: "No, your submission has set this up. You saying to me, 'I want to please you; I'm into submission' is what this whole arrangement is based on. Your safety is that and not about me holding you here. This is your desire being enacted. I make the space for it, but not the requirements."

There is sadness in the car at it darkens near 6:15-6:20pm. There is also now some rain. I say actually I didn't want to talk about this in the car but also, I want to say it sooner rather than later. I check the clock: 6:25. On the passenger seat, I open my belt and unbutton my levis and pull them down to my thighs and climb up on her lap. The driver's seat is reclined. "Fuck me." She fucks me and is crying as she does, fingers pushing into my cunt. It's fast, really fast—I got to be back at the register at 6:30—and I don't come but I enjoy her hand in my pussy. I climb off and then, c'mon, let's hurry.

Driving back on Folsom to the store, I'm buckling and buttoning and also pushing pieces of cheese and bread into my mouth, trying to get something in before going back to work. I'm already heady, dreamy and flying and walking back to my register across the front of the store, hurrying (I'm sure I'm getting back late if I'm getting fucked at 6:25!) and chewing and choking down a couple more bites of what I'm calling dinner and stashing my leather satchel under the register, keying in my pass code to the drawer and computer system while reaching across the belt to remove my 'closed' sign, signaling to customers 'I'm open' and making slight adjustments to the ergonomic keyboards and realizing as the first customers steps up and asks, "Are you open?" that I am; I'm open and feeling good. I'm smiling and I notice the customer, and the ones that follow for the rest of the night, like me smiling. They like me feeling good, it's that apparent, the goodness and the willingness I have to share that goodness.

As I got out of Bonarh's car on Folsom, her dropping me off in the rain, before I jump out to run in, she asks, "Can I see you after your shift?" Yes.

November 12, 2017:
Dear Bobby:
She asks, "Can I see you after your shift?" Yes. This is the first time that we'll meet this way: kind of spontaneously and to her bidding, from her ask. But things are really heating up now. In fact, it's getting hot everywhere. Michelle is texting and asking for more, and that she wants a commitment for more time with me. She's asking for reassurances I actually can't give and I'm getting resentful because I have fear I can't actually do this; I can't reassure her and I'm trying. Michelle is asking me to explain again what I'm offering or wanting. I have fear what I want is to go over her house a couple times a month and fuck her. Or, let me put it this way: I have fear we don't want the same thing. I have fear it's not worth it to fuck her. I have fear the price is too high. I'm under a lot of street trying to manage Canela and Leah living here with us, and Bonarh calling and seeing her and cashiering, even my ideas about trying to manage everything and everyone are so misguided, distorted and with the driving force of self-preservation. I get frustrated and after a bunch of texts back and forth that result finally in Michelle telling me to go fuck myself. I'd sent her a text that asked, "Who else pays this price to fuck you?"

Also, T The last time I saw her, we went to a lecture with Canela, the three of us sitting together. In the middle of the lecture, Canela wrote T a note, passed it to her and left. She told me she might have a date and would have to leave in the middle and then she did. I drove T home then and she was asking all kinds of questions. I found them irritating because they were unanswerable: How is Canela? What's going on with Canela? What does Canela think about me and you? Is Canela working? Does Canela care when we have dates?

I was driving the van up Mission Street to 26th to head up and then cross over to 25th. I felt the resentment starting to rise, and in my brain the irritation that was about to be discharged in a scream: "Please! If you want to know about Canela, goddamit, ask Canela!"

Instead, gripping the steering wheel tightly I said through clenched teeth: "I don't know. I honestly don't know what's happening." She then began to ask the same or similar questions about Leah: "Are you and she lovers? What does she have that I don't have? What's happening with the three of you in that apartment?" I said the same, I don't know. T said she wanted more attention from me. She said she wanted me to respond more to her and her emails. She said she wants more, just more from me. I pulled to the front of her building and turned the flashers on in the van, double-parked and said to her, "I don't have any more for you."

Yes, things are heating up. After work I ride my bicycle home then go down to the parking lot on Gough street to meet Bonarh. It's 10pm. It's late but at this time of year, the veils are thin and reality is revealed to be an illusion; time and space constructs of the human consciousness. The spirit world makes itself known palpably, albeit in the form of dark mystery. This time of reflection, celebration and great magick provides the communion with that which seems hidden; a spiritual connection.

I hop in her car and lean over and kiss her, quickly but I hadn't kissed her at all earlier in the evening on Enterprise. Then it's expansive. No, then there is expansiveness. Slow and long. Enterprise was so fast and felt rushed and so did the entire afternoon at the dance studio. This is slow slow slow. I sped a long time touching just her breasts. I don't even know how, how or what because it was a while before I unzipped her dress over her t-shirt and pants. Then lift her shirt and I begin. I say, "We've been a bit lax about how we've been referring to this harness. We've been saying 'the harness'. It's actually 'my harness'. You look good in my harness. My harness fits you so well."

I'm touching her breasts, belly and pulling on the thick strap between her legs. I'm feeling lazy and relaxed, kind of lounging in the slightly reclined passenger seat, leaning over to let my hand just pet her, rub her, feel her skin. She's been at a friends' house and I ask her what did she say to her friend about my harness. "I said I'm basically wearing it all the time," she said. When I reach into her pants the fucking strap is literally just that: pulled up so tight and deep into her pussy even I'm wondering: Wow, no wonder she's so turned on all the time. Her entire cunt has basically engulfed the strap. It's slick and wet and tight.

There's more touching and while I touch her, pulling nipples, petting, cupping her breasts, teasing her cunt, I'm talking in her ear. I'm half laying on the seat and my shoulders are against the driver's seat, my head close to hers. I'm asking questions.

What are you giving up, Bonarh? She's trying to come up with something. She begins to really get into a state now. Her brain is occupied with trying to answer the question posed and I'm continually touching her, building this into a lot of heat and excitement. It feels good. I tell her not to come.

"Flatten out this energy," I say, "real wide." I want it to feel real flat, like a sheet, no, not a twin, queen size. I'm gonna lay on it, on my back, real lazy, rolling the corner in my fingers. Then, face so close to her ear, fingers on her breasts, I'm telling her I like to see her in this state, like this. At this point, I'm actually really tired and I do want to just lay back on her as a sheet. It's also getting hard for me mentally to maintain stamina, like brain function, and I'm getting bored with it all, bored with even my own made up story.

I lay back on the passenger seat, rolled off of her, left her breasts exposed, shirt pulled up, dress unzipped and rolled up so belly is bare too. At some point, maybe now, I've undone her pants button. I've started pulling her pants down off her hips and even in the dark car I can see the even darker bruises on her hips from the other day which came up like a pair of chaps from the shape of her pants and where the belt made contact.

I'm laying back in the seat, smiling and on the one hand I want to just leave it like this: Bonarh bared exposed and actually quite quiet next to me, not panting nor breathing audibly and I'm laying with eyes closed, grabbing and rubbing my clit through my jeans. I'm smiling and thinking of leaving it like this.

Laying back, smiling really big with closed eyes, unselfconsciously though even at this moment my ego begins to assert itself much like it is now in the narrative: how do I look? My desire and ego flared at the same time. Is that not what desire is? Or ego is?

I rolled back onto Bonarh, clamping my hand over her mouth tightly and burying my mouth on her neck, deeply into her shoulder and yes, slid my thumb into her pussy. Oh yes, as I relive this moment I remember unsnapping my harness and laying the long strap, pulling it from her labia and laying it under her on the seat. Then yes, slid my thumb in her wet cunt and fucked her. It was sublime and kind of perfect: even physically, I mean, not awkward or taxing but some kind of easy, right leverage that held everything and I was able to fuck easily and smoothly but powerfully and to hold a rhythm against Bonarh, which wasn't actually against, but with perhaps. My hand is covering her mouth and she's screaming and moaning yelling through it even and the fuck is so good I actually don't want her to come at all, just be in it. Soon her pussy is an amazing fountain, soaking the seat, my hand, and still we are fucking with the easy smooth rhythm. My hips are in this too, pumping and my face near her ear again, I'm saying: "Yeah, spread you out like a sheet, all that energy wide and flat so I can fuck you, I want this, this is what I want…" and whatever else I was whispering. Meanwhile, she's spraying like a fountain. It feels so good and like one of those moments that one reads about: I mean, I could have gone on forever.

Also, meanwhile my hand is still clamped over her mouth and she's not fighting it at all, I mean she's screaming and yelling but she's keeping even her arms by her side as I instructed her to do earlier in this whole scenario. As I write this, my clit is swelling and my cunt, too. I feel good. After a while I roll off her again, partially, kind of still leaning on her seat with her and I reach through her legs and pull the strap back up and snap it back in place over her belly. She's kind of shaking and vibrating still and I slap her pussy repeatedly and hard and she squirts and sprays again wildly and asks if she can come. I don't actually say anything but she does and after, we lay side by side in the car. My eyes are closed again, my arm under her neck kind of cuddling her and Bonarh takes my hand and intertwines our fingers.

The next morning there is a text from Bonarh: 'Cashier, thank you for fucking me so beautifully. I am unwound.' And then her signature. I go to work and after I count out I buy half & half for Canela's coffee and then leaving the store, riding my bike to buy a lottery ticket and then home where Canela is at the typewriter on the red table in black bra and panties and knee-high engineer boots. I wash up and the sit on the couch. "Come get on my lap, c'mon," I say. One knee on either side of my thighs, she does and is smiling and when I'm rubbing her pussy through the panties, she's excited and pulling to the side. I find she's very wet. "I've been like this all day," she says, "wet and open." My thumb slides in and I fuck her on my lap like that, grabbing her belly in my fist. It's so good.

November 15, 2017:
Dear Bobby:

At this time, like I've said, everything is getting hot. Canela begins spending time at Jacey's house overnights to give us more space. Our tiny apartment seems not able to contain all of the honest expression which lately has taken the form of a lot of resentment. I'm alone then with the cats and at first, I feel relief and like, "Ah, finally, alone!" but quickly that turns to sad lonely depression. And when Canela and I are here, I try to avoid a fight.

I leave early and ride my bike to the tailors and then go to work and have a second cup of coffee there. I continue to take my personal inventory while I'm on the register, balancing a notebook on the top of the drawer next to the receipt printer. These damn steps work though. I don't feel better but I do feel bad enough to leave work early. I sign out and go upstairs and count my drawer and don't even go through the store on the way out, just leave by the produce door and walk along Folsom to the bike garage.

I ride my bike over to the main branch of the library, lock it on the Grove Street side and go in. It's often at the library I'll see customers from the store which always makes me feel good, like a part of a city, not invisible. I use the bathroom off the first-floor lobby (not the one in the basement next to the Koret Theater) and then take the stairs up. I walk around the third floor and don't find a space and walk up to four where I find an open desk near the window overlooking the Fulton Street mall and the Asian Art Museum. I get comfortable and fall asleep. I'd wanted to write but I was so wasted, all this fucking and fighting and just being alive sober is pathologically fatiguing.

When I wake up I ride my bike up the hill to the meeting at two.

I do want to say that the spiritual experience is ongoing; there is a daily reprieve with the steps, thank god. I'm too down, too resentful and too remorseful to stay sober. I mean, I'm an alcoholic. What I think I am thinking or feeling isn't relevant actually. The book says without a spiritual experience the alcoholic will drink again. So, I'm going to meetings. I'm doing the tenth and eleventh steps. At the meeting, I'm trying to share about the situation I'm in but I don't even understand it fully, nor why I am so fucked up. I mean, according to me, this is basically the most amazing time in my life: an amazing partnership with a woman I'm in love with who is, at least most of the time, into us seeing other women, and the other one I'm seeing is really into me and this situation and the arrangement we have set up. So why am I still so down and depressed. I mean, it's remarkable. And in the meeting the experience is shared while I'm sharing: "You know what Bill W. says about this?" and I say, "No! Please tell me! That's why I'm here! What does Bill W. say about lesbian polyamory?" The book is being held up and I say, "I mean, I've read the book and I don't know. What does Bill say?" The book is thrown to the floor as Tom exclaims: "Are we not victims of the delusion that we can wrest satisfaction and happiness out of this world if only we managed well?" Aaah, the complete psychic change. I'm off the hook.

After the meeting I try the third 'm': movie. So, I ride my bike home, down the steep steep hill on Gough from Ellis and at this time of year it feels particularly dangerous. The speed the bike travels, even when I grip the brakes; the damp street surface from the seasonal rains and the getting dark early; plus, all the traffic crossing town to go mostly to the freeway off of Mission and 13th has me holding my breath every time and riding and weaving in and out of lanes of cars at the lights and backed up, not moving.

But I am, quite fast, down the hill and while terrified, I love the feeling and the heart racing and adrenalin coursing through me. I reach the bottom of the hill and cross Market Street and bring my bike upstairs. I eat some cheese and a potato and then walk up Market Street alone.

I don't remember what I saw now and actually can find no record of this; which continues to surprise me when I come across glitches like this. I spend hours a day usually writing, recording what has happened, what I'm doing, how I'm feeling, what I'm thinking about, etc. and it's never enough. I can't write enough and the incongruity of it is that the more I write the less I'm actually able to record; the more detail I attempt the less I'm actually able to write in quantity. Of course, we hear about writers who in their obsession to write everything that happens wind up near-crazy writing "and then I'm writing 'near-crazy'" not living, just writing. Or living to write, writing to live. I'm not there yet.

I get my period at the theater and walking home down Market quickly then visible lesbian in denim jacket, levis and black boots, bleeding.

November 16, 2017:
Dear Bobby:

I'm alone on Market as I walk home that night, levis, boots, and bleeding obvious lesbian but alone. The female flaneur is non-existent for the very fact I'm experiencing: the female's tether of the physical needs of the female body. We can't, usually, go out for long strolling walks in the urban environment stopping along the way in cafés for another cup of coffee and then back to the streets for the physical need of a bathroom along the way. The male flaneur can step between two parked cars or even like the guy I just saw, open the fly of his pants and grab his penis and take a piss in the middle of the block. He'd simply stepped to the curb and unleashed into the gutter. Sometimes I carry a plastic piss funnel but even with its thin design it isn't stealth.

And this night is beautiful. Walking in the dark, alone, I'd like to cruise, perhaps along Noe to the park, sit on a bench there for a while or stand on the sidewalk along the side of the park and just watch but my female body has me walking quickly home to staunch the flow of blood, or at least to experience the beautiful flow without worry about my levis.

Peter Berlin talks about his high cruising style. He says he'd dress—tight shirt, tighter leather pants, his shaggy hair combed and hat on head—and he'd walk the streets of NYC, San Francisco, some European cities. Yes, he says, of course he was cruised and propositioned and occasionally he'd go home with a guy. But he wasn't that into 'sex'. The guy'd get him home and would ask, "whataya into?" and Berlin would kind of shrug. "What I always wanted in all my years dressing and cruising, and never found, was a guy who would dress up for me the way I was dressing up for him."

Douglas Crimp writes about cruising in NYC and he says as he walked the dark desolate streets at night alone he'd see a figure up ahead, a few blocks away. Walking toward him and the feeling of excitement with the thought, 'maybe this guy, also out alone at night in the desolate streets, is like me' and as the two approach and get close enough to begin to see each other, certain signifiers—oh, he's also wearing a leather jacket, oh, the middle button of his 501's is also open, oh he's walking in the summer in a t-shirt, not carrying anything, wearing cut-off shorts and has a handkerchief in the back left pocket of his jeans—provide the excitement of seeing one's desire reflected and explicit.

Crimp then goes on to talk about Cindy Sherman's work, the early work while not included in the pictures show, but which he writes about in a revised, expanded essay. Her untitled film stills show Sherman in a variety of stereotypical female roles. She is in the urban setting and alone and looks terrified. Here's no excitement. The fetish of outfit provides nothing but to signify female and her look, away from the camera signifies nothing but a vulnerable victim of prey.

I've been walking around in the city, going to libraries, public parks, riding my bike, taking the bus or the train and while I'm grateful to never have felt like the Cindy Sherman depictions I haven't ever felt like Douglas Crimp. Maybe a little like Peter Berlin, full of longing and desire to be met.

During this time of shortening days and getting longer nights, to be honest, despite trying to manage everything and everyone, there are moments of uplift. The meetings of course, and the longer I'm sober the more I can enjoy movies, having moments in a dark theater of forgetting myself even enough to laugh out loud. And the improved conscious contact in the eleventh step, I mean it's the reason to live. And with Canela, sweet sweet loving moments of deep reflection and care. We have an amazing time at the lake one afternoon, fucking in the garden and it's blissful and joyful and I'm happy actually. We go out to Baker Beach the next morning and the parking lot we usually have to ourselves is packed. We have to drive up to the upper lot to find a spot and the ocean's edge is filled, like lined up in a row right next to each other, one fisherman after another, all with poles in the water. Asking a guy who is getting his pole out of his trunk what's up he says the crab season just opened.

So Canela and I go to the far beach, the one that requires a hike down to the water along the steps. We climb over the rocks and the water looks so beautiful, thick and foamy. We strip down and wade in. The waves are rough and the tide is in just enough so that the big rocks on the shore are covered with every incoming wave. It's dangerous to get in, not just cold but the rocks disappear and the waves crash. We are talking, Canela and I. We are walking out a bit to water thigh high which quickly chases us back higher up the beach. We are laughing and lying face down in the water. It's amazing even like this.

November 17, 2017:

Dear Bobby:

While I'm treading water, trying to keep my head up, being grasped and developed in a manner of living ("the spiritual life is not a theory. We have to live it") the political climate in the US also starts to heat up. I don't know if I can even explain this. I might not be the best person to try and report this because I don't actually read the news; I don't follow the 'news'. I get my information from customers in bites at the register. I read widely and have a critical analysis of racial, economic and social issues, but I don't engage with mass media or social media or independent news outlets, neither read not listen to them. I rarely use email. I don't even have a computer, just a handheld device for calls, texts, research, including local movie times and addresses. Most current events are delivered to me word of mouth. At that point, I may go online and read a couple headlines but lately,

I wait days to read analysis of events, not about the events themselves. This is great at the register because I am very uncomfortable engaging with customers and this is a way I can do that: engage with them. I'm dangerously anti-social but find I actually need human contact.

So, while I'm pursuing my lesbian enactment of sex magick a parallel development is occurring: Trump v. Clinton, a tyrannical non-choice in an alternative universe. First there's been revealed that she has won the democratic nomination over the one who is a self-described democratic socialist, American progressive ("many scholars consider his views to be more in line with social democracy"). Many people are excited by the idea of the first female president but many customers are disappointed that the New Deal-era American progressive has lost out to a neo-liberal: I mean, they say, she's as bad as her doma-, NAFTA-signing husband of hers who was also a democrat. She's pro-war, pro-prison expansion, pro-exploitive trade agreements that allow child labor, and anti-immigration. And the other guy who she's running against in the Presidential election? He's an Atlantic City hotel developer. I mean, I don't support gay marriage, everyone knows I'm against any marriage sanctioned or required by the state. I'm for abolishing prisons, healthcare for all, universal housing. The idea that either candidate is anything but a corporate oligarch is laughable. The dubious luxury of living in the bay area allows me to cast my vote for the only true candidate: Jill Stein ("the answer to neo-fascism is stopping neo-liberalism…we have known that for a long time, ever since Nazi Germany").

The female candidate, not Jill Stein who is excluded from every single debate between the candidates, in fact she's arrested outside of one debate for trying to enter, is ahead in the polls. But I mean, c'mon, the other is an Atlantic City hotel developer. Then, less than two weeks before the election, the results from an FBI investigation are released. Hillary Clinton used her family's private email server for official communications rather than official state department email accounts on secure servers and though she was ahead in the polls, her lead drops heavily within days.

The morning after the election I'm at the register. Many people are crying, workers and customers. The hotel developer won. The guy with no political experience is the president of the US. No one seems able to believe it; how did this happen? I tell the customers I'm not on social media, I don't follow the news, but even I'm not surprised by this at all. I mean, don't people see what's happening everywhere? Especially in the US? The economic desperation that is happening in most of the country? All the racial killings by cops? All racism being expressed everywhere? And everyone was like, "everything's changed now" and I was like, what? Everything is exactly the same, more has been revealed, yes, but this is exactly how it was yesterday: desperate people taking desperate actions. There's nothing but misery going on but everyone's expecting that 'this time it will be different.'

I gave Bonarh very specific instructions to follow for our next meeting which is the night after the guy is elected. I sent her an email and told her what time I'd be to her house to pick her up and what to wear: "Please wear pants that give me access to your pussy. No tied drawstring or pantsuit. Button and zipper are acceptable if the waistband is loose enough. Skirt is a distant fourth choice. I want to be able to slide my hand in easily. Also, I like the red lipstick." I say that also we'd discuss being in public including "don't introduce me to anyone" and how she will stand when we are together. I'm excited.

November 23, 2017:
Dear Bobby:
    I sent Bonarh an email and tell her what time I'll be picking her up on my bike. ("We'll be riding bikes from your house to the theater at 6pm") and what to wear ("Wear pants that give me access to your pussy. No tight waistband.") And I say when I arrive to pick her up we will discuss how we will appear in public ("Don't introduce me to anyone; I'll tell you how to stand"). I'm excited. Bonarh responds with a generous email of her own, finding and then quoting herself and expanding on an idea she wrote to me about three months ago: that she will pretty much do anything if it means sex. It's a long email.
    It's november, but it's hot like summer. I work in the morning, a

208

busy wednesday the day after the election. Customers and workers both are crying about the result. Canela comes to the store and sits on a stool behind me at the register and behind the column that partially hides her. She's crying too and I wish I could be more generous with her but all I'm thinking, even without any boss or manager at our store, is how this must look. This isn't one of the times I yell at her, "Please! I'm at work! This is my livelihood!" But I come close. I want her to take care of herself. Or something.

After my quick shift I count out and then hurry home. I'm writing a list of all the things I have to do before going over to Oakland to pick up Bonarh at her house, including buy half & half for Canela's coffee in the morning. So, after I count my drawer and make the bank and log and drop it, I grab my bag and coat and hurry down to shop and then go through the register and out the door after saying goodbye to co-workers, customers and security workers and to the bike garage to unlock my bike and carry bag on my back, ride home.

It's just a five or six-minute ride to the front of my building where I lock my bike but I'm not off the floor until 1:00pm and the meeting I'm going to is at 2pm so I'm really hurrying. I lock my bike and into the building and up in the elevator to the 5th floor, hurry down the hallway to my place, 514 in the far corner. Canela's at work by now so I come in and unpack my bag, refrigerate half & half, cheese, veggies for Canela. Then take off work clothes, and in the closet, pull on my nice jeans (levis 501s) and black dress shoes, change my a-shirt but it's so hot, even up in the apartment, especially so in the closet, I can't put on my nice shirt so I put a t-shirt over the a-shirt. I begin to re-pack my bag: hat, sport coat, button down shirt (the nice one) but everything is taking much longer than I thought, trying on and taking off and very soon it's 2:45 already. I forgot my keys somehow and by the time I got down to my bike after making maté and putting it in a jar to go, I realize I've forgotten my keys, even though I have to use keys to lock the apartment when I leave, I don't have the bike key.

So back inside and back in the elevator and back down the hall, back to my apartment and when I got back there I thought: why not just meditate here on the couch? Fuck the meeting? And it felt so slippery to think that, I rushed that much faster back out, locking the door and down the stairs and out to the bike and unlocking it and with my heavy leather bag on my back and all my dress clothes in there, I rode up the very steep hill on Franklin up to O'Farrell, hoping off the bike the last two blocks—they're that steep!—to push my bike while I do a fast hurry walk and arrive at the meeting finally.

I have a great meditation in the meeting though, I can't believe it and it is so needed on a day like today. I'm at the meeting for like an hour, meditate and then listen and then share my gratitude at the door, "I'm so grateful to be sober and alive as a result of these steps!" and then still hurrying, ride to the bart on the bike: Geary to Powell and now I'm starting to get fearful.

I'm wondering even though I heard from Bonarh in the email about her doing pretty much anything for sex, I didn't know if she received my directions about our date tonight. And actually, she didn't confirm our date tonight…is she even gonna be ready when I get there? Am I gonna look stupid? Did she even get the email? Or was her email not one back to me but just coincidentally sent after I sent the one to her? Did she think the election results more important than our date? Was she going to some Oakland downtown protest instead of meeting me?

The bart ride is easy. I get off at MacArthur and ride my bike to 44th and stop at Webster, around the corner from her house. I'm perspiring profusely from being on the bart car and it being crowded and carrying my bike and riding and all the excitement and anxiety. I mean, really sweating. I'm glad I wasn't wearing my dress shirt. In Oakland it's even warmer. At Webster, I stop my bike and change clothes, taking off t-shirt and putting on dress shirt, using handkerchief to wipe my forehead, under my arms, tucking shirt in to my levis.

November 24, 2017:
Dear Bobby:

On Webster at 44th around the corner from Bonarh's house, I'm changing clothes for our date. It's hot like summer, especially over here in Oakland and I'm really perspiring. I'm nervous and excited about the date plus 100 forms of fear and waiting on the bart platform at Powell Street and getting off at MacArthur and carrying my bike down the stairs and then riding over here. I take off my t-shirt and pull on my really nice grey striped button-down men's shirt. I have cuff links in my pocket but I don't put them on yet. I don't even put on my sports coat. I put on my leather cap and ride the last block to her house, then locked my bike to the street sign on the corner.

Fearful. Fearful. I ring the doorbell, waited. Bonarh comes down and we say hello. I try to smile. She asks if I want to come up and I say yes, I want to put my bag up. We go into her house and up and into her room. I kissed her hello then. I asked her: "Did you get my email? Today?" She says, "No, yesterday. About that we're going to BAM and you liked the red lipstick? Yes." I took out the jar of maté and we drank it, me sipping and holding it to her lips and pouring it in, as usual.

I said, "So let me tell you how it will be: don't introduce me to anyone if we see anyone you know." Then I showed her how to stand in front of me: slightly to my right, off my right shoulder. I position her in front of me, where I want her and then I ask her: "Do you feel me right behind you? Do you feel where I am in relation to you? That's what I want from you for the rest of the night." I turn her then to face me and I slap her face a bunch, especially as we were leaving.

Down the stairs as we exited I realized I forgot my bike lights. "I gotta go back in." Back inside and up the stairs. She was crying then. I said, "It's no problem you crying, you can cry all day, all night. Don't worry," or something like that. "We're protected." At this point, probably earlier, I stood behind her and slid my hand down her pants. My mouth was close to her ear and I said with my fingers grabbing her clit: "Good choice." Holding her like that, I asked her, "Yeah, what else did the email say?" "That we'd ride our bikes to the museum, that you liked the red lipstick..." I'm pulling on her clit with my two fingers tight around it. Bonarh is breathing hard. "And what else?" "That you wanted access to my pussy." Yes, I want this. This is what I want.

We go down to our bikes. Hers is in the yard and I unlock mine from the pole. I put my jacket on before getting on my bike. It's still so warm, a beautiful night, dusk or twilight. It's the ride I've been so enjoying, between Oakland and Berkeley, flat and easy ride with so many trees and flowers and houses (that I find myself envying and then hating myself and thinking 'you think a house would be anything but a problem?') and the fall has everything smelling so good and rich. The ride between us is quiet and it's so warm I take my hat and jacket back off and put them in her bike basket. As I pedal I unbutton my shirt to my belly and roll the sleeves up past my elbows.

We arrive at the bike racks across from the museum after a final speed and race along Oxford from off of Bancroft and then locking our bikes. Then, pulling Bonarh to me, I put my hand down her pants to her clit, saying again: I want this. This is what I want," jacking her and myself, pulling/pushing that dick energy into her. I grab my jacket from the back basket and put it on and then my hat and take her arm and lead her across the street, opening the heavy door for her and inside to the ticket desk. In the hallway there, what passes as the lobby of the museum, she's excited by the posters on view. I say "I'll be right back, stand over here and wait." She does. I use the bathroom, ungendered and single user, to piss and take off my jacket, button my shirt, wetting paper towels to wipe again my back and neck and under my arms, trying to cool down. The ride, her clit, the maté: my head is spinning with excitement and desire, my body responding to ideas I don't even know I have.

When I come out she's waiting. She wants to show me a notice for an upcoming show on the electronic board on the wall near the gallery entrance. So, we stand and wait through all the slides. Bonarh is standing on my left and excited and nervous, I can tell. Her energy is so high up it's like its radiating from the top of her head and she's smiling so intensely and ceaselessly. I'm standing, still, strong and hard: this is how I show my excitement. Bonarh is talking and narrating the slides and laughing and then, like she realized suddenly and quickly, took her place on my right, slightly in front of me, feeling me behind her, quite closely.

November 27, 2017:
Dear Bobby:

Bonarh is standing on my left and excited. Then, like she realized suddenly, quickly took her place on my right side and slightly in front of me, feeling me behind her quite closely. She wants me to see an announcement of an upcoming show and we are waiting, watching the slides. There's so much excitement the run-through all the slides seems to be taking forever. "Oh, this is taking too long," Bonarh says, or something like that and I said, "You obviously needed the time to get yourself in position." In the Pat O'Neill video room, I slap her face. Everything else falls away when we do this, engage in this act, together: I'm calling her to the moment as I'm being called to this moment, now.

Down the stairs (all red) then to Mind Over Matter ('conceptual works that focus on performance and language') and that show is good, enjoyable. She wants to look at the performance part while I watch Antfarm 'Media Burn'. Somehow, we pass each other in the gallery space and she's gone. I wait watching the video until she circled all the galleries and she's able to come back and find me. She gets in position then, standing between me and the monitor, slightly to the side, and says quietly, "I thought I lost you." I put my arm around her and pull her close from behind, my arm grasping her around her ribs under her breasts. "I'm right here," I say. Bonarh cries then. I think she turned to me or I turned her around and slapped her again.

Earlier at her house when I picked her up she'd been crying about the election results, she said. She'd been up late the night before with friends waiting and watching as the polls closed and reported. This is the point I tell her I'm not surprised by the results; the effects of racism, institutionalized racism and misogyny, produce an environment of fascism. The gay agenda meanwhile has been assimilating with its policies, fighting for legislative changes rather than structural; promoting gay marriage, gays in the military, pushing for hate crime laws: basically, entering into a contract with the state for the myth of protection, state protection. I mean, pushing for hate crime laws when we are living in a prison industrial complex that jails black and brown males disproportionately should be a hate crime itself. What I'm trying to say is that expecting protections from the state promotes fascism. I said to her, "The production of culture is the only way to make fascism irrelevant. Opposing fascism is engaging fascism." (Though of course, fascists should be punched in the face at every opportunity.)

The Ana Mendieta exhibit is being shown at the museum tonight. It's what we came to see, the opening night. Once we enter into the gallery, which is showing her videos, basically which have been lost and unseen for decades, after being murdered by her husband Carl Andre in 1985, we are transported and the feeling of what can actually be accomplished with art and sex and darkened rooms, transpires.

All the videos are projected in the dark room, which itself is rather large though the monitors are small. They each require a standing close, intimately experiencing Ana Mendieta's work. Nature, feminism, femaleness, blood, spiritual and physical connection with the earth, water, mud, volcanoes, caves. "Her body was the subject and object of her work."

Bonarh and I stand together, Bonarh in position, and she's crying again. I put my arm around her waist and hold her. I tell her I told her that it's ok for her to cry, all night if she wanted. She's saying something about the news, the pipeline, the election. I'm not thinking of any of it, thankfully, and thankfully I don't say anything either. I just let her express herself. We watch the videos. During all of this, I'm touching her, grabbing at the harness underneath her shirt, sliding my hand down her pants.

At a certain point, she is crying, sobbing actually, and goes down on the floor like into a child's pose and is sobbing audibly. I'm standing behind her, arms folded, watching, but like watching to protect, to hold space for her expression. I'm actually wearing her bag on my shoulder because it was in the way as I was behind her, my hand down her pants. The young gallery monitor, a UC student, was fearful and approached me tentatively: "Is she ok?" she asked. I said yes, and then to reassure her further: "She loves and is deeply moved by Ana's work" and the young woman looked not only relieved but amazed and indeed, Bonarh prostrate in front of video monitor projecting light and image, it does seem like tears of devotion.

When Bonarh's up, I'm fucking her.

November 28, 2017:
Dear Bobby:

Earlier, standing behind Bonarh, I said in her ear, "Stay here while I look at you." I walked around to the front of her, stood a few feet in front of her, and watched her. Standing still, arms crossed, holding her eyes with mine, and then letting her see my eyes travel down her body to her tits, her belly, all the way down to her boots on her feet, then back to her eyes. I smile. Even now, writing about this kind of consumption, my clit is getting hard. Then I'm back behind her and standing a few feet from her again. She looks over her shoulder, but hesitantly. She sees me staring at her ass. She faces forward then. "You look so beautiful," I say, "your expression is powerful." I can see the effect these words have on her body as she stands still in front of me, like a shiver or vibration passes through her, almost imperceptible. Were I not staring at her, I'd not see it. "I want to lay you down on the bench, get on top of you and fuck you."

Of course, I'm not sure if I said any of this, ever. All of it is not being reported but written, now a year later. I thought the whole story, every episode, would be typed in three months starting last january. If I thought we'd still be at this queer project a year later—me typing, you receiving, me sending, you reading (presumably)—I perhaps would have offered a safe word to be used: "Ay, too much!"

And of course, a year later, a year after the election of which, of course, we saw the writing on the wall even then, no surprises but certainly I have little idea of what my response to the event was then. I mean, I'll be honest, I was thinking mostly of fucking: fucking Bonarh, fucking Canela, and in the larger sense: fuck everybody that comes as a result of the steps: the reprieve, the not thinking of anybody or hopefully, anything, because when I'm thinking of anything, it's a problem. It's not evil. It's evil corroding fears.

There's food being served at the museum in the lobby. Bonarh and I go there and I lead her to the end of the buffet table, effectively cutting the long line. We are like salmon swimming upstream as I juggle the canapes and slabs of cheese on my palms. Of course, the plates are at the beginning of the table and we've come from the other end. I lead Bonarh forward with my elbow gently in the curve of her back where shoulder blade meets her thick waist. Water is being served from pitchers, we help ourselves (the wine is poured by UC students working the event) and I'm feeding Bonarh, putting the food—little crackers with fish or roast beef, the cheese, she'd asked for some of the vegetables too—into her open mouth like a mother bird back to the nest to baby bird's open beak, then pouring cup after cup of water and pouring it into Bonarh's mouth.

At this point the room is filling, getting quite crowded, but we have a bubble around us. Bonarh is smiling at how much water I'm holding for her to drink. I'm laughing. Bonarh says, "I really want to kiss you right now." "Well, what's stopping you?" And this becomes the theme of the night.

Bonarh has a list of reasons why she hasn't acted on kissing me when she's wanted: non-romance requirements, being actually pushed away by me when she approaches, that she thinks it's not part of the arrangement. As the night continues, she's able to express more and more of her ideas about why she shouldn't kiss me which amazingly continued in the next morning when she's saying she has fear her touch is so toxic and ruinous that she shouldn't be touching me, and that she's trying to take care of me.

After eating we go back into the gallery again for the Mendieta films. The lobby got too full but it's crowded in the gallery as well now too. Groups of people standing and chatting in the dark. I turn and face Bonarh when we are near the bench in the center of the room and actually fuck her deeply then and there. Her cunt is open and wet and her pants to provide all the access I need. I'm standing close to her, very close with my arm around her shoulders and my face close to hers. I'm using my thumb and sliding in and out easily. At one point she asks to come for my pleasure. I'm deep into it, deep into her and I begin to lose myself with the flickering light from Mendieta's films on the monitors around the room. Everywhere I look is the female body: in water, on fire, blood dripping, in a cave, and I'm swirling inside Bonarh, my hand now tight against her clit and she's swooning and me too.

The room begins to clear when an announcement is made that the director is going to address the visitors and members. This becomes our wonderful opportunity I think as I dive in again but then a guy, still a student but not wearing the guard shirt, but maybe museum staff, comes over to us. My hand is actually inside Bonarh and I'm pulling out as he's next to us saying, quite kindly, "I'm sorry, there have been some complaints. People are uncomfortable."

November 29, 2017:
Dear Bobby:
My hand is literally wet with her cunt as I stand close to her and the guy, perhaps he's the gallery manager, stands very close to both of us. He's quite discreet. He leans into us, into the space I'm holding for Bonarh's submission to me sexually in the gallery, dark with flickering light from the Mendieta films on the monitors around the room. He starts out with an apology: "I'm sorry" and he's very kind and continues, "There have been some complaints. People are uncomfortable."

I immediately say, "I'm sorry. I understand. No problem." He smiles again and turns and leaves. I try again, putting my hand down the front of Bonarh's pants to fuck her, defiantly, which actually doesn't feel as good. "C'mon, let's get out of here," and we leave. I lead her up the back stairs and we exit from the main hallway, laughing and making jokes. I'm impressed, highly, with the guy's deescalating, nonviolent language, no blame attributed and no shaming. He's skillful and practiced, I say, I wish he could come to our store to give a training to all of us workers about how to defuse potentially difficult situations that leave the patron or customer feeling so good.

I hold out the heavy glass door of the museum as we exit, Bonarh in front of me as we get out to the sidewalk feeling happy and laughing. I hold her elbow as we cross the street to the bike rack. And at the bike rack is where it gets good.

I go for it right away and fuck her and jack her off from the front, then behind her from the back. I say to Bonarh as I grab and rub her clit, "I get behind you, I put my hand down your pants, feel your clit and say, 'I want this. This is what I want.'"

She's leaning her head back so it's resting on my shoulder and her neck is bared in the street light, her arms reaching behind her to hold me tight to her ass. Then I'm repeating everything we did in the museum. "The leather hat I'm wearing marks us as obvious dykes, slapping your face Bonarh, do you think some of the other patrons saw that, downstairs in the first gallery we were in? Do you think they saw me in a leather hat with a man's dress shirt rolled up to my elbows holding your face as I slapped your cheek repeatedly? Do you think the people were already complaining about what we were doing? Or how about when I cut the line and began grabbing food off the buffet table from the opposite end of the long line and began piling snacks and cheese and crackers on my outstretched palm, not using a plate and turning to you to tell you to also to hold out your hand while I loaded it up with canapés? It was the same dyke, they must have reported, the one with the black leather cap and levis. And then they said she held the plastic cup filled with water to the other woman's mouth and poured the water in while everyone else milled around them during the reception. And then in the gallery, in the darkened room they were, she was, she had her hand down the other woman's pants..."

I'm repeating this narrative and rubbing Bonarh's clit, leaning against the bike racks. I'm leaning back and telling this story over and over and picking up and twisting around and beginning again and again while Bonarh leans back into the front of my body fully. The deeper we go into this story of the museum, the heavier Bonarh feels, more solid and full and the weight of her and her desire in my arms which are now wrapped around her, one hand across her chest effectively pinning her to me, and the other hand down her pants, grabbing and rubbing her clit, fingers slipping in to fuck her—she's wet and open—and then pulling out to grab and rub some more, telling her in her ear close to my mouth, "I want this. This is what I want," while Bonarh is breathless, panting, moaning and sighing, and at one point I had the feeling of slipping in and not being able to hold the protection but this feeling was so sweet and then building and getting hotter and wilder.

For a moment, without leaving Bonarh's pussy or her pants, I step out of what we're doing and briefly look around. There's a coffee shop on the corner behind us, the entrance to the university campus is across the street, there's a stop light on this corner, so cars line up waiting for the light to change. Drivers in cars and then their passengers are just a few feet from us when this is happening, plus the many, many pedestrians walking behind us on the sidewalk. This block has many restaurants catering to the UC students. Two people are sleeping, or at least have spread their cardboard and bedding out on this corner as well. What I mean to say is that it's quite busy and full of traffic where we stand and engage like this.

Then I dive back in, having assessed the surroundings. I'm back with Bonarh in this. The inexactitude of memory is a dark murky causeway, like a slightly raised paving over the marshy sand dunes, slipping away, shoulders, shifting grains beneath what seems so solid and sure. Be careful going there, you may not like what you find, or find a way out.

November 30, 2017:
Dear Bobby:

I'm mostly recording these events at the register, a year ago, writing with a notebook propped open on the cash drawer, in between customers while I cashier. I don't know exactly what I was thinking while all this was going on; I'm so distracted by the rushed frenetic energy of this time period, the texting with Bonarh, Canela, Michelle and then T. And on my break, either seeing one of them or on a call with another and over to Oakland and back and falling into bed to be with Canela and an alarm in the morning to wake and then really wake up: continue to take my personal inventory, an easy and simple meditation technique and then racing out to a meeting or to work and then to a meeting and hurrying through dinner or to whatever's next. What's been recorded is the highlights, I think, but what's actually recorded is this narrative. What I was thinking, and what I'm thinking now, is that public lesbian sex is a political act.

The day after the election when I'm fucking Bonarh out on the street, I'm fully aware of my intention: to disrupt, and my hope: to bless the world. Not just a sex magick but a visible presence of female bodied sexuality powerfully embodied, not hidden, not implied, not suggested but overt. I have fear I'm being too grandiose here and fear

I should just stick to the notes but I have an idea that as obvious as I am as a butch dyke, as outspoken as I am about my lesbianism, I feel this is then reaping of the benefits of that very public position.

Having assessed the surroundings, I dive back in with Bonarh in this on the corner of Center and Oxford Streets in Berkeley at the bike racks across from the museum. I'm deep in fucking Bonarh and holding her against me, front to back. From this position, her front body exposed, every car passing can see my hand down her pants. I'm holding her and holding a space for us to be in, to come into together. My mouth is close to her ear and I'm telling her everything we did in the museum earlier: the feeding, the fucking, the watering, and crying. The laughing and watching and being watched and it's getting, through every turn through this recitation, getting hotter and wilder and Bonarh is panting and says, "Please can I come for your pleasure? Please, Cashier, can I come for your pleasure?" and I say only yes in her ear and then grab her even more tightly with my arm around her and my hand pressing harder and grabbing firmer as she explodes, soaking her pants and my hand, coming in a yell and a cry.

A couple of days after this, I'm at the meeting. I'm doing the steps and then making notes and then when it got too dark in the room, I listened to the shares. The meeting ended at 7pm and I was getting a burger. I'd forgotten my bike lights so I rode over to the bike lane on Polk Street and I was wondering, 'am I gonna ride down Polk and then go back across to Hayes Valley to get a burger?' I called Kim on my way down the hill. Not only is it dark with fall-time but the city is also dark. Many street lights are out I notice as I ride, even along Market Street. Kim on the phone talks about the election when I ask how are you, saying, "Well, I mean considering the circumstances..." As if the circumstances are any different from monday to tuesday; as if the circumstances are what have us feeling bad. Kim and Joe are in the city. They came in but the MOMA is closed. I say I'll ride down and meet you two near the Yerba Buena for a burger.

Most of the talk is about the election though I try and divert this by talking about the ocean swimming, the Mendieta Exhibit, the ant farm video, the Obomsawin film about the crisis between the

Mohawk Nation and a town in Quebec, mostly white, but none of this gets a bite.

After a burger, I ride home along Market and at Van Ness I looked ahead up to Octavia where both sides of Market Street were blocked by cop cars with lights flashing. I ride past our apartment. Across the street, the streetlights in front of Zuni were out making the café seating on the sidewalk seem extra unappealing, especially with the traffic backed up now on Market: all the buses, the 6, the F-car, and the Gough Street traffic to the freeway all have to turn onto Valencia. I ride up past Octavia in the dark and the freeway entrance is blocked by cops, cop cars, lights flashing and a mob of CHPs on motorcycles. By the time I get there, the cops and the CHPs were all standing on the small dirty plaza at the freeway entrance across from the record store. I pedaled on and finally caught up to what was 'happening' at the Safeway and Duboce alley bike way: a very small protest, people chanting, holding up signs. Here too, Market is dark and with all the police, it's intimidating. There's more cops than people protesting, plus cop cars and SUVs with the lights flashing and motorcycles surrounding the protest on all sides. I was fearful and rode up, got off my bike, walked on the sidewalk, got to the front of the march, saw a banner that said, "Hate is not unifying" and crossed over, caught a cop's eye and gestured, can I go back down Market, and did.

December 1, 2017:
Dear Bobby:

I walk my bicycle across the street, away from the small crowd and past all the cops standing in Market Street and past their cars and SUVs with lights flashing. I walk a bit further with the bike. It's so dark along this stretch of street and I don't have lights. Then I hopped back on my bike and started home down Market Street. The freeway entrance was open again, cars flowing through the intersection as if nothing had happened.

But I'm getting ahead of myself. It's during these few days that I get a call from Bonarh. I surprise her and answer the call, picking up because I've called in sick to work so I can stay home and write. I don't feel well with so much in my head wanting to be expressed.

Bonarh's call is a question: asking me to come for my pleasure. My response is a question: Is your desire to cum or to please me? What is your uncomfort? The harness itself? Or your desire? Are you not in an impossible position?

But I'm getting ahead of myself. We are back at the bike rack, in front of the museum, across the street. I'm fucking Bonarh deep. I don't want to go in too deep. I want to be aware of our location; we are on the street, literally, in public, and I have fear to dive in too deep could be dangerous or leave us vulnerable. Standing in front of her though with my fingers deep in her cunt, fucking her, I feel myself, both of us, slip in such that as I slip in, I catch myself and pull back out to the street.

I pull back from being transported to 'lesbian public sex' which isn't a place. Or is. Or something. But it's not in front of the museum because when I do come back from it, it is from another time/space; I'm actually feeling myself 'return,' which means I was somewhere else, we were. For safety sake I say to myself, "Be careful" or "Don't go too deep." Bonarh is so willing, though, so obedient (and has such a wet pussy) it's like it's easy to go there, deep.

Though it's not. All of this, every part, is hard, a part of being hard and her ready for and choosing hard. I pull myself back, return, and with my hand still down her pants and pulling her close, I look at her and begin to say, "What pleases me..." I start from her reference again to the letter (from september 16-october 1, 2016), in the gallery while I was watering and feeding her. She brings up the section in the letter, where I wrote when she pushed me against the wall of the Oakland Hotel on 14th Street (I say, "Out of that entire amazing letter, this is what you remember? From all the images described, this is the one that sticks?").

"Speaking of the letter," I say, "one image that remains with me is the walk we were on the evening I read the letter to you. There were cats everywhere in the golden hour. And as we walked you said, 'I mean, you can't dominate me in public, you can't slap my face in public. I have an image to uphold.' Remember?"

On the street then, with my hand in her pants, grabbing her clit, stroking her, pulling her, Bonarh says, "Yes, I remember." "I held back that day," I said. "Maybe you felt me, felt my energy as we walked down Linda Street. Maybe you felt I was ready to slap you then?" Bonarh is panting. Me too, breathing hard and heavily; the expansion of energy required to keep us here and safe. "What pleases me, Bonarh, is this: you doing what you said you wouldn't or didn't want. What pleases me is you going over the edge of what you said you wouldn't," and then as I start to say it, say what she's done or accepted or allowed or desired: "after you make clear what you won't do, what you won't let me do, just a few weeks later, huh? I'm fucking you in the museum, out on the street, fucking you in public," I pause to slap her face, "doing whatever I want, whenever I want."

Now, during this whole scene, cars are passing close by, a person and a dog are laying on the corner, bikes and pedestrians are crossing the street to reach campus, all close by and when I turn away for a moment from Bonarh's face, I see the people looking over at us. I'm trying as much as possible to keep my eyes open, to stay here and to look at her to keep her here too. Mostly the people quickly look away, either not interested or don't even see what's happening. At this point, it is heavy breathing, Bonarh moaning, my laughing and growling. Bonarh mentions lesbian invisibility and I concur: how can they understand what we are doing?

Then we are back on the street. The bike racks are perpendicular to the sidewalk, taking about the length of a curbside parking space. I'm slapping Bonarh's face and telling her how much I like it, like how much she lets me do and how much she wants it. Then I step behind her, which is riskier—when we are facing each other, we can stand close enough that our actions, me fucking her, are shielded with our bodies. I can press into Bonarh enough and tightly so that my hand, down her pants, thumb in cunt, is kept from view.

December 2, 2017:
Dear Bobby:
    Then I step behind her, which is riskier. When we are facing, we can stand close enough so our actions—me fucking her—are shielded from view with our bodies. My thumb pushed deep into her cunt

on the street is not evident and what we are doing falls into a seen/ not-seen expanse of not time/not space.

I'm behind her then and laying out a kind of force field around us, using the energy of the sex to protect us. I'm looking over her shoulder at the UC campus ahead and the busy corner of Center and Oxford Streets and then pushing my fingers deep into her cunt, my thumb pressing on her clit: the pulling, pushing, building, flying. And then everything recedes and a light surrounds us, like a beam from above shining down like a spotlight upon us but rather than making us like stars on a stage, what happens is that everything else, I mean, everything, seems to disappear or be revealed for what it is, unreal. No café, no bicycles, no museum, no one else around. Outside of this light, nothing else exists and in this light, which it becomes more apparent isn't from above but from between Bonarh and myself, and is like a powerful glowing, a radiation emanation, that disperses around us and we are held there in this unspace in un-time: now. The feeling of protection isn't either, but is in fact a feeling of being fearless; that whatever I'm thinking may cause us harm is only my fear or false evidence appearing real and, in this light and ecstasy, disappears and is therefore revealed as the false evidence (reality doesn't disappear) and then it's here in this light-energy we seem to be traveling in a vacuum—there isn't anything else—except Bonarh and I in or of this light, this ecstasy.

In this, I'm leaning into Bonarh and whispering in her ear: the museum story, the gallery, the walk up Linda Street with cats every-where in the golden hour, the pulling the wanting of this; I want this. This is what I want. I grab her clit and then I'm whispering breathily about fucking her in public, here on the street and as we do this, me pulling her close from behind while I jack her off and fuck her and then just jack her off, she asks, panting, "Cashier, please can I come for your pleasure? To please you?" and I say yes and she begins a loud, strong yelling and then yes yes yes.

I'm holding her tight and laughing with relief myself and look-ing at all the people on the corner waiting for the light to change so they can cross and the guy on his bike also waiting for the light and in the cars next to us—2 or 3 feet from where we stand—and they are confused or surprised or disgusted. They are all scowling or frowning, and I'm laughing and Bonarh is shaking and the light turns and they disperse. Bonarh is smiling so happy, so wet. She's sprayed as she came and has soaked her pants. I buckle her back into the harness, the strap between her legs, quickly. She's saying, "Oh, something else. Another reason I haven't initiated touching you or kissing you when I want is because I'm trying to take care of you." I think, what? She's a little confused, post-orgasmic fog and when I realize this, I quickly unlock our bikes and walk us out of there. It's harder to hold a field of protection without the sexual activity and I suddenly feel our vulnerability.

We walk our bicycles along Oxford for a few blocks. I hurried us out of there and put everything into the basket on the back of her bike—our jackets, bags, bike lights, my leather cap—so that we could get even a short distance away from where we were. I ask then are you ok to ride now? And put the lights on the bikes, put the locks from the bikes into the basket, put on jacket, and we ride through Berkeley. My pussy feels so good. I say, "That was amazing."

Along Shattuck we ride and talk about surfers on Long Island, surfing in the Atlantic, the taco shop in Rockaway, Trouble coffee in the Sunset and why San Francisco is so dirty (I say, "During the boom times there is such a rapid influx of people who come to pan for gold, for a chance. No one wants a job picking up trash.") And then we are back at her place, bringing our bikes through to the backyard, using my bike light as a flashlight to illuminate our way and locking them together. And then back through to the front where Bonarh's neighbors and roommates are standing on the sidewalk in the warm night looking at the waxing gibbous moon and the rainbow corona.

I'm jacking off now at the typewriter, sitting here in front of the humming machine, first touching my nipples through my shirt, then reaching down into my pants, keeping my belt done and buckled. It's tight getting my hand in and jacking off and I've touched myself through my jeans a bit while writing this, letting myself build and then stopping to hold here. And then now, so excited by this, writing and all of it, I come hard and then a second time, tilting back in this chair, stretched out, spread out, yelling.

December 4, 2017:
Dear Bobby:

At the typewriter at the desk, I'm jacking off writing remembering, reliving the night at the museum, at the bike racks, in the galleries, the walk up Linda Street with cats everywhere and telling Bonarh this story over and over and she's crying in front of Ana Mendieta's films, prostrate on the floor and I'm putting snacks in her mouth at the reception and telling her I'll lay her on a bench in the darkened room and lay on top of her, whispering in her ear, my mouth close to her ear, then my fingers inside her as the gallery manager comes up to us: "I'm sorry, there have been complaints," he says, "people are uncomfortable." and then outside on the street near our bikes, I don't have to whisper anymore, she's already here, no coaxing necessary at this point, no gentleness needed, I'm already fucking her and I say to her looking at her directly in her face with my fingers sliding in and out of her cunt in a beam of light that spreads around us, "You think I can't dominate you in public?" Bonarh explodes with this and me here too.

The bike ride across town to her place. The putting the bikes away in the yard. The neighbors watching the moon and rainbow corona on the sidewalk. Bonarh and I go up to her room. Bonarh takes off her shirt and jacket. I take off my shoes and shirt. She lays on the bed in pants and harness. I pull a low stool over to the side of the bed. I'm wearing my a-shirt and levis. My sport coat, dress shirt, denim vest, t-shirt for tomorrow and hat are folded neatly in a pile on the couch. My bag and shoes are placed neatly on the floor.

Bonarh asks, "Are you surprised that you're the one taking all the initiative?" I leave and go to the bathroom to piss and come back and ask her to repeat the question. My feet are on her sheepskin rug, my toes curling in the soft long fleece. It feels good. She asks again. I say I am a hard woman, very dominant in general. I kind of draw this out with pauses and thoughtfulness.

Bonarh's room is a sweet calm space, a square with two big windows onto 45th Street. A tree is out front, the leaves and branches a lacy screen for inside. The leaves now are aflame, bright, bright red with fall but California or global warming keep them on the branches, most don't fall off so the tree blazes. Her bed is covered with a quilt of the october night sky, stars and constellations threaded and knotted on a dark blue background. She's laying on it and I'm on the low stool next to the bed.

I laugh a little and I'm looking at her now. She's listening. I say, "What I like about being dominant is the results it brings, results I find highly erotic."

Leah and I drive out to the beach to swim one day. Leah says, "Men don't hit me hard enough." She's talking about her dates. "They don't give me what I can take," she says. I explain to her, that for me, I don't want to beat a woman into submission but instead a coaxing of surrender, taking a woman to her edge, holding her there and then a little more and the gently falling over that edge. I have fear this now sounds like a cliché but when she and I talked about it that day it was hot.

I tell Bonarh this story in her room. When I described this to Bonarh it was hot. I was saying that the place I find so exciting is when a woman is on the edge, unsure, unsure footing, the unstabling. I said, "I like when you have nothing to rely on, Bonarh, no ideas of yourself or how you are in the world or how you will be or should be, when your footing is destabilized enough that it is easy to catch the wave and we can just get swept up into it."

At this point Bonarh asks, "But are you surprised at how good I am?" "Good?" I ask. "Good at not taking initiative?" "Yes," she says. I climb up on top of her on the bed. "It is persistent, huh? The wanting to be the best?" "Yes," she says.

I'm sitting on her chest, my knees on her arms pinning her down, and her face as I look at her like this, from above, is so beautiful, it's almost painful. I've never seen her like this, what she's showing to me, a classic female feminine beauty that breaks me open, or turns me on, because this look is coupled with the harness which is visible on her shoulders and palpable under my ass. I'm slapping this face soon and she's smiling. What I'm not mentioning is that her features from this angle are quite semitic and of course this is the painful beauty I'm responding to: my wreckage. Fear that jewish girls are better than me. They just are and it's obvious and that jewish girls would never be with anyone like me: dirty, lower class. catholic.

Slapping Bonarh and she has to piss. I move down her hips and she's asking if she is the best. We play with this back and forth a bit until we arrive at this idea: are you the best at waiting, Bonarh? Are you the waitingness-est? She laughs. Yes, I am.

December 5, 2017:
Dear Bobby:

On the bed with Bonarh, I tell her her waitingestness has been noteworthy, literally. I describe the first time she picked me up in her car on Folsom Street in front of the store. We were going out to the beach. I came out of the store, having bought some snacks for the day there. Bonarh was standing, waiting for me on the sidewalk. "I made a literal, an actual note of that, Bonarh, I like it very much." In the car then, I pulled pen and paper from front pocket and wrote down, 'Bonarh waiting on the sidewalk outside the store'. "So yes, let us say your waitingestness is notable."

I'm slapping her arms now, watching the color come up, her arms spread above her head. I'm slapping biceps and forearms and she's explaining some qigong ideas and I'm saying, "Well, the color is coming up, qi following circulation." Bonarh pisses and comes back.

I'm lying on the bed now, on my back and she climbs in next to me. "Read to me," I say. She's written an email on tuesday which I asked her to print out so she could read it to me now. Ok, she says but she's printed out two. One included my instructions for tonight and one is just her email. "I printed out that one first and then I didn't know which you'd want so I printed out the other just to be sure." I'm lying next to her, running my hand across my torso. In the thin a-shirt, slowly gently, it's quite sensual and erotic. Soon, I'm rubbing myself through my jeans and grabbing a fistful of denim and pulling it with my hand. A powerful charge races through me as Bonarh describes printing out two copies. Then she asks, "So, I'm not sure which one you want me to read." She pauses. Then, "Which one?"

I don't answer. I lay slowly slowly touching myself, my belly, my breasts with the flat open palm of my hand and I'm on the edge now, too. "This is where I like you, Bonarh, on this edge here." I'm throbbing and pulsing with a powerful turn on and then the edge I fall over isn't the one I expect. I begin to cry. Not actually crying or sobbing but tears, a couple, fall.

I've just said to Bonarh, "I like you like this, this edge of unsure, this edge of insecurity, this point of trying to guess or figure out, wondering, 'what does she want?'" Then I understand almost everything in that moment, and I mean, everything: my entire cosmology.

I say to Bonarh, "Let's pause for a minute. I want to explain what's just happened. As a woman, perhaps you can relate. You see your mother, you think I'll never be like her. So, you become a hard leather butch dyke and think you've gone as much opposite from you mother as is possible. Then you hear yourself say something and it's like it's the mother exactly, as if it's from the mother's own mouth not your own."

I don't explain to Bonarh what I heard myself/my mother say, just the explanation of the phenomenon occurring. But I'm actually shaken to the core with what I've heard, with what I've suddenly understood, which is that I've eroticized and perpetuated/perpetrated my worst trauma. As I write this, I'm ashamed. This seems kind of stupid and not so profound, or just very obvious and not surprising. For me, though, this was a huge and rather disturbing realization.

I'm laying back, Bonarh is kind of sitting up, almost kneeling next to me, a pile of notes and papers in front of her, waiting, in the harness. I'm describing to her what's happening which is I'm extremely turned on and excited. My own gentle touching of myself is building my desire and arousal. Bonarh asks me, wondering, "What do you want?" and I say this is the edge I want you on, this unsureness, this unknowing, this insecurity and then the awareness oh, I'm recreating my entire childhood, trying to please an unpleasable mother, trying to figure out what the mother wants in an ever-changing, chaotic environment. Oh, what I find so erotic in women is actually the situation of insecurity that is terrible for a child: the feeling of being constantly unsure, no security, nothing to rely on, no way to rest in previous experience. This part is hard to write, the intensity of mind/body shift in awareness that seems huge but after that moment is just considered a new baseline of understanding: I am the unpleasable mother as disappointed dominant.

Before this, maybe just moments before this, I was taking inventory 'fear I can't be touched.' Even at the time, I was laughing through the fears, through the tears, not actual tears but a profound sadness to see that same line again. And then that line always leads to fear I'm untouchable and then the pariah/dirty monster/undesirable inventory follows. And then thinking of what suddenly seems like my cocky bravado, sitting on the stool bedside, I'm sickened by the brain and how it operates: the eroticizing of not being able to be touched.

December 7, 2017:

Dear Bobby:

I'm stroking myself, petting my torso, and I'm wanting Bonarh to touch me this way but she won't because I've already set forth some treatise about my hardness or made an exposition of wanting women to be unsure of how to approach me and have it all go down to the same old inventory. By the time I've continued to take my personal inventory and the lines about 'fear I can't be touched' are taken and then throw in 'fear I'm a failure', just for good measure, laughing while I do it, so common is that line, I can't help but laugh to see it again. But by the time these lines are all taken I have fear I've lost the lead or dropped the reins. I'm tired and frustrated by my own inability and though I've said to Bonarh, "I'm going to say this (about my mother/myself), then drink some water and we will pick up where we left off," I find it hard to do; I've lost the thread or something. It's hard being a hard butch and then crying about not being able to be touched.

I've asked Bonarh to touch me but I find her touch lacking, distracted or just not enough to counteract the ruminating inventory ('fear I can't be touched, fear I'm untouchable, fear women aren't that into touching me'). So Bonarh is reading and re-reading the letters to me while I ask questions and have her re-read passages again to me aloud. I drink water and get up and piss, then return and take off my pants and say it's time for bed, read to me until I fall asleep. I think I fell asleep ok but I woke at 4:30am and I'm still tired but can't get back to sleep—hot, restless, ruminating. Finally, at 6, my alarm goes off. I get up, go on the little couch in Bonarh's room, do the steps and have a good meditation. I piss then and make coffee and bring it back to the bed.

Sitting up in bed, drinking coffee and Bonarh laying with her head in my lap and I'm combing her hair with my fingers, collecting the pieces and rolling them in a ball. I'm telling her: "After my talk last night, I want to be clear with you: I want you to touch me." Bonarh then explains her idea of not touching me to take care of me; she's trying to protect me. "I think I'm so toxic and ruinous that I shouldn't touch you."

This is such a relief to me and I say I completely relate. I explain my own ruinous inventory, namely that people would be better off if I were dead. And the nature of the brain: that thinking I'll take care of someone or I won't take care of someone is the exact same thing, the same exact neurons firing over the same exact neural pathways.

Then there's a second cup of coffee. Back to bed. Bonarh is kind of diving into my pussy and I actually hold her back and then I'm fucking her, from behind with her on my lap and then I flip her over on her back and get up on top of her and have a great time fucking her, hand on her neck ("I love when you fuck me like this," she says), she's looking at me like this. She comes. It's great and then I spread her legs and stand over her and slap and slap her pussy hard. It's amazing. I jump up soon to get to the 8:30 meeting which is actually the 8:15 meeting and so I'm late. I drink a shake and ride instead to the 9am Rockridge meeting which lands up being a great event, post-election the speaker says we neither endorse nor oppose any causes; aa is not allied with any sect, denomination, politics, organization or institution. Our primary purpose is to stay sober. The speaker announced having 31 years sober.

Resentment has no power. Blaming people for their predicament only creates more powerlessness for everyone. There's no figuring out what the problem is. There's just getting rid of it. On monday night, I'm working at the register. It's very busy and Bonarh, who comes to meet me for my break, has to wait for me by the water cases. Finally, I'm off and we walk to her car which is in the back. "Drive to Enterprise," I say. It's taking me a while to shake off all the customers who are all fucked up about the election results. When we arrive at Enterprise, I actually step out of the car, piss and then get back in. Bonarh puts her head in my lap, let's me pet her. Then I lift her off, open my jeans and say simply, "Fuck me."

It's good. Soon she's taking off her shirt and her body in the harness looks great. Sexy. Strong. Thick. I open the car door again, get out and tell Bonarh, c'mon. I pull my levis down further and face the car and she fucks me from behind, burying her face in my ass. Soon I turn around, lean back against the car and jack off while she fucks me. I'm holding the harness as she does and I come hard. She's still fucking me, vans and trucks are passing, she's topless in the harness. I'm in t-shirt, levis down and I'm rubbing hard to come again. Almost give up, don't think I can pull it off, but then she shifts something and I yell to the sky, head thrown back, hot and hurried and then a kiss between us, and I pull up my pants, button the fly and get back in the car. "Drive me back to work."

December 8, 2017:
Dear Bobby:

"Have you tired of this situation yet?" I ask Bonarh at our last meeting. We sit in her car on Enterprise and I'm trying to settle from a busy day and a busy cashier shift and I want to be here in the moment with her but it's really just a moment. I'll be back at the register trying to write all this down in half an hour. So, this is a hurry up: a meeting, a leave the store together to walk to her car, to get in and drive three blocks and then a hurry up fuck before I go back to work, basically buttoning my pants and pulling my undone belt as I arrive back through the front Folsom Street door.

Any reality can be reproduced on the pages.

We think we are experts in our own narrative but memory is utterly fallible. Once the re-telling begins, we remember more. Bonarh is marveling about this. I say I'm not remembering what you're saying. I'm writing it. And it is this record recreated that I use for the repeated incantation whispered and breathed between us: I want this. This is what I want.

Then the end is near now. Everything is happening so fast I can barely keep up. I'm working at the register cashiering and writing and when I wake up after I do the steps, as much as possible, I write a bit before actually going to the store. At the store I use the top of the cash drawer as a desk I stand at, handwriting the events and results of this story. At this point, the end is coming fast seemingly from the future, racing toward me at the register, cashiering while I'm trying to pull what's happened from what seems to be the past into this now. Everything is happening so fast and all at once, the threads of every story is overlapping and spinning with an increasing-ness that it feels like time. I'm not sure how else to say this: time is slowing and simultaneously hurrying. I want it to be december because that's when Bonarh and I will take a trip but then that means it's over; she's leaving december 31.

So, the hurtling feels like I'm being tossed about, like in the waves out at Baker where Canela and I are still going to swim. As we stand on the beach in our bathing suits, the sky a cold grey and the water a colder grey, holding hands before we jump in, I say to her, "This is what we'll remember from this time; that   we came out to Baker Beach to ocean swim in the winter." And then the jumping in and being caught up and thrown about in the salt water, legs kicking, arms stroking, finally able to roll over to my back and to lay like that in the arms of the great mother as I look at the sky, the red bridge and turning my head at Canela, running along the water's edge on the beach.

It's through this time-warp that time is proven for what it is; which is, that it isn't. The backwards forwardness of everything all at once reveals time to be merely a construction; a clock or a calendar marking increments of delusional existence in a delusional world. The writing, that's all this writing is for, to reveal time as simply a slowed attention to details and a hurrying over where I'm cringeworthy, regretful, remorseful.

This is the beautiful queer vulnerability of returning to where I am shameful in my memory and the recreation not of the memory but of myself. And here, to extricate from this story which is mostly an attempt to prove my queer existence; those places, those memories, those untimes where I am reminded of shamefulness and to explicate them in the writing. The present hasn't created these unresolved issues. It is a reminder of where they are in this story.

I begin during this time to prepare for an overnight Bonarh and I will take at Orr Hot Springs. Even six years ago, Orr was often full of land dykes, polyamorous dykes, cute dykes, dykes up for the weekend to celebrate a birthday. I begin during this time to write lists of everything Bonarh and I will need: the food from Rainbow, What I'll pack, what I'll bring to wear. I send Bonarh an email and tell her to dress warmly, wear boots, wool, leather. I will pack radishes, salt, butter, cheese, persimmon, lemons. I tell Bonarh to buy steaks at the butcher: "Very lean cuts, sliced very thin for pan-frying."

After the swim at Baker, Canela and I strip off our bathing suits in the parking lot next to the van. I've started the van so the engine is running and the vents are blasting hot air. The sand is so sticky it's hard to brush off even with a towel, especially off our feet. I pull on levis, wool socks and a sweater with a hat. Canela does the same but adds a hoodie and puts the hood up over her head. We slide the van door shut, and shiver together, laughing and smiling.

December 9, 2017:
Dear Bobby:

So much of what's here is done at the register and is like this, then this, then that; not really lifting off. I'm ready to just get to the trip to Orr, just get there already instead of all this trying and trying to build up something, trying to do something, trying to prove something. It takes a lot of power to not try and to just be. Fear I can't.

After the meeting on wednesday, which ended weirdly early, I drove the van over to Oakland. It's already packed with my clothes and gear and food for the trip to Orr. I go to the fried chicken place in downtown Oakland, get chicken and rice and eat it on the couch in the van. I'm already, or still, feeling anti-social and self-conscious, so that I don't want to sit inside at a table. Or was the inside seating already gone. The chicken is amazing as usual though, so I enjoy it even like this: by myself, eating alone in the van.

After I eat and go back across the street to compost my little paper tray and napkin and chopsticks, I set up in the van. I pull the curtains on all the windows, make the bed with sheets and wool blankets, turned on the propane for the morning coffee. Then I went and got gasoline and drove to Howe Street near the hospital. I found a spot on the street there and once the van was parked at the curb I put up a rod behind the driver's seat with a sheet over it. Anyone approaching the van from the outside would see only darkness inside but wouldn't see a curtain covering the windshield, which I have fear looks too much like someone sleeping in their vehicle. I don't want to attract any attention or suspicion.

As I got into the bed, which is so amazingly comfortable and cozy, I was already down. I have fear I didn't get a good feeling in the meeting, fear I didn't share honestly. I mean, this is the usual for me, even in alcoholics anonymous, or, especially in alcoholics anonymous: I'm trying to prove something, I'm trying to pull something off (what even?) and not fully taking control, which isn't even what I want to be doing anyway. I want to slip away, to transcend, to feel as good and as disappeared as alcohol once provided for me. But I'm filled with fears about I gotta do this, fear I should be better. Anytime I'm thinking about what I should be doing I'm feeling bad with the bondage of self. And it's hard to share from that place, the place of the self asserting itself, because what's required to even say anything is ego-deflation at depth, the self-searching, the leveling of our pride that almost none of us like but which the process requires.

But we saw that it worked in others and we had come to believe in the hopelessness and futility of life as we had been living it (aa, Big Book). So, that's the rub.

I'm trying to plan a trip with my lover. I'm wanting to pursue this sexual situation. I mean, even just the idea of I'm driving the van across the bridge is hope in a trip, hope in a woman, hope in fucking. And it's hard to share in a meeting based on the spiritual principles of anonymity: "Oh yeah, I got hope that this trip is gonna make me feel good." If the trip feels good, or if I enjoy the trip it means I've removed enough inventory to sufficiently forget about myself and all my ideas about what's gonna make me feel good.

Somehow, with all this and plenty more, especially logistics about tomorrow ('gonna wake up, gonna turn on the light, gonna put water on to boil, gonna make the bed, gonna do the steps, gonna figure out how to take a shit in the van…') ruminating and running like a computer program running in the background discovered once all the other windows are closed, I put my head down on the pillow and I did sleep well. I slept deeply and for 8 hours or so, getting up at 4am, no problem. Which shows the steps work, even if I don't think they are.

And then I put the water on, turned on the light, made the bed, did the steps while waiting for the water to boil, make the coffee and as I drank it, climbed into the driver's seat, started the van and drove while drinking coffee in the pre-dawn darkness the few blocks from Howe and MacArthur to 45th and Webster.

I felt so strong and good then: the excitement of stealth city camping, the feeling of freedom and waking up, driving away, drinking coffee. The windows were fogged over from condensation and the cold overnight air, and with my denim jacket on over a wool sweater, I drove with the radio on and the window rolled down.

Bonarh is ready when I pull up on 45th street and park the van in front of her house. The light is on in her room upstairs and is visible from the still dark street: I can see her walking around up there while I sit and finish my coffee. Then she turns out the light and a moment later is down on the street. We pack her car with my bags of clothes and gear and with the boxes of food. I make a second cup of coffee before turning off the propane, took my belt from the loops in my levis and put the belt around Bonarh's neck as the sun started to rise, though passing cars still drive with their lights on.

December 10, 2017:
Dear Bobby:

Our suffering is the pain needed to prove the existence of our spiritual experience. Our pain is our thirst for a spiritual experience, our thirst is to find god. Our pain and humility allow us never to be arrogant. The reprieve is loving everybody and not hating myself.

At the register during this week a famous poet comes through my line. I recognize him by the huge crystal he wears around his neck and I introduce myself as a fan: "I heard about your crystal," I say and pull mine from my front pocket to show him. It's wet and it's raining today and he says he's driving to New York. I read him the poem I wrote in

Bonarh's car while driving to Orr: don't drive/back and forth/across the country/between xmess and new years,and after I read it to him I say you're not quite in that window but since it is winter, please be careful. He paid for his car-trip groceries, left and then came back with a poem of his for me. It's a busy winter sunday at the register before the big hellish day on thursday with no time to write.

Earlier in the week Bonarh and I drive in her car up to Orr Hot Springs. After loading her car and closing up the van, I put the belt around her neck and with my second cup of coffee we got in her car to drive north. I'm driving. I take the back way down 45th Street to the entrance off of MLK up to 24 and over through the slow-down as it swings around 580 then up on 80 north through Emeryville, Berkeley, back to 580 toward the Richmond Bridge, where it jams up again.

When I was first sober, I saw a therapist in Fairfax and I was living in Oakland. I'd ask for the morning off from work and drive up this way, 80 to 580 to the Richmond Bridge and over through San Rafael, passing San Quentin to Fairfax. On 580 the traffic slowed as we approached the bridge and having quit smoking as well as starting to go to aa, sitting in my truck—a little pickup with no radio—I'd be just about crawling out of my skin, wondering what to do in a situation like this. I got the idea to memorize the third step prayer from aa: 'god I offer myself to you to build with me and to do with me as you wish. Relieve me of my difficulties that victory over them may bear witness to your love, your power, your way of life. May I do your will always.' Which isn't that long or that hard but seemed impossible and like a major accomplishment when I'd repeated it enough to actually remember it.

I can't imagine the level of alcohol dementia I'd had after drinking for so many years (25+), like near retardation at that point. The prayer was so heavily judeo-catholic, and that seemed offensive but I didn't care. I couldn't care at that point. The serenity prayer, which I'd heard people in meetings say that when they were agitated or doubtful, they'd say the serenity prayer. Well, after just a couple weeks sober for me, that thing had already run out. 'Grant me the power to kill myself' is what I was praying and since that was what

I'd been praying for mostly my whole life, it wasn't giving any relief.

But memorizing this third step prayer, well, I actually felt like I'd accomplished something pretty magnificent. And for a couple months maybe I'd be saying this near-constantly, over and over in my head, wondering what's wrong with me, if this is how people stay sober in aa, I knew it wasn't going to be enough for me to not drink doing what they said they were doing. I knew I'd drink again.

We drive north in Bonarh's car. I have to piss and the traffic is tight and slow. I exit in Richmond and find a gas station that's actually very clean. I got out, run to the restroom, text Canela, piss, maybe even poop. Bonarh washed the inside of the windshield and then she went in and pissed too. Then we jump back in and get back on 580.

Bonarh begins to tell me the way she's been jacking off: pulling herself to a peak then not coming, not actually climaxing. I say, "Yes! That is my work jack off, the way I jack off at work," I explain. "There's only two bathrooms for 240 workers upstairs and there's often a line. As part of the cooperative spirit, I don't go in the bathroom and go all the way but I will go in and jack off and bring myself close, hot, tight, excited and then wash my hands and I'm ready to cashier."

Once over the bridge, traffic lets up and soon I'm speeding, racing, driving recklessly. Bonarh's wearing one of those t-shirts that is so thin it's barely even a shirt. The harness is visible as if she's not wearing a shirt at all. Her tits, too, completely revealed or exposed, seemingly more so than if she weren't wearing a shirt at all. Driving one handed, I'm grabbing and reaching over to grope her. She's got the belt, my belt around her neck buckled with the long end hanging loose.

December 11, 2017:
Dear Bobby:

Bonarh is wearing the belt, my belt, around her neck, buckled, with the long strap end hanging down between her breasts, over her belly. She's in the passenger seat while I drive fast. Once we've gone over the Richmond Bridge and I've thought about early sobriety and then pass through San Rafael and get on 101 north and the traffic lessens, I can really speed. I'm driving with one hand on the steering wheel and one hand in Bonarh's lap, on her breasts, slipping my fingers under the belt around her neck. I'm smiling.

The ride is mostly silent after our masturbation stories. I don't have much to say and driving this fast, on a two-lane freeway, changing lanes and passing cars I deem too slow while groping Bonarh is requiring quite a bit of concentration. When she puts her own hand down her pants I tell her no, you can touch yourself through your pants, but not inside. Bonarh is wearing brown corduroys and she moans and sighs heavily, pulling her hand out of her pants.

Up to Cloverdale happens before we know it and I pull off to piss again. I park the car at the curb. It's still early here in town, like still a bit of wet frost on the ground, the sun not having reached over here yet in the winter. We try to go to Karma Café but it's like in some mall or something and the bathroom is locked and through the mall which because everything is closed, seems creepy. I really have to piss though and even though we don't want to we have to go to the place for urban refugees/hipsters which are now up in Cloverdale too, an hour and a half at least north of SF. This place is called 'Plank' which sounds like Brooklyn, but doesn't everything now?

Actually, Plank is where I'm able to poop and get another cup of coffee, which is ok. There's also another butch dyke here too, who I recognize as a customer and as the girlfriend of an ex-girlfriend of a friend of mine. The butch doesn't let me catch her eye, though, and hurries from Plank before I can say hello, which feels bad. And the café, while nice enough, also has a bad feeling because it looks so much like Brooklyn or Oakland or everywhere else. It's like we drove for over an hour to get here, which is the same as there? With bare, reclaimed recycled lumber for the walls and some deer antlers and a couple of wool blanket throws with hand-thrown ceramic mugs for the coffee for here. Again, not like there's anything wrong with any of this stuff in itself, but when it's the only thing, it doesn't feel good. Sitting here in Cloverdale, much like in Berlin when I went in 2016 with Michelle, is a white-haired, extremely well-dressed in wealthy casual attire woman drinking coffee and reading the New York Times. Like I say, nothing particularly wrong with that, it's just that Cloverdale's 2010 census population is about 8,000 and it is in Sonoma County. Brooklyn, here?

We pull back onto 101 north then, continuing the drive. By now, the 101 is quite open and I can go really fast. Driving, speeding, changing lanes. As we hit Ukiah, I pull over to explain something to Bonarh, some clarifying point I feel I need to make, though what at this point I can't imagine. The rest of the drive is as quiet as the first part. Not much has been said on most of the drive. It's around 11amor so by now. I'm still driving and pulled over in Ukiah we talk for a minute. Then it's on to Orr Hot Springs Road, twisting and turning down into the valley to actually pass the hot springs and continue to Montgomery Woods. It's here that a forest of coastal redwoods stands.

Down in the valley here, the ground is cold, wet like a redwood forest. The sun had barely reached down here and the air is cold. We've been driving in t-shirts and as we stop the car in the parking lot and even before we get out we can feel the temperature change. I look at Bonarh and say, "Let's go." In the back in my bag I have some tall boots, knee high engineers and a pair of faded levis that I change into in the parking lot. I also pull on a thermal shirt over my a-shirt and then a pair of chaps over my boots and levis. Bonarh has a sweater and some boots as well. I take the bag of gear from the trunk of her car and we begin to hike in.

The trail is easy and wide with a few slight inclines. Our car is the only one in the lot at the trailhead, not surprising at this time of day or this time of year; mid-week also. The forest is the way the redwoods like it: moist and cold. We can see our breath as we walk through. I'm looking as we walk for a good spot. I want to tie Bonarh to a tree, to one of these majestic redwoods so I can use a couple of floggers I bought from Worn Out West (in their new location on Market Street) on her. The sun now is beginning to crest over the sides of the valley and dappling the path a bit, shining on some of the fallen trees and over the tops of some of the tallest trees. After a short hike I see a spot that has the most light and a clearing around the redwood's base. Ok, here, Bonarh.

December 12, 2017:

Dear Bobby:

It's still morning when we arrive at the Montgomery Woods parking lot and trailhead. We walk in, an easy trail, well maintained, cold, wet. The sun barely peaks over the tops of the tall, dense redwoods and over the mountain side. I find a spot at the base of a redwood, but medium sized, not one of the largest her—I don't have a long enough rope for that—and begin to set up. "Ok, here, Bonarh," I say.

I begin the preparations. I place my bag of gear on a fallen tree trunk, which lays like a shelf across from the tree at whose base we stand. The thick fallen tree is behind us then, making an enclosure for us to stand in. I start by pissing around the base of the tree to cleanse this area and to claim it for our use as it begins to approach noon. But in this woods, it's like a slip back to primeval. I sing then to the forest and to this tree, "Oh, mighty redwood, beautiful tree protect us with your longevity and timelessness. Thank you for your broad canopy and vast underground roots. A-men."

I tell Bonarh to unpack my bag and lay everything out on the tree trunk. I'm walking around this tree trunk, clock-wise, then reverse, calling in directions and forest-ness and light and love of the mother. In this type of place, even so close to the road, in relation, so close to the town of Ukiah, relatively, even so close to San Francisco, where there are aspects of this land being the same, or has the feeling of being untouched, or at least, at the very least, respected; for as I said there is a trail well-maintained through this woods, but the feeling stepping off that path and standing under the redwood is of stepping out of time. This is mostly what I'm seeking everywhere: out of time-ness. And that is what I call it here, under this tree, quite majestic and the looking up to its canopy—the top can't be seen—I have the feeling of losing myself in the branches and soft fir leaves, like looking at a star-filled sky. Behind this tree or on the other side of this tree is the rest of its ring, the other trees it grew up with and that side is also a clearing though at this time of year, no sun is reaching the inner circle of this fairy ring.

Everything is laid out on the trunk. I approach Bonarh. "Are you ready?" I ask. She nods yes. I slap her face a few times with short hard strokes of my open-handed fingers, holding her chin with my left. "Please give me your verbal consent," I say, and I repeat: "Bonarh, are you ready?" "Yes, Cashier, I'm ready," she says. I smile. "Let's begin then."

I undress Bonarh, taking off her hat, the belt from her corduroys, her sweater, coat and shirt and then the belt from around her neck. Each item as I remove it I fold and place in a pile on the trunk. She's standing now in front of me. I'm wearing my levis and chaps and thermal shirt. She's wearing only her boots and corduroys. The sun has moved and is now dappling her bare chest which is crossed by the harness. I pick up the wrist cuffs, leather and fur-lined, and place them on her wrists. She shivers a bit as I buckle them on her. "Cold?" I ask. "No," she says, "excited."

"Come stand by the tree," I direct her. And Bonarh does. "No, please face the tree," I correct her. And then I tie rope through the ring on the wrist cuff. I look at her, smiling. I walk around the base of the tree then with a rope in my hand as if I'm walking around a may-pole and as I get around pulling the rope taut, I'm back at Bonarh's side and tie the end to the other wrist cuff, pulling tight and causing Bonarh to reach around and hug the tree trunk tightly. Then I pull a little tighter, so her face is actually up against the bark, the rough thick bark of the redwood, cheek against the tree quite intimately. Standing behind her then, I kick her feet apart so her stance is wider and her feet back slightly behind her. I lean into her from behind like this, my front torso and hips pressing into her back and ass. I breathe into the side of her face.

Then I step from her and step slightly to the side, behind her field of vision. I stand there looking at Bonarh, tied to this tree, shirt off back bare but for the thick straps that cross her shoulders and meet in a large ring in the center of her back and then into one thick strap, continue down under her pants, between her legs. I can't see the leather wrist cuffs unless I step even further around and then there is her arm, stretched completely out in front of her, grasping the tree trunk.

I turn back to the trunk behind me where my gear is laid out. Bonarh has laid all the items neatly and individually, nothing is piled together here. From here, as I begin to touch what's here, I pick up the heavy handled floggers and begin to swing them one in each hand, swirling them alongside me and they make a quiet sound in the still forest.

December 14, 2017:
Dear Bobby:

I had fear I hadn't prepared enough for this trip. I had fear I wouldn't have it to bring. I had fear what with everything going on and everything happening I wouldn't be able to be present. I have fear I was exhausted already and really just wanted to use the time to be relaxing, maybe sitting in a hot tub soaking. I had fear I wouldn't be good enough.

By the time we are in the car with me driving though, racing north and then the exhilaration of the ride and excitement of seeing Bonarh in the harness under her thin t-shirt and then exiting the freeway at Ukiah and beginning the long descent curving ride on the road to the springs and the woods, I feel excellent.

Bonarh is tied to the redwood tree and I'm standing behind her, just watching her and letting the long leather thongs from the flogger dangle and then jump as I lift and swing the tails behind her; swinging the flogger so in the quiet forest the tails sound a soft swoosh. "Can you hear that, Bonarh?" I ask. "Yes."

I begin by approaching Bonarh, standing so close behind her my face is in her hair and my hips pressed against her ass. I stretch around her, aping her arms spread around the trunk of the tree, front to back. I grab the cuffs on her wrists and pull myself in to her body very tightly, hard, and then I step back. I begin to stroke her skin, her shoulders and bare arms, reaching my hands through and petting her belly, then pushing her back into the rough bark of the tree trunk and holding her there with one hand.

"Let me ask you something, Bonarh," I say to her while holding her, pushing her into the rough bark of the redwood trunk. I'm spun off of her so most of my weight is on my arm, leaning into her. I'm looking at the forest, bright green and crisp in this diffuse winter light, sun visible in beams between the branches landing on ferns and mossy patches. "Have you tired of this situation?" "No, Cashier," Bonarh says. "You're not tired of this arrangement?" "No, Cashier, I'm not." "I'm curious then, Bonarh, since on the drive down here you mentioned you jacked off without asking if you could come for my pleasure." "Yes, Cashier, I did."

I step back fully from Bonarh at the tree now. The sun in this short time making its short trip across the low sky has now come to where we stand exactly. The sun shines on Bonarh's back. "Let's try and understand the agreement we have, Bonarh," I say to her. I begin at this point to lightly caress her back and shoulders with the flogger's long tails. Bonarh shivers against the tree. "How does this feel?" "Ohh, I like it, Cashier," she says. The leather straps are stroking her gently. I ask her why she happened to mention to me the fact that she came during this week without engaging me. "I'm not sure," she says. "I'm wondering because that's actually not our arrangement, is it?" "I'm not sure," she says again.

Now I am putting a bit of my arm into the flogger. I begin to actually lift my arm each time the leather strokes her skin and as a result, I feel the strips land on Bonarh's shoulders and back. It's not quite hard, not yet, but more than a caress for sure. "Well, Bonarh, we don't have an arrangement that you will call me every time you want to come, do we?" "I'm not sure," she says. I'm keeping a steadiness with the flogger both in pacing and in stroke, steady and easy still. In this cold, I really want to warm Bonarh up before going further.

"How do you understand our arrangement, Bonarh?" "I'm not sure," Bonarh says again. Bonarh's back and shoulders have begun to take on a pink-ness at this point and I increase the force I use when striking with the flogger. I increase the speed with which I strike her and also put a bit of my own shoulders into each thrust, lifting from not just my arms but now throwing each stroke with my arms lifted, from my shoulders. As Bonarh feels these, even with the soft leather, in this cold air on bare skin, there is a sting not just a thud, and she says ooh and aah. "Do you like this, Bonarh?" "Cashier, I want to please you." "Bonarh, I'm trying to be very generous with you," I say. "Yes, Cashier, I understand."

I've now got both my arms up and extended from my shoulders.

I've got a flogger in each hand and I'm hitting Bonarh's shoulder blades simultaneously with each of them. "Is there anything you want to tell me, Bonarh?" I ask. "Like what?" she responds. "I'm not here to chat, Bonarh," I say, swinging the floggers more rapidly now. "Is this your poor memory or are you playing dumb?"

I step closer to Bonarh at this point, letting the floggers drop from my hands and hang on my wrists (the loops on the ends of toys always seem silly until it's useful to hang from a belt or wrist). I push up behind her again, letting my body fall onto hers and I caress her.

December 15, 2017:
Dear Bobby:

Standing behind Bonarh, I'm caressing her pink skin and pushing my hips into her ass. "This feels good, Bonarh," I say to her. I put my lips on her shoulders and kiss her warming skin, getting hotter with the flogger's strokes. She, with me pressing on her, begins to sway her ass, so slightly but with a powerful effect against my levis and the button-fly pushing on my clit. Yes, it feels good.

I step back and pick up from where I left off, striking her with two floggers at the same time starting at the top of her shoulders and working down along her shoulder blades. My arms are extended from my shoulders and the swing I'm using is almost like a flick now, really not a stroke of leather but instead like a blow. Bonarh is really feeling it and in the pauses I'm giving her, after her shouts when the flogger tails make contact, she's shifting her hips side to side. "Yes, Bonarh, dance with me," I say and laugh. I feel good, strong and turned on with the sight of her enjoyment and also with the exertion of the beating I'm imparting.

I lean into Bonarh again and press her with my hips, pushing her against the tree trunk. "Bonarh, I want to be clear we understand each other," I say while slowly thrusting on her ass, fucking her ass through her corduroys and my levis. "I want to be careful with our arrangement," I continue. "We don't have an agreement that you will call me every time you want to come, do we?" Bonarh is moaning against the tree trunk, sighing and breathing deeply. "Please, Bonarh, I want to make sure our arrangement is one we both are agreeing to."

I step back from Bonarh again. The forest is so beautiful, so cold and so quiet. Now, when I'm hitting Bonarh with the flogger I'm lifting my arms all the way above my head and I'm putting a lot of force into each blow. I'm alternating sides, left and then right, but without a direct rhythm so that I'll strike right left right right right left right. Bonarh is crying now. "What is our arrangement, Bonarh?" "I'm not sure." She's crying harder now and so I match her with the pounding of the flogger, pulling her and pushing her as I repeat over and over, "What is our arrangement?"

It's getting really good now. I put the floggers down and grab my belt which was around Bonarh's neck in the car ride up here, then removed when I took off her sweater and shirt. The belt is easy to use, so supple and I have so much practice with it. I am able at this point, to simply pick it up and strike Bonarh's ass. I hold the buckle end in my right hand and just swing the belt back and forth over Bonarh's ass. I'm able to hit quite hard because she still has on her corduroys. I'm feeling so good and when I ask Bonarh she says, "Oh, yes I feel so good."

"Bonarh, isn't our arrangement for you to please me?" I ask as I fold the belt in half and grab the two ends in my fist. Now each strike is loud as well as delivering what feels like a punch rather than a whip. There's less sting and more thud. And more moaning from Bonarh. More of Bonarh's hips moving, and now she's thrusting into the tree trunk. Rather than side to side, Bonarh is thrusting and pounding into the tree trunk. "Bonarh, isn't that what you said at the beach that day?" Bonarh says yes, yes yes. "What did you say at the beach that day?" "I said I want to please you. I said I'm into service. I said I wanted to please you, Cashier." "Yes, Bonarh. What did I say would please me?" "Oooh, I don't remember, please Cashier," Bonarh is in a frenzy-like state now.

In the middle of this, during this frenzy, I hear voices on the trail. Do they hear ours? Is that why they are also talking in fuller voices, to warn of their approach? But as they pass I stand in front of Bonarh, between us and them, so they aren't fearful about seeing a woman tied to a tree topless wearing just a thick leather harness. I put down belt and as two women with babies strapped to the front of their bodies I look at them directly and say hello. They return the greeting and pass then.

"Bonarh, we don't have an arrangement that you need permission from me when you want to come." I'm standing now to the side of Bonarh, turned from where I blocked her from view so that now I am in her view. "Look at me," I say, and touch Bonarh's face, lifting it a bit. "That's not our arrangement, is it?" "No, Cashier," Bonarh says. "What is our arrangement?" "That I will ask to come for your pleasure," she says. "Yes, that you will ask to come for my pleasure."

I step back behind her and pick the floggers back up. I begin now fully in earnest swinging each flogger and striking Bonarh quite hard. The flogger normally can't deliver what say a thick belt or strap can but when held and thrown hard these can hit with quite a punch. And this is how we finish off: Bonarh cries again as I ask, "Do you understand me?" Yes, she cries, yes, yes yes.

December 16, 2017:
Dear Bobby:
Now, this question I'm asking Bonarh over and over arises from something she told me as we drove down deep into the rolling hills of the Mendocino coastal range from up in Ukiah. The road is curving and sharp-turned and I drove fast, spinning the wheel. At one point, Bonarh says to me, "I wanted to tell you something, Cashier" and she says that during the time between the last time we saw each other and this time, she in her bed late one night had jacked off and come without calling me; without calling to ask for my permission to come for my pleasure. I listen to her while I drive and in fact I actually don't say anything while she says all this. It's my silence I think that Bonarh interprets as I'm angry with this information because as she talks, as we drive fast down the hills, she begins to explain to me what happened. It's not that the hour was too late to call since many of Bonarh's calls to me during this period came while I was sleeping, at even 3 or 4 in the morning. At this point, during this period, remember that Bonarh is wearing my full body harness basically 24/7 with the thick leather piece crossing down her belly over her clit, between her legs and over her cunt, ass, and up her back

before spreading out into two straps that crossed her shoulder blades and wrapped her ribs. Any time I checked this harness, putting my hand down her pants to feel it, it was almost always very wet and firmly embedded in her cunt, definitely pushing and rubbing on her clit and I say this simply to say that often when she did call and leave a message, asking for permission to please me she mentioned the harness, how it felt and waking up in it; she woke, she said, turgid, tumescent and swollen.

And it's not as if Bonarh is motivated by some consequences for telling me this or even doing it in the first place: there are none. In fact, as I remind Bonarh later when she is tied to the tree in the redwood forest, "Bonarh, our arrangement is not that you ask for my permission to come. Our arrangement is your desire to please me." Now, if this seems only a difference of semantics, or a splitting of hairs, that is just an unintended benefit of this arrangement. I repeatedly tell Bonarh, almost every time we are together, that she set these terms for our arrangement; this isn't something I'm calling for and that in fact the way she presented her desire to me was that she wanted to please me. "I'm into submission," she said, "in every way from being a hole to service."

At this point, in the redwood's shadow, it's getting cold. In fact, I can see my breath, especially now as I'm really beginning to breathe heavily, lifting the floggers overhead and swinging down with the force of my shoulders, arms and also torso. Bonarh has asked for her wool cap for her head. When I walk around the other side of the tree trunk, I touch her hands in the cuffs, tied and spread, and they are getting cold too. The sun has shifted in the sky and now isn't visible at all where we are. I untie the rope holding Bonarh's arms around the tree and gently hold her arms in mine as I pull her to me; not letting her arms just drop.

But I'm getting ahead of myself. This was after the final questioning I put to Bonarh: "Do you understand me, Bonarh?" This is while I put myself fully into swinging the floggers onto Bonarh. Bonarh has begun to cry, and she's saying she's not sure what our arrangement is, though she agrees, or finally says, she wants to please me; that in fact, that is what she wanted from the beginning: to please me. I explain to Bonarh now that I'm actually not interested in when she comes for her own pleasure, that our arrangement isn't about me regulating her behavior, but accepting pleasure from her. Bonarh is crying now as I hit her and swing the floggers. I stand close to her and pause for a moment petting her and then starting again. "How will you know when it's done?"she asks.

I'm holding Bonarh's wrists close to me with the rings in the wrist cuffs. I'm petting her gently and then unbuckling the cuffs. I put her shirts on her, her sweater, hold some water up to her mouth and we each drink. I have fear things got a little away from me at the end here. I didn't know how cold it would be or how that would factor in to the whole scene out here. I pack up the gear, put my belt back around through my belt loops, hand Bonarh her jacket. I put the wrist cuffs, the floggers in my canvas bag. Then we walk out.

When we reach the parking lot, there is only the one other car there, though we didn't see the women and babies again. I check in with Bonarh, ask how is she. She says she's thinking about buying new boots and her trip to Indonesia in january, like should she get the boots for that trip. Whatever ride we were on I have fear it's come crashing down to this.

December 19, 2017:
Dear Bobby:

It's cold and damp in the woods as we walk the trail out to the parking lot, it's a bit abrupt from the high flying we were in a few moments before: the heat and the heated-ness of the floggers and leather and talking and building. Now, it's back to our physical selves again and we are on the trail, well-maintained, and thinking each of us of our cold feet, our cold hands and what we have to do later and next week. I feel like a failure and have fear I am a fraud.

In the lot I unlock Bonarh's car and start it. I let it run and warm up with the heat on and the vents wide open. She has a thick moving blanket in the back of her car and I get this out and wrap her in it, crossing her arms across her chest and then swaddling her with the blanket as we stand near the hatchback. I stand behind her and wrap my arms around her in the blanket and pull her tight. "Thank you for a nice time, Bonarh." I say to her gently. In the car is a jar with some water. It's cool but we drink a tiny bit each. "C'mon, let's go," I say opening the passenger side for her and she slips in. I shut the hatchback after putting in my canvas bag and go around to the driver's side and get in myself.

We pull out and make the short one-mile drive back up the road a bit to the entrance of Orr Hot Springs. I haven't told Bonarh this is where we were coming and she is surprised; she says she's never been. For me it's been years since I'd been, coming alone in my little truck and staying the night in one of the little cabins. The one I reserved has a bathroom inside the room. It's too early to go into the room but we can check in and unpack our food in the kitchen. There is a large hand cart that we fill and then roll inside the gate. Bonarh goes back to park the car in the overnight parking lot.

I'm wearing levis, engineer boots and my black leather chaps. With a sweater over my t-shirt, the chaps keep me warm enough for us to eat outside on the small patio. We made a steak inside on the stove and packed cheese and crackers and persimmon and butter. Bonarh has on a wool serape over her t-shirt and a wool cap on her head. The lunch is sweet and from the one plate of food I feed her across the table. She opens her mouth like a small bird waiting for a worm to be delivered in her mouth.

The grounds here are quiet. It's a grey wintery day, not sunny at all and that adds to the quiet-ness, I think. A few other white people walk past or bring their own gear in and smile at us as they pass. After lunch we clean up, wash our plate and then to put on water for my coffee. I'm going to the room now to meditate, continue to take my own personal inventory and then meditate. Bonarh grabs the handle of the cart, loaded, and pushes it to our room.

The room is one of the older ones, further back but, like I say, with a bathroom. It is decorated in a rustic-style, meaning wood paneling half way up the walls and a wood plank floor. There's a bed and small desk with chair. I put my clothes bag on the desk next to the french press coffee pot I've carried while Bonarh pushed the cart. I've taken a coffee cup from the kitchen and place that there as well.

I've brought my best levis and second-best levis and the pair I'm wearing now under my chaps. I have a thick sweater and a flannel shirt, plaid, and a chambray cotton shirt. Plus, my underwear and socks. The bag is quite full also because I'm wearing my boots and have another pair of boots in the bag. Across the room is another smaller bed, like would be for a child and it's here that Bonarh puts her bag of clothes. Now that we are inside she's put a pink sweater on over her t-shirt and over the harness. I begin the steps.

When I come out of meditation, I press and pour the coffee. It's still hot, or warm, but not unpleasant. Bonarh who was on the little bed while I meditated in the bigger bed now comes over and lays on the bed next to me. "Read to me what you've prepared for me," I say. Earlier in the week, when Bonarh and I emailed back and forth about this trip and its preparations, food, clothes, etc., I'd written to Bonarh, "Please prepare something for me to read; for you to read to me while we are on this trip."

As Bonarh sits on the bed, she tells me this has been challenging for her this week, the wanting to please me with something to read. She has interpreted this request as I want her to write something to read to me, not as simply a request to make a selection from another source and bring that; that has been the difficulty. I laugh as I explain what I meant but I am quite pleased, I tell her, of her efforts here, in the writing to me.

December 20, 2017:
Dear Bobby:
I lay in the big bed at Orr, drinking coffee after meditation. Bonarh comes and lays next to me. It's the afternoon. "Read to me what you've prepared," I say. Bonarh goes to her bag on the littler bed across the room and smiling, shuffles through a book and her clothes and pulls out a letter, handwritten, and brings it to the bed. "I wanted to take time with your request," she says, "but I was so busy this week, I only had time last night before I went to bed." "I'm happy you wrote to me," I say, "but I wasn't expecting it. I said prepare something to read to me but I thought you'd bring a book or a passage from something you read."

Later, a few weeks from now, I'll tell Canela that in 25 years of writing letters to women, Bonarh was the first whoever wrote back, and even that's not true, of course, I realize later than that. I have a stack of cards and notes from Canela, all sweet and sexy and loving and daily and engaged. Everything that I think is happening for the first time isn't actually and that's been the hardest part of all of this; the continual waking up to the experience that my brain is like a record player and I have only one record. Every day, I'm putting the needle on the record and I'm playing that sad, sad song: 'They don't love me, they don't care…', and every day as if it's the first time I'm playing it.

The letter Bonarh has written, the pages she's prepared to read to me are a description of our fucking. It's beautiful. While I lay in bed, drinking coffee, listening to her read the pages, I feel relaxed. I'm enjoying this. "Again," I say when she reaches the end, "read it again." And Bonarh re-reads then re-reads the pages.

It begins with, "I fucking love this situation" and then there's a description of the time we were in Bonarh's car on Enterprise and she fucked me against the side of the car in the dark. I've exited the vehicle and she's followed me out and I'm standing against the side of her car. She fucked me in the front seat, with the seat reclined, her sitting on my lap and facing away from me, "ass to you," Bonarh writes in her scrawling black penned penmanship. Bonarh describes me, sitting in the front seat, taking my own personal inventory when we park on Enterprise. 'I want to please you," she writes, is not enough. I'm scrawling on my paper, leaning back in the seat and my harness, Bonarh writes, is wedging into her pussy, the thick strap spreading her lips. She wants to lie her head in my lap, wants to touch me all over, she wonders, how?

The next line is: 'How do you like touch? To what extent? What're your ranges of pleasure?' And it's here, hearing these lines that I feel the disruption. Each time Bonarh reads these pages, these lines are where I get stuck and while she continues reading through, I'm asking myself those questions again and again.

We are in the front seat of the car, parked on Enterprise. I say to Bonarh, she writes, 'C'mon.' Finally. The time is rushed here, though

I don't want to be fast, this is the fastest, my hand inviting, bringing her hand down into my cunt.

'Would I be bold enough before then? when does the thought enter, the desire, in my waitingness, in this state of excitation, yeah,' she reads her writing.

How do I relate to demand, request, command, instruct, require?

'I want to know what the situation requires, what the situation wants,' Bonarh continues.

The room is in late afternoon light which in the darkly paneled room with the curtains drawn and the bedside lamp on, is very yellow. It's cozy inside here, and through the windows through a split in the curtains are light, it's that winter grey light outside, not bright. The sound of the stream that feeds the pools and springs is outside as well, water running. It's this sound of water that provides such good sleep here at night.

And then the questions again in Bonarh's writing to me: 'what gets you off? What gets you to feel yourself in the deep? To unleash, to open up new tones, spaces, the velvet feltness of all of you? Slapping, the belt, yes. But inside of you? Burrow. I want to master fucking you,' Bonarh writes, 'I want this so bad I want this more than cumming myself, but cumming feels so fucking good, and the twist is I want to please you and if my cumming pleases you, of course that comes first. It's complicated. My own desires and then agreements and the desire to please you as base. My body, our arrangement... there is no clear line. No binary here, where your harness envelopes me, encases me, so much of my days, and now.'

And I'm asking myself in the car, and in the bed in the room, what gets me off? How do I like to be touched? What pleases me? Inside myself deeply. I have fear I don't know.

January 5, 2018:
Dear Bobby:

I have fear I don't know what pleases me, what gets me off. It's from here, that, on the bed in the little room at Orr Hot Springs, I lay Bonarh out, the afternoon and evening quickly, with the help of the hot waters and darkness in the cabin room, coffee in the middle of the day, blended into the morning, such that nothing in terms of time stands out; it's all the trip to Orr in my memory.

And we do go in the water, the big cold plunge pool and the hot little pool at the end near the steam-room and sauna. The hot pool isn't as hot as I like it but it feels good to be in the waters, ritually, soaking and talking quietly. And then slipping up over the edge and pulling myself up and out, using the stairs into the cold pool and swimming the length of that and back. Then again, a pulling up and over into the small hot soak. My hips are tight and my shoulder sore from over-extension repeatedly at the register. The water feels good on my head and hair when I pull my head underneath.

Bonarh is wearing the harness. Tell them it's a European bikini I say if anyone asks, which seems funny until some actual Europeans come around the pool and wearing tiny European bikini. I say their consciousness is that they can be protected by a small piece of material. Later, in the tubs, up on the deck, I'll piss in the water and over Bonarh's body and she'll discreetly fuck me. My piss and my cum have already, I say, anointed the tub energetically, how can a bathing suit protect them.

The sauna is what appeals to me most this trip, more than the pools and the steam room. Being in the close, dim tightly closed room with the wood benches, sweating deeply feels so cleansing, so relieving and so damn good, I spend most of the time in there, leaving when I get a bit light-headed and jumping in the cold plunge, then swimming the length and back and jumping up and out at the end and back in the sauna. Again, Bonarh has on the harness. "What do you think?" she asked, "Should I wear it in the water and sauna?" "Why would you take it off, Bonarh?" "The leather," she says, "I'm concerned about the care of the leather itself." This leads her to ask me about the harness again. "Me in the harness?" I say, "I was drunk and smoking."

"Hard isn't in opposition to easy," I tell her. "When you chose hard you didn't even know what you were agreeing to." "I didn't," Bonarh says. "I offered you hard or easy, but it's not about difficulty. It's about continuous engagement. The questions aren't to be answered; the intention is to occupy your brain with your submission." The same with the requests to come for my pleasure. Not a claiming or claim of ownership but instead a way to have her constantly thinking of her submission. "Bonarh, you asking me is my desire."

The difficulty for me in this scenario is getting fucked. I have a lot of ideas about how I should and shouldn't be getting fucked, mostly how I shouldn't be getting fucked. Most of the ideas, I don't even know where they came from or how they started. Some of these ideas, like 'butches don't get fucked' seem so archaic and out of date and actually against my other beliefs about queer sex, lesbian sex, sex between women—that it's not based in agender or sexual identity, that a sex act isn't proscribed by a gender or sexual identity—that I find this other belief, 'butches don't get fucked' to be confusing and limiting but none the less, a belief I am strongly at the effect of having.

Of course, my personal wreckage, already mentioned at length here: 'fear I can't be touched; fear I can't be held; fear I'm untouchable' is persistent. Difficultly so, and certainly cunning as well. My hardness comes from this belief, a pursuit of the delusion that I don't need to be touched. I force myself to take it from Bonarh, making it a key part of our arrangement. I take the belt to her and then, tell her to get me off.

While she fucks me, I'm crying. It's as if every time is the last time. There's a sense of the dire in me getting fucked. And as usual, I overreact to even my own reaction so that the dire crying quickly becomes a deep sadness and feeling of the world annihilation. Bonarh fucks me. I cry and come and think of the end of it all and then she fucks me again. My pleasure increases and my orgasm begins to mount and I fall again, push myself over the edge into tears and cries out of yes, yes. Despite the completion, I've always thought this situation marked my coming death.

January 6, 2018:
Dear Bobby:

At this point, I'm about to throw in the towel, so to speak. It's so close to the end and I don't know if I can finish this story. I'm kind of sick of this story, actually. Especially because I know the end, which

I won't give away but I will say I started in the beginning writing the way this ends, is me fucking myself and crying. So that's out of the way, again. Trying to build this into something good is too much pressure. This story, like all stories is chronic and progressive, fatal. If there is anyone who cares about this story I don't think I'm one of them.

Here's how this whole story starts: I'm ashamed from the beginning.

It's so close now, to the end and the repetition of all of it, the brain patterning and the brain trying to figure out how exactly to do this, to pull this off, to work it out, to wrest satisfaction and happiness if only I manage well. I mean, this is all I have. Literally.

Are all things permitted in this story? Then this has to be included as well. I've been trying not to include this part, the part that isn't just sad and depressed but the self-hating part, the part of the story that wonders, even while all this is being told: what am I doing? And I started out in this place, but I thought somehow all of this would have changed me, made me a better person, a good person, or at least a person, I'll be honest, who has a good story to tell. I've said from the beginning that what I want most of all is to be seen that way. Of course, in moments of grandiosity, I want to be a good person in the world, in these dark times, to have a reason for living, to be alive for a reason. Is this not what everyone wants? I actually don't know. After so many years of drinking to live and living to drink, what's the point sober. Of course, this is that sad and lonely outlook (or is it an in-look?) that I'm talking about.

The moral complexity of doing what one wants puts one in a difficult position. For one, doing what I want doesn't do anything but give me the experience that I have the freedom to do what I want. Not necessarily satisfaction, but freedom, and that actually cannot feel that great to the other people involved. I mean, even this whole year of letters has left me wondering has this even been the right thing to do, the right action for this time, and implicating you in all of it as well. I still question the consensual aspect of it all. What I'm thinking is this, which is what perhaps seemed like an exciting prospect, loosely defined as 'sending you a series of letters that describe a highly charged sexual affair' (and it might be argued, there was a precedence for this between us, during the fall of 2016) has become a powerful obsession, one I seem driven by but also fearful that without which, will I be able to finish this whole story.

And that is the parallel. As I near the end of the predetermined time frame of said affair I begin to wonder how I will be without it. And that will I, in fact. be able to just stop thinking about Bonarh.

With Canela everything is getting quite difficult, and that puts it mildly. She is wanting me to stop seeing Bonarh and I'm telling her, alternately, that I can't and, that there is an end date which is when I'll stop seeing her.

Myself, all I feel is that Canela is trying to thwart my happiness and when we talk and it quickly leads to a fight I'm mostly yelling the same thing which is: "Don't you understand how bad I feel most of the time? Can't you allow me this one happiness?" or something like that. But my agreement with Canela is that I have to be allowed to pursue what I want, that my life depends upon the freedom of doing whatever I want, whenever.

What do women want, I ask myself. And when I'm lying in the bed with Bonarh and she's reading to me the piece she's written for this trip and I'm listening and she's asking in the reading, 'What gets you off? What pleases you? How do you get off? What do you really like?' I'm feeling bad, jammed up and not free, not even free enough to say, "I don't know, I've relied so much on alcohol, been so in love with alcohol, my sexual experience seems so limited. I can't say I've ever really been able to explore what I want. Plus, with all of my ideas about not being touched or getting fucked I don't know." I don't say any of that.

January 10, 2018:
Dear Bobby:
What I do say to Bonarh as I lay her out in the bed in the little room at Orr in the afternoon or morning is about the beach. Bonarh is spread out on my lap and I'm touching her labia, clit, cunt, gently stroking and stroking, petting and rubbing and telling her about the day we spent at the beach.

"I was behind you, Bonarh, and you were facing away from me and into a tiny cave-like space where the waves had washed away a portion of the cliff, creating a double-sided open crevice that we crawled into and spread our blankets on the damp sand. We could sit up in here, this washed out area that afforded privacy and a bit of shelter from the wind and the spray of the waves as the tide went out. It was there that we kissed, and then, with my request, you sat up and stayed like that as I rubbed the crotch of your pants with the heel of my hand."

Bonarh on my lap is writhing and shifting her weight from side to side. I sip coffee from the cup on the small table with the lamp between the beds. "Please, Bonarh, be still."

"I was behind you at the mouth of this small covered grotto, facing your back as you knelt in the sand. I reached my arms around your thick waist and pulled your ass against my hips. Your shirt was already off and I paused to lift my own shirt over my head and then thought 'fuck it' and pulled my undershirt and a-shirt off as well. Now, I'm topless, too, and when I lean forward with my weight on your back, you can feel my naked breasts and belly on your skin. Your pants were already unbuttoned and I pulled them further down your thighs."

I'm getting excited now too, sipping the coffee which has gone to room temperature, no longer hot. I'm watching Bonarh as I stroke her cunt and tell her this story, slowly and slowly. As I repeat everything and ask her as I tell it again, "Is that what happened, Bonarh? Do you remember what happened next?"

Bonarh is slick and open and wet. The little room with a heater on is quite warm, warm enough for us to lay above the blankets and sheets. Bonarh is spread out across my lap and I ask her, "Bonarh, what happened next?" She shakes her head, "I don't know."

What happens next, I tell her, is that I pull her pants further down her thighs. "You were on your knees facing away from me, Bonarh, and I pulled your pants down your thighs. I pushed against you from behind and youbegan to fall forward and I pulled at your hips using your bunched-up pants as a tool, like a handle, and said to you again, 'stay up here, Bonarh' and pulled your back against me. Your bare ass was against my hips and the seam of my button-fly levis. I'm pushing into you and leaning forward on your back and expecting you to hold my weight and all of what I'm putting forth."

Rubbing stroking not fucking Bonarh I ask her again, "Do you remember this, Bonarh?" She shakes her head yes and I gently continue with her labia and clit and cunt but not fucking her. My cunt is wet.

"I reach my arms around your waist and pulling you tight against me again, I slip my hand down to your cunt. I grab your swollen clit with my fingers and begin to pull on it, jacking you off, your clit in my hand and I lean into you further and say in your ear as I grab that clit, 'I want this. This is what I want.' And as I pull you like that, pull you and push you from behind and hold onto your pants and hold you up, we begin in earnest to make an ascent, together, climbing."

Bonarh has actually begun bleeding in the little bed, her cunt reddening and her wetness thickening. I pull on her lips and spread them with my fingers, the thickness of blood inside and pooling and about to drip out.

"'I want this, this is what I want.' Do you remember I said that to you, Bonarh?" My fingers are now at the mouth of her cunt, not inside but between her lips. I slip up again to her clit, rubbing the thick hard shaft of her, grabbing with thumb and finger underneath and behind and pulling out from there, grabbing her and then again with fingers soft, stroking and stroking, and then back to her cunt. With the coffee here, bedside in the french press, with my cup from the communal kitchen here as well, I can go like this for a while.

Bonarh is worried about the blood. "Soiled the sheets? No, Bonarh, you're in danger of spilling your precious blood," and I begin stroking again, with a towel underneath her ass across my lap. "This is what witches were doing: fucking with blood and cum, drinking piss, enchanting, charming, incanting and spreading the power of their female fluids to bless the world and ride the stick of a broom. This is what witches are burned for, for slick cunts and red blood licked from fingers with no regard for anything but a circle cast to fly from," and Bonarh, when I slide, finally, my fingers inside, takes off.

January 12, 2018:

Dear Bobby:

From here we are flying then on the little bed in the little room at Orr Hot Springs, me drinking coffee and fucking Bonarh and then telling her about why the witches are burned, what the witches are doing with blood cum and piss and the rides they took on long sticks between their legs.

I pulled from my bag a bag of the clothespins and covered Bonarh's thighs and inner arms and breasts and the length of her torso, along her hips pinching just the thinnest skin with the wooden clips over her thick muscle. While she watched me, I clipped the very sensitive skin on her neck, along the sides onto her collar bones. I save for the end the area between her legs. I'm going slowly now, placing each clothespin gently on her inner thighs now. Her skin is almost hairless here. Then, closer to her lips, separating her labia and affixing four clothes pins in this small tight area, four on each side and then lining her cunt so the mouth of her cunt is framed in wood, spoke-like or the petals of a flower.

As I place these pins on her, circling and being symmetrical in my placement, I'm talking about Gayle Rubin writing in The Leather Menace, quoting Susan Sontag who writes that sexual behavior has been concentrated by christianity as the root of virtue and that everything pertaining to sex has been a 'special case' in our culture. Rubin describes the right wing in the US tapping into this erotophobia in its ascension to state power and the legislative and cultural bans on the erotic and non-reproductive pursuit of sexuality. And this was in 1989. Rubin talks about arrests at bars, porn shops and stores selling sex toys by reclassifying certain items—leather items, enema bags, dildos—as pornography and thereby having their sale fall under very strict statutes.

We have passed the right's rise at this point and the restrictions being called for by the newly elected potus speak more clearly of fascism than simply a business-as-usual, right-wing attempt to gain power. The calling for bans on immigration especially from certain countries, the calling for deportation of very specific groups of people heretofore given asylum in this country, the specific racist and misogynist vocal-ness that is being flamed with inflammatory speech. I don't want to go down this trail again, as things get worse I actually feel less and less capable of writing about this analysis. This story of a sexual affair though, during this moment, cannot help but call into question the idea of what is happening and what am I doing.

And it's here that Bonarh and I begin a discussion of what is female desire and how can it manifest personally in this political climate. Our desires for dominance and submission, for the use of leather belts to whip and bruise, for violence to be eroticized and enjoyed while fascism is prevailing, while rape culture is becoming the go-to entertainment online, narratives describing what has happened to women presented in an electronic/virtual reality and not actually bringing forth anything except that narrative, joined with others in a long scroll. I'm not an activist, I'm a woman who likes to have sex, to read about sex, to write about sex.

How can d/s be enacted without misogyny? How can an actual queerness be enacted without assimilation? Is any of this possible? How can female desire be developed in a culture of misogyny, of domination, submission, rape?

On the drive home from Orr, in Bonarh's car we stop in the town of Ukiah at the Army/Navy men's clothing store. I buy levis and socks. Bonarh buys a hat. After we go to the thrift store. It is picked over and messy, disorganized shelves and clothes on the tops of the racks, the racks full of empty hangers. Plus, the store is being 'freshened' with a chemical aerosol delivered by a device that meters the scented spray regularly. Immediately upon entering the store I can smell this chemical poison. I get a headache and fuzziness right away. I'm completely irritated as well. The device is high up on the wall of the store on the column between racks and every few minutes a soft hiss is heard and the spray can be seen. Bonarh looks at the women's clothes, I hurry through housewares. "C'mon let's go," I say after just a few minutes but on the way out the door in the case by the register I see a typewriter.

"Please may I see that machine," and it is pulled up and out for me. There was another typewriter on the shelves near the electronics but upon opening the case I see the keys all jammed together near the platen roll and the ribbon in a rat's nest of a mess, all pulled from the spool and tangled in a knot. But in the case? A hermes 3000.

January 13, 2018:
Dear Bobby:
I think the first time I came across the hermes 3000 model it was at T's house. She'd called me and said she'd done a work trade for a friend and got this portable typewriter in exchange for the work she'd done. I was kind of scoffing about it, as usual, hearing almost anything, but also because I'd ridden across town on my bike one afternoon to bring one of the many typewriters I had to give to T and now she had one she thought was better.

Let me say something about the typewriters. Most of them are portable though I do have two selectrics, and at about 40 pounds each, are anything but portable. Though this one has gone from SF to Long Island—it was my fathers' wife's—in 1994 in my postal jeep when I was driving from SF to New Mexico then to NYC and out to Long Island, spending time in NJ with my mother and then out to my Dad's in Wantagh. Out there, from his garage, he gave this model, tan selectric II. I used it to write the first letter to Michelle at his kitchen table. Then he and I made a sleeping platform in the back of the postal jeep and put the typewriter underneath. My brother and I then drove back from Queens, NY to Albuquerque, New Mexico.

The second selectric is blue, quite beautiful, the one I got while I was at his house a year ago, to begin to write to you from there. I said I wouldn't go to NYC and begin to go online and look for typewriters but I did even though I'd bought an electric typewriter with me from SF to NYC. This was the one I put in a banana box with tons of wrapping and inside it's thick-walled heavy plastic case, checking it at the curb when I got to the airport.

That one I actually brought back with me from NYC in august, carrying it on the plane this time, when I came back from NY and my brother's house, so I could bring it down to LA to continue to write you there. It's portable but heavy.

Let me say this. The machine I'm working on right now has been a work horse. I've had it now almost 25 years and it has been back and forth to NY and SF, from SF to Chicago and from Chicago to LA and back again and then down to Fort Wayne where I had it repaired by a guy who was doing 'business machine' repairs out of his garage. There was no typewriter repair shop in Fort Wayne in 2004. I can still, occasionally, by going to places like Scrap or Creative Reuse, find cartridges, high-yield correctable film. Last year, I found a place online that sells new ones.

When I've moved it, I've had to build a box to send it in, it's too long for a banana box and too heavy for just about anything else. So, with a box cutter blade and a roll of thick packing tape, wrapping, taping, adding extra cardboard and then writing fragile and 'This side up please!' put it on the truck or in the container or on the pallet myself.

As for the other machines, a few have been given to me, friends finding them in basement or garages or at their parent's houses. The portable electric in the plastic case was in a basement clean out I did for a non-profit that was worried that all the dust and dusty papers stored in the basement of their office was perhaps making some of them sick. I thought it was the work: prison reformation.

I got a couple of typewriters that type script which I know you have one too. For cards and notes, I love the idea but for longer pieces, I mean, my work is impenetrable enough. I have a couple in storage that need new ribbons. I have one little electric I gave to a kid friend. I gave another to my ex, Pristine. I have the one I found out at Scrap last year that the case smells musty and after the guy cleaned it I bought a new case for it. The guy even said it's nearly impossible to get that smell out of a typewriter but try the new case ($25). Then there is the remington rand which is quite nice though very difficult to type on, the keys so stiff and like they have no spring at all. I pull it out every once a while and try it but it's hard on the hands. I got that one to replace the one I left in Florida in 1999 at my mother's house there. She was acting crazy and I left quite suddenly, slipping my bag into the back of the car and when my parents and I were driving my girlfriend to the airport, we pulled up at the curb and I said no problem, pop the trunk and I'll get her bag from the back and then pulled my bag out and I told them I was going to see my dad but leaving the typewriter and coming back for it. But then I went from Lake

Charles to Chicago and left the typewriter in Florida. I asked them to ship it or send it or give it to a family member but my mother sold it. This portable remington looks exactly almost like one, my early 1990's typewriter from SF, when it was still easy to find typewriters in thrift stores or at yard sales.

January 15, 2018:
Dear Bobby:

All this is to say while I do have a collection of typewriters I don't consider myself a collector. I want a machine I can use, that has a good feel and the keys a nice touch, a machine that will go the long haul easily and one that can travel.

When I gave the typewriter to T, I put the machine in its case and strapped it to the front rack of my bicycle and rode across Valencia Street near the end then pushing the bike up the steep hill to her house, rang the bell of her building and she came out on the steps to meet me. It was a sunny day and we sat for a few minutes in the sun, chatting. I told her where to get the ribbons for the typewriter, over in Berkeley, but without a car it's hard to get to either of the two places. The one on University isn't too close to bart and the other on San Pablo doesn't open til noon and then sometimes when you get there at noon they still aren't there til close to one.

T sent me one or two cards typed on the machine with very light ink so that just the barest impression of the letter could be seen. It could be considered beautiful especially since this typewriter, I seriously don't even remember if it was electric or manual, had a ribbon that was red for making corrections. Not like the glorious selectric where typos can be corrected as one types but this was like black ink and then red to type over the mis-keyed strokes. So, the red portion of the ribbon, while still as dried out as the black, which is very faint like a shadow or hint of mark and then the red was darker and able to read a bit easier but the ink, like I say, was so dry that it made the typing likedusting or powdering on the page, with a lot of spray next to the lines of the letters. Like I say, this could be beautiful but I'm a typist. And I'm trying to communicate. And when you're waiting for a woman to send you a letter and then it gets there and when you open it and it's a piece of paper with some individual letters all over the paper, line breaks and most of it illegible, I don't know about anyone else but I'm disappointed. I need the substance.

Then T says she got this new typewriter. It's beautiful, she said. And the next time I went over to her house to see what she'd been working on she pulled it out. It's the hermes 3000. In a teal plastic case with a teal metal base. It's the kind of typewriter that when people see it they say oh it's so beautiful.

I don't wish I was that kind of person, though I wonder about how they are sometimes, how people like that live in this world. I mean I seriously don't relate. Now, I know most people would never want what I have, the way I am, but I do wonder. Part of what I'm thinking when I see this kind of typewriter is the way that a certain kind of store has begun to feature manual typewriters in their front windows or display cases, along with deer antlers, sheep skin rugs and hand-thrown ceramic mugs and coffee urns. Or tattoo shops that also sell jewelry will sometimes, in certain cities it's quite often, have the typewriter on display next to the flash.

This kind of harkening of hand-made-ness, juxtaposed with the naturalness of animal products, calls back 'earlier times' or frontier-style, non-electricity, homesteading lifestyle. I mean, what's next is the remington rifle, used by the genocidal militias as they pursued a 'manifest destiny' belief of expansion. But which everyone knows that lifestyle now is really only available as a result of late-stage capitalism, and that it's really only a choice for people who've made a lot of money in an industry that is completely opposite of the 'back-to-the-land-ness' that those commercial windows sell: tech in a large city, Hollywood or the movie industrial complex, working for big pharma. So, when I see a typewriter in a window of a crystal shop, that's what I'm thinking. I'm not thinking, 'oh, here is a comrade, a fellow typist, a person I can relate to'. I'm encountering someone who is basically like: "Oh, I love typewriters! They're so beautiful!"

At T's then looking over her new hermes, sitting in one of her chairs with the machine on my lap, all this hateful judgment going through my head, I lifted the top off the typewriter and rolled a piece of paper in onto the roll and began to try it a bit, the roll felt good, smooth and the platen itself grabbed the paper gently and smoothly. And then I began, typing on the top up in the corner the date and it was amazing.

The feel of the keys was perfect, so tight but with a spring behind them so that the keys felt like they were almost lifting to meet my fingers rather than being depressed, they were calling my fingers, showing my fingers without my thoughts, which letters to form which words were next. And the return and paper advance: like in a movie, left hand pushing lever and carriage sliding over to the right while paper rolled on platen and as smooth as silk. This was beautiful, this was the meaning of the beautiful. hermes 3000.

January 16, 2018:
Dear Bobby:

The meaning of the beautiful is in the action, the practice (process, praxis, practice).

Now, of course I hate being so hateful. Which is why this story meant anything at all (if it does mean anything at all) and why I had to write to you any of this; why I have to explain any of this. which is so beyond belief, it's unbelievable. It's not the sex, which of course I hope excites, the way I'm excited, still but an experience of something greater than the sum total of all these words. And by that I don't mean that the letters, both the individual stroke of every key and then each correspondence building to this long series. But, instead the act of me sitting here, sober, often—near as daily as I could imagine and manage—with enough of the sad resentment removed to express any of this.

I hate myself and I hate my condition.

Which I don't even think I have this hateful condition. I'm thinking, if only I pull something off in this world, if only I could be better or be a better person, then I'd feel better and if I felt better by being better I could be better in this world, too. I'd be a better friend, a better lover; I'd be a better cashier and a better worker. I'd be a better writer. I wouldn't feel so goddamn bad all the time and I wouldn't be so full of hate. If I could pull that off, I think, I could fit into this world, like a person.

But when I look around this so-called world, I'm sickened. I don't want to fit into a world where people are living on the street, living, literally, in their own shit on the street in a tent in the winter, in the shadow of a 40-story crane, building more luxury condos. I don't want to fit into a world where health care bankrupts the people needing care financially, and bankrupts the caregivers and everyone working in this industrial complex, spiritually. I don't want to fit into a world where health care is an industrial complex instead of just care.

I mean, I'm crying as I write this and this is just a couple of things off the top of my head from leaving my apartment this morning to go out to a meeting, walking over to the MUNI stop two blocks away and avoiding pile after pile of shit on the sidewalk. On Market Street, in San Francisco, wondering as I walk, how do people live like this and by people, I mean all of us, walking together to the train or the bus. It's 9am and rush hour.

So, I think to myself I guess if the choice is my intolerable condition requiring a spiritual solution for living in this world, I'll take being hateful because it has me having to reach for that solution the way I once reached for a drink.

When I first got sober, even after 25 years, more or less insanely drunk, I thoughtI wasn't that bad. I heard people sharing in aa and I thought, "Well, I'm not that bad..." which translates basically to, "Well, I can come back to aa, sober up, get a job and my own place, maybe convince my girlfriend to come back and then after a little while and things are going good, I can drink again." And now, every day that's what I'm gratefully reminded of: the hopeless condition.

And so then, sitting at T's apartment with the hermes 3000 on my lap, T gets out her electronic tablet and we look online for a manual for the typewriter: how are the margins set? How is the carriage release released? Why is the carriage continually re-locking? The selectric is so easy. The manual is found on a typewriter site some collector has posted and we read together the directions ('pull forward lever b while simultaneously depressing button c') and I'm doing the actions on the machine. On my lap it has a nice feeling, a good weight and even though the chair—itself, a beautiful mid-century modern style with leather seat and wooden frame, arm rest

267

on either side—I'm able to type with it like this and I write a short tiny paragraph about being at T's house with her, in the front room which is empty and by empty, I mean completely empty. Just a white space—she's in-between shows at this point—but the floor, wood, is very clean, very un-dusty even, as though it's been swept and wiped with a damp rag just before I've arrived.

And the machine on my lap. hermes 3000. Isn't it beautiful, asks, T again and again. I scoff. And then I'm typing, a short paragraph describing being with T In her clean but quite cluttered apartment (this room we're in is empty but the other two rooms are packed literally floor to ceiling with books, papers, archives, ephemera, records, paintings, plus all of this in the kitchen too and in there as well bags and jars and plates and cups and saucers and on the stove a pile of papers that is moved to the other burner when that one is needed) and it's beautiful.

January 19, 2018:
Dear Bobby:

The hermes 3000 is like slicing a warm knife through butter or a loaf of bread with a serrated edge, so easy but an ease that feels good, that the effort expended, though slight, feels effortless and in the effortless there is the feeling of as if no effort is being spent. That's beautiful.

And at T's house, there in the chair with the arm rests and the typewriter on my lap, I'm feeling this. T is at my feet, on the floor, watching as I'm on her machine, enjoying myself. I'm typing a para-graph-sized story of being there like this. She got this machine in a work trade with someone who got it on a European trip, perhaps in Switzerland, I don't remember, but T said this guy had a friend who she also knew who also had a hermes from the same trip. Should she contact him for me? Perhaps I'd like to buy it from him?

At the same time, like most of the time, I'm not in the market for another typewriter. As I said, I'm not a collector, I'm a user and now that I was in the small apartment with Canela, there wasn't room for a typewriter, or at least not another one. The selectric was under the bed in its vinyl cover. The portable I liked was in the closet and

268

could be brought out when needed but even that's hard when one is laying abed, one is usually not thinking oh, I need to take out the typewriter. So, it came out for special occasions. Plus, there were two or three typewriters in the kitchen up high on the cabinets, a couple in storage and one or two in the closet. I told T I'd think about it, but mostly my answer was no.

The second time I came across a hermes 3000 is at the place that used to be on Telegraph Avenue: Total Estate Liquidators. I was on a date with Michelle one Sunday afternoon and maybe we had her dog in the car or we were going someplace else but we stopped here. This place bought entire households and then sorted the stuff and sold it out at Alameda (the good stuff) or in the store front (the ok stuff and some jewelry and paintings) and then in the back yard of the store there were piles and piles and stuff piled on tables and under a shed and then also toward the back, under a big blue tarp (the crap). We looked around. I looked at the huge selection men's ties and found a couple I liked but when I asked I think it was $8 or something like that (it's hard for me, after being in Chicago in the early 2000's to pay more than $1 for an old tie, even if it is silk). I went out into the yard. It had rained that day earlier or the day before and there were still small puddles both on the ground and in the coffee cups and bowls on the tables. And then way in the back, near the shed I saw the hermes case.

I grabbed the machine and brought it inside to the store because even though there were so many tables outside in the yard there wasn't a drop of space to put the machine on. So inside, I put the case on the floor and from the front pocket of my levis I pulled a piece of paper. I rolled the notebook paper in the typewriter and felt the beginning of the good feeling as the platen roll grabbed the softened lined paper and rolled it on. And then the trying of the typing. The ribbon was old and dry, for sure, and it was difficult to make an accurate assessment with me and my body hovering over the machine on the floor, peering forward and squinting, since I'd forgotten my glasses.

Something was not quite right. Yes, the ribbon was bad and the machine needed cleaning but also...well, I couldn't put my finger on it. Was the type size smaller than the machine at T's? Is that it? It seemed tiny (this is 12 and I wouldn't go smaller that this). And like I say I'm not a collector so I really don't know anything about the hermes or its many options. The type seems tiny, the ribbon dry (a ribbon at my repair shops cost $25) so when I ask them at the liquidators the cost of this machine and they say $25, I balk. I think about it for a second and then a second more. I show it to Michelle and the soft paper in my hand. "I think the type size is too small," I say. And we leave.

And then think about it for the next few weeks. Was the type too small? How could I compare it to T's machine without making a plan with her and going over and asking if I could use the hermes? It did have that feel though, that's what I kept thinking, the feeling of rolling the paper on the platen roll, the feel of the keys under my fingers, the page return lever in my hand, ah, so easy, so smooth. The feeling, yes, the feeling was there. But was the type too small? It seemed tiny. When I looked and looked again at the sample I'd typed on the notebook paper, it did seem small, squinty small. But was T'S like that?

Michelle later said she went back to the store to buy me the hermes but it had been sold.

January 20, 2018:
Dear Bobby:
After the trip to Orr then as we are leaving, checking out, Bonarh went to get one of the large open two-wheeled carts from near the front gate. We loaded our bags and then while I went into the kitchen to get our food from the refrigerator and from the back shelves, Bonarh went to the parking lot across the road to bring her car to the closer lot for loading. I piled the bags and boxes of food onto the already full cart and left it for Bonarh to wheel.

It was not afternoon, I'm sure. We probably ate lunch already and went into the tubs on the upper deck. The water isn't as hot as the waters at Wilbur or Harbin but it's very pleasant to fill a tub of the deck under the redwoods and read a book like that. We'd fucked all morning in the bed, me talking and telling Bonarh about fags and dykes and witches and blood and cum and piss and then I cried.

As we got into the car then I was going down. It was time for me to meditate. I'd already drank as much coffee as I could and I had a jar of brewed maté for the afternoon but I was getting irritated and annoyed. Time to meditate for sure but how to meditate in the car while Bonarh is driving uphill along the long windy road back to Ukiah. I'll try, there's no choice.

It's terrible. Usually car meditations are great, when the car isn't moving. Meditating in a car parked in a sunny spot, or in the shade if it's summer and hot, windows slightly opened, especially with another person in the car meditating together it's like the meditation fills the car and then the meditation is deeper. But in a moving car, this is like only when nothing else is available. Of course, I should have said to Bonarh, 'pull over to the side of the road in a sunny spot while I finish my meditation' but I didn't. It's like my vanity. I want to look good and for some reason I don't think it looks good to be like, "I NEED to meditate." I want to look like I got this and like I'm meditating as a spiritual person. I don't want to look like I'm about to go crazy and tell her to go fuck herself. But I am. And a meditation of going uphill in a car and being shifted left to right as we go curve to curve doesn't provide the relief I need. When I come out, after opening my eyes repeatedly during the 20 minutes to check to see what Bonarh is doing, I don't feel fantastic. I'm still down, I think, full of self-centered self-pity, but I notice that I haven't told her to fuck off, so something must have happened even if I don't think so.

In Ukiah, the first stop is the Army/Navy Men's store. Most of the clothes: wool shirts, especially, but also duo-fold thermal shirts and some quilted jackets, are all too big. I think most of the sizes started at 'L' and went up to 'XXL' and bigger in some cases. I looked at socks too but them also, too big. Bonarh got a hat. Just about as we were leaving and I was telling the two guys who worked there that my men's store in San Francisco that I'd been shopping at for 25 years had just closed (Kaplan's: RIP) and then in the front I saw their levis 501s. I looked through them quickly and found a pair of 32/29's! I bought these and was quite happy.

Then we went to the thrift store with its air freshener being pumped into the sore and quickly giving me a headache and making me foggy. I was nauseous and sick to my stomach. Then I saw the hermes 3000. It is a beautiful machine, since I've had my experience on it though I personally don't like that seafood teal color that got popular in the 50's and 60's. I opened the case on the glass case it was in, near the front of the store. I tried it out and it had that feel. Now I was sure it hadn't been a coincidence at T's house on her machine, that I hadn't imagined this was an amazing typewriter to type on. Now, I'd had the experience with hers and then at the estate sale store and now here in Ukiah. I had a headache, and no glasses on though, and the smell seemed to be getting stronger. Then I heard the sound 'pssssss' and looked over at the top of a column in the store and saw the industrial strength air freshener pumping the chemicals into the store. I felt worse.

I asked the manager how much for the typewriter and he said $85. I made a face to show him my displeasure and then turned to leave. I'd put a piece of lined notebook paper on the machine though, from my front pocket of my levis and when I look at that paper scrap even now I wonder what I was thinking because the letters are clear. The ribbon wasn't too dry, I can see all the letters. But I was sick.

Outside on the sidewalk for some fresh air I begin to tell the hermes story to Bonarh. "The bottom line," I say to her, "is that I don't need another typewriter and not for $85." Bonarh offers to go in and steal it for me. She says, "I'm here to serve you."

January 21, 2018:
Dear Bobby:
What I want is to slow all this down so I can experience it. The days are getting shorter, nights longer and the store is getting busy as the big fall meal approaches. Bonarh is spending the meal and that weekend in NYC with her family so before she leaves we meet on monday night during my evening meal break.

Bonarh arrives, as instructed without lipstick and waits by the water cases. I smile to see her and the next time I look up and over at her, she's applied the lipstick, red, and is holding her new crushable hat from Ukiah in her hand. The last few customers go slowly, it seems, the orders are large, everyone buying for the big meal later in the week, everyone excited and wanting to chat, as usual, I'm conscious of performing 'cashier' for her, for the customers, for myself. The actions arranged, enacted, choreographed: 'This is how to ring up groceries in a worker-owned organic market.' The ease at these moments makes me so happy, as I forget myself as 'cashier' and simply execute, carry out, each movement and gesture ('lift the keyboard to fit holiday celery—extra-long with leaves—fully on the scale to be weighed, greet customer with a silent but welcoming glance, slight smile of hello') an intricate dance with conventionalized movements feels so grand and suddenly grandiose as I reach for the receipt from the printer on the cash drawer, tear it off and half turn, smiling to the customer, hand them the long strip like a banner, a flag unfurling overhead, the finale. "Thank you so much for shopping here" and a slight nod of my head. And, on to re-enact.

I have fear I'm running out of time, even here. My brother is coming from NYC and then immediately after Leah coming to stay. During this is the last time Bonarh and I will see each other. I'm trying to keep up with all of this and also trying to work it out with Canela. Plus, the usual fear I can't do this. I mean, what am I doing.

I put the closed sign at the end of the register, begin to gather bag and books and pen from cash drawer top and put the lid on my water canteen, tightly. My relief is here. Swinging bag onto my shoulder as I log out of the register, I turn and look at Bonarh. She's waiting for me, looking at me. I walk over to her and lightly touch her arm to lead her outside the store. As we walk, she says her car is in the back lot. "We don't have time for that tonight," I say. We exit the store onto 13th Street and cross under the freeway overpass. It's already dark outside and so this then is quite dangerous: jaywalking four lanes of traffic, crossed with hardly any light from street lights even.

On the other side we walk around a bit. Bonarh will wear the harness to NYC, during the time she's gone. And I say, "You will write to me your experience of wearing the harness like this, in NYC, with your family, during the big meal and whatever else you do." "Yes, Cashier," she says. The time seems to go quickly though in the way the night does when it's darker longer but so fast. My excitement from seeing her without the lipstick and then looking over again, seeing her with lipstick on has swept through me deeply and quickly. Since I'm at work during this, though, all of it doesn't fully register in my thoughts until later, when I'm back at work, back at the register.

During the time we are out on the street there are questions and concerns and directions for Bonarh. I'm slapping her face, kissing her and lifting her shirt to see her bare breasts outlined with the harness. I'm pushing my hips into hers, pushing her back against the old warehouse on 12th Street. I'm holding her face with her hand, lifting her head up slightly and slightly turned away from me so I can leer at her with my mouth close to her ear. I'm stepping back away from her, telling her, "Lift your shirt for me," and then watching as she almost blushes, lifts her shirt above her breasts, baring them to the passing cars' headlights. I'm smiling and excited and then hurrying back to the register.

Back at the register, I'm wanting more time, time to lay and listen to Bonarh read to me the stack of letters she's written to me. Time to look at all the bruises that have come up since the week before with the flogger and clothes pins. In the street lights, they appear as shadows lining her arms and the leather straps under her breasts across her ribs seem to make shadows as well: these places where the flogger reached around her thick middle and bit her in the front. And then, yes, my teeth marks on her shoulders where I bit hard and long, leaving the snaggle-toothed impression that identifies me. There's too much I want to do, too much I want to listen to: her comments, questions, assertions, and to hear her through all of this.

The next morning at 4:30am Bonarh leaves me a message: she's begun reading Genet to me.

January 29, 2018:
Dear Bobby:

I communicate with Bonarh. "Please write to me of your experiences in the harness while you are in NYC: who you see, what they do, if they encounter the harness, if you show them, when you wear it, etc. I want a lot," I say.

In the morning, Canela and I have a fight. We are driving out to Baker beach. Do you piss on her?" She asks after reading that section in Urban Aboriginals. I say, after a lot of talking, "Listen, I don't want our relationship based on a mind-fuck, bondage situation. That is not hot. I don't want to be a lazy, self-hating asshole ordering you around. I want to feel confident, assured, finding what's erotic to me." We jumped in the water and the tide was so low we got tumbled back on the shore repeatedly and couldn't swim.

The post-climax letdown of the trip the previous week settled in saturday and sunday. After all the preparation and excitement and physical-ness, the regret shows up as fear: fear I should have been better, fear I should have been more present, fear I should have praised her more. Right now, I'm at the effect of how this will end and I'm stuck, stumped. I don't have any more ideas.

Bonarh is on her way to NYC. She doesn't wear the harness through the TSA check point, which I think is wise. It's in her bag and when she gets through security she goes into the bathroom and puts it on in the stall, removing her shirt, jacket already on the hook, (brought for NYC but too hot in SFO) slipping the long thick strap down the front of her pants and grabbing it between her legs and then snapping it closed in the front on the cock ring. The heavy shoulder straps go on like a shirt, staying buckled and Bonarh's arms go through and then the whole thing is on, heavy. She puts her shirt back on and then at the sink, hand washing and lipstick application, bright red.

I send her a text from work, 'Come for me at the gate while you wait for your flight to be called and imagine me standing, also waiting to board the plane with my carry-on bag at my feet, my arms folded over chest and I'm watching you.'

Bonarh doesn't get the text until after she's already boarded so in the moments before all devices must be turned off and all trays in their upright and locked positions, she responds: 'I'm on board already, in my seat but wanting to take advantage of your permission so quickly given and on SF soil and so I squeezed my thighs together and looked from my window seat, past my seat mate across the aisle and saw you, Cashier, turned from your seat, leaning slightly into the aisle, watching me and without touching myself, came almost immediately: squeezing with some heavy breathing and the harness pressing on my clit, it's enough, especially with you watching and knowing what I'm doing for you.' She continues, 'As we take off then, I turn from you and look out the window and there is a big fucking rainbow in the sky. It seems like it's right outside my window and the crest of it is in the clouds. What is this divine, again, upon coming for you?'

My brother comes from NYC tonight. The store is busy and after a few days of cashiering I'm glad for the holiday closure. My shoulders, arms, and hips are sore from standing and pushing groceries. Canela, my brother and I drive up north and have a meal with friends. While there, in a back room, Canela and I fuck quietly while everyone else is still at the dinner table. Her pussy is as sweet and soft as ever, and I'm smiling as I slide my thumb in easily and gently, looking in her eyes and both of us feeling the surprise and joy of this ease and practice.It's so good.

When I go back to work on saturday, it's the rotate, 9am-3pm. It's mostly relaxed, though I'm on the express lane. I text to Bonarh in NYC that I will call her at noon today. It's my break and I am upstairs in the lounge, leftovers spread before me with cheese and chips.

Bonarh is in Brooklyn. "Are we chatting, Cashier?" She flirts as we talk about the past couple of days and she's telling me about the NYC weather. "Is this the chatting you don't do, Cashier?" "No, Bonarh, I'm waiting for you to express all your nervous excitement and to land in with me." I hear her gasp on the other end. I say I've missed her and then send a text while we are on the call: 'the definition of 'tether': noun 1. A rope of chain with which an animal is tied to restrict its movement. syn: rope, chain, cord, leash, lead. verb 1. Tie (an animal) with a rope or chain so as to restrict its movement, hitch.' I tell her it requires a lot of energy, focus, holding the cord so tightly while she's been across the country.

As we speak, Bonarh says she got the text. "I accept," she says. I laugh. "You already have," I said, and then I said, "Say it again." And she did, and again, same thing and then I said, "Do you feel me slapping your face every time you say you accept?" She moaned.

January 30, 2018:
Dear Bobby:

Bonarh is in NYC, wearing my harness. I've written to her, before she left, that she should make extensive notes of her experience wearing my harness as she goes on her trip. Please, I add, but it isn't really a request. Include, I continued, in the documentation as many details as possible. Bonarh, please include when and where you put it on, when you take it off, what clothes you wear over my harness, your sleep, your other activities in my harness. I want a lot.

After Bonarh has been in NYC for a few days, we are able to speak on the phone. I call her during my break at work from upstairs in the lounge. Bonarh is in Brooklyn and on the call, she's telling me about the NYC weather during the last week in november: "It's cold, I'm wearing layers of wool and the grey sky overhead feels low, like a curtain held by the leaf-less tree branches in the park, a fine gauzy fabric draped on top of the bare trees." Lovely. Bonarh thinks we're chatting. No, Bonarh, I'm waiting for you to land in with me here.

Yes, she says, I accept. I laugh finally, my own excited energy dissipating and allowing me to be here too. You already have, I say. She laughs, the small sound of breath escaping that sounds almost like a 'yes'. Say it again, I say. "I accept." Again. "I accept." The same thing and then, "Do you feel me slapping your face every time you say it?" and she moaned.

I want to see you after work on monday, clear off tuesday morning as well. But before she can answer, we are at the end of the call. My break is over, time to get back on the register and finish the shift. I'm telling Bonarh, as we near the end, that we have to put the dick through the harness again. Then, Bonarh, you'll stand real close to me and I'll put the dick between my legs. I was grabbing the straps of the harness, even with Bonarh in NYC, I can feel the leather straps in my hand already, thinking about her fucking me on monday.

On sunday my brother and Canela and I have dinner. He's talking about our mother, her violent outbursts and her pathological remorse after these insane violent overreactions. She was full of self-pity. Meanwhile, we're like "We're hungry." Our mother's constant selfishness and self-centeredness.

Right now, I'm kind of disappointed and sick with myself and my failure and my inability to write any of this. Canela and I had a great scene the other night and then she went to a movie and I cleaned up after a roast chicken dinner. I said to Leah, "Yeah, this whole thing has been great, new heights and amazing experiences but it's like I have fear I haven't even been able to fully enjoy this because of Canela's overreactions. I can't even think of Bonarh, let alone process any of this with for myself. I can't share any of it, any of what I'm doing, experiencing or learning, with Canela, not because I'm keeping it from her or because I'm developing intimacy but because everything I say, Canela twists around and throws back in my face."

Now, I can't believe I'm saying any of this. I'm sure I've said it though, exactly, these exact lines over the past 6 weeks so many times I can't count. But, I mean, I can't believe I'm still writing the same things about my mother either.

I'm trying to explain this, to explain how the wreckage of the past is being displayed. Manifest? No, seen; I'm seeing my inventory, again. Which there is relief, with that experience. It's never the other person. It's always the wreckage of the past. Which in itself is basically unbelievable, basically requires a spiritual experience to even write it. It's not happening now.

But meantime, this kind of inventory does make it seem impossible to try and write any of it. I mean, all the inventory makes it all impossible. Doing anything for that matter, anything that doesn't have anything to do with trying to make 'mommy' happy: laundry, cooking, vacuuming. Does any of this even make any sense or is this just more excuses? I can't write about any of the scenes or ideas I'm having, I mean I haven't been able to write almost anything except the barest description of being at Orr with Bonarh or any of the ideas, which seemed so great, I was thinking up there. Then my brother here and Leah after him and the big meal day that has work so busy I don't have the capacity to write between the customers while cashiering, and then everything so fucked up all the time with me and Canela. Near constantly.

Fear Canela needs constant attention. Fear I can't actually see this project to completion, fear I can't write any of this. Fear I won't remain principled.

February 1, 2018:
Dear Bobby:

Around this time, I begin finding playing cards on the street regularly again. The three of diamonds shows up twice in short succession: works. "I am now ready to give everything and receive everything." I take this deeply to heart even while being aware of the extreme grandiosity of this charge. I mean, everything? I'm trying and feeling the futility.

Bonarh arranges her schedule to be available to me monday night to tuesday morning. She contacts me to let me know. She says she wants to be ready for me when I come and want her. She really looks forward to seeing me. In the morning, there is another call and installation of Genet being read for me. She texts, 'She who wants a lot gets it,' and adds, 'I roil with question marks sent, the no's, the commands, they thrill me. I am wet for you." Later, Bonarh calls and asks to come for my pleasure.

I call back and tell her, "Bonarh, your message was so clear. And your voice so loud and clear, too. It pleases me so much to hear you, to hear you speak about being so uncomfortable, either way, calling or not. And then of course, you asking to come for my pleasure, is so pleasing to me. Thank you. I feel quite good, so looking forward to seeing you tomorrow evening."

Bonarh responds quickly, via text: 'does it please you to fuck with me?'

'I'm not fucking with you.I'm saying no, Bonarh. And telling you how much you please me and telling you what pleases me.It will please me for you to wait for me.'

Bonarh texts, 'spell it to me, yes'

I write: 'I want you ready to please me tomorrow night. I want you to be ready and wanting to please me. I want you hard and ready and hot for me, to please me.'

Bonarh: 'yes I want this so much too ok soon, yes finally soon enough' and she reads the final installment of Genet for me.

After work, I've borrowed the truck from Leah, I drive over to Oakland. (The way the bay area is now even driving over the bridge at 10pm there's a lot of traffic.) It's late when I arrive and so I quickly greet Bonarh, a quick kiss hello, and pull her close to me, hold her tightly for a few moments. "You landed?" I ask and she says yes. "Are you ready?" She says yes. "Ok, I'm gonna go piss. You get a chair from the kitchen and bring it in here. I'll meet you back here momentarily." I piss and wash up after work, wash the money off my hands and face. Back in Bonarh's room, I take off my shirt, stand in a-shirt and t-shirt and from my bag I pull out my dick. I toss it to Bonarh. "Take off your pants and shirt and put this through the cock ring in the harness." I stand in front of Bonarh while she prepares.

Bonarh sits on the kitchen chair. She's wearing the harness and she holds the dick in her fist. She's pulling on it and already she's turned on. She lifts her hips as she pulls and makes a hissing sound through her teeth. It's late so I don't fuck around. I take off my boots and pants and then pull my boots back on. I rub my clit a bit watching her sit on the chair. She looks up at me.

I sit on Bonarh's hips, facing her. I grab the straps of the harness, the thick leather up near her shoulders in my hands and lean away from her, holding myself up and pulling her toward me. The dick is between us and pulling this way and shifting my hips forward, I can get the dick tip to rub against my clit, from underneath, like a pulling there too. My cunt is wet and I shift on her lap again.

Sitting on the dick then, using my hand to hold it while I slip on, I let myself go. I'm on her hips as she sits on the chair in her room and I'm really riding it, fucking on the dick on Bonarh and going for it. Enjoying it, actually. My boots are braced on the rungs under the chair and I'm able to lift up and slide down pushing with my feet and on Bonarh's shoulders. I lean and kiss Bonarh, open mouthed. With our mouths together, I lean in deeply and then I'm fucking the dick with just my hips, slamming myself into Bonarh hard and fast and liking it.

Suddenly, the rumination in my brain starts: "I've never been fucked like this before." I want to say this while we fuck, I want to say this and forget it but I know that that is what I always say. But it's distracting, meanwhile. The dick feels so good and I've told Bonarh "sit still" and I'm taking the dick deeper in my cunt and leaning again forward, pulling Bonarh to me, and with the harness straps in my hands, the harness rubs my clit and I'm brought close to the edge repeatedly.

February 2, 2018:
Dear Bobby:

Sitting on Bonarh's lap as she sits in a chair from her kitchen. It's late after work on monday night. I'm just off of work and she's just back from NYC. She's wearing my harness, thick leather straps with wide buckles that cross her chest under breasts around her ribs and then down her belly, around her thick middle and between her legs. The cock ring holds my dick. Is she fucking me or am I fucking myself up on top here like this, lifting and thrusting against her hips in the chair, sliding myself on the dick, pulling off as far as I can while the tip stays in my cunt, just the tip, and then slowly pushing myself back in, back on, until my clit rubs on the edge of the harness. I'm pulling and pushing with the straps of the harness and telling her to sit still while I ride like this, on her.

As I start to build, as I start to climb, as I start to feel really good, forgetting what I want to tell Bonarh about how I've never been fucked like this before and then explain that even though I'm trying to say that, it's not true and not understanding that either and then feeling my orgasm start to mount and I'm getting closer and tighter and I reach between my own legs and start to jack off my clit, rubbing as I slide off the dick and then rubbing harder as I push back on the dick. Bonarh is watching me and as I come close to her, grabbing the harness and pulling her closer to me, I kiss her. Her hands are on my hips and I'm rubbing and fucking and then I roll off of her lap.

Then I'm on my back on the fur rug on her floor and Bonarh is fucking me again. The dick is too loose to fuck this way so she switches to using her hand. Again and again and I'm coming. It's great and I say don't stop. I come again and again, Bonarh fucking me and I'm rubbing my clit, hard and swollen and thick and tight as my cunt gets stretched around her hand. She's leaning over me, in the harness and the is dick hanging limply off her hips. I reach up with my other hand and fuck her from underneath and she's spraying and soaking us and the rug and I'm pushing myself to come again, my clit now getting raw and sore and I'm straining on my back, holding my legs tight and clenching my belly and getting it, again.

Then I flip Bonarh over onto her back and I'm on top and I fuck her straight up, my fingers pumping her cunt and I'm holding her by the strap of the harness near her shoulder asking her, "Isn't this what you wanted?" Yes, yes, she says and the rug is wet beneath us. The next morning, Bonarh fisted me just about, very close and I came many times again. I thought of the time Canela fucked me like that in the morning, with the sun on my bed.

Through this whole thing I'm wanting to get approval, I'm wanting to impress this one or that one and then I'm reminded I have to do this for myself. If it doesn't feel good what's the point. This better feel good to me or else why do it any of it. I'm still wanting to be seen for what I'm doing but my experience is that what I'm doing doesn't feel that good. What I'm doing is wanting to get approval, wanting to be taken care of, wanting to find what I need and none of that feels good.

The next day, the obsession with Bonarh is growing, the idea of Bonarh is growing. There is the element of this situation in which the turn-on isn't felt physically, as not necessarily 'a hard dick' but it's felt in my brain, like as an intellectual stimulation. What can I say, what can I do to get what I want from Bonarh.

Leah, Canela and I drive out to the beach. The water is cold and we had to swim at Crissy Field today with all the dogs. Aquatic Park was the finish line of a big race so we couldn't get close and the waves out at Baker are too rough to get in. Canela, Leah and I wade into the water at Crissy Field and swim with the dogs.

I'm sad and lonely. I'm bored and comparing myself to Bonarh, feeling bad about all of it: fear I missed an opportunity, fear Bonarh had a better time with this, fear Bonarh's gotten more out of this. It's evil, it's evil corroding fears. I got to feel more than good because I feel worse than bad.

I work on sunday morning and then ride my bike home to meditate on the couch before getting in the van and driving across the bridge to meet Bonarh.

We meet at the butcher on Broadway in Oakland. There is the

extreme turn-on of Bonarh's waitingestness. I pull up from over the bridge and across town and park in front. Bonarh is inside sitting wrapped in wool with bright red lipstick, just applied, waiting with water. We then wait at the counter, pacing heavy breathing. If this was on Long Island or in NYC there would be a second butcher working who'd ask whose next. Instead, we're waiting while this guy takes his time making sliced beef. Finally, our turn: bologna and steaks.

February 3, 2018:
Dear Bobby:
We're at the butcher and if this were Long Island, there'd be another butcher asking whose next. Instead, we're waiting while the guy behind the counter slices beef thinly, with great care. Finally, it's our turn: bologna. Steaks. We'd drunk the medicinal strength maté while waiting and by now, I'm shaking. I might be shaking by now anyway, I'm so excited to see Bonarh. I'm then paying and gathering packages of meat and crossing the street to the van, opening the slider side door, putting in the packages—I forgot a bag so they are just laid on the floor—and turn and slap Bonarh. I talk about waiting, how tired I was of waiting.

We are in the same spot we were weeks ago, 40th and Broadway, 'kink corner' reads the graffiti on Mama's Royale Café. Passersby ignore us as I slap her face and grab her collar and pull her towards me. I get behind her there and then in front of her and kiss her and then I shape her hands like a yoni on the back rack and fuck her like that too.

We get in the van then and drive up behind the Claremont Hotel. We park on the street up there, where there are signs posted on the telephone poles and some of the security gates, warning that this area is under video surveillance with a picture of a video camera next to a video camera. I lock the van, we gather our few things and walk the half block to the entrance to a little park up here, behind the hotel, above both Oakland and Berkeley. It's dark and the park is empty but the sign says it's open til 8pm. The wide dirt path is easy to walk on. Bonarh says in february baby owls are in the trees with signs posted 'keep your dogs on leash'. Lights from the cities below twinkle, and then, behind and above us, lights from houses up on the crest, also twinkle. It's a clear night tonight but still there's a stream of pollution lightening the sky like a klieg with the lights from planes, looking like drones or space craft from our position, looking up at the stars, as Bonarh begins to call out the constellations by name.

Up here is another sign about video surveillance so we cross off the path to a large eucalyptus on the side of this hill. There's a large log here too and this is where we set down our bags and coats. I begin to gather a handful of sticks and stones and with breath and intention, throw to the four directions for protection. Then, "What do you want to tell me, Bonarh?" Bonarh says she has intense gratitude for this experience. She says she's not analyzing, not being nostalgic, not writing it either, but expressing it live. "I'm so grateful for your exquisite care, Cashier," she says, "Thank you."

I stand from where we've sat on the log. I put out my hand to Bonarh and bring her to her feet as well. I toss the rest of the sticks and stones and lead her to the base of the large eucalyptus. "Are you ready, Bonarh?" I ask as I take off my belt. It's windy and cold up here.

It's windy and cold up here, even in the lea of a tree, with its strips of bark flapping like a flag blowing in the wind. Once I've taken off my sweater and blue shirt, and stripped to my skin, pulling off my double undershirt as well, I move to Bonarh. The belt pulled off my pants didn't go around her neck but hangs down from my back pocket while I unbutton her wool coat—her serape is already on the log near our bags—then her silk shirt, and I lift her undershirt, a ripped cotton thin tank top, up over her head. Once we have our shirts off and are standing bare, we barely feel the wind, it's that cold.

I lean Bonarh forward against the tree. It's a eucalyptus grove again. I tell her how to take the belt: "Don't tense up and resist me, absorb it." And then I begin with the belting of her. Her belt is removed as well, also now hanging with her undershirt from my back pocket. I'm swinging my soft belt doubled in my fist, swinging, hitting her ass, hips, shoulders, repeatedly and then with my hands. She's screaming. No, she's actually not screaming, she's just saying ouch but two or three times after I've struck her she's walked away from the base of the tree. The third time I go to her and take her hand and place her in position against the tree again. "Lean forward, don't tense, step your feet back and wider apart; absorb this." Behind her I'm standing in levis, topless, engineer boots on.

My open palms now are hitting her, not slapping her and now she is screaming. and in the midst of this, her crying and the breaks, I'm bending down behind her, squatting and kissing all the spots the belt has licked. Then standing and pulling her ass against my hips to fuck her, grind against her how she likes it, how she's come before for me, for my pleasure. Then another time, I'm squatting and leaning against the tree myself, between her and the tree trunk, kissing and caressing her, taking her nipple in my mouth.

February 4, 2018:
Dear Bobby:

I'm squeezed in between Bonarh and the tree trunk, squatting and leaning with the trunk against my bare skin on my back. The smooth eucalyptus feels warm like life. I'm caressing her and taking her nipples in my mouth. I'm not wearing a shirt, just levis and my engineer boots. I have on nipple clamps, tweezer style with a medium length chain, and also my crystal which is re-hung on a leather cord. Of course, Bonarh is in the harness.

And then the beautiful fucking, the wet messy beautiful fucking; I've laid my sweater on the ground and Bonarh lays on top of it. I pull her pants down and then her voice is carrying, the yelling and screaming up the hill is rousing the people who live here, outdoors, to reveal themselves, turning on their flashlights to signal to us with their hollers and shouts of, "Oh yeah" matching our laughter, back and forth, up and down the hill.

Up behind the voices, past where their light is flashing to us, is the lights of the large house. The stream of light that emanates from the very large picture window—the glass seems from down here to form one wall of the house—overlooking all of the lower Berkeley hills, the campanile at UC, the marina, then the flats of Oakland and its docks and container cranes and all the way, on a night like tonight, to San Francisco's skyline, across the new bridge to Treasure Island

and past to the old span: this multi-million dollar view, from this window, streams a beam of light as if it were a signaling flashlight itself, the light reaching into what would out here otherwise be a dark sky, light pollution filling this night, pouring out.

Yes, I say, signaling to us the problems of money, property, and prestige, that's what is being communicated, not success or wealth but problems, obviously, if so much pollution is coming out, what could be happening there that is good.

In the shadow of this Bonarh comes and anoints the ground and soaks the leaves and strips of bark on which we lay, calling out her pleasure and mine, to the lightened sky and passing planes and drones and surveillance cameras and the people up on the hill, in their hidden tents, laughing.

Laughter is a signpost for a new freedom and a new happiness.

Later, Bonarh and I drive to Piedmont Avenue to get something to eat. It's almost the same problem as last time: a sunday evening in Oakland on Piedmont Avenue means most places are closed but this time the burger place is open and we go in. There is one other small group in there still eating and we get our burgers and fries and hurry up and eat it all.

I'm smashing the meat into my mouth with one hand, I'm so hungry, I haven't eaten since 11:30am, and shoving a burger into Bonarh's mouth with my other hand, feeding her in public the meat with no bun and telling her, "Wait, here are the fries," stuffing her mouth full.

Back at her house that night, I'm sitting on the little couch in her room. After eating, I'm calmer, resting a bit, deeper in my body as I land from soaring above it all in the hills. Bonarh is between my legs on the floor in front of me, her back against the couch. She's reading to me from the little book she wrote while she was in NYC wearing my harness. I'm running my fingers through her hair, petting and fingering and combing while she reads to me. My head is thrown back on the back of the couch and my eyes are closed listening to her experiences and her descriptions for me.

Suddenly, I start to cry, hard. This beautiful time is almost over, that's why I asked her to write this in the first place.

I've slept over, and the next morning, I wake and do the steps.

Bonarh makes me a cup of coffee and while I drink it, she lays in my lap. I'm combing her hair again with my fingers, pulling lose strands and rolling them in a ball. She begins to express herself: "When I came back to the tree," she says. "You mean when I led you back to the tree?" "Yes," she says, "when you brought me back to the tree, I thought, 'you can hit me forever', I mean with breaks of course." Of course.

Our ritual on the hill, shirtless, fucking, drinking cum.

Bonarh continues: "I have fear you feed me too much."

"Too often?" I ask

"No, too much. Too much food at once and too much food overall."

"Oh, yeah, I like your mouth so full you can barely close it."

"I don't have fear you will kill me, but I thought I would mention it."

"You thought you would mention that you don't have fear I will kill you?"

"Yes, I mean, the thought has gone through my head, but I don't have fear you will kill me."

We speak next about the ending. Next week will be the last time we are together. Bonarh will remove my harness and we will part. This is what both people want. She said, "I can get behind the idea."

February 6, 2018:

Dear Bobby:

The next morning, we are lying in bed, talking about, among other things, the problems of money, property, and prestige. ("It's not that those things might cause a problem if you get them; They are a problem. Pursuing them, getting them, keeping them, what to do once you get them. A problem." "Well then," Bonarh asks, "What to do? What does someone do in this world? What's there to do if you aren't pursuing money property prestige?" At this point I interject: "Sex, security, society..." "Yeah! What?" "Thank god for the steps. Thank god to be able to do something with all my ideas of "I gotta be somebody!") Bill says there's 100 forms of fear and they boil down to two: fear I'm not going to get what I want; fear I'm going to lose what I have.

The end is rapidly approaching. Bonarh and I will be separating. We will spend next weekend together and then, at the end of the weekend, with intention and consideration, Bonarh will remove the harness, return it to me and we will separate, end this arrangement. I said to her, "I mean, we both want this, or more accurately, this is what both people want." She said, "I can get behind the idea."

We're fucking while we talk about this, in her bed in the morning. We both have to be at our work today but as Bonarh puts it, "Time doesn't exist with you, Cashier." I laugh and say, "I don't exist," as I fuck her, squatting between her open spread legs, my hand sliding in and then just pumping her cunt as she's coming, shaking, soaking the bed beneath us. She's saying it's so good, so good. "Oh, Bonarh, nothing good ever came from me."

She has questions about if she's sexy enough. But what does that mean, sexy? I ask her and she doesn't really know. Does she just want to hear that from me? But it's not what I'm looking for, I tell her, sexy? No, I crave power and honest expression.

Then we flip and I'm fucking her from behind in the ass, lube my thumb and fingers, push her face in the pillows and my other hand holding a glass jar beneath her as she comes. This is the cum we drink while I tell her what to do, what to say, how to come back to me, the raveling, cording, tethering to call her back, all her ideas of hitting her forever.

The next day I'm working. My body's sore. In the morning, Canela generously massaged me and I had a breakthrough, crying and I really let go with it. She asked have you been writing about this? I said, "Write? I'm on the register and there's not much time for exploration there. I'm basically just getting down what's occurred and hope it can be filled in later."

I spent the day thinking of the trip. Bonarh and I will go out of town on thursday and come back on monday midday. And then, as I think to call or email Bonarh with instructions for preparation, I remember what the trip is for: the ending and I'm so full of sadness I can't contact her. I'm fucked up about being so sad, crying so much too, like not just sad and crying but judging myself for crying and being sad, asking myself who wants to be fucked by a crybaby like this? And I have fear I can't hold a space for us like this, or that I'm not able to plan anything.

Canela asked where Bonarh and I would go for the weekend and in my stress, I snapped, "I don't know! I don't know where we're going!" and she said, "How will you plan which meetings to go to then?"

Leah said, "You think you're doing any of this?"

Canela followed up with, "If this is how you feel why are you ending it?" I don't know how to respond. I don't know what to say.

The idea still persists that the reason the situation with Bonarh has been so good so strong so powerful is because of the strict protocol and containment, and that the idea of ending has been in place from so early on. For me, I have an idea it's allowed me to really go for it with everything I've wanted, all the ways I've wanted to fuck and be fucked.

I work a double today to make up for the time I'll take off to go away. In between shifts I get a haircut, go to the library to drop off and pick up books, stop at the bank to get cash, go home to meditate on the couch and then go to 18th and Guerrero to get my knife sharpened and then ride through a light rain just starting back up Larkin to the barber to get my glasses which I left during the cut. Then back to the store for coffee and back on the register.

I'm looking at the calendar full of sadness and dread. I'm fearful I will, still, even with the end, be yearning, pining, waiting, trying, obsessing, paining. And that I won't actually be able to end it. Fear I will be thinking about Bonarh too much and also fear I want the situation and not just Bonarh. Fear I'll never have another situation like this again.

Canela and I just ate dinner upstairs in the lounge on my break. She said: "We are rewiring ourselves with this way of life around relationships: beginning middles and endings; exclusivity, transitions. We already have the high level of intention that's required. Nothing's wrong." It's such a relief.

February 7, 2018:

Dear Bobby:

Canela goes to work early this morning. I jump up too, after the steps and coffee, to pack for the days away. I've gotten some cheese and butter and rice cakes plus coffee and maté from the store. Plus, some clothes and some gear.

Bonarh and I still haven't decided where we will go; I haven't been able to talk with her at all, to be in any communication with her at all this week, I've been too sad. But we have decided that she will come to the little street behind my building at 9am on thursday

I've put a box and a bag in the van ahead of time so that Canela isn't disturbed seeing my stuff packed in our little apartment. So then, in the morning I go down and wait. Bonarh pulls up and I'm excited. I haven't exactly planned anything but I have some ideas about what I want this weekend, what I want to carry out sexually with Bonarh before the end. There is one thing though that I have to do before we leave: stop at Foods Co. Our store doesn't sell crisco. So, on Brady Street, Bonarh pulls up and I say pull next to the van. I open the slider to the van and then load my stuff into the back and the back seat of Bonarh's car. There is a slight rain this morning which is good because there has been such a drought for so long in California. As the customers say, we need every drop. Yesterday as I rode my bike across town back and forth doing errands between shifts at work, it was a light drizzle, enough to make the streets slick but not much else. This morning seems like actual drops are falling, but we'll see.

I'm so excited I'm feeling almost manic. I can barely land in with Bonarh, just telling her what to do, bring the car around to the parking lot, pull up next to the van, here hold this (my jar of maté) while I get the bags, grab that box from the van, etc. Bonarh does what I say for the most part but then says at a certain point, hey can we land in? This isn't really her role between us, the calling in or the holding of space, but I stop for a second and we hug. My body, though, is already revving and excited, like I've said, and I want to get going. I jump in the driver's seat, call to her to get in and then I drive us over to the Foods Co. parking lot which on a rainy morning at about

9:15am is like a mad house, tons of cars and limited visibility in an already high stress situation. I pull into a spot that says 'no parking', tell Bonarh "Wait here, I'll be right back" and then I run in.

Foods Co. stinks. Literally. The chemicals they use to cover up the smells from the meat counter alone are quite overpowering plus the fact that they sell tons of chemicals for household cleaning whose phthalates leach right through the plastic they are sold in and the whole store gives me a headache right when I walk in. I run through the aisles, looking for the baking supplies and run up and down that aisle looking for the crisco. I grab the can off the shelf and begin to run to the front checkout and as I do I wonder if there is anything else I need while I'm in here. There never is. The checkout line is long, even the express and I stand with my one item, dancing from foot to foot, waiting.

Outside it's raining a bit more now. Bonarh is in her car waiting. I jump in and turn on the windshield wipers and begin to maneuver how to get out of the parking lot, which is now even more crowded than before. There are two exits but one goes on to a one-way street, 14th, and I suddenly remember that I have to go back home for some supplements which I realize I forgot so I pull out onto Folsom but turning left from the parking lot is long; a lot of cars and then the bus and bicyclists. And then, finally through, but I have to go all the way over and go around the long way to get back over to my place.

I'm driving fast and running yellow lights and being careful in the rain and then finally, coming back up along Mission to Brady at the end, and up the street to my corner, which is also now, weirdly, like Grand Central Station: tons of cars pulling in and out of the parking lot and the other parking lot and going down little Colton Street to the back parking lot and then a lot of cars coming down Stevenson, too. I think because it rained, more people drove to work or something. I double park Bonarh's car on Brady, put the hazards on and jump out. "I'll be right back," I say to Bonarh. "Wait here." And I run upstairs. I run in the building, wait for the elevator, get in, go up and then at five, run down the hall to my place, unlock the door and come back inside.

Leah is here and she's having another cup of coffee. "I'm depressed," she says but she's surprised I'm back. "Are you ok?" "Yeah, I forgot something." I grab the supplements and turn to hurry back out. I say to Leah as I'm at the door, "I have fear this is a mistake," she laughs and says, "Yeah, of course, what else would you have?"

February 8, 2018:
Dear Bobby:

I run back down, saying goodbye to Leah at the door of the apartment and jump in the car. I look at Bonarh before I start the car and say "ok." She smiles a bit. "Are you ready?" she says I think so. "What do you need to express before we leave, Bonarh?"

Now, she has a different kind of look on her face, I can't quite tell what it is or what it means. I mean, let me remind myself at this point, I barely know this person, this woman. At this point in the story, I've been intimate with her on a regular basis for three months but even that doesn't mean weekly and most of the time we've spent together we haven't spent talking.

So, I look at Bonarh before starting the double-parked car. "Ok, Bonarh, go ahead." "Well," she says, "first of all where are we going?" I laugh and reach again for the keys. "I have no idea!" "Wait a minute, please," she says, "Are you ok?" I say yes, yes, yes. I say I'm just excited and anxious to get on the road. Bonarh says again she wants to land in before we leave, to feel we are together. I actually don't know if I'm capable of being that present, not right now. I don't want to launch into some long explication of how we are taking this trip, spending these few days together to end our arrangement, to acknowledge what's been done, to thank her for submission and desire. I want to just get going to wherever that is.

I lean over, I kiss her cheek, I grab her face and turn her head so her lips face me, I kiss her lips, I put my hand on her thigh. I pull back, look into her eyes and say, "I'm ok, I'm excited to be taking this trip with you. I have a lot of ideas. Let's go, huh?" She says ok. "Is there anything else you want to express before we begin here, Bonarh?" She says no, she's ready. "I'm ready. Is your seatbelt buckled? Let's go." I start her car.

"I thought we could drive south," she says. "I brought my tent and some blankets."

I pull the car backwards into the parking lot entrance behind us and then turn the car around on Brady Street, drive toward Mission. Then swing around to 13th Street to use the spiral entrance to the 101south near South Van Ness. The advantage to the false start is that the rush hour traffic has lessened and especially going south, away from the city, the freeway is clear and quite soon we are at the 280 and then a moment later, on the hwy1, headed south out of the city and on that turn just at Pacifica where the road curves right and the Pacific Ocean suddenly sweeps out a vastness of horizon: majestic. I still have the wipers on, though on intermittent as the rain is again a light drizzle.

The first hour on the ride goes very quickly, mostly because of how fast I am driving. I don't remember if I ate breakfast or not but I don't feel hungry. The road is open, hardly anyone out today especially after we pass Pacifica and then begin the real drive on hwy1, getting past Half Moon Bay and then it's just beautiful and beauty. The ocean on our right is wild with waves splashing and crashing and then suddenly with a cove or a cliff and the fog and the rain increasing, the ocean disappears and it's all thickness with a light light shining, clouds and wave crests meeting and also disappearing into sameness.

One of the things I want to do with Bonarh is swim and I have a favorite beach I like to go to down here. But by the time I realize we are coming close to Santa Cruz, I realize we've past it. It's just south of Pescadero, when did we pass that? How fast have I been going? But now, well, we are coming into Santa Cruz, the north side, quite fast, and it's raining and I say to Bonarh, "There was a place I wanted to stop, but we passed it." She says, "Where? And here? In Santa Cruz?" "No, no, north of here; we passed it." She says no problem, she's hungry already, anyway but I see it as a harbinger and as an indication of my failure.

As we drove, I was talking to Bonarh about how she's taken to the harness, how she's been in it. "Your progression is beautiful," I say and while we drive, while I drive, I tell her my memories of the past few months, the resistance she had both of the harness and her own excitement about wearing it.

"Oh, Bonarh," I say, "the texts you sent about not being able to spend the night in the harness, your texts and calls about waking in the middle of the night in the harness and feeling so constricted and confined, twisted in the straps and sweating, twisted in your sheets, blankets thrown off and your body, naked but for my leather, rising up into your cunt, swollen clit being pressed by leather so tight your every shift or move rubs the straps against you, through your cunt, across your ass and you calling in the middle of the night asking to cum for my pleasure and thinking you won't be able to or that there will be relief in throwing off the heavy harness, or at least unbuckling it, loosening it, taking the strap from between your legs, releasing it or just wearing it across your chest or on your shoulder, slipping out of the leather in the heat of the night, under one arm pulled through, the harness then gathered next to your body in sleep, rolled up and almost like a purse.

"The heat of the leather is like an animal alive more than a totem, more than a fetish, leather and all its connotations is flesh becoming word and word is desire and the harness itself is not just desire, but actual submission; not just symbol, but a yoke, yes a tether but also to focus attention: for my pleasure; and the constancy of the harness, wearing it not just to sleep but during your day, all day (you do, you've said, remove it for swimming) going about the tasks you do and call a life: shopping, walking, seeing friends, at home with room-mates, making your meals and eating, driving in your car, working, on your bike, all day you feel, you are aware, you are wearing my harness which is on your skin, being heated and returning heat, to and by you and against your cunt and clit and you think there will be release in calling, or in coming, so you call and ask to come for my pleasure with your fingers slipped through the cock ring in front, the big stainless steel ring that's thick and heavy and lays at the bottom of your belly, just at your pubis bone, fingers slipped through there and then hand resting on other side as you rub and rub and rub your clit with the leather at your cunt heating and getting wet and slick and swollen itself, seemingly to fit between your lips, to spread your lips with the thickness and then the thick leather strap becoming engulfed in your engorged-ness, as you pull on your nipples, lifting your tits off of your chest by your nipples, pinched between fingers of your left hand, lifting your breast, your now-heavy tit also getting engorged as you begin to mount, to build, leather straps across your chest, your ribs, you've tightened them to better feel me, my hold, you've said, these straps now feel tight, a bit constricting as your heaving and heavy breathing quickens.

"Oh, Bonarh, your progression has been beautiful," I say as I lean over, taking my eyes off the road to look at Bonarh who is looking at me. Her seat on the passenger seat is one of squirming and adjusting, pulling the seat belt as she shifts again, her hips, from side to the other on her ass, adjusting adjusting shifting in the harness now, as I drive down hwy1, the ocean coming into view, dropping behind a dune and the coastal cypress and then the rain and around a curve, appearing again. I look over at Bonarh again and reach over, one hand still on the wheel while driving, reach over to grab her tit framed perfectly by the harness which is visible through her thin t-shirt and on her shoulders at the stretched-out scoop neck.

"You've taken the harness as a lover, Bonarh, like a second skin, as a part of yourself, deep inside you've been fucked by the harness and hoping that by coming you'll be able, as one rolls off a lover post orgasm, to lie in that moment of loneliness, alone next to the beloved, that sublime supreme alone-ness that can really only be achieved when in the company of another, the harness is still holding you, my harness is still wrapped around you and your body sweated and slick and now cooling but wrapped tightly and restricted in thoughts where as one may, on those moments after coming, laying with a lover be thinking of laundry or what to eat, what's available to eat in the kitchen cupboard or fridge, or, most deliciously in those moments, of other lovers, past or not here now, the other lovers who brought one over the edge, the lovers who laid next to oneself as one lay in that little death, those that witnessed the passing, and in that luxury of aloneness and being held in my harness, you've written to me of your desire, to be fucked by me on the street, whenever I want, wherever I want, doing what I whatever I do to you, Bonarh. This is the harnessing that you've accepted, that your pleasure is for my pleasure and even at this point, when you are out of the actual leather, heavy straps around your body, across your chest, framing your amazing tits, buckled tight around your thick middle, bulking you up under clothes to make your body feel, even to yourself, felt or looked at, to be unfamiliar in its shape and feeling, to feel as though your body isn't even recognized by yourself and when you lay down in the bed by now, when you get on your bike to ride around Oakland, when you feel that strap slip up into your cunt, which even in the middle of the day is wet and open and ready and receives the harness, leather wet and slick and then spreading you, as I would do, with my fingers, spreading your lips with my fingers, pulling you apart and asking you as I do, 'Are you ready, Bonarh?' then you feel me fucking you and understand and accept my harnessing. It's beautiful."

February 10, 2018:
Dear Bobby:
   The car feels like it's flying, like we are just soaring through the coastal farms and pass the pie place and then Pescadero and all the state beaches as we go south. No one else, it seems, is on the road and it's clear.
   Suddenly it's like a crash landing after being on a rocket. Suddenly, lost in my reverie of Bonarh in my harness, we are pulling into the northern edge of Santa Cruz, along where campers and vans and other house-trucks are parked near warehouses under some trees. "What? Santa Cruz?" I say, "How did we get here so fast?" Bonarh says she's hungry though I wanted to stop along the way at a beach I like north of here, to swim. It's raining now, lightly, as I pull into the parking lot of a burger place.
   I go around the back, pulling in from the side street, and park along the side of the place. I have no idea what time it is but pulling into a parking spot and stopping the car and then turning it off has the effect of as if I'd been driving all day, like on a cross-country trip: my body still feels the forward motion of the vehicle.
   I turn to Bonarh and she's smiling. "I'm hungry," she says. Though I'm crashing now, sinking low without the propulsion of the driving,

suddenly still and then I'm sinking. "Yeah," I say, "maybe time to eat." I start to gather my things together. I'll put on a jacket but when I look at my device from the bag, there's a text from Leah: 'you left your keys here' it says. Oh no, since Leah was in the apartment when I went up to get my supplements, I didn't use my keys to lock the door behind me. Leah had stood in the doorway as I went down the hall to the stairs, saying goodbye.

I mean, it's not like I need the keys this weekend, obviously. The car is Bonarh's and I don't need keys for home or for the store, it's just that this realization, leaving the keys (I mean, I want to say losing the keys but they aren't even lost, Leah has them) coupled now in my brain irrationally, with passing the beach I wanted to go to, seems a compilation of evidence proving I'm an idiot and a failure. This rumination hangs on me heavily; my selfish self-centeredness bondage of self upon me. Bonarh asks what's wrong? But how can I explain something so trivial and silly, so petty as having such a tremendous impact on me. I'll sound crazy, or worse, unattractive.

Leah's second text says, 'what should I do with the keys? Should I put them at that store? Or what? Leave them someplace for you?' Bonarh says great, no problem, she has the keys, she'll leave them for you, let's eat. Lurking in my brain still however is the beach I passed. I'm still trying to figure it out, how did we get down to Santa Cruz so fast? How did I not notice the beach, even though I was looking at the beaches and the ocean?

C'mon, let's go, I say to Bonarh. Out of the car then, I pull on my jacket. My belt hangs around Bonarh's neck, buckled with the long end hanging down her torso like a necktie. Come over here, I say. And she stands in front of me. I take the long end and tuck it into itself, tucking the end into the part around her neck, pulling it through two or three times and then adjusting the little piece that's left, gallantly. Her shirt is askew, and her hair is also a mess. C'mon now, I say, what'll people think when they see you wearing my belt around your neck like this, so disheveled, and unkempt looking. C'mon now, if I'm gonna let you wear my belt around your neck like this I want you to look good, huh. Bonarh nods her head yes. And then we go inside.

This place is order at the counter, pay for your food, then take the number to the table of your choice. At the counter, I get a burger, no bread, no bun, no sauces, just meat with a lettuce wrap and fries. Plus, a cup of coffee. I ask Bonarh, "What do you want?" and I turn and tell the guy who's working the counter, "She also wants a burger in lettuce with fries, just meat, nothing else." The guy says without looking up from his computer screen, "Does she want any tomato?" and I say, "No, no tomato." I pay for lunch and tell Bonarh, "Grab the number he gave us." It's number 25. There's a table in the back, farthest away from the seventeen teevee screens that are broadcasting basketball, golf, and the news with a news feed scroll along the bottom. And the weather: overcast and rain, light showers.

The food comes, I grab my burger, hot and juicy and slippery in the thick iceberg lettuce and shove a huge bite in my mouth, wiping my chin with a napkin. Bonarh sits patiently and then after a couple sips of the terrible coffee to wash this down, I swallow. I pick up Bonarh's burger and lift it to her mouth, which is already open. I push in this mess of meat and leaf and say "Ok" and Bonarh takes a big bite. She begins to chew and I pick up some fries and bring those to her mouth as well, open, I say and push in the fries. I say to her: "Everyone is watching you open your mouth so wide and wondering, how'd that butch get so lucky as to be feeding her a burger like that in public?"

February 11, 2018:
Dear Bobby:
Bonarh is obedient. I'm choking down my own burger, washing it down my throat with the poor-quality burger joint coffee. I'm eating the fries as quickly as possible. Let's get this over with is what I'm thinking, as usual. The burger and fries make a lump in my throat and the coffee helps but still, that lump is then in my stomach. Meanwhile, Bonarh is here, next to me in the booth. I've tucked a napkin into the stretched-out neckline of her t-shirt but that doesn't work so I re-tuck it into the belt. Her nipples are hard through her shirt and when looking at her nipples, hard like this, one can't help but

notice her tits, which are quite spectacular as they are full and round and the t-shirt so thin and the tits, one can't help but notice, are framed perfectly by the straps of the studded leather harness across her chest.

Ah, Bonarh, open that mouth of yours when I hold the burger in front of you, open your mouth wide as I push the cooked and falling-apart meat into your maw, pushing in with my fingers and laughing as you realize the size and amount of the bite I'm expecting you to take. Bonarh, the sweet tears that form in your eyes as you try to chew and not choke on the burger and soft lettuce and when I lift four or five fries to you, Bonarh, for not shaking your head no, but instead opening your mouth and accepting, though there is not really any room for more, accepting more.

"Everyone in here is wondering how'd I get so lucky," I say laughing. I've stripped down to a t-shirt as well, though my tits have never been anything to talk about, lying flat unbra'd on my chest (even my mother said, "No, your tits aren't your strong point"), only there it seems to signify my femaleness, my womanness and to everyone everywhere to show that Bonarh is being dominated by a butch woman, not a man, let my hips and tits scream out my femaleness, their curves and roundness, even in the tits' flatness, when I take off my shirt or my vest and stand next to the table in front of Bonarh,

I've gotten up to get more napkins, feeding Bonarh with my hands, this burger juicy and greasy and the lettuce too, is everywhere, and in this burger place then everyone sees what's happening. "Oh, Bonarh, they like what they see, they like how you open your mouth for me, they wonder how'd I get so lucky so as to have you wearing my belt around your neck and they are wondering, Bonarh, what you are wearing underneath the thin, thin t-shirt you have on, they can see the straps and they are wondering, is that a harness she's wearing and also mostly, what they want to know is how did this butch get so lucky? How did I get so lucky, Bonarh?"

As I push the remaining burger in her mouth, she coughs a bit and wipes her eyes with the napkin in the belt around her neck. "C'mon, let's go," I say, and take the rest of the fries and gather them like a little bundle of sticks, a fat faggot and then close to her mouth, close to her face, "C'mon," as Bonarh is trying to swallow a bit, her eyes red and then she opens and I say, "Good." Still standing, I slug the rest of the coffee. I wished this mid-day cup had been better, stronger and tasting better than this brown piss. But Bonarh has bought, especially for this trip, an electric kettle and adapter for the car that plugs into the cigarette lighter. Perhaps when I stop to meditate later, she'll make the coffee for me. Meantime, let's go.

I actually feel better after eating and the coffee, while terrible to drink, does seem like it helped a bit. I've forgotten about my keys, left at home in SF. I've forgotten about the beach I wanted to go to. Hey, this is an adventure, right? (This, I notice, is what normies say when things don't go how they've planned: this is an adventure!) but I'm actually able to get on board and we go back out to the parking lot, go to Bonarh's car. Bonarh asks if I need anything. "Like what?" I say. "Oh, I don't know, you want me to drive for a while?" No, let's go.

I open the door for Bonarh on the passenger side, she gets in and I close the door. I go around to the driver's side, get in. I lean over Bonarh and grab the seatbelt, pull it across her body, snap it into place. I grab the belt around her neck and slap her face. "You looked so pretty in there, Bonarh, opening your mouth like that for me, letting everyone see how I do what I want." I start the car and we begin again, driving out of the parking lot and then back onto hwy1 which goes through Santa Cruz.

As I drive I'm thinking again about the beach, is there another place that is as easily accessed from the highway as the place I like, or is it all now wide sandy expanses that Santa Cruz is famous for? Maybe a bit further south, outside of town. As we are driving this is what I'm thinking about.

February 13, 2018:
Dear Bobby:
Through Santa Cruz the traffic was heavier but like driving through town heavier, with the rain and wet streets and mid-day-ish people going places, not terrible just cars going slow, especially as hwy1 curves around through Santa Cruz to the left over the river.

South past the state beaches, past Capitola and then there's a turnoff for a beach or something but I take it. Maybe there's some beach access here. The sky is grey, really thick and heavy and low, especially out over the ocean. The turnoff, an exit south of Santa Cruz, leads down a long road lined with low trees up to the dunes and then a guard house. There's a price to get through to the beach, I think it's $15 which now doesn't seem like that much but at the time I thought it was too much.

So, I did a u-turn around the guard house, speeding back to hwy1. I'm frustrated and also needing to meditate soon. Oh well, got back onto hwy1 and continued south.

Bonarh sitting next to me in the passenger seat, I'm getting kind of manic with ideas. The coffee didn't taste very good but I'm feeling the effects. I'm talking to her about wearing my harness, and about the arrangement we've had. I have a list of things—people, places, and things—from the past couple days in my front pocket. I pull it out and look over it while I drive: items to get from the store, the item from Foods Co., the days off I needed, covered, plus the name of a customer who introduced herself at the register (I wrote down her name to help me remember it) and then reaching around to the back seat, left hand on the wheel, right hand through the seats to my bag back there and I pull out my notebook. Now I have paper, pen and notebook on my lap.

One hand on the wheel, all this stuff on my lap and my right hand is on Bonarh. I'm petting her breast, pinching her nipple, then reading to her from my notebook. "I wanted to read this to you," I say, or something like that. And I flip through the book to read to her the selection I wrote about being in the hills up behind the Claremont Hotel: "…swinging the belt, my soft smooth belt doubled in my fist swinging, hitting her ass hips shoulders repeatedly…" and as we drive now the rain is increasing and I put the wipers on again, with the headlights too as the oncoming cars have theirs on.

My hand on the wheel, holding the notebook open while I read to Bonarh, pen and paper in my lap, I keep looking over at Bonarh who's looking back at me. I tell her to sit still. I lean over and with my right hand, I unbuckle her belt. She's wearing red corduroys which are rubbed smooth between her thighs and this is where I place my hand next, to this smooth area where the fabric is almost rubbed through but so soft and with the backs of my fingers on the smoothness and then my knuckles are resting against the seam at the crotch and I'm pressing my hand there. Bonarh responds, pushing into my hand. She's leaning back against the seat and shifting her hips, lifting her hips onto my knuckles.

I'm going a little too fast now, and when I look back to the road I'm way over the line. I swing the wheel and the car back into the right lane. I use the pen and paper to take a few notes, the way Bonarh looks now in the car, so soft, so open, so wanting and ready, harness through the thin t-shirt, and me driving this whole thing, reading and writing and then leaning over and unbuttoning and unzipping Bonarh's pants. Of course, Bonarh doesn't wear, hasn't worn underwear on this trip (from NYC, Bonarh wrote to me of wearing underwear over my harness under her wool pants for fear of being itchy in the central heated apartments of Manhattan and Brooklyn), so that when I lean over further, glancing from the road for a moment, to Bonarh's lap and reach my hand into her pants it's easy.

Is this not a moment to live for, I wonder to myself, the moment of opening a woman's pants and reaching in with my hand, nay, the moment before this moment: of opening a woman's pants or lifting her skirt and the smell of her pussy, into my nose, my mouth, like a shot to my brain, lifting me, heady musky delicious ready wet scent calling me or at least offering to me herself, her deepest self and then from there, my nose my brain taken over and the swooning, rapture, yes, of pussy, exalted exaltation and like a blanket going over me or I'm putting on a new coat, slipping my arms into the sleeves or as if I'm stripping and removing all my clothes, everything I have on, giving everything up, the smell caresses me from literally head to toe, but now mostly, concentrating on my clit, in my own cunt, my own wetness flows, I can feel it, and in this moment, her smell, released with such force that it's obvious she's been wet a while and it's for me, and we take off.

February 14, 2018:

Dear Bobby:

Reading, writing, driving fast in a car that has filled with the scent of Bonarh's wet obedient pussy—I'm alive. And despite all my thoughts otherwise, my whole life of wishing I was dead, or wanting to be, are forgotten for this moment and does this sound like an exaggeration? Well, we all need a reason to live and I'm grateful this is mine: the emanation of smell that overtakes me when a woman's skirt is lifted and her cunt, still covered by panties, is so powerful and pervasive I'm at its effect without touching her or even seeing it, her fur-trimmed bush, her slick-skinned shaven snatch, or like this with Bonarh, reaching over to unzip her pants, from the way she's sitting in the passenger seat I can barely see anything except her open pants and in this case, the harness which lays on her belly, down from sternum and across belly button to enter pants and then between her legs and this is what I see when I look over again.

I'm hot, really hot and getting hotter. I'm speeding and racing the car down hwy1 and wanting to get to where we are going, though I don't even know where that is, where we are going, and in the meantime, wiping my mouth with the back of my hand, lips dry but so much saliva as I tell Bonarh about fucking her, about the harness, about the customer I met the day before and with the wheel held by my knees, I write in my notebook, on a piece of paper from my front pocket and then again, read to Bonarh from what I've written last week, yes yes, I'm saying this is what I was saying and writing and I'm reading and wanting it all.

I lean over again, push my hand into Bonarh's open pants and slide my knuckles against the leather strap that is becoming more and more, as she gets wetter and more open, embedded more deeply into her cunt. The strap covers her clit but it's so swollen I can feel it behind the leather and I press with my knuckles against her.

Pulling out my hand, bringing my hand to my face, I inhale deeply, deeply the scent on my hands of Bonarh's pussy. And then I keep my hand there, at my face, other hand on the wheel again and do my eyes shut slightly for a moment in this reverie?

Suddenly, too suddenly, there is a turn-off from the highway, off to the right, that looks like it goes right out to the beach. I've never been off the road here, Moss Landing, but let's try it and with a quick movement, turning the wheel to catch the last second of turn before it's too late and we pass it completely, I turn the wheel and hit the brakes and realize just as quickly, I've lost control of the car, the road is too slick, the speed too fast and the turn too sharp and suddenly the wheel is spinning or I'm spinning the wheel to avoid going off the road but it's too late and the back end of the car fishtails a bit. Another car is coming up behind us, seemingly just as fast still on the highway and passing us who are now in the timelessness of the moment before something terrible happens.

There's an embankment and a drainage ditch and it's this we crash into hard. The car has driven off the road and into a ditch and across the ditch into the embankment with such force we are both shocked and stunned. The windshield is ok and the engine is still running but I'm thinking I got to die. How could I have been so stupid as to do something like this? Haven't I learned my lesson ever about driving so fast and so crazy? And what about all of wanting to look good, to impress Bonarh with what? I wonder now, even now, what was I thinking I was going to be impressing her with? I'm hating myself.

Bonarh and I look at each other. I don't know what she says. I think I say oh no. But I can't manage much else. There's a cursory are you ok kind of thing exchanged and then we start to climb out of the car. The car is in water, the drainage ditch with the rain has done its draining and it's full, with cattails growing tall. There's a way, once we open our doors, which thankfully do open, that we are able to climb on the car and hop to the side of the ditch from there. Once we are up there, on the road, we see another car has stopped, is calling to us, "Are you ok?" They tell us something, like that they've already called the highway patrol. Before we got out I tried to just put the car in reverse to back us out but no, we were jammed in where we were.

We were pretty shook up at this point. We told the people we were ok. While we waited we climbed back into the car, Bonarh's boots getting wet when she slipped into the water, we got our phones and I found my book and pen and paper which had slipped to the floor of the car. Bonarh got her shirt and her jacket. Then we climbed back up to the road to wait for the highway patrol. I reached over to Bonarh and took the belt off her neck, putting it back on through my own pants' belt loops. "We don't want to have to explain something like that after something like this."

February 15, 2018:
Dear Bobby:
At this point everything seems to stop. Bonarh and I are standing on the side of the road, hwy1, in the rain, drizzling lightly. Cars are passing on hwy1, most cars going too fast to even notice our car which is in a ditch on the side of the road. The cars pass spraying water from their wheels and only tap the breaks as they pass, a kind of 'ah, forget it' sentiment. Highway Patrol arrives soon after, while Bonarh is on the phone with aaa, on hold. I've called the woman who passed the steps to me in aa. She lives in Georgia and is at her son's basketball game. It feels good though to have something to do and I think she says 'take your inventory'.

Later, Canela will call while we are here, on the side of the road, then she'll call Bonarh's phone and Bonarh will answer and hand the phone to me. "It never occurred to me to call," I'll say to her. "I mean if you didn't know about the accident in the first place what would it matter to tell you we had one and that we are ok?"

I'd forgotten, in my shock, that I also called Leah who was driving down to L.A. on this same day. I called her on the off-chance that she was taking hwy1 down instead of 5 or 101, but she wasn't. "I crashed the car," I said, "I want to kill myself, I'm a complete idiot. This is me trying to pull something off." "Are you ok?" Leah asked. "What? No, did you just hear me, I'm an idiot, I want to kill myself. I'm not ok." "I mean from the accident," she said. "Oh yeah, we're fine." Then the call cut out; she was probably going through the Altamont Pass. But on the other side, the first call she got was from Canela, and Leah thought oh, she's calling about the accident so that's what she led with: "Yeah, bad news, but at least they are ok," and Canela said, "What?!?" and called me and when I didn't answer, was increasingly getting anxious and called Bonarh.

Highway Patrol said, "Forget about calling aaa, on a day like today, they'll take hours to get here. Call your insurance and I'll call our Highway Patrol-affiliated tow service." I can't believe Bonarh knows what to do or can even do it. This is an example of alkie v. normie thinking: I'm so self-centeredly fucked up with how I look after crashing a car, I'm not even able to think of what to do. The only thing I can think of is sitting at the side of the road and ruminate with self-pity, useless.

So Bonarh is then on the phone with her insurance, giving them the info and location and my name as the driver. I'm writing my inventory on the piece of paper from my front pocket that we retrieved from the floor of the crashed car. Highway Patrol is in his car, radio-ing and writing forms.

Quite quickly, the tow truck is here. It's a big flatbed truck with a winch and cable but, unfortunately, Bonarh's car doesn't have the screw-in hook as part of the jack kit. Tow Truck tries a bunch of different ways to drag the car out of the ditch, hooking or trying to hook the cable on various parts of the car. Meanwhile, it starts to rain harder, really coming down now. Highway Patrol is wearing a rain jacket with safety stripes but we are basically in wool: wool hats, wool sweaters, Bonarh has her wool serape. Highway Patrol says to us, "You can sit in the patrol car while Tow Truck gets your car out." He opens the back door for us and we slide in and he turns on the blower with the heat; he gets in the front seat. He finishes asking us questions for his form: "Yes, the road was slick and wet…no, normal speed… ideas of going to the ocean…" Then he says, "Yes, you're lucky you are ok." And then when we say what happened, no, we didn't hit the windshield, the air bags deployed, Highway Patrol says, "Oh, the air bags deployed? Oh, you won't be able to drive that car. Insurance is most probably going to total it, if the air bags deployed."

Now we are thinking, 'oh no.' Highway Patrol says, "Well, I guess I'll go check on the tow truck," and he gets out and goes over to Tow Truck who is half under Bonarh's car, with the hook on the cable looking for someplace to hook it. The two of them chat, Highway Patrol in his rain coat, kind of following Tow Truck around.

I'm in the back seat looking out the front windshield, watching them. Bonarh says, "This morning when I was packing this car in front of my house I thought, 'I hate this car. I wish I had a different car.' Can you believe that?" I can't, but I smile, or try to smile. Then she says, "This was an accident. I don't think it's your fault." "What?" I say. "It was a single car crash into the side of the road because I was speeding and driving recklessly!" "Yes," Bonarh says, "but I've been in the car with you plenty of times when you were driving like that—too fast and wild—and you never had an accident before." I don't know if this kind of reasoning makes her feel better but it has an effect on me and I notice that I am wondering if maybe the accident wasn't my fault. It's enough relief, coupled with the inventory I'm taking while she's talking, for me to turn to Bonarh in the back of the patrol car with me and ask her, "What about you? How you doing?" She looks at me and says, "Oh, hello." I laugh and say "I'm sorry, I'm really self-centered."

The patrol car is like cop cars are, with a thick grate between the front and back seat, a thin slot in the grate for passing a license or documents between cops and people in the back, plus built-in, and in its own grated cage, is a camera. Of course, the doors have no handles for opening the windows or the doors from inside. Looking over the front seat I see the radio mounted on the dashboard and a special holder for Highway Patrol's nightstick, which he's left here in the car with us. There's a computer on the seat next to the driver's seat, also built into its own console. The radio is making announcements but the volume is on low so we barely hear anything that's happening.

"What about you? How you doing?" I ask Bonarh and she smiles and says, "Oh, hello, you're back." Yeah, I say, with a little laugh to shake off the rest of my bullshit.

In a moment, Bonarh is on my lap. She puts her arm around my neck, kind of reclined sideways on the seat. Her feet and boots are wet, so she's taken off her boots. She's reaching up and kissing me, pulling herself on to me, in my lap. Now that she's on the same side of the bench seat as me, I can see on the floor the thick ring that's been mounted there, obviously for detaining people in the back of the car.

Bonarh begins, "If I had still had the belt around my neck, if you hadn't taken your belt off my neck, you could lay me down on the floor and attach the belt to that ring, with my face away from you, on my stomach on the floor of the car."

I pick up from there then, "Yeah, right in front of the camera, everyone in the highway patrol depot will be gathered around the screen watching the footage of two middle-aged dykes in the back of the patrol car following a routine traffic accident." I continue while starting to pet her breasts through her shirt, hand under wool serape, "I'll pull your pants down to your knees and you'll barely be able to twist your head, that's how tightly your neck will be tied to that ring in the floor. You won't be able to look over your shoulder at what I'm doing, you'll just feel me doing it: pulling down your corduroys, grabbing your hips, pulling you closer to me." Quite quickly Bonarh in my lap has shifted and now the way she is across me gives me access to her pussy without unbuttoning her pants; somehow there's a looseness here and I slide my hand down the front of her pants.

Bonarh's clit is so hard and I start to rub her and she is wet and I pull my hand out and begin again, holding my fingers to my nose and face and inhaling deeply. "Bonarh, Highway Patrol is gonna come back after Tow Truck has the car on the flat bed and when he opens the door he'll smell your pussy. Bonarh, he'll see the look on my face of smug satisfaction and he'll wonder what happened to that sorry pathetic butch and I'll put my hand to my face right in front of him, smiling.

"Bonarh, with your neck belted to the ring in the floor of the car, I'll do anything I want. Just like now, which with you on my lap, this is probably more visible than on the floor to that camera." I slide my hand back into the front of Bonarh's pants, the soft, nearly-rubbed away part on the back of my knuckles and my fingers grabbing her clit, "yes, I want this. This is what I want, Bonarh." And I begin pulling her clit and rubbing the length of it and then squeezing it and while Bonarh's arms are around my neck, I whisper in her ear that she can yell as loud as she wants the camera has no audio, only video, so go ahead.

Bonarh with the sound of my voice, starts to rock and buck on my hips against my fingers and hand and soon, quickly, she's fast and wet, and into her ear again I say, "the cop is on his way back to the car here," and Bonarh explodes and soaks her pants, my hand and right through, soaking my pants on my lap and screams as loud as she can, the sound reverberating with the car windows rolled up and getting steamed.

Tow Truck has gotten the car attached and he's gone around to the side of his truck and turned on the mechanical winch and the car is being drug backwards out of the ditch. Then, Tow Truck goes to the other side of the flatbed and raises the bed at the steep angle required for the car to get lifted on it. Highway Patrol is standing in his rain jacket watching the whole thing. Once car is up on the tow truck, or half way there, he starts back to the highway patrol car and says to us, "Ok, you're all set! Tow Truck'll drive you to a shop. Just call your insurance and tell them where it is."

February 16, 2018:
Dear Bobby:

We are in the tow truck with Tow Truck, driving Bonarh's car to the auto body shop in Salinas ('Salinas Auto Body'). Bonarh is on the phone with her insurance. I'm sitting between Tow Truck and Bonarh, in the middle on the bench seat in the big truck and up high like this, above the road and close to the windshield, I feel exposed.

Bonarh leans on the passenger door which gives me a little space in the middle. I don't want, in the twisting turning drive from Moss Landing into the Salinas hills, to be leaning on Tow Truck while he drives. Even though this is his job, getting calls and being dispatched to accident scenes to load a car onto the tow truck, I feel the way I always do, which is like he's doing us a favor, really something extraordinary, like I really owe him. At the end of this, when he's dropping the car at the body shop yard and I'm trying to meditate on a chair in a warehouse with a phone ringing and it's quite cold and dirty, I'll come out of the meditation to make sure I catch him before he goes on his next call—"Rain makes for work"—and I'll tip him $40.

But now, in the truck in the middle, staring out the windshield listening to Bonarh, wondering if I'm supposed to be chatting with Tow Truck (he's not saying anything so I don't either) and taking inventory. I feel terrible and I don't think the steps are going work about this. I mean, crashing a car while on a date. No, crashing her car while on a date, crashing her car on date because I'm speeding, driving recklessly, reading and writing while driving in the rain and reaching over, with one hand on the wheel, to pet and fuck her. What can the steps do about that?

The next series of events is just logistics: Tow Truck brings us up into the hills of Salinas to the auto body shop and drops off our car, we check with the woman who is the receptionist or secretary here, she says we wait now for our insurance company to call back, I try to meditate in the vast auto body shop and find I can barely shut my eyes for even a few minutes in a row, I'm too hepped up, too wasted, too still in shock, too much needing a cup of decent coffee, then we get the ok and clear everything out of Bonarh's car, of which there is a lot not just stuff for this trip but stuff she drives around with every day: thick heavy moving blankets and shoes for qi gong, a hat, and we pile everything in a pile in the auto body shop yard while we wait for the rental car that the insurance company will provide for the rest of our trip or for today or for how long I don't know and I have no idea how insurance even works and never in a million years would I think that I was entitled to get a car to replace the one that I crashed (at some point in the day I tell Bonarh a bunch of car accident stories including the fender bender on the southern state when my brother was driving in bumper to bumper traffic; he'd picked me up at the airport—this was in the early 90's when it was still easy to get flights from SFO to Laguardia airport—and he hit the car in front of us and when we got out my brother was in boots, shorts and a t-shirt covered in grass and grease from his job as a lawn mower in a huge Queens apartment complex—by the time he finished all the sections, it took a week and he'd have to start again on monday back in the first section, mowing grass all week—and I was in a dress with combat boots and I'd ripped the sleeves off the dress on the curb at Laguardia because july is so different on Long Island than july in SF but either way long dresses and black boots were very popular for dykes in the very early 90's—and the guy who's car we hit was very well-dressed and he was very pissed and we looked at the cars and saw nothing wrong and then he sneered at us, he pulled out his business card and it said he was from the FBI and then I noticed the gun strapped to his ankle where he'd put his foot on my brother's bumper to use his own knee as a surface to write my brother's info and then since there was no damage, he said before getting back into his car, "Well, let's hope we don't have any problems," and the time I'd gotten off work, waitressing in the popular family-style Italian restaurant (I still have never had a better spaghetti marinara with a side of meatballs) and I was driving not home in Long Beach but from a bar in Freeport to my grandma's house where I was repainting her dining room and living room, my grandfather was teaching me how to paint, and for some reason, I didn't drink at the Freeport bar but then drove north on Milburn Avenue and as I hit Sunrise Highway, I had a green light and started to go through this big intersection in my town and I heard sirens and a mack truck-like horn blaring and I looked to my right and saw a fire truck racing through the intersection I was in! I hit my brakes, luckily, and then slammed into the side of the truck which is something like 15 tons, I don't know, but the entire front end of my little Toyota was smashed,obviously but what could have happened if the truck had hit me sideways? And with that accident, I just got a ride home from the tow truck and parked the car in front of my mother's house, I had no idea what to do with a smashed car nor did anyone ever mention to me that I should call my insurance or even, best case scenario call the fire department's insurance or something, I think the town finally came and towed the car to the junk yard as 'abandoned' and I went back to riding my bicycle to and from work and I painted at my grandparents only on my days off) but Bonarh knew all of this kind of stuff, like how to get a replacement car (I was thinking we'd have to call one of our friends to come down and pick us up) and soon after her smashed car was empty, here comes the rental car driven by a guy from the rental car office on the other side of Salinas and he's driving a huge Ford Expedition for us. This is about 3 times bigger than Bonarh's Honda Fit, but ok! And we load everything into the back of this big truck and Car Rental drives us to the rental car office. I sat in front with him and Bonarh sat in the back and this guy was easier to talk to, so the three of us were laughing pretty quickly, mostly we were making jokes about how nice this big vehicle was and how we could just sleep in it for the weekend. Then the paper work at the office and showing our licenses and signing papers. And then I'm mostly focused on getting the adapter for the hot water kettle to work in one of the various plugs that this truck has and neither of them are working; not the AC nor the DC converter, whatever that means, but by now I'm getting really desperate for a cu p of coffee (I passed up the one they offered to make me at the auto body shop, holding out a styrofoam cup with a pot of hot water) and so I finally get the whole rig together, plastic drip cone and filter with coffee and go into the car rental office and use their bottled water which has a switch for hot water and I make a cup that way. Bonarh is filling out the forms and then talking to Car Rental and asking him directions but where are we even going? I actually don't care. I feel terrible, need coffee, and rest and probably to meditate for real and take more inventory, though I don't want to, nor do I think it will work. I feel so down and leaden it's like I'm dragging a carcass around instead of being in my body.

Bonarh gets directions back to hwy1 and she's driving ("I think it's best, don't you?") and I nearly lay in the passenger seat, defeated, drinking coffee and hoping something will happen to turn this whole thing around. We drive through the hills but the easier way this time and come out just a bit past the crash site which is good and then soon it's dark, or getting dark, and grey and rainy still and we come into the town of Marina. We debate about whether we should stop here or not and try and find a motel for the night or what, and then we are taking the next exit and swinging around out to the ocean again and there's a couple of motels and at the first we pull up and I jump out and run into the lobby and ask is there a room for us? And the woman at the desk says yes, it's $79. I say ok. How are the rooms, I ask. And she says, "about what you'd expect a $79 room to be." Ok, fair enough. I get the room and go back to Bonarh in the car. We'll stay here.

At the room we bring in most of our stuff, bags and boxes of food, our clothes, etc. I've brought a typewriter with me but now that seems a joke. We are both hungry, we've not eaten since our stupid burgers in Santa Cruz when I was feeling so cocky and strong.

Now, we each fend for ourselves and stand at the motel desk and eat cheese and spread butter on crackers with fingers. Hungry and tired, wasted. I finish my coffee and make another cup and then I lay on the bed on my back staring at the ceiling (which is stained and disgusting; in fact, the whole room is dirty and behind the chair in the corner not just dirt but trash: paper and a plastic spoon are visible, I don't look further). I'm sad and impotent, laying. Bonarh asks, "What's up?" "I'm insanely distracted with my self-pitying remorse." "What do you need?" she asks. "Probably to take more inventory, though I dread trying to write the same thing over and over... I got to go to a meeting!" I jump up and forget the internet, trying to look something up and figure it out, I call the aa Hotline directly: "I'm in Marina and I need to go to a meeting. Please help me." "Yes, there's a meeting for you 3 minutes from where you are in 5 minutes, at 7pm." I jump up and say, "Let's go, c'mon" and we hurry out the door of the motel into the big truck, drive to the meeting 3 minutes away.

Bonarh is a bit pissed, I'd say, like it's become all about me and what I need but I'm thinking it's everyone for themselves, each person selfishly seeking their own salvation and I don't have anything but the steps to do to not be wallowing in the slough of despond.

The meeting is at a park facility and in the park Bonarh is able to do some qi gong while I'm in there. And the meeting is terrible, basically a non-alkie telling how they don't drink but it's a meeting and I'm grateful to get there and share that there's no way I could be sober without the steps.

February 17, 2018:
Dear Bobby:
I get to the meeting of alcoholics anonymous in Marina—it's just a three-minute drive from the motel, which is amazing because when I call the aa Hotline for help, it's 6:55pm. Bonarh and I have just eaten something, bread, butter, cheese and I drank another cup of coffee and then lay on the bed, depressed and full of self-pity. "I just can't keep writing the same inventory over and over." I say meaning mostly 'fear I'm an idiot; fear I'm a failure; fear I've ruined the trip.' The meeting's a drag, but I'm able to share my gratitude, "I'm grateful

to have made it to a meeting of aa, grateful for the steps, grateful to be sober as a result of the steps."

This is what I share at every meeting of aa I go to but after this meeting, a lady came up to me and said, "Thank god you were both ok, thank god neither of you were hurt." And then a guy came up to me a few minutes later and said the same thing and then I was grateful for having had the spiritual awakening as the result of these steps, to have the much-needed psychic change that I can't produce for myself when I'm completely consumed with myself. "Yeah, thank god neither of us were hurt. Thank god Bonarh didn't go through the windshield."

Then I hurry out of that meeting because it seemed like everyone was going to stand around chatting for a while. I found the truck parked in the lot and when I approached and looked close through the tinted windows, I could see Bonarh sleeping on the big black seat. I tapped on the window and she woke up and let me in and we drove back to the motel. Back there she ate a bit more. I basically washed my face and brushed my teeth and lay on the bed again. After the meeting, I'm down again, it feels like nothing's been shattered; I'm at the effect of my fears again. Bonarh tries talking to me but it's like every time I open my mouth, I'm expressing that sad-ass self-pity and pathological remorse. It's so un-sexy and that knowledge, instead of preventing its expression seems only to feed it so that soon I'm adding that litany to Bonarh: 'fear this is so un-sexy, fear I'm so distracted with myself and with my failure, fear the weekend is ruined.'

I do tell her about what the people said at the meeting, about thank god I didn't kill her, basically. She said yes, everyone she spoke to on the phone: insurance, rental car, even the tow truck woman at the shop, they all said thank god you both are ok. Yes, she said, we are both ok.

I suddenly say to her: "I'm sorry for the way I am, believe me I wish I were a lot better than I am, namely, not the kind of maniac who reads and writes while driving fast and recklessly, and fucking you and then crashes and totals your car but also I wish I were the kind of person who when that happened, I was able to just take care of it all, not just the calls and the tow truck but also not be self-centered and self-pitying, able to just stop thinking about myself for a fucking second, long enough to just take us out for a meal, even in Marina, and maybe say thank god we're ok (but if I was this kind of better person I wouldn't be thanking god, I'd be saying 'I'm glad we're ok') and maybe get a laugh about it all and then come back to this motel, which might be cleaner, or nicer, and put you into bed and give you all kinds of care and reassurance or something, but that's not me and I mean, it's really not me.

"I have an idea that if I could just live like a normal person I'd be more attractive, and basically, just better, a better version of myself." Now of course this is the same self-pity being expressed, just the other side of the same coin, but it is a bit more empowered, so I'm being taken by it. "I'm sorry for the way I am but the way I am allows us to experience a power greater than ourselves. Seriously, I'm such a failure in this world, trying to pull off anything has me in a big mess or a problem. When we see ourselves protected, when I see myself sober through something like this it's evidence of a power greater than myself, than ourselves, even if we don't think so."

I've rolled on top of Bonarh now and while I'm reciting this I'm pushing my pussy into hers. She's wearing underwear and the harness and I still have on my jeans. I'm pushing the button fly of my crotch into the leather strap that crosses her cunt and I'm pushing on her shoulders, bringing my face close and then pulling away. We do this for a while and then I roll off. My fears again, have me feeling so impotent and un-sexy. But Bonarh follows this time and shifts down the end of the bed, between my legs and she unbuttons my levis and pulls them down enough to fuck me. I'm on my back on the bed and I'm wanting to tell her 'no, don't' but I'm so lack of power and tired I can't. So, she fucks me and I come.

February 19, 2018:
Dear Bobby:
That night in Marina, Bonarh fucks me and then we fall asleep. The fuck is fine, more like one of those fucks that is like a stress reliever rather than a sexual experience, just to kind of release stress, re-set the physiology, not some amazing fuck that one later jacks off

to remembering it. In fact, I barely remember it, or any details from it, just that I know it happened.

And I'm glad because the next morning waking up, my body is sore. Head neck and shoulders feel like I got hit by a truck....oh yeah, the car accident yesterday. We both wake with symptoms of whip lash and just like tight and sore. I have coffee and do the steps. I remember last night and laying on the bed, weak and full inertia, staring at the stained ceiling and going down, fast and hard. 'How did this happen? How are we in this terrible place? How am I ever gonna feel any better? Fear I've ruined the weekend...' This is in meditation and I'm going over and over these lines again and again, and then after a while, thinking 'this meditation isn't working either' I remember it comes to me what Bonarh said to me as I lay there after the meeting, trying to explain to her how bad I felt about everything and by everything, I mean every single thing, everywhere. That bad. Bonarh is sitting up in the soft bed with its thin mattress and polyester sheets, leaning on the pillows propped against the headboard and she says to me, "You know, I know you feel bad and that there's nothing I can do or say to change that or help you, but I want to say that I'm not actually thinking anything different than I was before the accident. I'm not thinking you're weak or impotent, I'm not thinking the weekend, or anything, is ruined. I'm not feeling less turned on to you than I ever have been. I'm still wildly attracted to you and everything you do. Really."

After meditation we put on our bathing suits and grab some towels from the room. In the big rental truck Bonarh has a wetsuit and she grabs that as we cross the parking lot. And then we see how close we are to the ocean, across the street. Dirty little motel off the highway drops us right at the beach with an easy access to the state beach across the street.

It's early morning still, I don't think either one of us slept very well, waking early and now as we approach the ocean, there is a low fog still hanging about over the dunes and the restored wetlands and Monterey pines, permanently in a windblown pose even on the calmest day, which this morning is: the fog keeps the air warm and there's no wind, even on the beach and actually getting down to the sand, getting to the ocean looking out at the Pacific, over the water, there is no fog, just blue sky, bright over vast ocean and as we watch, in that first moment, there's a dolphin and then another, cresting and jumping past on the horizon but close in, arching out of the water and the spray of rainbow behind them before they dive in again and again, over and over til they disappear. Of course, all things are connected. Of course, all things have meaning, but what is that meaning now.As we walk across the sand to the water, I see and pick-up a small piece, coin-size, of burnt driftwood. It's smooth in my fingers and hand and I put it in the pocket of my levis, already nostalgic for this moment.

I stand near the ocean's edge, putting my feet in, testing the water. Bonarh puts on her wetsuit. I've piled my towel and hers in a tower-like structure with my boots as the base, providing the height to keep the next layers of clothes and then towels on top, dry. The water is warmer than in San Francisco at Baker Beach, warmer water and softer waves. The beach here is wide and so the waves come in and lick the sand no crashing smashing and fight to get in, just walk out and then dive under, kind of like Jones Beach on Long Island. Easy and enjoyable and I swim around and float on my back and swim twenty strokes parallel to the shore then roll over on my back and do a slow back stroke watching the sky and the birds flying overhead. And then another forward crawl and then just floating on my back. It's that warm. Well, not that warm. I have to keep moving to not start shivering but I can stay in a bit longer than at Baker. For a while, I ride a few waves and laugh because getting tumbled here is really just that: a tumbling. No being slammed into the sand with waves pounding and crashing and being dragged along, coughing and choking. Here it's fun and like a little game and when I'm back on the sand again, I get up and run back in, right back into the water jumping over waves and diving under and just playing and laughing. By the time I'm done, just about too cold, I see Bonarh is already out. She's laying on the sand, face down. She's crying.

February 20, 2018:

Dear Bobby:

Bonarh is in her wetsuit lying face down in the sand. She's crying. The water is warmer than in San Francisco and the waves gentler, it's like Jones Beach on Long Island in the summer, easy soft waves of the Atlantic, perfect for playing and just floating. The weirdness of the universe is that after our accident, on our way to nowhere, after all the car towing and car renting and Salinas and Moss Landing we wound up here, in Marina, right at the state beach, within walking distance to the motel we stayed at. I mean, pretty good. I never even heard of Marina before and if I did, I didn't notice it.

And now, in the morning we wake, muscles and body sore from the car crash, we pull on our bathing suits and walk across the street, through the parking lot, filled with tons of surf vans and campers, and onto the beach, make a pile of our clothes with towels on top to keep them dry and then into the ocean, great mother, healing divine body of water, salt-sister, to float, rest and cleanse. Forget the accident, forget your failure, forget about everything while you float on your back, looking at the sky, so blue it's almost painful, the infinite blueness of sky never-ending and birds, flying, soaring and diving seems like right in front of you, so close, beak first into the ocean and then a moment later, to pop up and fly again. I swim and float and swim and float and laugh.

It's warm but actually not as warm as the beach in the summer on Long Island and if I don't keep moving, swimming really, can only tread for a minute or so before shivering and then I'm riding the last wave, letting myself be carried ashore. Bonarh is there already, in her wetsuit, lying face down on the sand, crying. I walk over and climb onto Bonarh's back, lay myself down on her, my face into her wet hair at the back of her neck.

Oh, Bonarh, this is what I wanted from the start, to be with you on the beach, in the water. In the summer before all of this, we were overlapping in NYC and I wanted to pick you up at the airport, borrow my brother's car and pick you up from your late flight and then in the morning, we drive out to Riis Beach and swim, early before it's crowded. On the way down here, yesterday, I told you the story of Mr. S's boy Antonio, who was trussed up in a wetsuit at the water's edge by Mr. S himself and then photographed by him, and the boy writing in the book with the pictures of this: boy, in wetsuit, tied with arms behind his back, left at the water's edge, face turned to the camera with the look of absolute devotion and terror: "I can't swim," he writes.

Rising then, we get the towels from the motel from the pile and dry ourselves off a bit. The California sand, though is so sticky, so wet even when the skin is dry, the sand doesn't brush off with a towel, even when we take turns brushing each other off. And out of the water, now not swimming, in the air—the fog has lifted and the wind is up a bit—it's getting cold. So, pulling off bathing suit, pulling on pants, maybe just the towel and a shirt, if we hurry. Up the dunes in the sand back to the motel, there's a hot tub there, let's try it. And so, sandy, we hop in. It is warmer than the air and so we float in there too, for a while and make a plan for the next couple of hours. Yeah, a meeting, there's probably a noon in Monterey, we can eat some of the bread, butter and cheese that's in the room here, pack everything back into the truck, drive down to Monterey, how far is it I wonder.

Back in the room, we jump in the shower, her first then me. The water in here is hot! I stay in for a while, my toes are cold! Her wetsuit is laying in the tub, full of sand. In fact, there's sand all over the bathroom. By the time I'm out and getting dressed, Bonarh has begun to load the big back of the truck. With the seats down, it's like a huge bed. I'm finishing another cup of coffee and hurrying to eat the bread, load my own stuff in.

As we finish, after I've been back into the bathroom to try and wash all the sand in the tub down the drain, hang up the towels on the rack, look around the room, did we forget anything? I see the trash behind the chair again, and laugh, well, at least this provided what Bonarh said she wanted in the patrol car: "Let's hurry and get to a motel so we can have sex," plus the beach and the hot tub, not bad. The cleaner, the woman who cleans the room is outside in the breezeway as we are leaving, so I give her a $20 for the sand left.

Then we climb into the truck. Bonarh's driving. I'm looking up the location of the nooner in Monterey. Oh, it's just 15 minutes away.

So, we continue down hwy1 and go to the meeting that seems easiest or something. Who knows what I based it on. But we find it, I hop out of the truck, Bonarh gets out on her side. I'm gonna grab a jacket from the back and while the door is open, Bonarh uses the window as a mirror to apply lipstick.

February 21, 2018:
Dear Bobby:

I stand on the other side of the open truck door and watch her apply the lipstick. Listen, I'm not going to go into a long description of a butch watching a femme put on lipstick partially because I think this is one of those sacred acts of desire that are best left unsaid. I watch Bonarh apply her lipstick, using the truck window as a mirror.

I'm still not quite feeling myself, after the accident yesterday; I'm still kind of shook up. I go to the aa meeting behind Trader Joe's and even though I'm resentful when I come out of the meeting, relief was gotten, I notice. And let's be honest, this is more like myself than mostly anything else: my critical, judgmental resentful nature. I mean, it's a boost from self-pitying depression, that's for sure.

After the meeting, Monterey is warm and sunny in the mid-day-ness. I get some canned fish and bottled water from the store and go back to meet Bonarh. She's sitting in the sun, smiling, near the truck. She looks happy. As I approach, she's happy and excited, she says. "I found us a place to stay tonight," she says, and then adds, "I mean, a couple of places, do you want to look at them?" I said no, wherever she wanted. "I'm happy you took the time while I was in the meeting to find us a place," I say. And we get in the truck and drive around the corner to the motel she's picked. It's quite lovely, with a long driveway and a courtyard and our room has a fireplace. It's great, I say.

In the room, believe it or not, I have to do the steps again. So, I sit on the bed, take inventory and meditate. When I come out, Bonarh's made some lunch for us and she spreads a sheet from her bag over the bedspread (this room is very clean, very.) and I feed her bread, fish, cheese and some pieces of cucumber she's brought while I tell her about the meeting.

I'm also not going to go into too much of my resentment about aa meetings here for fear of this part being misinterpreted but suffice it to say that if I was the boss of aa I'd be the only member. At certain points through this recitation to Bonarh I pull out from my bag my little Big Book and read sections to her. This is actually more for me, though it looks surprisingly like I'm trying to teach Bonarh something, I need to hear the spiritual experience that I'm reading, I need to hear my only dilemma is lack of power.

After lunch, I lay down in the bed. Bonarh and I have talked a bit about the car crash while we ate and while I read and we are both kind of surprised: "Oh, yeah, the car accident yesterday." Everything is in an interstitial-ness, an out of time-ness but the reminder is in our bodies, stiff, a little sore and maybe a headache, too. So, we lay down and both fall asleep.

The bed in this place is very comfortable and the sheets seem like they are cotton and a really nice cotton and the pillows are of varying plumpness and fluffiness (I like flat pillows mostly and there is one like that too) and the fireplace, gas powered, is at the foot of the bed and so the whole scenario is quite pleasant.

When we wake up, it's still light out but late afternoon winter light, the sky is kind of yellowing in its greyness, and the windows of the room (we are on the second floor) look out over and into some trees which the branches of the far one are bare, leafless now, but the up close is a cypress and full and big and old and its canopy is making this a bit like a treehouse. The louvered blinds we left open and I slept on my side and when I woke from the nap I looked out the window and had my initial feeling of 'oh no it's already late, we slept through the day I'll be down all night.' I feel Bonarh stir next to me and I tell her, "Hey, get up and make a pot of maté, please."

As I drink the maté she's made and brought to me in the bed I begin to talk about the end of our arrangement. I want to remember, I say, "why we are here, to bring intention and care to the returning of my harness to me, care in her removing the harness, intention in the untethering." This is getting to an edge I'm not that into, like the sky and the ending and still lying in bed doesn't seem like a recipe for anything good. I get up and pull on my levis, my boots, and a shirt. I tell Bonarh to get up, get out of bed.

Bonarh wears a blue leather dress. The top part of the bodice is sky blue, light blue and from a piece of very thick leather and the bottom part, the skirt is royal blue and here the leather is thinner and grabs Bonarh's ass and fits like a glove. Overall the dress isn't very tight, but like a sheath for a woman larger. Nonetheless it is quite flattering, if only for the fact that it's a leather dress which Bonarh has worn for me. While she stands near the bed, I continue to dress which in this case means pulling on my dick in its harness. I unbutton my fly, thread the straps through my legs, inside my underwear, then pulling the straps over my hips and buckling them on the side, slipping the dick through the cock ring in front as I do, pulling tight so the dick sticks straight out from my button fly. I pull on suspenders to hold my pants up while they are open, unbuttoned and hanging off my hips. I have on my engineer boots, my belt.

I call Bonarh to me. She's been watching my preparations and I ask her, "Are you ready, Bonarh?" "Yes," she says, "I'm ready." "Ok. I'm going to the bathroom and when I come back we'll begin."

And we begin. Bonarh, stand in front of me please. I'm sitting on the small settee at the front of the bed in front of the fire. Bonarh, stand in front of me please. She stands between my legs between me and the fireplace. "Oh," she says, "It feels nice, the heat on my back." I've begun to caress her body, rubbing my hand over her body over the leather dress. I'm telling her how good the leather feels. "Oh, Bonarh, the leather is so soft." From her breast down along the side of her belly around to her ass, long slow strokes with my palm open, fingers together. I'm being very gentle but deliberate. "Bonarh, this dress is amazing." Underneath I can tell Bonarh isn't wearing anything, just the harness and then the leather against her skin. I stand for a moment and pull the dress away from her body at the neckline and pass my hand and wrist and forearm down the front of her dress. I've caught Bonarh unaware and she's surprised after being lulled by my petting. Inside the dress there isn't a lining, just the rough side of the leather, rubbing, as I pet the outside, against her breasts.

Now, I'm two-handing her, standing in front of her, one arm

322

down the front of her dress and the other hand lifting the dress from the bottom up, pulling the skirt up toward her hips, gathering the leather in a bunch in my fist and looking into, holding Bonarh's eyes with mine. Bonarh is quite still and the way I've grabbed the dress and I'm pulling it, she has to stand on her toes a bit to stay steady. I'm kind of shaking her the way I've grabbed the dress.

"Ok, Bonarh, what do you want to tell me before we start?" "I'm excited." "Yes, what else?" "I'm always a little afraid when I feel your desire like this." "Like what, Bonarh?" "Rough." "Yes, rough. I'm being really rough with your dress, being rough with you." "Yes." "Anything else, Bonarh? Do you want to tell me anything else?" "I wore this dress for you tonight."

Oh, Bonarh, the way you give yourself to me has my cunt pounding in my levis, my clit hardens to hear you. "Yes, the dress for me, Bonarh." I remove my hands and let go of the dress, of the leather I've grabbed and let Bonarh stand again for a moment and then I turn her to face the bed. "Kneel here on the settee please Bonarh and lean over on the bed." Now, with the royal blue leather over her ass, held prominently and raised, I begin here to stroke the dress again, over Bonarh's hips and across her ass, pausing for a moment to lean my entire body over hers, much the way I climbed on her back, while she was in her wetsuit on the beach, laying curving around her from behind. My dick is pressing the cleave of her ass which is held flat by the dress. My arms I reach forward to the straps on her shoulders; to stroke her hair and then to the leather over her shoulders and upper back. My thighs press her bare feet, tucked under her knees on the little couch.

Standing then again, asking again, "Bonarh are you ready?" and I take off my belt waiting for her to answer. "Yes, I'm ready." I begin to swing the belt across her ass, of course gentle at first, but quite quickly the feel of leather on leather excites me furiously. "Here are the wonderful parts about this dress, Bonarh. One: it's made of leather. Two: the way it looks on your body, your body really enjoys the feel of the skin on your skin; I can tell by the way you move. "Yes," she says, "it feels amazing to wear it on my bare skin. I've never worn it this way before." I'm beginning to hit her ass harder now, swinging the belt with wider swings of my arm. "Third: the leather you're wearing protects you enough that I can hit you as hard as I want and I won't be able to break your skin."

By now, Bonarh is moaning and her ass is swaying back and forth over her heels. Oh, Bonarh, you look good. I'm striking and swinging quite hard now and the leather dress is taking it all. From my bag I pull the floggers out and during the pause Bonarh is looking at me over her shoulder. I pet her, stroke her sides, her ass, her hips with my flat palm a few times and when I see she's watching I ask, "Do you like what you see, Bonarh?" "Yes, I like it," she says.

The flogging I give her is beyond anything we've done until now, with me letting it fly, unleashing, unfurling, a furiousness that is wild with desire and I'm able with the leather dress to let myself go. As I swing the heavy leather, I feel my wet cunt behind my dick.

February 22, 2018:
Dear Bobby:

Now of course, Bonarh is naked under the leather dress except for the leather harness she wears. The dress is slightly too big and by this, I mean only that it's not a skin-tight sheath but hangs a bit from her shoulders, catching on her breasts and ass especially. And then with certain movements, her bending over or a certain stance she takes, the harness becomes visible as a thick bulge under the leather, the lines of the leather straps, outlined in leather, here sheathed in leather, is especially arousing. And when I reach my arm down the front of her dress, lay my wrist and forearm flat in the space between her breasts, my arm is laying then on the harness. And also when lifting her dress from below, pulling the leather up from the bottom, inching it up, gathering the leather in my left fist, pulling the dress over her thighs and then to her hips, a thick fat gather of leather in my fist getting to the straps on Bonarh's hips and stopping there so she is now bare legged, pulled toward me such that she must stand on her toes, my right arm almost completely down the front of her dress and then grabbing between her breasts the fat d-ring which lies on her solar plexus, pulling her toward my face: "Kiss me."

Now, Bonarh is on her knees in front of me, bent over the bed, kneeling on the little couch at the foot of this big nice bed. Her torso is on the bed and ass in the air and this is one of the positions that allows the harness to be outlined so definitely under the dress, the leather here stretched tight over Bonarh's hips and ass and I'm petting her with my hand gently and firmly for a long time before I actually begin to hit her with my belt ("No, Bonarh not this time, the belt isn't going around your neck this time") and then feeling leather striking leather, feeling and hearing and seeing leather striking leather, the effect on Bonarh—she likes it—and feeling my cunt, wet behind the dick on my hips, an excitement takes me and I let go into it.

I pull the floggers from my bag, long leather heavy tails on a short handle provide versatility: heavy thick thudding or an all out swinging almost like a whipping, and begin on Bonarh bent over like this. It's amazing how much I can give now with the leather encasing her. There isn't, or almost isn't, any stinging, just the solid thudding that enables us to lift off and fly quickly.

I'm smiling. I'm feeling good, really good and Bonarh is moaning and when I go around to the side of the bed to look at her face, pausing with the hitting, she is laying on the side of her face and smiling, her eyes are closed. I touch her cheek gently, she opens her eyes, looks at me and smiles hugely. "Bonarh?" "Yes, Cashier," she says. "How do you feel?" "Oh, Cashier, please don't stop." "You're ready for more?" "Yes, please."

I begin again standing behind Bonarh at the foot of the bed. The gas fireplace is on my back and feels good, the heat back there. I stroke Bonarh's back and shoulders with the tails of the flogger softly, then slowly increase the speed and intensity, hitting harder slowly and building, building again and then increasing the speed until again I'm hitting her, striking her quite hard and quite fast, over and over and while I do I'm asking her, "More? You want more?" and "You think you can take this?" and "How much can you take, Bonarh? Can you take as much as I want?"

Now, I'm striking her back and shoulders and ass with both floggers at the same time, double. I'm sweating and getting hot, sweat is running down my ribs from under my arms which are raised at this point, and there is a flash or something. I look to my right and it has darkened sufficiently outside such that the windows in the motel room are now like a mirror. I catch the look of myself, levis, unbuttoned, dick hanging erect from the fly, white net a-shirt, and me in my glasses. For a moment there isn't recognition, I'm not used to seeing this self reflected, but when I see Bonarh's ass raised so close to the tip of my dick, I'm embodied there. I'm smiling, I see.

"Oh, Bonarh can you see yourself?" Bonarh needs to be called back a bit, to where I am now. "In the window, look." From where she lays she can't see, the window too high and her head too low on the bed so I begin to build up with the bolsters and pillows from the bed a little pallet for her to lay atop. Increasing the height little by little, and in this kind of place, I think I mentioned, there are a lot of pillows of varying thickness plus the many bolsters and decorative pillows as well. I'm adding and adding until finally she says, "Oh, yes!" "Oh Bonarh, you look good" and then "Bonarh please watch this:" as I raise my arms over my head and begin where I left off: full strokes of the floggers both at the same time. The way Bonarh is positioned, now especially, with torso raised, my target is large: ass back shoulders and I'm able to hit as hard as I want. Soon we are both watching as I hit her as hard as I want. And when I do we both yell, "Yes, yes."

The window is great because the reflection is so dark, we can't, or let me put it this way, I can't see myself truly, just as if I'm maybe like in a nightclub, or some kind of dark club, where I'm disguised slightly. Though I do look happy, and excited and I'm not just talking about the hard dick. There's an aura of excitement about me that does seem visible in this darkened window reflection.

During this session with the floggers and the belt and my hands on her dress, I've been asking Bonarh questions about every time she's been ass fucked. "Please Bonarh tell me every ass fucking experience you've had." "Starting when?" "Bonarh please tell me every ass fucking experience you've had." Of course, like most, Bonarh's begins with the handle of a hairbrush. She's quite young but realizes that the shape of the handle could, perhaps, provide pleasure. And then as a young woman, still as masturbation, she's inserting various objects up her ass. "And getting off on this?" "Oh yes, I liked it a lot."

Bonarh's ass is raised, but because of the pillow pallet so she can watch herself being beat; it's not offered, per se. Her whole body is raised, as I described. But still she is kneeling on the little couch, the settee at the foot of the bed which she's folded over. I'm behind her, alternately standing barely brushing against her thighs with the front of my own thighs and then pushing in a bit against her or folded over myself, with the dick hanging down off my hips, pushing into the leather of her dress. The feeling is quite arousing. I get stuck in this feeling now for a while.

I lean forward and push the dick into the leather and then as I raise to standing again, I slowly drag the dick against the smooth leather. Soon, I lift the skirt of Bonarh's dress to just under her ass, that incredibly sweet spot on a woman where ass becomes thigh in a curve, this curve holds the dress as does the dress itself, the rough inside of the leather. "Oh Bonarh, you look amazing." Bonarh, kneeling on the little couch, laying then on the pillow pallet raised, dress raised now too to just under her ass, and just the beginning of the curve is visible. I stand behind Bonarh and lean forward so my thighs are against her bare feet. "Look at yourself" I tell her and our eyes meet in the window's reflection.

Now when I lean forward, the dick is between her legs and Bonarh gasps with surprise and pleasure. The dick is so smooth and easy, it gently parts the parts of Bonarh's thighs that are closed together, near the top. I can't see the harness over her cunt and asshole, the dress isn't that high but its outline across her back and around her hips is clearly seen. I push in slowly, the dick between her thighs, and then I'm still for a moment, very still, hanging there like that almost. In the window, I look over at myself, levis, dick, suspenders, glasses. And then, still watching, still looking, I begin to pull out slowly, but just my hips. My thighs are still against Bonarh's feet, only the dick is moving. Bonarh moans. And hearing her, I do too. I'm so slow with this withdrawal it's like I'm... I'm lost in it all. The slow teasing isn't even teasing because it feels so good to both of us, obviously, there's nothing more to even want, just to enjoy this slow slow fucking.

I'm watching the dick, watching my thighs, watching myself in the window and watching Bonarh. "Oh Bonarh, you look amazing."

I pull out and before I'm out I'm going back in. "Do you feel me watching you Bonarh?" My eyes on Bonarh, my eyes on the window's reflection, I'm catching her eyes in the window, I'm smiling and high now, really going high. I'm back in again, tight against Bonarh's ass with the dick between her thighs and she's moaning when I push and press, just a bit. I'm coming out so slowly again and the dick's shaft is wet. Now, I'm moaning. Slowly, almost to the end, just to the tip of the dick, just to where the tip gets caught on the dress' edge, the hem of leather there catches under the head, or just at the head, and for a moment, the dress is slightly lifted, the dick is being pulled slightly down, there's a thick tension between dick and leather and dress and me and Bonarh and then, I let go and the dick releases and pops up, bangs my clit with the base.

February 23, 2018:
Dear Bobby:

I'm excited now, seriously. I step back away from Bonarh, bent over the bed, and grab the dick in my fist and push and grind it against my clit, pushing the base against my clit, against myself and really getting turned on.

The dick is in my right hand and I've turned to face the uncovered windows, reflecting myself. My left hand rests on Bonarh's haunch. Her head rests with her shoulders on the large pallet of pillows I made on the mattress, piling them up high so she could also see herself in the window's reflection.

With my hand on the side of her ass like this, I have to admit, the image is extremely appealing: Bonarh bent over the bed in a leather dress, two shades of blue, the dress pulled up to just the curve of her ass, her thighs bare and she's kneeling on the little couch at the foot of the bed, her bare feet just at the edge, just hanging off the edge of this couch, and she's turned her head so she's facing the window, watching me pet her ass and stroke and pull and push the dick in the harness from my hips, grinding the dick in my fist onto my clit. I'm kind of dancing there like that, levis, black engineer boots, button fly unbuttoned, dick out in my hand, leather suspenders holding my levis up, white net a-shirt. I'm a little scrawny but in the window, it doesn't look like that. The darkened image has even produced muscles in my arms when I'm moving, kind of dancing. My cunt is wet, my clit is hard, and through the net shirt my swollen nipples have my breasts looking full and round. "Look Bonarh."

My left hand begins to slowly lift her skirt a bit higher. Both of us are watching my hand do this. Ah, slowly baring more of Bonarh's ass, gently while I hold the dick in the other hand, still now but pressed on my clit. Slowly lifting a bit higher and then before the full cheek is exposed I pull the leather back down to the curve. Ah, we moan. This I do a few more times, I'm lost; the image of us together in the window, darkened but alight and so appealing, this enactment, projected and reflected, and then repeated, again and again and in the action which I first feel in my hand, my arm, my other hand, the lifting the smoothing the pulling the pushing and the grinding and the stillness and the dress held for a moment before it's pulled back down to the top of her thigh, then the action is seen as it's done and so felt in my brain and in my eyes and in Bonarh's eyes watching the reenactment of the same action again.

With each reenactment, with each reaching of the peak where after a pause the dress will be pulled back down, the excitement builds considerably. We're getting higher and higher. I'm sweating quite profusely now, really wet with sweat under my arms, at the back of the neck my hair is wet and my cunt, wet. The gas fire behind me is blazing and this helps keep it hot (I'm thinking of Bonarh's bare feet not getting cold) but the building of heat is between us and I'm watching Bonarh's skin begin to glisten as well. Her eyes are sparkling, alive and as the dress reaches the top of her ass, baring her cheek, as I pull the leather slowly across her skin and then pause and hold still for a moment, Bonarh is still with me and the moment I begin to pull the dress back down, her moan and eyes closing, a look almost of her eyes rolling into her head and she shakes, her body shakes with a release of this building but also the release of the repeated motion: "Ah, yes, this…"

I take again my position directly behind Bonarh: my thighs against her bare feet bottoms, I'm leaning into her as if she's supporting my weight. Again, the dick slips between her thighs which are now slick with perspiration and my entry here is easy. Bonarh watches my slow slowness in the window and is gasping as I've been able with a slight shifting of my stance, to have the tip of the dick rub across the leather strap between her legs. Again, the feeling of the dick on the leather of the harness is different from that of the dress and this new feeling has me wanting to feel it so bad I fall forward on my hands, feet still on the floor, propping myself above Bonarh so she only feels me on her feet and on the leather of the harness covering her cunt, an almost chastity belt that keeps the dick from actually penetrating her. This thought, of not being able to fuck her, or of her desire being denied, or just the thought of leather straps crossing a wet cunt of which I'm experiencing myself with the harness of the dick I wear, has me pounding quickly, pumping my hips.

The dick is sliding on the wet leather easily and my cunt is sliding on wet leather too. There's a moment when while I'm pumping, the dick is pulled slightly away from my body, very slightly, and then as I pull or push, continue, is on my clit again, slipping on my swollen wetness. I'm watching Bonarh, watching her body move with me, respond and receive this attention and her own pushing pulling pumping groaning moaning and I'm watching her body and her ass and thighs and shoulders take all of this and then I'm watching my arms, planted alongside her on the mattress, fists on the bed holding me above her and then the way the dick looks as it plunges between her thighs rapidly and then from the corner of my eye I catch a glimpse of motion and oh, yes, the window.

When I look over at the window, Bonarh is already there, watching me fuck her from behind like this; she's watching my hips and my arms and her ass and yeah, here in the watching being watched is where I'm gone, literally, I disappear into a state of transcendence, of beyond this and this means all of this, like a time distorting hall of mirrors, like a space distortion of image action and idea occurring at once and then though I'm experiencing my body, in fact I'm literally looking at my body, I'm gone and it's amazing.

The fucking continues like this and also stops. I pull the nipple clamps from my bag and I lift my shirt, watching myself in the window-mirror and I put the clamps on my nipples, tight and hard and then take up behind Bonarh again and now added to all of it, the chain hanging between my breasts, shirt lifted up above my tits and the rest: Bonarh, her ass, her cunt, my cunt, the way she looks, the way she looks, the way I look and my cunt and my dick and the harness and the leather and the image and the image and the image and my feet in boots, her thighs bare, her ass cheeks bare and her eyes watching us, her eyes meeting mine, behind glasses, in the glass of the darkened window, and how hadn't I noticed this before, but when I let my gaze relax a bit, out the window and not at it, I see the cypress tree, permanently its canopy in the windblownness, vast expanse of flat-topped leaves just outside the window.

During this, intermittently, Bonarh has been telling me her experiences of ass fucking. Ass fucking has never really been my thing and so I'm interested and curious and asking her questions with each of her installations. "Yes? And then?" "Well, I was living in New Orleans and I had a lover who was very gentle and very into anal and so…" even just that line alone is enough to rabidly excite me and my fucking begins seriously in earnest now. Increasing in pace and speed and thrusting harder into Bonarh's thighs with the dick. Bonarh's telling becomes more and more breathless and distracted. She's panting and I'm asking her to repeat, "Ok, you have a gentle but persistent lover…" "Yes, and we were together one…" Is it her voice, is it imagining her getting fucked by this gentle lover gently, is my desire such that I've reached a peak where I don't even care what's being said or how or why, just the vibration of sound to this scene.

Which though I've been fucking her for a while, intensely actively and with serious attention, I'm not inside her at all and this is, no question, a huge part of the turn on for me. Both of us are sweating and panting and breathing so heavily and seriously so excited, my head is spinning, swirling. Bonarh can barely talk, her eyes aren't really open but they aren't shut either. She has that look again of her eyes almost rolled back into her head. When I call her to me, in the window, she takes a moment to be able to focus her gaze which is completely elsewhere now. I don't care about anything at all.

Bonarh is telling me about being fucked slowly, slowly, first a finger and how slowly and I collapse on her back letting myself fall forward onto her and I lay still and beneath me Bonarh is kind of spasming, shaking and I receive the vibrations now, through my body fully. I close my eyes to rest, to pause, to receive only this between us. Ah.

In a moment though I'm back up and telling Bonarh roll over, get up and I'm grabbing her hand in mine and pulling her hand into my pants, behind the dick to fuck me. I'm standing, Bonarh's kneeling on the couch, facing me and she's swooning as she feels how wet I am and then I'm falling back on the bed, onto the raised pallet of pillows onto my back and I'm loosening the harness around my hips so Bonarh can really get into my cunt and fuck me deeply.

The dick lays limply to the side of my open jeans and though the strap is still between my legs, it's loose enough for Bonarh's hand to get behind it and fuck me. I hold the dick in my left hand and direct Bonarh as she's inside me. "Very slowly pull out almost the edge of my cunt and then push back in quickly and slowly slowly pull out again." I allow myself the feeling of falling and being caught, being held by her hand as I lift my hips in the slowness of her fucking, using my slow rhythm to show her what and how and she's holding it steady, slow and then fast and slowslowslow yeah, then push in hard and fast, yeah, fuck me like this, slow and then feel me wanting it and fuck me there, yeah.

February 24, 2018:
Dear Bobby:

Bonarh is fucking me. I'm on my back in the bed in the motel and I'm giving her the directions: yeah, pull me right to the edge, pull out real slowly, then push back in hard and fast, yeah, like that fuck me. Bonarh is using her hand and I like it. I'm still wearing my dick but the straps are loosened sufficiently such that she can get behind the strap into my cunt; the dick hangs limply to the side. I drop the dick which I'd been holding in my left fist and grab the chain of the nipple clamps that hangs between my breasts. I lift the chain up off my chest and pull my breasts by the nipples straight up. It's painful and with my right hand I'm slowly jacking off my clit.

Yes, Bonarh, like that, real real slow as you pull out. I'm lifting my hips to slow her hand even further, yes, like you're pulling me over the edge, yes fuck me and she does, her hand pushing in hard, yes, push in deeper and then the slow slow pulling out and as we reach this point, the point of her hand almost out of my cunt, almost about to push back in, I'm reaching a peak, I'm mounting and moaning and it's amazing and then as she pushes her hand back into my cunt I rub my clit a bit harder and faster and then again, slowing slowing my pace to show her again, slow slow ah, slow.

Round after round of this has me shaking and writhing, my cunt is begging for her hand even when she's inside me. I pull the chain higher, flattening my tits with their height, searing my nipples and feeling as though I'm pulling my clit up through the center of myself as I pull the chain. And it's there then that with Bonarh pulling me from the inside out and the chain pulling the outside in that I come. And it's good. I'm thrown into an almost convulsive state where my pulsing has me off the bed, lifted off the pallet of pillows and my head is thrown back and I'm not saying anything.

Bonarh comes to lay next to me but she's on the mattress and not on the tall pallet so it's slightly awkward. I roll off and roll onto her and roll her onto her back. I lay like that on top of Bonarh, just still, a bit disheveled, shirt up over my breasts, dick kind of stuck between us but to the side and the nipple clamps are really paining now. I'm up in a minute, piling the pillows back on the chair in the corner of the room, taking them all off the bed. Then, while Bonarh lays there on her back, I readjust the straps of the harness I wear, I loosen the nipple clamps and pull them off. Ah. It's painful and behind the dick, my clit responds and is hard on the base of the dick.

I pull my shirt down and then lean over and pull Bonarh's dress up. I gather the leather up past her hips and it's gathered at her thick waist. The harness over her cunt is so wet and slick, her swollen lips have basically engulfed the strap. I slip my finger behind the strap and just slide my finger up and down, knuckle rubbing over her open cunt. Oh, Bonarh, are you ready to get fucked? I unsnap the strap and Bonarh is so open I can dive right in, kneeling now myself on the little couch and propping myself above Bonarh with my fists planted on the bed. My dick hovers for a second and then with just a slight shift of my hips, plunges deep into Bonarh's cunt.

With the couch and how good I feel and how good Bonarh feels it's easy to fuck like this and by easy, I mean really easy, smooth and good and once I start, a rhythm comes quickly and without thinking I'm on the ride too. Bonarh has her eyes open and our faces are close together. I like fucking you Bonarh, I say. And she nods her head, not saying anything. It doesn't take long before I've built according to Bonarh's pace, into short hard thrusts of my hips and the dick and Bonarh is grabbing me around my shoulders and begins coming in a long strong yell of pleasure and while she does I just ride and follow as she rises and falls repeatedly.

As we are reaching what feels like the top of this wave, I hold myself still on one hand and reach into my pocket for the razor blade I have there. It's wrapped in foil, from a snake bite kit I've also brought. I unwrap the blade, carefully. It's never been used so it's really razor sharp. Bonarh is still thrusting against me and I'm meeting her and as she slows and starts to close her eyes, I call her back: Bonarh. Still on one hand, the dick still inside her, still still, I bring the blade to her face and draw it across her cheek, lightly. Bonarh moans, says oh no. She moans again and I ask her, no? And she says no, yes, please. I place the blade there again and cut Bonarh's face, slice it.

February 25, 2018:
Dear Bobby:

I place the sharp blade against Bonarh's face, her upper cheek just beneath her eye, the line of her cheek bone and I slice it. The drawing is so quick, the blade, brand new, so sharp. It takes a moment for the blood to flow, for a moment there's nothing visible, that's how sharp the razor is, and then a red line appears and then the blood. I lean forward, I kiss Bonarh and then suck her blood into my mouth and then kiss her again. She tastes the blood and is startled, though of course she felt the cut I made. I push up from her again, dick still on my hips and still inside her cunt and balancing on one hand I take the blade to my own cheek and slice there too.

I immediately understand why Bonarh is startled tasting the blood. The cutting causes such a flood of feeling it's disorienting. For a moment, I'm not sure what's happened though I know because I did it. And then the same, the blood is flowing down my cheek now too. I kiss Bonarh again and pull the handkerchief from my back pocket and alternate pressing her face and mine, staunching quickly the flow.

At this point, everything is falling away. Everything is falling away now: work, home, the election, memories of Jones Beach, even the car accident. And thank god for the car accident because aa would fall away too. Coming down when Canela asked what meetings I'd go to, I kind of secretly had the idea 'maybe I'll take a few days off...' and so far in less than two days I'd been to two meetings. I mean, I'd never make it to any meetings of aa if it were up to me.

I roll off Bonarh, sliding the dick out as I do. We lay on our backs, side by side for a while. The fire is blazing still. We get up, we each piss, I take off the dick, Bonarh takes off the dress. We decide to go for a bite before we go to sleep. We'd been in the room since about 1pm or so, though who knows what time it is now. Outside its winter now. We have on our coats and hats but still we must walk briskly through the little town. But no matter, it's really now all geared to tourists and so as we walk through the streets and the plaza, it's all closed except for the bar way at the end of the street our motel is on. Everything is quiet.

And then back to the motel. The bed. The fire. The window, still uncovered. The pillows piled high on the chair in the corner. The little couch. And again, once inside here, everything falls away outside. No time, no place or at least no space that isn't anywhere else the way a motel room is, isn't this why people come to motels. Of course, to rest while traveling, but also the anonymity of self and of place too, one like another anywhere. What is this moment worth; to enjoy myself doesn't describe what I want. I want to forget everything, including myself.

It's almost, this feeling, high from bloodletting and fucking and coming and feeling young, but a youth I never felt. For a moment to forget every regret, a lifetime of regret, including the regret of the future. Disappearing while I watch, flooded with feeling good and nothing else. This is what I want. I want this.

Bonarh and I get into the big king size bed. Without all the pillows, the expanse seems vast. I pull her toward me, moving to put my arms around her. I'm on my side, facing her and my arms underneath her shoulder but the harness she's wearing is bulky in the bed like this. It's kind of uncomfortably digging into my belly and chest. I try to shift Bonarh's position, try to get comfortable, but that only puts it at my arm, the soft under part. I try and shift her again and that doesn't work either. "I mean, this isn't comfortable. How do you sleep in this?" and I realize no wonder she's up every night, waking in the middle of the night in a state of excitation, reminded of her submission.

I'm beat though. I fall asleep and don't remember dreaming or if I woke at all. I only remember waking when I heard the door to the room close, very gently. I open my eyes and Bonarh's gone out. She's left a note I find when I get to piss 'taking a walk' but I'm up now and weirdly already looking at my device and for fuck's sake! There's a meeting at 6:45am across the street from the motel room! Well, I continue to take my personal inventory, meditate then make a cup of coffee while I dress to get out the door. I bring the coffee with me, aa coffee as a way to start the day puts a bad taste in my mouth. And I judge every single thing about this meeting: what they say, what they share, fear they all sound like addicts watering down an alcoholic group conscious, but I'm moved to share and I put my hand up, get called on and say, "I'm grateful to be sober as a result of the steps."

February 26, 2018:
Dear Bobby:

It's actually amazing, again, to experience freedom from the bondage of self as a result of the steps, so much so that in a room full of strangers, I'm able to raise my hand, say my name and that I'm an alcoholic, but more amazingly, to say I'm an alcoholic who is grateful to be sober as a result of the steps. Which is the reason for the steps, I'm getting what is described, which is incredibly unbelievable, in fact rarely seen. Most alcoholics of the hopeless variety, hoping against hope that we are not true alcoholics, meanwhile sitting at a bar, ordering a drink: "here's how!" and then slamming our fists on the same bar, wondering how did this happen again? To be among the most hopeless, self-pitying, self-centered in the world is to be among the most fortunate and to be bearing witness to this power, arrived at with these steps.

So, after the meeting, with a complete psychic change, I return across the street to the motel. Bonarh is in the bed, under the covers, wearing the harness with wet hair, combed. "I took a shower," she says. I pull the little chair over to the side of the bed, next to the night stand and sit. "What else, Bonarh? What else do you need to tell me." She went for a walk this morning, she was up early... "I know, I woke as you left at 6am." Oh, she thought she was being quiet enough. "No, Bonarh, if you wake and are up and leaving, you need to make me coffee before you leave. Make the coffee and put it by the bed on the nightstand." Ok. She went out and it was cold but she had on her wool serape over her sweater and pants and she had on her hat and also a scarf. She walked a bit and then not too far from here found a park where she could do qi gong. She liked it, she said.

Bonarh asks if I'm hungry and I'm not, I just want more coffee but it's right to eat in the morning especially after not really eating dinner the night before. I want to be hard but not mean. There's still bread left and some butter; Bonarh take the bread to the kitchen here and ask them to toast it, please. Put the kettle on with water. Coffee's made and then I get into the bed Bonarh's left, taking off my 501's, and button-down shirt, slipping into the still warm sheets in my a-shirt and underwear. I drink the coffee and write a bit. It's already a swirl of everything.

Bonarh's back with the toast on a big buffet plate. She's got an order of bacon and sausage too. Sit in that chair, Bonarh. She puts the plate on the night stand and sits in the chair and I sit up higher, propping the pillows behind my back in the bed. I hold the toast to her mouth and she bites and then I'm feeding her the breakfast meat. Like I say, I'm not that hungry, so I drink my coffee and have some of the bread with butter, a few bites of bacon but the sausage is like breakfast links and I'm not sure what's in them, but I don't like it. So mostly it's putting food into Bonarh's mouth, telling her continually, "Open your mouth." I like it when her mouth is so full she can barely chew, has to kind of choke the food down. The final piece of sausage

I put into her mouth without letting her bite a piece off, sliding the meat down her throat as far as I can. Bonarh does cough and choke, her eyes tear and then she smiles deeply at me. I'm happy.

After breakfast, I get back into the bed for real, like laying down head on the pillow. Bonarh gets in behind me and we lay together, despite the harness between us. As we lay there, Bonarh tells me she had a terrible dream the night before. "You had killed yourself," she said. I laughed. "It was terrible," she said. "Yeah, your nightmare is my dream come true!" Bonarh's told me she's dreamt this dream before. "You dreamed this again, huh? Is this some kind of wishful thinking?" I ask, trying to joke with her. "No, I'm really afraid of this," she says. "Really?" I ask. "Do you know how much you talk about killing yourself?" she says, "Really, it's disturbing. I mean, I like you, I would miss you, but also the constant talk of wanting to kill yourself is really intense."

I try to explain "this is alcoholism." I try to explain the meeting this morning, the steps, the result of the steps, of the first time I went to an aa meeting, of the meeting the day before, this morning, the steps being passed onto me, Bill's spiritual experience, Bill writing that his guilt and depression were made so worse for the fact that he was unable to work the very steps he wrote; I try to explain no one could do the steps, that if we aren't grasped and developed in this manner of living we can't stay sober, not the real alcoholic; I try to explain that my first memory in my life is walking down the street I grew up on, 5 years old, thinking, 'I gotta kill myself" without even understanding what that meant or without even having an understanding of how or why or anything and that that was what alcohol provided relief from: a brain that says I have to kill myself. Thank god for alcohol, thank god for every drink I took. I don't think Bonarh understands.

February 27, 2018:
Dear Bobby:

Ok listen, so we're at the motel. We had some disgusting meat off the buffet table, bacon and sausage that felt like it was loaded with chemicals. At least we had the bread and butter. That, and the coffee, which after I drink a cup and eat even a bit of that meat, laying back in the bed with Bonarh, I fall deeply asleep, like a coma. That kind.

I wake, if there were dreams I don't remember, with Bonarh at my back, behind me in the big bed. She comes at me. Quickly, unexpectedly, she's in my underwear with her hands. I feel her breath at the back of my neck, hot and she's breathing softly through her mouth. I squirm a bit. Honestly, I'm uncomfortable and hoping to discourage her. But waking like this, now must be near midday, having already woke, drank coffee, been out and more coffee and then so solidly asleep again, I'm disoriented. I squirm again. Bonarh's arms are around me now, at my waist and hands going into my underwear in the front.

I roll over. As I say, I'm uncomfortable. And the truth is, I'm uncomfortable being touched. Especially like this. I'm not really awake, though waking more by the second. And without coffee, I'm distracted. I want to actually tell Bonarh, 'if you're going to touch me, get up and make me coffee before you do' but that seems antithetical to what's happening. Which is that for basically the first time, Bonarh is initiating. That alone, that kind of switch-up, is enough to have thrown me a bit. By this I mean, the waking, the lack of coffee and her initiating together has me confused enough that I haven't pushed her hand away or actually gotten out of bed. That would be usual for me.

I roll over. I'm wondering if perhaps I can regain what I consider to be my position in this way. But the result is that I've kind of rolled closer to Bonarh and somehow her hands are deeper inside my underwear. She's kind of grabbing at me and I'm trying to try this. C'mon, I think to myself, how bad can it be? Now, I know for most people that's not super sexy but I also know that for most women, this is exactly what they've said to themselves before having sex, at least once.

And I'm not that comfortable being touched. I'm fearful of the vulnerability, of allowing myself to want that way, or to desire that way. I'm fearful I won't respond the right way, meaning fear I can't get fucked right. Fear I should enjoy this more than I do which is the same as fear I don't enjoy being fucked. Fear if I say what I want, I still won't be satisfied.

I'm grateful for the compensatory, some might say, behaviors that have developed into what I consider my sexuality. I love to fuck; getting fucked, that's more difficult. And negotiating what I consider my own rigidity regarding sexual positions or activities is also a challenge, one I've mostly managed to avoid with reliance on a kind of taking the reins in my own hands, so to speak. But, c'mon, I say to myself, you wanted to be uncomfortable sexually, specifically.

And I am uncomfortable. Bonarh's energy is high. Her mouth is now on the back of my neck. Or, am I on my back. She's got a hand down the front and a hand down the back. Am I kind of laying on one of her hands, I'm not sure. She's fucking me soon enough that I'm not wondering that anymore. She's got her fingers in my cunt and a finger in my ass and she's got her mouth near my head. I want this to feel good. I want to enjoy this. I tell myself to enjoy this, to at least try to enjoy this, but as we know, as most of us have experienced, telling yourself to just enjoy this while having sex kind of guarantees you won't.

And listen, I hate sounding like this. More, I hate being like this. I want to be better than I am, that's for sure. So, I go along with this, with Bonarh fucking me. The bed is piled with blankets from her smashed car and also sheepskins which Bonarh brought on the trip. So, I am getting fucked under skins and blankets. And, when I, even just for that length, say 'I'm getting fucked under skins and blankets' to myself, I'm able to forget myself enough to enjoy being fucked under skins and blankets.

They say that a spiritual experience is one that can't be measured because, namely, that it is a spiritual experience, outside of the time that doesn't even exist; that reality is revealed for what it is and that is that time is a delusion. So even the most profound of the saints and prophets' spiritual experience, that when it is described goes on for perhaps pages and pages, "...the light, the light and the ecstasy! No matter how wrong things seem, they are all right! A feeling of love and of being loved!" that most of these experiences, if they could be measured, would probably only be just a few minutes, maybe like five, and that's the ones we heard about, like I say, the great prophets and saints. Mostly though, what is experienced and described by many (turns out when through the ages, spiritual experiences are compared, many have many of the same components) is a flash of light. So how long does that last, yet the people are so profoundly affected as to have life altering, complete life changes.

So I'm not comparing the sexual experience that morning with Bonarh in the bed to a spiritual experience, but I will say that yeah, like a few moments of enjoyment, of being able to forget myself, to think of instead the sheepskins and blankets weighing heavily on my body, to think of the weight of the blankets and skins, plus the sheets and blankets from the motel, on top of me, got me enough outside of my head, for a moment to slip into the body I don't even want to admit to having and to experience something other than fear, I'll take it. So Bonarh fucked me. And I let her. Or it's what's occurred and the rest of this is what I tell myself to explain what happened, like how else can I understand lying there and being fucked like that unless I have a whole story about it.

After, I get up and from being under the skins and blankets and getting fucked, I'm hot. I jump in the shower and use only cold water. Remember I've been swimming in the ocean for the past few months and I'm used to cold water. Or I crave it. But it feels good, like a real wake up after getting up. I put water on for coffee before I went in and when I came out, wrapped in the thick motel towels, I made a cup of coffee. Bonarh is up too, getting dressed, putting on a shirt and pants over the harness.

And then it's out to the truck. We'll go to the beach. The sky is blue. We bring towels and our bathing suits. I bring the typewriter, the portable I've brought on this trip. I've made another jar of medicinal strength maté too. And then we're off in the big truck with a crazy good sound system and heated seats.

The drive through Monterey is full of traffic and slow, plus we don't really know where we're going exactly. Even though there seems to be only one main road, something about it is confusing. It should be easy, the water and everything, but we're driving through Monterey a while before finally winding up at Asilomar Beach. Plus, the motel had told us some other beach to go to and that was what we were looking for when we found this one. By the time we got there, on the other side of the peninsula, it's kind of raining again.

But once there the beach is lovely. It has a wide expanse of sand and the waves here too, are easy and look soft. The rain has made it empty. Most of the cars that are parked along the road here are leaving. The surfers who are in their wetsuits, tourists who got out of their rental cars and stand on the side of the road to look. It is beautiful.

And speaking of wetsuits, Bonarh is climbing over the seat to the back to get hers. I pull the typewriter onto my lap and open it up, lift off the carrying case that is the cover and set it on my lap. Bonarh has a playlist playing through the car sound system and now that we are still and not driving, it is incredible how loud and clear the sound sounds. The sun is still out, but it's drizzling kind of heavily, rain and mist from the ocean, which in this light has turned grey. I begin typing, I'm writing about the water, the sky, the music and now about Bonarh putting on the wetsuit: she's undressing and then squatting on the front seat and singing along with a Phil Collins remix (Against All Odds in dance version, it's actually quite beautiful and the pounding beat like this, at the beach and the pounding waves and the typewriter pounding, I think you get my drift) "How could you just walk away/leave me standing here alone/just the memory of your face…" and then she's taking off the harness while I watch.

The whole day so far has been emotional, waking early, too early, and then still kind of recovering from the car accident, and then the meeting, a powerful experience there, and then Bonarh fucking me the way she did and us getting up, my cold shower and now, here again at the beach, getting ready to get in the water and Phil Collins and Bonarh singing and taking off the harness, I start to cry while I'm typing about watching her take the harness off, what it's meant, the last time I saw her with it off we were about to swim at the Albany Bulb but now, knowing that it will all soon be over, here is the prelude to that, to Bonarh without the harness on: she's naked on the seat.

March 1, 2018:

Dear Bobby:

Bonarh's got the driver's seat reclined completely. She is undressing, squatting and shifting on the chair, in the harness, about to unbuckle the straps to take it off before swimming. Of course, this is the part I don't want to type: the removal of the harness, which is the idea that has been agreed will happen this weekend. Bonarh will take off my harness, which she's been wearing for three months, with attention and intention.

I'm typing with the small portable typewriter on my lap in the passenger seat of the big truck. The seat is heated and the sound system is really incredible. Bonarh is playing a playlist that includes Phil Collins' Against All Odds (I cried in 1985 at house parties, drunk, my girlfriend going to college, "Take a look at me now! /You're the only one who really knew me at all!) singing along while I type and cry. I look over as she pulls her bathing suit from her bag in the back. she's naked, wearing only her socks. It's almost like I don't recognize her body, she's been defined by the leather through all of this.

While she pulls on her bathing suit and wet suit in the front seat, I get out of the car. I need some fresh air and I put the cover back on the typewriter, put the whole thing back in the back and then pull my suit out of the bag I have in the back. With the passenger door open, the music fills this space around the parked big truck. I undress there in that space made by the door, pulling shirt overhead, pants down after boots are off. When I look at Bonarh again, she's watching me now, and she's crying a bit. I pull on my bathing suit.

It's cold here out of the truck, naked and bare feet. A light rain falls. I'm wet before we even get to the water which is soft and the beach here is wide, a wide swath of sand and gentle, playful constant waves. We put the electronic key under the back wheel and then run down to the water's edge. Two surfer guys, standing in their wetsuits, holding their boards, say as we pass, "Wow you're going for it, huh?" and I smile and say hell yeah. And actually, on a day like today, cold rain, wind, the water, the ocean actually feels warmer getting in. I run into the little waves, then to my knees and up to my mid-thighs and kind of bend my knees, sinking in a bit deeper, shiver, yell and push on. I dive under the next wave and on the other side, swim a bit.

I'm not a strong swimmer but I love the ocean, the open water swimming is like life and un-life, negation of self, no sound, floating, salt water buoyancy, salt water equilibrium, like a balancing of or between me and the ocean, great mother, the return to that moment of pre-existence; sure, some forward crawl strokes, sure some back-strokes but mostly just treading water and floating and being carried along and looking at the sky and the birds and waves, way out and then approaching. The cold water of the Pacific is mind-numbingly cold, thankfully: an extra benefit.

And because of the rain, we have it all to ourselves. Bonarh in her wetsuit is swimming. I'm floating rolling laughing. The break today is easy and not too far out. Getting up on top of the waves is easy and feels exciting, not dangerous and the wideness of the beach here too kind of just deposits me up on the sand, doesn't throw me and tumble me like at Baker. And plus, the waves aren't tall enough for surfers, it seems; they've all packed up and left. I'm running in and out of the water until I'm shivering too cold. My teeth are chattering and I'm smiling and laughing and Bonarh is out now too. We run back up to the truck.

Which, arriving back at the big truck parked on the road, we find we forgot to turn it off, the stereo was playing too loud so we didn't hear the engine and since it doesn't need a key to start it, well, it's running. We got the key from under the wheel and unlocked the door and as we got in, the seats, still with seat warmers on, were like little griddles. The playlist was still playing and the heat blowing from the vents. So, no problem getting in after taking the towel from the back and drying off. So many people had left, I just took my bathing suit off there on the street, threw it in the truck back and went around to the front and dressed, socks and pants and shirt but no jacket needed. The truck is like a sauna and it feels good.

Bonarh is driving today, I don't feel comfortable yet getting back behind the wheel of a car. The accident is still too fresh and I don't really trust myself with an even bigger and more powerful vehicle, especially not in the rain. So, once we are back in and driving, I give directions to get us over to hwy1. There's a backup nearthe entrance to the 17 Mile Drive, one lane of traffic in each direction, and then the same on Route 68. I'm getting irritated now, the crawling along like this and the wanting to get some hot tea or coffee. Then ok, things move along and there's a shopping center with a thrift store and a place to get coffee. Let's go there.

As we are driving, we start talking about the accident. There's still a lot left to discharge about the whole thing, though Bonarh doesn't seem completely fucked up about it. I am, feeling guilty and all the other things I've described here. "I'm glad about the motel we found though," I say, "I mean we never would have found that spot and swam in the morning, just walking over to that beach and seeing the dolphins. I'm glad you said you just really wanted to get to a motel so we could fuck."

"Yeah," Bonarh says, "but too bad we didn't."

I am so surprised, so caught off guard, fuck, so resentful, I don't even know what to say. Plus, while we are talking, I'm giving Bonarh directions to the shopping center.

"What are you talking about?" I ask.

"Well, I just mean, we got to the motel and then we went to your aa meeting."

"Yeah, but when we got back from the meeting, you fucked me. Don't you remember?"

Oh, why is this the thing that brings me back from gone to myself again; why is what makes me remember myself this resentment? How can I be here again?

I'm actually angry, hurt and I yell in the truck as we pull into the parking lot, "Don't you remember fucking me?" I mean this is my worst nightmare, and my worst inventory, the generating principle of my life: 'fear women don't want to fuck me; fear women don't want to touch me; fear fucking me is not important to women; fear women just want me to fuck them; fear women don't recognize my vulnerability.'

"Oh yeah," Bonarh says. I can't be sure what that means, like is she saying that like she does remember or is she saying she doesn't remember.

I'm spiraling down. And I mean down. I know it's my inventory,

I recognize it as such and therefore false evidence appearing real, but shit, this is mesmerizingly real. I feel like I'm falling down a dark hole. This seems proof of Bonarh's betrayal, proof I could never trust her, proof I've been mistaken about all of this, proof that this trip is a mistake.

"What does that mean?" I ask Bonarh, trying to not lose my temper. I've pulled a scrap of paper from the front pocket of my levis and I'm scratching down these lines but fear it won't be enough; fear everything is ruined. I'm putting my fears on paper, asking this power to remove them.

"Listen," Bonarh says as she puts the truck into park. "Turn it off this time," I say. "Yeah," she says, then "listen, I forgot that I fucked you in the motel. It's not that it's not important to me, it's just that with the accident and then everything else plus the meeting, I mean, it's been a lot. Not to mention last night and this morning. I'm in a swirl with it all. I love fucking you, I think about it all the time. I wish you could believe me when I say how much I think about fucking you, how much I'm wanting it and how glad I am every time you let me."

It's like I'm viewing this scene through a dark shadowy thick glass, like I can see her, and hear her, but it's like I'm stuck in this unreality of my belief system, I can't reach her and actually I can barely even understand her, that's how foreign what she's saying is to me.

So, I say, "C'mon, let's get some coffee." I'm hoping maybe if I sharpen up my head, it will all make sense but I know that is just more of the same self-will asserting itself. There's no making sense of delusion, no matter how much coffee I drink. But I'll marshal my will and push on. The line for the coffee is long, I'm not being patient, I'm holding Bonarh back and from me with a strong hard energy field. I'm squinting my eyes at her with an uncertainty as if I'm trying to assess the situation. Bonarh is the one with patience here.

Then we're served, coffee for me, some kind of green tea for Bonarh, water. I almost buy the rotisserie chicken in plastic that is available but by the time we are paying I put it back on the shelf. I'm still out of sorts from it all and now, doubly confused Bonarh has her hand on the small of my back, a gentle gesture that actually, in hindsight, works. By the time we are back at the truck, climbing in, and planning the next part of the drive, I've forgotten the inventory. The waiting for the coffee was enough of a distraction and irritation that my resentment shifted there. That, or the steps worked. Bonarh starts the truck

March 2, 2018:
Dear Bobby:

Bonarh starts the truck and we make it back out to hwy1 and begin driving south. At this time of year, the day is darker early and I don't know what time it is but by the time hwy1 swings back out along the coast it's dusk. There's too many clouds to see a sunset but it's obvious there is one. The road is empty and dark. I'm looking out the window for a place to pull off. I'm looking for a space that's a bit deeper than just off the shoulder. Suddenly, in the darkening ahead there is one. "Pull off," I say and Bonarh hurries to obey. "Here?" she asks. Yes here.

I direct her to back the truck into this spot which is off the road in a clearing under some trees just a short walk to the edge of the cliff that hwy1 rides tightly along. It's started raining again and we sit in the truck after we pull in and listen to the rain on the truck. Bonarh doesn't know what's happening but I have a plan. I get out of the truck and walk around the truck, I take a piss near the back and then walk around the front and toward the road a bit and then turn around and walk back toward the truck. I'm looking to see how visible the truck is, this big white truck here off the road but it's far enough back and the way the road curves and the small bushes provide enough disguise for us. I go back to the truck and get in the passenger side again. From the back I pull my bag forward and take out some nuts for protein and the large jar of medicinal strength maté and hold the jar to Bonarh's mouth and pour the maté in then fill my own mouth with it.

"I'm gonna go in the back and get the truck ready," I say, "you put on a sound track while I make the preparations." I set up the back of the truck, moving the blanket rolls, the typewriter, our wet bathing suits and the wetsuit, folding the seats forward, opening the back tailgate door. Then I pull out my other other bag and take out ropes, leather cuffs, get a towel, and the rest of the stuff I want.

When everything's ready I tell Bonarh to come back. She climbs over the seat from the front not wanting to get out and walk around because of the rain now. In the back I tell her to take off her pants but keep on her boots. We had the heater on before we turned the truck off but it will get cold again, I can feel it.

Bonarh is laying in the back of the truck then, shirt and sweater, no pants or underwear, boots on and the harness visible at her pussy. Lay down I say. I pull the ropes through the handles up near the ceiling by the back door, one on each side and let them hang. I take the cuffs and put Bonarh's ankles into them, buckling them, not too tight but it's good she has the boots on. Then I lift her legs, spread and tie the cuffs with the rope to the handles, again on each side. When I'm done Bonarh's legs are spread wide, the width of the truck and in the air. I reach out to Bonarh now, my hand pets her face and then her hair, gently. I'm smiling. I tell her to let her hair down, and I reach around back to take the hair tie from the little ponytail she's got back there.

I reach and unsnap the harness and tuck one end back behind her, the thick ring rests on her pubis bone just above her clit from this angle. How do you feel I ask her and she says excited. The music is playing and the sound is good. From the bag I pull the can of crisco and open it. Bonarh twists her head to see what I'm doing. I grab a handful of the grease and roll it between my fingers and begin to fill her ass with it. I make a few rolls of this and push it as much as I can. Then I start to fuck her ass, slowly, just finger at first and with this much lube it is so smooth and easy, like a hot knife through butter. Bonarh likes it. I pump a bit, pushing in and out and she and I are smiling at each other. I grab more crisco and cover my second finger and slide that one in too. Of course, ass fucking should go slow but Bonarh's wide open and with this much crisco she's more than ready. I feel her ass pulling my fingers in, hard. I pump her ass like this, two fingers feeling the smooth muscles of her ass and rectum and it's good.

As I begin to get ready with my third finger, I start to feel Bonarh's shit approaching from her guts. "Uh oh," she says, "I'm gonna shit."

"I know," I say, "I feel it." She's worried but I don't care. I push in deeper with my two fingers and dig. I make that freaky shit come up and out of her. "Push," I say and when she does Bonarh deposits a shit in my hand which I've held at her ass hole, taking fingers out and kind of pulling as she's pushing and there it is. I turn around and toss shit out of the truck into the bushes, I wipe off my hand on the towel but I mean c'mon, there's not really danger of contamination: the shit came from her ass, I'm just putting the same bacteria back in. Bonarh seems upset about this or embarrassed but I reassure her. It's not ass fucking if there's no shit, something like that. Or that I'm not disgusted by shit while ass fucking. I slide three fingers in.

March 4, 2018:
Dear Bobby:
I'm squatting in the back of the truck between Bonarh's spread and cuffed legs, raised to the roof of the truck, tied off on the handles there (for what reason I wonder?) and I have three fingers in her ass. She's opened herself to me, like this, wide. I push in more of the crisco from the can I brought and it's messy: melted crisco and her shit and the mud from the rain and the back door of the truck is open like a small canopy behind me and from the speakers, I think there must be 8 in this vehicle, a sound track of dance music plays loudly, heavy beats thumping and I'm pounding now with this beat. Bonarh and I look at each other, I call Bonarh to me: "Look at me." I pull my fingers from her ass and hold my hand between us while applying more crisco. I show her that I'm greasing my whole fist and down to my wrist and up my forearm. "Yes, Bonarh," I say, smiling, "it's all for you." Bonarh moans and as I begin again at her ass held open for me, pushing in fingers again, I start slowly and build quickly. My fingers curve and curl into a cone shape that enters easily. I watch her thighs contract and release when I ask for more. "C'mon, Bonarh, give me a little bit more. I want a little bit more. Let me fuck you deeper." And again, a breath and a sigh, a groan and I'm in deeper. "Bonarh, look at these hooks back here in the truck where I've tied your feet. What do you think they use these hooks for normally? Or is this model as big as a bed when the seats are folded down, actually usually rented

as a sling on wheels? Do you think that's how they sell it, Bonarh? As an ass fucking utility vehicle? With this sound system, pounding woofers and a hose-out carpet covered area here in the back?" With these questions occupying Bonarh's brain, I'm able to slip in my fist, just past wide knuckles of my left hand and then I hold still.

Now, I'm into this, this whole scene: the music, the beat, Bonarh with her legs in the air, the rain, the open back door which opens into tall trees that line the edge of the famous California cliffs that drop sharply to the majestic Pacific below. The interior light is on in the truck and also some small accent lights near the back doors and front cockpit. Bonarh looks incredible like this, with my fist stuck up her as and both of us still now. Watching and feeling each other, yeah, tears come to my eyes. I want this, this is what I want.

The rain and the clouds make the stars not visible, but I know they are up there, or must be, aligned to allow this incredible event, this amazing occurrence. I'd say it was like a dream come true but this is something else. I'd want to but I'd never do this. I couldn't. My desires were so convoluted, a mixed up thanatos obsession which meant marshaling the will and is in such severe opposition to itself, to oneself, that one is left prostrate as if paralyzed. Hating to live but too cowardly to kill oneself. I wanted to stop drinking. Well, actually, I wanted to not drink so much. No one wants to get drunk like that. I wanted to be able to control and enjoy my drinking. But like the lady in the book says, 'When I controlled it, I didn't enjoy it and when I enjoyed it, I couldn't control it.'

I wanted to be able to do even half of the things I thought about, ever.

And then suddenly, some arrangement of the stars, some middle life crisis, some power greater than myself that I don't believe in but have turned my will and my life, to has be with my fist up Bonarh's ass. Her legs are spread in the air, she's opened herself to me like this and I'm diving in. "Oh, Bonarh, I wanted this, this is what I wanted."

I shift on my heels, kneel rather than squat between her knees which are up near my head and shoulders. I barely move my hand through this. I'm coaxing her and sweet talking her and her ass. "C'mon, give me this. C'mon, this is what I want. C'mon, let me take this…" and Bonarh is moaning and after I've shifted she begins.

Bonarh now relaxes even more, her ass opening further so that she's actually pulling my fist in deeper. I'm crooning to her encouragement and praise: oh yes, this is so good. I lean a bit forward and with my right hand I lean on her swollen clit. It's pounding, coursing and hard and thick, turgid. Yeah. Without moving her hips, just with the muscles of her belly, Bonarh starts to pump against my hand and my fist, sucking in, pulling in and bucking against me. For a moment, I slide fingers into her cunt, which is surprisingly tight but then I feel why: my fist is already there. From inside then my fingers and fist slide against each other with just the thin membrane that is Bonarh inside between them. It's so tight and so much of me is inside Bonarh that rubbing my hands against each other I can feel the ridges of my finger prints. Yes, Bonarh, I'm leaving evidence behind inside you.

It's in this fucking with hand inside ass, fingers in cunt and thumb on thick hard clit that I suddenly see blood, it's dripping or oozing from Bonarh, that's for sure, but with the crisco and cum and slickness and mud it's hard to tell from where, but you're bleedingBonarh.

Hold on a second, I say and pull my fingers from her cunt. From the back pocket of my levis I pull out my handkerchief, red, and wipe away some or all of the blood from Bonarh. Bonarh is still in a spasm of muscle and cunt and belly and this stopping hasn't stopped her, but I'm concerned. I need to check. My fist is still in her ass, still slow and mostly pulsing with energy, not full-on fucking. As I gently twist my fist, just to wipe the edge of my wrist with the handkerchief, I see the blood is from Bonarh's cunt. "You're bleeding," I say. And Bonarh says something that's like a grunt. "It's from your cunt." I say. "Yeah," with voice hoarse, she says, "I wondered if I was getting my period." Oh well then, c'mon.

I push fingers back into Bonarh's cunt, twist fist again, slightly so both hands fit like this, thumb on Bonarh's clit and say "You can scream as loud as you want, as loud as you can." I'm loving the feel of this as we take off. Bonarh begins to scream and by scream I mean full voiced out into the darkness, into the trees and cloud-cover sky, raining back down on us like an echo, reverberating through the truck and through my body, my hands my fist my arms and then through Bonarh and her ass and cunt and her voice, so loud, so clear now, screaming my name out into it all from deep inside her, deep, deep inside where I am, pulling and pushing and being pulled and pushed and taking off like in flight and getting lost, already lost and yet found. The vibrations of this all have the truck a-rocking and as we ride like this, high baby, it's good. Bonarh's shaking and then me too like I'm just holding on for dear life.

The light from inside the truck casts just the smallest circle around us outside and then just past that edge, there's nothing. It's all darkness. I turn my head to look out the back door and don't see anything. I hear the rain still falling and once or twice during this ride here while we parked, the car was beeping. With the radio on, the stereo on, the overhead light on, the battery was getting low and so I have to leave Bonarh's ass to crawl out the back of the truck and go around to the front and start the car. The vents are open and the heat is on full blast and so even with the back door open, it gets hot. I climb back up and it's hot already.

Bonarh's screams of joy and pleasure, I'd have to leave it to her to describe her ecstasy, fill then the darkness and the vibrations seem felt that much more with less to impede them. The sky begins to fill and then the trees and then also from the muddy ground up, meeting, then, at the level of the truck in a crescendo that falls like rain heavily on the roof of the truck. A wind picks up and begins to blow through the truck and with it, Bonarh's wet hair, from her exertion and everything wet in the back and greasy and muddy and rich.

This richness has me feeling so good, so full so strong and so swept away. I'm here and still in Bonarh, both hands full inside and that feels like all that is keeping me here, not blown away or taking off with the sounds that Bonarh is still yelling. Her cunt is spraying and soaking us further, ass oozing the crisco I packed in. I'm happy.

Who knows how this ends or if it does. At some point, I do begin to slowly pull my fingers from Bonarh's cunt, back out gently from her ass, even more slowly. I grab a towel from the pile of bathing suits and etc., and begin to wipe Bonarh between the legs, wipe my hands, take the other end of the towel and wipe her face. Then we lay in the truck bed together. I take her in my arms like that. If there is still time, if it passes still, it's hard to say if it's fast or slow, so gone from here I feel. The music still plays and the truck still feels like a spinning dance floor with the darkness and the rain, which, now that we are quiet, can be heard on the roof of the truck and its soothing. Interior lights in the truck, the music, and now beginning to feel more too the cold wind from the Pacific. Trees rustle in this wind and heavier drops fall on the roof and the music still plays. We lay still like this.

Suddenly, it gets uncomfortable: the truck back, unpadded and uncushioned, has me trying to adjust under Bonarh's head and shoulders. Even in my arms, tired, I'm trying to shift without disturbing the mood. But the mess and now being cold and coming down; landing is a bit rough.

Bonarh doesn't want to put on pants or even underwear so I wrap her in the towel and tuck it at her waist. I kind of help her out of the back after untying her feet from the hooks near the roof. I walk her around to the front passenger seat and then go back in the back and kind of roll everything up into a big roll of the other towel. Then, I reach up and shut the door and get in the front driver's seat. I'll drive, I say. Yeah, good Bonarh says I don't know if I can. I reach over her and buckle her in with the seat belt, then my own. I start the truck and begin to drive very slowly, entering the highway from this opposite side. It's so dark and the road here curved in such a way that I can't see if any cars are coming from either direction, not even their headlights. I say to myself oh well and have to floor it and just go for it. Then, once on the highway, I maintain a steady speed. I'm driving this big truck very carefully back north to the motel. Bonarh's kind of still out there and not grounded and I'm worried I lost her, that maybe I went too far tonight. She's not saying much except that she's hungry and tired and wants to wash up. Ok, Bonarh and I drive us up to Monterey. As we drive I try to entertain her with a story about how scared I was to drive over the Bay Bridge.

March 5, 2018:

Dear Bobby:

I'm driving really carefully in the dark along hwy1, going north back to Monterey. I'm trying to entertain Bonarh by telling her the story of trying to drive the van across the Bay Bridge on a windy day. With its boxy shape and tiny wheels, the van feels like it will be blown right off the side of the bridge, and though I think I'd probably die that way, it doesn't really hold any appeal. Plus, I'm worried that instead of going over the side of the bridge (I've asked my brother in detail and repeatedly, "Do you think the van could be blown right off the bridge?" and he said, "Yeah, it could, but probably not.") that the van would be blown into another car on the bridge and that it would cause a big pile up, that the van would be wrecked and it would be a terrible accident.

It got so bad that while driving I was starting to have a panic attack. My lover lived in Oakland and I'd spend the night and drive back in the late morning and after a few weeks, as I'd approached the toll plaza and see the palm trees blowing in the wind or hear the wind against the side of the van or worse yet, see the big sign posted over the roadway that says: 'Use caution! High winds on bridge!' I'd start to sweat so profusely that my shirt would be soaked to my waist and I was worried my hands would slip off the steering wheel.

And on the bridge, it would be bad, or seemed bad. I could feel the van being rocked from side to side and I wasn't sure how to drive in this. In snow of course, the rule is to turn into the swerve and if the road surface is covered in water causing a hydroplaning there is something to do then too, but I wasn't sure what to do, how to drive in the wind on a raised surface. Like, hold the wheel so tightly it feels like I will break the steering wheel. or try and let the car just float with the wind, maybe steering it like a boat, gently with the waves but to be honest, I wasn't exactly sure what it meant to turn into the swerve in the snow and I didn't know what to do when hydroplaning just that there was something to do then.

I tried breathing; breathing deeply when I'd get on the bridge and start to panic. I'd try to focus on inhaling and exhaling but the sweat still poured down. My hair'd be wet by the time I got to the other side. I tried praying. I tried listening to the radio. I tried talking to whichever woman I was driving with, I tried asking that woman to just not say anything, just let us get to the other side. I couldn't tell if it was worse driving by myself or with another woman in the van with me. It helped to think I wasn't alone but then of course I'm feeling like a complete failure, exposed for the terrified little girl I am, not a tough rough butch dyke, but shaking crying sweating mess who shouldn't be driving. I mean, I know that one of the traits that make butches so appealing is their sensitivity, but this is ridiculous.

One evening, Canela and I are coming from a day in the east bay. I'm driving the van and as we approach the bridge I start to panic. Even the memory of going over the bridge in a panic is enough to start me in a panic. Canela is offering encouragement and etc., being very kind and loving. I think I can make it but once through the toll plaza, I feel the wind on the van and I say, "I got to pull over! You have to drive! We have to switch!" Canela says, "What?! No!" But I've already crossed the four or five lanes on the other side of the toll plaza, just past the metering lights and pulled to the narrow shoulder. Canela is pissed; she thinks this is dangerous. "More dangerous than me driving on the bridge?" At this point I'm basically fearful that once up on the bridge, especially on the other side of the island on the old bridge with its towering dizzying towers that one can't help but look way up at as one approaches, that I will be frozen with fear. This vertigo doesn't help the driving either.

I hurry to leave the driver's seat, squeezing between the seats in the front to the back while Canela slips from passenger side to driver's and then putting on her seat belt, looking in the mirrors puts the van in gear and basically floors it from the shoulder into the flow of traffic. Her brow is furrowed. I've already pulled the paper and pen from the front pocket of my levis and have taken inventory: 'fear we won't be ok, fear we are in danger, fear we won't be safe' and by the time Canela asks me, I'm already saying, "I got relief."

It's my experience that taking the inventory keeps me sober, that's the evidence that it works, and in reflection of a group conscience, I'm reminded that it is a spiritual experience. Mostly, though it seems rote: pen to paper and asking this power to remove the fears. And then mostly, going about the rest of the day. But occasionally, there is a powerful profound experience taking the inventory. This was one of them. As I wrote those few lines I wrote, and it probably wasn't much more than I've conveyed here, a palpable feeling began in my feet and quickly and steadily rose through my body, up my legs and thighs and through my guts and belly and across my shoulders and through my arms and also continuing up my neck into my head, like an electricity. It was what I imagine it feels like when a computer is being re-booted. The screen asks, 're-start?' the system will power off and then re-boot. It felt like a complete psychic change.

I turned to Canela and said "Wow" and I described the electric feeling through my entire body, the re-starting, the way I felt now, healed, I said. And then I explained that my mother had been very phobic when we were growing up: a paralyzing fear of snakes, of heights, of bridges. These were the ones I mostly remember. She'd drive us across the Verrazano Bridge, which is really tall and really long and a very high suspension bridge, then half way across she'd start screaming at me and my brothers because she was near paralyzed, driving so slowly that all the other New Yorkers and people from Jersey even, were coming up behind us at speed and then have to slow way down and swerve around. They'd lean on their horns of course which only set my mother further into a spin and she'd be yelling and cursing at the other drivers too: "Go fuck yourself, mister!" and she'd be hunched over the steering wheel, fingers white from gripping it so tightly, sweating.

Once it was fourth of july and fireworks were being set off below the bridge in Bay Ridge and the rockets' red glare and bombs bursting in air only caused to inflame her hysteria. The fireworks seemed like they were landing right next to us on the bridge, that's how tall the bridge is, how far above the water the road surface is suspended.

Now, of course I completely recognized myself when I remembered my mother driving like this and I felt compassion for her. She actually didn't let her phobias keep her from trying to take us places or show us a good time. She tried, it was just that the phobias always kind of ruined it.

Once with a snake at a public zoo that was very crowded, a handler brought a snake through the crown of us who were looking forward at the dioramas of stuff reptiles. Coming up from behind us, some in the crowd started to turn around and smile and tentatively pet the snake that was being offered. My mother hadn't seen it and so she was startled when it was suddenly right behind her and she yelled and screamed; everyone in the place ran out, then it was just me and my brothers and the snake and the handler and my mother who was crying and screaming and falling to the ground and couldn't move and we were little, and somewhat embarrassed and also trying to help her, only that made it worse and the handler was trying to show her the snake was harmless and trying to bring it closer to her so she could see it was fine but it wasn't. It was quite terrible or felt that way for all of us, I'm sure including the snake.

But in the van, Canela driving us in the fierce wind, I said, "I'm ok" and I meant it. I mean, I was actually ok, all my fears about not being ok, not being safe were false evidence appearing real. And not only that but these are the fears I've been at the effect of my whole life. And the fact that here I was, a 50-year old woman driving in my van with my girlfriend across the bridge proves that the fears of then and now, which since there isn't a time, it's all the wreckage of the past, are false. I'm ok now and then and always.

Driving north from the pull out near Garrapata State Park back to Monterey, I try to relate this story to Bonarh. I'm driving so carefully, so just below the speed limit, the truck is so big and it's so dark on hwy1 and the recent accident is still so fresh and the road is still wet as it's still raining off and on. I'm not sure if it's right to tell Bonarh a story that features Canela and I'm not sure I'm telling it so that she understands it. I can't tell if she understands it or not. But I can't stop myself from telling it once I've started. It's like I'm trying to prove something but I'm not sure what.

We get back to the motel and I park the truck and we get out and go upstairs. Once up there, Bonarh goes in the bathroom. "I had to take a shit," she says, "and I want to take a bath." Plus, we are both really hungry. So much maté in the truck and maybe only snacks after the breakfast we had early this morning. So, I clean up too, change my shirt and Bonarh comes out and she's wearing the harness and she gets dressed and then I hug her, tightly. "How do you feel?" I ask. I'm feeling so insecure after a big scene like that but I'm trying to just hold the space for Bonarh right now. "I'm hungry and tired," she says. There's a restaurant around the corner from our motel, around the corner and across the street, so we go there. There's beef soup on the menu and fish with rice, warm tea. We sit and when the soup comes, I feed Bonarh with the spoon. The server asks shall I bring another bowl? I say no.

March 7, 2018:
Dear Bobby:
    Bonarh and I sit at the restaurant around the corner and across the street from the motel. We order some beef soup with seaweed and raw fish with rice. The food is good. The server brings the bowl of soup and asks shall she bring another bowl and I say she eats from mine. I serve Bonarh the soup then, spooning in spoonfuls to her mouth. She has a thick paper napkin tucked into the front of her shirt. Once she's eaten a few spoonfuls, she's back to normal: smiling and obviously happy and joyful. This puts me at ease.
    I begin to talk about the film Nemo. It's about a fish who loses his mother and father, then has to find them, I think. It's funny I can't remember it now, but that night at the table I am able to entertain Bonarh with the story of Nemo and also a few other animated children's programs. "Nemo is like the Bambi of our generation. I mean, a hunter kills Bambi's mother? That's how a kid's story starts out. I couldn't take it as a kid. I was distraught even watching Lassie, I was devastated! A boy down a well? And only a dog knows where he is? I couldn't take it. My mother said, 'You're not allowed to watch anything on television anymore' because I was inconsolably crying after almost anything. I mean, even watching Mr. Rogers, I was terrified about Bobdog. And then Nemo, the same: the opening scene in Nemo, a little disabled fish is caught in a scuba diver's net and brought back to a dentist office and put in a fish tank! What? This is our idea of entertainment. Though," I continue, "it is wildly entertaining, but with this other animated show about dinosaurs, I

mean, it is so stressful! The music, crescendoing, building and then building and crescendoing! And then dinosaurs are basically at the moment of extinction so every episode they have another crisis such as earthquake or solar flares or drought. It's terrible. The kid friend I have and used to watch these shows with and I couldn't take it. My nervous system felt like it was on a roller coaster."

Bonarh hasn't seen Nemo so she loves this story. It's only much later that a friend tells me Bettelheims' theory about fairy tales, that it's good for children to experience these kinds of stories, that it helps them to process their own difficult feelings of abandonment, or fear of conflict or sibling rivalry. Oh, well, then I kind of understand what 's intended but, still, I don't enjoy them.

After dinner we walk back to the motel. We are both tired, such a big day, beginning at 6am even though we took an after-breakfast nap, then the whole rest of everything including swimming, and driving and crying and fear Bonarh doesn't care about touching me, fear Bonarh doesn't recognize my vulnerability, fear fucking me doesn't matter to Bonarh, and then the whole scene in the back of the big truck. I'm exhausted, I'll say that. Plus, everything we did but also the whole wild ride of being sober in these steps, the peak emotional experiences experienced as a result of the steps: despair, terror, crying, laughing, sexual joy and pleasure, crying there, wow.

And as we get back to the motel, there's still another ride. I'm thinking I stupidly talked too much, on the drive back from the pull-out sex spot and then in the restaurant too. Nemo? I mean, what was I thinking? I mean, we laughed hard at the restaurant but now, back in the room, I'm fucked up and hating myself. I'm tired, I say to myself, but that doesn't help. Trying to talk myself out of this involves talking to myself and the problem is the bondage of self and self-centered fear, so it doesn't matter what I say to myself. I need to be entirely rid of self or it kills me. Or at least, has me wishing for death.

So, we get into the bed but I have to sit up and continue to take my personal inventory. It starts as I suspect it would; 'fear I hate myself, fear I talked too much, fear I'm a failure' and then quite quickly and surprisingly what shows up, what's surrendered on the page is, 'fear I can't be touched, fear women don't want to fuck me, fear women just want me to fuck them, fear I'm not being touched right, fear she doesn't recognize my vulnerability, fear fucking me isn't important, etc.' I'm kind of belaboring this because it is the generating principle of my life: 'fear I can't be touched' is actually the same as 'fear I'm untouchable,' and to make the point that the self-will is cunning. All of this belief system is false but it manufactures slightly seemingly different ruminations that are mesmerizing. And I'm believing them. Even though I've taken this inventory before, even though I know it's not true, despite even what Bonarh (and other women) have said, tonight I'm believing it's all true.

How is this how I come back after all the ride all day.

I'm lying in bed next to Bonarh, or I'm sitting up next to Bonarh who is laying there. I'm humiliated, basically, doing the steps of alcoholics anonymous. I'm crying and in a fast and furious fierce surrender and I'm humbled. What I think isn't right, but I don't think so.

March 8, 2018:
Dear Bobby:

I'm sitting up in the big bed in Monterey, pillows behind my back, Bonarh is laying in the bed next to me. I'm taking the steps of alcoholics anonymous; the steps are being done. I'm humiliated. How is this how I come back to myself? I'm unchanged, the same as always. What was I thinking, I thought. I thought I was better than this, better than these same childish fears, better than having had fucked a woman to have to come home and cry like this. I'm in a fast and furious and fierce surrender, pen is flying across the page, the notebook on my lap is bearing this burden. What I'm thinking isn't right but I don't think so.

The notebook is bearing witness. I'm crying, and crying like sobbing. I'm remembering Bonarh not remembering fucking me the first night in the motel in Marina now. It wasn't stellar, I don't think. The truth is I barely remember any standout incident from that night. I was glad to be pulled back to the physical realm from my ruminating head trip about crashing Bonarh's car. Bonarh said we need to get a room so we can finally have sex. This was after the sex in the back of the cop car, so I'm thinking what? Or was this the next day? As we left marina and headed to Monterey? Is that when she said it? I was going to a noon meeting and I'm thinking "Have sex? Need a room? I fucked you in the car and the cop car and you fucked me in the motel last night!?!?!" She says oh yeah.

I'm taking this personally but I know it is my own inventory. And here it goes again: 'fear women don't want to touch me, fear women just want me to fuck them, fear fucking me, touching me isn't important to women'. Bonarh sent a text while I was at the meeting which said, 'last night was amazing' and then when we were driving in the big truck in the afternoon after swimming she explained, oh yeah, she sent it to kind of make up for forgetting. And we had talked about this then but I was still fucked up now, really believing it. I'm putting Bonarh in an impossible situation. If she says again now that she did forget, then I'm gonna use it to prove my inventory. If she says she didn't forget, it's gonna be a fight: "What? You said you forgot! And now you're saying you didn't?!?" Somehow, she just doesn't say anything.

Now all the telling myself anything doesn't matter a bit. I'm in a brainstorm of resentment. I'm probably just crashing from such a wild ride fucking Bonarh in the truck back. I'm probably just tired from waking up early. I'm probably still in shock a bit from the crash, I mean, my shoulders and neck still are a bit sore. But this isn't what's being revealed on the page. My fear that my vulnerability isn't respected is what I'm writing.

This is all painful, the belief that I'm not important or cared for respectably. But what is really painful is the knowledge that this is my inventory, that this is false evidence appearing real, and that I'm still at the effect of this. This is what is so humiliating, my inability to be better than I am. My inability to just talk myself out of this. My inability to stop crying like a big baby and to stop writing like this. I mean, how many pages have been written already?

My hip hurts during this and so I flip around on the bed, put legs up on the headboard and lie on my back. The notebook is now on my belly, my ass on the pillows. Bonarh is still silent, laying with her head on the pillow there, next to me, still. Of course, some of the lines are 'fear I look like a crazy person' and at this point, turning to look at Bonarh who is looking at me, I laugh. She is patient or patiently waiting and still. I'm laughing quite hard now. I'm incredibly surprised because I thought no way am I going to get relief, the best I can hope for is to be able to fall asleep tonight. But laughing like this, this is better than expected. No one understands how it works.

At this point, Bonarh reaches out and puts her hand on my leg or belly. I swing back around to upright in the bed and then lay down next to Bonarh. Wow, I say. It's unbelievable. I never think the steps will work and then they do, or something like that. Bonarh now begins to express her self-centered fears, verbally. She says, "fear I didn't know what to do, fear this was all my fault, fear I can't take care of you, fear I should know what to do." And hearing these fears expressed only lightens me further; now, I'm really laughing. It feels so good, this honest expression, it's really a tremendous relief. I'm off the hook with my own fears that I've ruined everything thinking about myself and then I'm reminded oh yeah, all anybody has is thinking about themselves.

I said thank you so much for expressing yourself. And then I said it's difficult to bear witness to god, difficult to see this power exposing unreality, difficult to have our fears revealed as a result of this power. But, I said, for me to go from that self-pitying sad crying to this elevated laughing relief is evidence of a power greater than myself. I couldn't do that. In fact, everything I tried just made me feel worse: telling you stories, trying to entertain you, eating some food, laying down to rest. I can't manufacture a good feeling; I'm too down and despairing, too manufacturing misery.

I began to talk about how with the car accident, Bonarh was brought to the place where I've been recovered, which is the gates of insanity and death. Most people, even if they are there, at that gate, they spend most of their lives trying to pretend they aren't or to somehow backtrack from that place, the edge of insanity and death. No one wants to be there, let alone live there. But there is no going back, there is no backward. I'm extremely fortunate, I say, I've been recovered at that edge. It is where I live, thankfully, at that edge because it means requiring constant care and protection, it means daily surrender to a power greater than myself. It means, no choice, I have to accept spiritual help. And to be conscious of that fact, to the nearness to death or insanity, or to have a way to be reminded, daily, how close one is to a drink, that is fortunate. To have the awakening that says oh, all of my best efforts, all of my trying, all of my marshaling of my will got me to this place. Left to my own devices, I'd slip through this gate, gladly. I need a power greater than myself to restore me to sanity.

Now, of course, normies don't want to hear this kind of grandiose proselytizing. And god bless Bonarh and every other woman who has been kind to me. Every other woman who wanted to care for me or help me. Every other woman who loved me and patiently listened to my shouting from the mountain top. Every woman who loved me when not shouting like this but laying abed, sickeningly depressed, defiantly depressed and full of self-pity. God bless everyone. I mean, I don't even want to hear most of what comes out of my mouth.

But Bonarh is patient and listens, or seems to listen, laying now curled up next to me. I'm trying to explain a spiritual experience to her; and now, remembering, I'm ashamed of my arrogance. But at the time, I know I was crying, again, but now tears of gratitude. I mean, when one is entered into by this power, when one turned one's will and one's life over to this power, there is nothing to do then except bear witness to this power. So, no choice, I have to express my gratitude. I'm so grateful to be sober.

Thankfully as well, I think I fall asleep after this, reaching up and turning off the bedside lamp then rolling over and trying to cuddle with Bonarh. The harness is so uncomfortable against my belly, I don't understand how she's been able to sleep in this leather at all.

In the morning, we sleep late, til 8:30. I don't remember dreaming, just waking and rolling over and looking out the window at the big puffy white winter clouds which crowd the sky. The sky is blue, bright and seems happy. Of course, I wake and continue to take my own personal inventory, meditate and then tell Bonarh to make me coffee. Then we lay in bed while I drink it and a second cup.

Bonarh has laid her head in my lap. I'm sitting up in the bed, back against the headboard and I'm combing my fingers through her hair, grooming her and petting her head. There's more talking now but mostly now I'm asking Bonarh questions. I'm asking her about her life, what she's done and what she's wanted to do, where she's been. If feels relaxed and easy, actually, just running my fingers through her hair as she talks and I encourage her with "then what?" type of questions. I don't want to get up, I don't want this day to end because tomorrow, we drive back to the city and this whole arrangement will end. I don't want to talk now about the harness, I don't want to talk about tomorrow, I just want to pet her like this and watch clouds while I drink cup after cup of coffee.

Now, this is amazing. Last night I'm completely believing that basically I can't trust Bonarh and now, this morning I'm relaxed with her in my lap. It proves the inventory is false because it's disappeared; reality can't disappear. The only thing bothering me is delusion. There's no figuring out what the problem is, there's just getting rid of it.

Bonarh is telling me stories of her life. She's telling me about one person in particular. I'm reminded, listening to her, our common problem is resentment. And by our, I mean people in general. Everyone is at the effect of the idea that it's someone else's fault; that the reason I feel bad now is because something someone did in the past. There's no way out of that. Just get it out. So, I let Bonarh talk for a while, just listening, stroking her back and head and shoulders.

Soon, I'm asking her questions about sex, who she's done what with. I'm not asking specific names, just activities she's enjoyed. I want to be entertained now. Bonarh begins with a story in New Orleans, a party she went to and describes what she was wearing: she'd just found a short skirt at a thrift store, denim with a zipper all the way down the front and high high heels; she could barely walk, she said. And a tight tight shirt.

March 9, 2018:
Dear Bobby:

I'm looking out the window of the motel at a blue sky filled with big puffy white winter clouds. I'm lying in bed with Bonarh's head in my lap. I'm listening to Bonarh describe a sexual experience she had in New Orleans.

Bonarh was wearing a short skirt, high heels and a tight t-shirt. I think of her younger self and try to imagine if she was different and how. What did her body look like? Basically, the same she says. And your hair? How did you wear your hair? I'm running my fingers through Bonarh's hair while she tells this story of being at a party, wearing this skirt and shirt, no bra, she adds and very high heels, she could barely walk. So, what did you do? "I kind of leaned up against a wall for a while, my back up against the wall, just looking at the party from the side."

Bonarh's hair now is messy, or wild. She never combs it except when she showers, putting in a part on the left side and combing the top flat across her scalp. "I mostly wore my hair the same too, just a little longer maybe," she says. Bonarh's torso is on my lap and when I finish my cup of coffee I have both hands free now. "The party was at a friend's apartment, she says, and the apartment had a big living room and then also double doors that opened on the dining room and for the party the doors were opened and then there was one big large open room. There were a few lamps around the rooms on low tables but mostly the room was dark."

"Not too dark to see," I ask.

"No," Bonarh says, "not too dark to see. People were mostly dancing, there was a dj. This was a while ago so the dj was at an actual table with a turntable set up and spinning actual records."

"The person was an actual disc jockey," I say.

"Yes, and very good," Bonarh says.

"Did you dance?"

"No, I really couldn't, that's how high these heels were."

"Wow."

"Yeah."

With a slight shift underneath Bonarh, basically lying face down on my lap, my hand in her hair, I'm able to subtlety position her so that I feel her weight on my clit. She continues: "I'd had a crush, or a whatever, on this person in New Orleans for a while, but we didn't really have any overlap in our friends or circles. I'd really only seen this woman a handful of times around the city. I smiled at her when I saw her but I could never even tell if she saw me or not. She was hard, very hard."

"Hard how?" I asked.

"Hard like she didn't give anything away at all. I'd once been introduced to her at a dance event and I was so excited and tried to talk to her but she seemed to look right through me."

"But that hooked you?"

"Yes, I was hooked. She was so handsome, thin and seemed strong and quick, she looked at me while I asked her about the dance performance, looked at me like she listened but she was so hard she didn't even answer me. She stood there while I was smiling and chatting and she folded her arms across her chest and just looked at me."

"Wow."

"Yes, that hard and then that brazen. I watched as she very clearly and pointedly looked me up and down, I could feel her eyes on my body while I stood right in front of her. She was shameless. Yes, shameless and I was hooked. That night, after I met her I went home and jacked off for hours, feeling her eyes on me, feeling her looking at me. I imagined her across the room, leaning in the doorway of my room with her arms folded across her chest, just looking. I came so many times that night I lost count."

"The next day," Bonarh said, "I couldn't stop thinking of her. I called friends and asked who is she where is she where does she live, and work, etc. I started riding my bike all over New Orleans hoping to run into her. None of my friends really knew her. They thought she was here for the summer but I looked everywhere, glad to expend some of my energy riding my bike because mostly I was just lying in bed all day otherwise jacking off."

I put my hand on Bonarh's lower back and press slightly as she talks, just enough so she feels me. I'm getting turned on, slowly my excitement is rising. Bonarh continues: "I don't know how I got the idea that she would be at this party but I did. And I got there early, like took my position basically as the dj was setting up. I'd found this skirt at the thrift store, and really high heels—I put them in the basket of my bicycle as I rode to the party barefoot, and put them on once I got upstairs—and the tight t-shirt and wore no bra and no panties."

"Hot."

"Yeah hot."

"Did you think this was what she'd like? Or what?"

"No. I had no idea, like I say, no one I knew knew her or her friends or who she went out with, I mean I knew nothing about her."

Just that you couldn't stop thinking about her.

"Yes, I couldn't stop thinking about her and all summer I jacked off to her: the idea of her. It was incredible, going on these long hot humid bike rides around New Orleans and leaning forward on my bike seat, pushing my clit onto the edge of the seat, kind of lifting my ass slightly as I did it, balancing like that and then riding my bike back to my apartment and running up to my room and throwing myself face down on my bed and basically fucking and riding my fist pushing into the mattress. It's so hot in New Orleans in the summer that even just lying in bed still can break a sweat, let alone the way I was going at it, fierce. And near constantly, it seemed."

At this point, I'm really getting hot, my clit is pounding beneath Bonarh, her shoulder is just near my clit and the way she's talking, kind of dreamily, and almost distractedly, has me really like this whole thing. Bonarh is across my lap, my legs are out in front of me, I'm sitting up in the bed, against the headboard with the pillows. Her torso is on my lap, her head near my left hand, shoulder at my crotch, and then the rest of her is along my right side, perpendicular. I have my right hand resting with slight steady pressure on her lower back. Bonarh's is facing head away from me while she's speaking. My fingers are untangling the tiny snarls in her hair at the nape of her neck. She lays very still while she tells this story.

"Ok, so then what?"

"So, I'm standing there against the wall of the party room. The music has started and I'm still just standing there. I'm watching from my spot as everyone comes into the party, as all the people arrive, but where I am, I'm kind of in the shadows, like kind of in a corner. I can see everyone but I'm hidden. And I'm like that for hours in these high heels, just bare feet. I'd found them too, at a thrift store, oh, the thrifting in New Orleans in the early 2000's: it was so good."

"Yeah, Chicago too."

"So, I found these shoes. I was with a friend of mine and we were having fun and I saw them and put them on as kind of a joke, we were laughing but when I put them on, they fit kind of perfectly and when I looked in the mirror, I couldn't believe how they made my legs look, so sexy, so tight and sleek and I got turned on just looking at them in the mirror. They were like $3 so I got them, then threw them in the back of my closet and then somehow remembered them when this hard woman came into my consciousness. I found them the in the closet and I pulled them out and put them on and started masturbating that way that summer. Riding my bike everywhere, looking for that hard woman, riding home, grabbing the shoes and then throwing myself face down on my bed and going for it.

"So, I kind of practiced wearing them but wow, I'll tell you, it is nearly impossible to even just stand in them for a few hours."

"I wouldn't know."

"I mean, it's nearly torture."

"But that added to the appeal for you."

"Yes, of course. This tortured waiting for her. So, I'm standing there, back against the wall, feet really throbbing, but also very turned on, just there by myself, no one really knowing I was there, I'm watching everyone coming in. I'm still while everyone is dancing. I couldn't move a bit, that's how bad my feet were hurting by then. I kept thinking I'd take off the shoes and just dance with my friends but I didn't, I just stayed waiting where I was.

"Then it was like magick, I was about to give up, in fact I'd moved off the wall, when I let my eyes drop from the doorway, as I did, I saw her arrive. My eyes were a bit lowered so we didn't make eye contact but what I did was turn around and face the wall and then took a few steps back and I bent over completely at my waist, I put my hands on the wall in front of me and just put my ass in those heels out there for her. I mean, the skirt was so short and with no underwear, and the whole time I'd been waiting, I was very wet, very wet and open and I just bent over like that."

"Wow."

"Yeah."

"And then? What did she do?"

"Well, I actually don't know. She didn't come over to me, if that's what you mean."

"Of course, that's what I mean, I want this story to end with you getting fucked like that, bent over in front of everyone at the party."

"Yeah but it doesn't end like that. You asked me if I had some idea she liked this kind of look and I didn't have any idea. But it was for her to look at me this way."

"So, she didn't fuck you?"

"No, she didn't fuck me, in fact I don't even know if she actually saw me, if she actually stood there and watched me bent over like that."

"You didn't look?"

"No, that wasn't the point, I didn't need to see her, I wanted her to see me."

"Wow."

"Yeah, so I saw her walk in just as I bent over and when I stepped away from the wall at that point, I was closer to one of the lamps in the room, just inside its light cast, I was quite visible and now, in this position, the weight on my feet was different so I was able to stay like this for a while."

"Hot."

"Yeah, I was dripping wet, literally, I could feel my come running down my bare legs. Meanwhile, the music is still pounding and now, in this other state and bent over in this other position I started to buck my hips, following the beat of the music and feeling her watching me and so I was in a wild frenzy, hips shaking and bucking and I came like that. I'd never come like that, it was incredible and when I stood up after, I didn't even look for her. I took off my shoes and got on the dance floor".

I can't take it. I roll Bonarh over and fuck her. She's still in my lap, still in the harness and I grab her shoulder and pull her toward me, kind of cradling her now on my lap, face up slipping my arm between her legs and lift her like that so her hips are against my thigh and her mouth near my breast. I'm still in what I slept in, which is my underwear and a-shirt. This happens so quickly, the rolling over and positioning her and then just as quickly I unsnap the strap between her legs, I make her cunt available to my finger.

Slipping in one finger only, Bonarh still has a tampon in, I push alongside the tampon in her cunt. I can't with the tampon actually fuck her, can't push in and out, but I can have my finger inside her, still. From this angle too, my thumb can rest on her clit and then it's on. My cunt is wet, throbbing and my clit too, pounding with excitement. I'm looking into Bonarh's eyes as this all happens, she's surprised then thick with desire.

"Ok, so you're bent over, hands on the wall, bent at the waist."

"Yes, like a 90-degree angle. Yes, ass out. Yes, my skirt was so short it didn't even cover my ass when I bent like that."

"And you stayed like that."

"Yes. I stayed like that but my cunt was literally dripping."

"You didn't know if she was there or not."

"No, I didn't but having seen her for just the second as I turned around was enough."

"And then?" I'm pushing Bonarh's clit with my thumb and then flicking it harshly. Her clit is thick and hard, engorged.

"Yes, and then I started bucking my hips, thrusting kind of, with the thought that she was standing there. I was so turned on I was shaking. The party was crowded by now, I was in a circle of lamp light, at least my bare legs and ass were, and I again, with the thought of her standing there, arms crossed, I didn't care if she liked it or was disgusted; I didn't even care if she was there or not. I squeezed my thighs together, squeezed my cunt, I was thrusting wildly, shaking and I came."

At this point, Bonarh is breathing heavily. As she retells this story with my prompts her breath is heavy and full of pauses and gasps, sighs. My finger is still, her cunt is so tight with my finger and the tampon and I'm pushing, flicking her clit. My left arm is around her shoulder, cradling her head and shoulders, I pause and lift my shirt and put my nipple in her mouth. "I love the idea of her standing with her arms folded just watching you, Bonarh." She nods her head yes but keeps sucking my tit. I've shifted her on my lap so I can push up from beneath her with my clit, kind of fucking her from below with my clit.

I like how I feel which is a steady burn, no building here just a steady tension that I stoke with clenching my ass and a pushing up against Bonarh. "It'd be great if she came in the door now, wouldn't it, came in and stood there by the door to the room and watched me fuck you, with her arms crossed across her chest, not smiling, just watching, hard." I pull the tampon from Bonarh's cunt and throw it across the room. Bonarh is sucking wildly, fiercely, her eyes still open watching me tell the story of her being watched and now, with open cunt I can actually fuck her and I do, one finger just poking her hole and I tell her this. "Yeah, while she watches, I fuck your hole with my finger", and I only have to say this a couple of times, I'm nearly out of breath myself, before Bonarh is crying into my breast, mouth still full, she's good and doesn't stop her sucking while inside her cunt she's flooded, wet soaking my hand and she's trembling shivering writhing in my lap, eyes rolling back and lids falling. Yes, Bonarh I like this.

We're still for a moment or so, laying and resting and catching our breath. I lean over and kiss Bonarh's hair. I think about jacking off beneath her but I like the way my clit feels, which is still pulsing, electric. I think about sliding my hand flat between Bonarh and myself to fondle my clit but then don't even do that. The sky is still blue and crowded with clouds.

I don't know how this has happened but now it's near noon and there's a meeting across the street. I have to make that one, I say, kind of pushing Bonarh off of me roughly and getting up and getting dressed hurriedly. Should I make you coffee, she asks. No, there's no time, just cut me some bread and butter it, please. I'm pulling on levis, a t-shirt over my a-shirt, levis over underwear, I'll change later I think, if I bathe. Socks and boots and my jacket and grabbing thread and smiling and kissing Bonarh's cheek, I'm rushing out the door.

At the meeting, I get a cup of the aa coffee. This isn't recommended, aa coffee. It's weak and too hot and then gives a strange sick buzz and usually a stomach ache. I have a half a cup just to wash the bread and butter down my throat then listen to the shares and share myself. Wow, I got a complete psychic change in this meeting, I'm so grateful to be sober.

March 10, 2018:

Dear Bobby:

When I came back from the meeting, Bonarh's got a plate of food ready and the water on to boil. She's smiling. I'm hungry, I think, or sick from the aa coffee. Something. Instead of eating though, instead of sitting down with Bonarh on the bed and having some lunch, I stand in front of her and ask her to open her mouth. "Please open your mouth, Bonarh." I put my finger in her mouth deeply like to the back of her throat. She begins to pull away but I hold her with my words, "Relax." Now, I'm smiling. One finger becomes two and then quickly three, but gently not rough. "I'm giving you time to get acclimated," I say.

I start to talk about the night before, in the back of the truck. "This is how I fucked your ass last night, Bonarh," I say, "slowly opening you up with my fingers so you could take my whole hand." I'm holding my hand still in her mouth; I have my left hand on her shoulder to steady her and keep her still. My three fingers rest all the way at the back of her mouth at the root of her tongue, which I'm pressing down. Bonarh begins to gag a bit. "Oh, Bonarh, you're gonna tell me your ass can handle more of my hand than your mouth?" I push in deeper, a bit. Bonarh does gag and pulls away from me to run to the bathroom. I hear her coughing and spitting and I say "Come back in here."

Bonarh comes back and I say again, "Open your mouth please, Bonarh," and, "we'll begin where we left off, which is three fingers in the back of your mouth." I smile at Bonarh to show her I'm pleased. She sees I'm happy fucking her like this. "Let's go a little more," and now I've pushed in four fingers. Bonarh's mouth is stretched, her lips pulled wide, I'm past my knuckles, fingertips just curling down her throat. She's struggling now, trying to pull away again as she gags but I'm holding her tightly by the shoulder. Her hands come up to her mouth, to my wrist and I ask her, "Are you thinking you'll pull my hand out?"

I take my hand from her mouth and Bonarh again runs to the bathroom, coughing and choking. In the bathroom, I hear her gagging, spitting. I go to my bag on the chair and pull out the cuffs from last night, the ones I used to tie her feet to the truck roof. When Bonarh comes back I turn her around and cuff her wrists behind her back and then spin her around to face me again. I tell her the cuffs are the same and the way I'm fucking her mouth is the same way I fucked her ass, sliding my fingers in slowly, gently but deeply. "You liked it last night, didn't you, Bonarh?" My fingers are already in her mouth so Bonarh just nods her head. "Yes, I liked it last night too," I tell her how deeply I was inside her and how much I liked it and liked feeling her like that: open, willing, giving. I say, "This is the place last night we got right before I pushed on, with my four fingers inside you past the knuckles and just about ready for my thumb to follow." This is the part I really like, which is looking into Bonarh's eyes, holding her there and she's tearing up. "A little more please, Bonarh," I ask and she shakes her head no and runs again to the bathroom. This time she's throwing up. I'm laughing because I like to see her lose control. "Come back in here please," and when Bonarh comes back in, hair sweaty and wet on her forehead, eyes wet and tears staining her face and cheeks, she returns and stands, and without my asking this time, she opens her mouth, wide. Oh, Bonarh, I get hard when you're so obedient. I grab Bonarh's face with my hands pull her towards me and kiss her deeply, pushing my tongue in her mouth and behind her teeth. Bonarh moans, stands, arms cuffed behind her, slightly swaying while I bother her with my perversion: her mouth and breath stink of vomit. "Please," I say, pulling myself away, "give me just a little bit more." Bonarh is crying openly now, and she shakes her head yes in consent with her mouth hanging open, her mouth dripping thick spit. I grab her head from behind and roughly put my entire fist in her mouth including my thumb. "I'm so happy Bonarh with how you let me do whatever I want." I tell her she looks beautiful and I gently twist my fist inside, fingers and thumb knuckles rasping on her teeth. "You want this, Bonarh," and with her tears and gagging ("Don't worry, your stomach is empty. You have nothing to throw up.") and even my fist like this, fully in her mouth, I hear Bonarh say, "Yes."

With my left hand then I reach down into the shorts she's wearing and grab her hard clit, slide my fingers along her wet pussy and smile. "Should I," I ask. Bonarh is shaking and her mouth is stretched around my fist and she's looking at me and standing with her legs slightly spread. She shifts her hips as if offering me her pussy and

I slide in. I shift myself, again twisting my fist, so I can fuck her properly, sliding my finger in and out of her cunt. Bonarh comes and collapses on my shoulders.

I pull out of her all the way, both hands. I pull her toward me in an embrace. I reach behind her and unlatch the cuffs. I sit on the little couch at the end of the big bed and pull her on my lap. I hold her like that, again like I'm cradling her, holding her tight. I'm kind of rocking her while she cries. I reach my face down to hers and kiss her mouth softly. She quiets soon. My clit is hard and throbbing.

"You hungry?" I ask. And she says yes. She's smiling again.

We get up and she restarts the kettle for coffee, brings the plate of food to the couch. We're leaving tomorrow so we have to eat a lot of what's left: daikon radish, kefir, the rest of the bread, some cheese and also chips. While she's finishing the preparations, the housecleaning woman knocks on the door. I go to it and open it. "Good morning, no thank you." "Nothing?" she asks. "No thank you, nothing." "Make the bed?" she asks. "No, it's not necessary." "Nothing?" she asks. "No thank you, nothing." "You never want nothing," she says laughing. And I laugh too but when I come back in I say to Bonarh, "She says I never want nothing. Is that your experience, Bonarh?" "No, it's not." "No, it's not," I agree. "I want everything."

We sit on the little couch at the foot of the big bed and I feed Bonarh from the plate, alternating bites myself. The room has become less like a room and more like a portal, a place to go somewhere else through, not to be in. Except for the meeting and the restaurant, I haven't been out it feels like in days, though yesterday we swam at the beach and were driving in the truck, that too felt some other place or space, not the west coast or the ocean even, but like the space for Bonarh's submission. This is what is being held, I tell Bonarh, space for your submission.

After lunch, I say to Bonarh, "It's time to put you to bed." She's yawning and I'm ready to lay down. I put Bonarh in the bed and I sit up and do the steps of alcoholics anonymous. I continue to take my own personal inventory and then meditate. And when I come out of meditation, I allow myself to slip under the skins and blankets that are heavy on the bed and sleep next to Bonarh.

When we wake, the sky is now a grey winter-ness and the cypress is blowing in the wind. I didn't drink the coffee at lunch so I ask Bonarh when I feel her stir, please make me some coffee. Even though the light is decreased and it's our last night here, after the nap and the steps, I feel expansive. The coffee is good too and I start to talk about going to the meeting earlier. It's incredible to be traveling and to be able to go into a meeting and have it be aa. They read how it works, they read the preamble, then they read from the book or people share their faults with each other. Amazing. I said I went to Berlin, in Germany, and while there I found the aa meetings. They were listed as 'english speaking' and so when I saw that I was thinking, 'oh, it's probably a bunch of ex-pat drug addicts talking about how great their life is now that they stopped using and that now they live in Germany and everything is great!' but when I went to the meetings, it was a bunch of alkies. Many of them, English was their 2nd or 3rd, in cases, 4th language! And when they shared, they shared how fucked up they were. It was amazing.

One meeting I went to, I could barely find it. There's no 4-G there and I didn't have a plan for my device so I'd have to look up the directions before I left the place we stayed and the read the directions from what I wrote as I took the bus or subway. Of course, I'm, as always, in a rush and late so I'd write really fast then not be able to read my writing or decipher the shorthand I tried to employ and then, since I don't speak German the shorthand didn't make sense when I got to the subway and tried to match my notes with the station map. The meeting this day is at noon in a place called 'American Church'. I follow the directions get there and come up from the subway and have to walk 5 blocks but I have no idea which direction to walk in. I try asking some German police but they don't know or pretend they don't know what I mean when I ask for the street names or for 'American Church'. I start just walking then, hoping, wondering, panicking, cursing and sweating and knowing I'm late already, probably and then suddenly as I walk another block, there is a big open field like a block long or more, huge and in the center? Of course, a big church with a very very tall steeple. I start to run toward it, I mean, this must be it, right? And I'm fearful of the time and running but I really can't run more than 2 minutes or so. Then I'm walking fast and I get to the church. I start to go to the front door but it's locked then around the side, also locked, in the back, locked, it actually seems deserted, empty, nothing open. And then, all the way around the back I seethe little blue circle sign hanging on a doorknob, 'aa'. Whew. I run to it, open it and there's another sign with 'aa' and an arrow pointing up the stairs. So, I start up the stairs and at each landing there is a door but each door is locked. I go all the way up and as I go, I realize this is the tower, the very very tall steeple I saw from the street. Up finally to the last landing, there is an open door and a tiny room, a few chairs, some aa coffee and a bunch of alkies! I flop into a chair, breathless and the meeting begins. The secretary is American and he reads the preamble. The guy who reads how it works sounds African. When the meeting begins, most of the alkies who share say, as is expected, their name and that they are alcoholic and then pretty quickly add where they are from, their nationality or ethnicity. One guy was like Soviet-era Bosnian or something, I mean it was incredible. Everyone starts to share and English is the common language but with some people, the accent and pronunciation are so wildly different from what I'm used to that I can barely even understand the words they are saying, or what they are saying.

And then, something incredible happens which is that I start to completely understand everything that is being expressed and I feel so good, so good, hearing this expression that I'm laughing, but like really hard, laughing really hard and I'm feeling incredible. And this tiny dark low-ceilinged room at the top of a steeple suddenly seems to light up and I hear this power being expressed, that my fellow alkies are bearing witness to this power when they say they are alcoholic and sober, grateful to be sober. We think it's the words that we relate to but obviously it's this power.

Of course, as soon as I start talking about the 12th step, I get boosted up and I'm expressing this and that and really laughing and tell all the details, anonymously of course. Bonarh is patient. I can't tell if she likes hearing these stories or not, but she lays at my side in the bed, seemingly listening. As we are under skin and blankets, plus I'm drinking the coffee, I'm soon sweating and excited. I throw back the covers and kind of stroke myself a few times. I haven't come yet today at all and my clit feels hard and throbbing.

Bonarh gets up when I uncover. She takes a piss and comes back, again laying her head on my lap. She wants to eat, she says. Let's go to the place around the corner and across the street. Ok. We get up, we get dressed. I thought I'd change my underwear and a-shirt but then I though oh, why, just pull on my levis and shirt, socks and boots and jacket. I sit on the little couch then, finishing the coffee, putting on my boots. The fire is blazing and the room is hot. The lunch wasn't substantial especially since it was about all we ate today so were are hungry now. Even I feel hungry.

Bonarh is wearing a pair of fuzzy animal print leggings. Even though they are leggings the harness isn't visible underneath them. She has on a shirt too and then some sweater. "C'mere," I say and when she's close I run my hands over her body to feel the harness I can't see. Yep, it's there. Bonarh smiles when I touch her. She's putting a scarf around her head with her hair visible over the top. She looks now like all the jewish mothers I had crushes on growing up on Long Island. "My town was segregated," I say, "Jews in one part, catholic business owners in another part, other catholics in the middle and way up north, on the town line near South Hempstead, blacks lived." I babysat for some jewish mothers and also in the 80's was heavily influenced by these then middle-aged women's style. I tell Bonarh about this and her scarf and I start telling her the towns on Long Island and their racial and ethnic make-up in the 80's: Baldwin, Freeport, Rockville Center, Merrick, I sound like the conductor on the Long Island Railroad announcing stations.

Then, there is the five towns I say. Yes, she knows, the five towns. Ok, well, list them. She can't. Bonarh is sitting on my lap, facing me, straddling my thigh with her arms around my neck. I'm holding her hips. "C'mon, tell me the five towns," I say. Bonarh is grinding on my thigh, riding me as we talk. "Well," she says, "I know there's Lawrence, that's where my grandma lived before Rockaway." "Ok, Lawrence..." Bonarh rides. "Yeah, Lawrence..." "C'mon, what else?" "I don't know." "Ok, there's Lawrence, Hewlett, Inwood," "Yes, yes" she says, riding harder and faster, putting her lips against mine. "C'mon,

377

tell me." "Yes, Lawrence, Inwood,..." "C'mon, Bonarh, what else? Lawrence..." "Yeah Lawrence." "Cedarhurst," "Yeah, Cedarhurst" she's increasing her speed and pressure. "Should I tell you about Rosa's Pizza?" I ask. "What? What's Rosa's?" Bonarh is beginning her panting breathless frenzy, pushing on my thigh, riding and then staying still, breathing, saying yes, yes.

"They say Rosa's is the best pizza on Long Island, it's in Maspeth." "Yeah, Maspeth," she pants. "No, Bonarh, not Maspeth, Maspeth is America but it's not one of the five towns." She's starting to soak my levis now. And as she gets hotter and hotter, I can feel the leather strap between her legs. "C'mon now, five towns." "Yeah, but what about Rosa's?" "Fuck Rosa's. Joey's better." "Ok, yeah, Lawrence,..." "Are you ready, Bonarh?" "Yes. Yes please. I'm ready please." "Lawrence." "Ooooh, yes, Lawrence." Bonarh's teeth are clenched and she's looking at me, breathing through her mouth. "Ok, drive out Sunrise Highway toward Valley Stream. Turn right on Peninsula Boulevard and go all the way down, past Hewlett, through Woodmere, then Cedarhurst, Lawrence and turn right on Nassau Expressway to Inwood," "Yes, Inwood." Bonarh is panting and moaning through the recitation, my pants wet and I say, "Please Bonarh, before we eat, please, list the five towns." Bonarh riding, thrusting on my thigh. "Lawrence..." "C'mon," "Lawrence..." "Oh, you like this, huh?" "Yes yes yes," "Ok, together, let's list the five towns: Inwood, Woodmere, Cedarhurst..." Bonarh is echoing each town as I say it, repeating it after me. "What's the last?" "Oh, I don't know..." "How many times have you come like this Bonarh?" "I lost count." "More than five, you think?" "I don't know." "Let's try one more time: Lawrence, Cedarhurst, Woodmere, Inwood, and?" "Hewlett" and Bonarh screams. Her pants are soaked. When I reach my hand into her leggings I feel the strap which is basically fucking her, her cunt is so open and wet, I push the strap to the side a bit and with my fingers I grab her clit, swollen and hard, I squeeze it with my fingers and say, "This is what I want. I want this." She comes again.

"It's cold," I say. "Change your pants before we go out." Bonarh hurries now, what time does the restaurant close on sunday night, we don't know. She pulls on something else, what, a skirt, or other pants, I don't know. I'm too hungry to notice and then we are going out the door. We walk around the corner and across the street and order basically the same thing as yesterday: beef soup with seaweed and this time two orders of fish with rice. I barely say anything while we wait for the food to come, I'm that hungry. When the soup comes, one bowl is fine, thank you. I feed her and myself, alternating.

Haven't I said enough already? And now, like this, in the evening, coffee wearing off, long day again, even with the nap, I'm going down. But it's the last night and tomorrow we will be driving back to San Francisco. Bonarh will have to take the harness off tonight but I'm fearful to start to talk about it. Listen, I don't want to cry about this, this set ending and the arrangement ending and all of it. I know that the success of this arrangement has been in its very clearly defined terms and conditions and also in its agreed-upon ending. That, I believe, was the one way both of us could have given ourselves in the way we both did was because we knew there was an ending we both agreed on. I'll speak for myself and say that knowing there was an ending allowed me to give and take as fully as I would and could without the risk of anything outside of this arrangement being expected. Why not fuck open-heartedly, why not express my every desire, why not say or do anything, why not grab for it all. The very specific parameters contained this, allowed that to be the only limit: this end.

But now that we've been in this room for three days plus the night of transition at the Marina motel I've really dived in and I'm not thinking of anything else really. At this point, I'm just thinking about the fish and the rice. The soup barely scratched the surface of hunger. Finally, here it is, the two bowls piled up with fish on a big bed of rice. I dig in. Bonarh sits patiently. And then it's her turn and my turn and her turn. I lean across the table during this meal and through her shirt I grab the harness and pull Bonarh to me to kiss her. She smiles. This has been a good trip, Bonarh.

The meal is over. Let's get back, maybe take a bath or a shower. Yeah, sounds good. Outside and walking back, just a couple of blocks, it's cold. It's winter now. The little town is quiet on a sunday night. In the room again, the bedding is kind of in a pile half on the bed. A couple dirty plates, the french press still with left-over maté, and pillows seemingly everywhere. Bonarh's wet leggings on the floor. I turn on the gas, re-light the fire, and tonight I shut the blinds over the windows. I turn on the lamps and turn off the overhead light. Bonarh begins to pick some of the stuff off the floor. I pull the blankets up onto the bed.

March 11, 2018:
Dear Bobby:
"Ready?" Bonarh says yes. We've kind of straightened up the room here, picked up plates and blankets from the floor, and put pillows back on the bed and the extras on the chair in the corner. The blinds are closed and only the table side lamps are on, no overhead light. As we walked back from our meal, I said to Bonarh, when we get back to the room, you'll take off the harness. This is what we've been talking about all weekend: this moment.

I won't go into it now, the idea of Bonarh being released, I mean I think it's obvious that's what this has been about, the feeling of freedom that a woman experiences through her own submission, being harnessed, tethered, and restrained; that that restraint results in a spaciousness; that constraint provides expansiveness.

But before we start, Bonarh asks for some water. "I'm so thirsty," she says. "Sure, I mean, I'm sure you're thirsty, the way you've been panting all day, huh?" "Yes," she says, "I'm really thirsty." The agreement is that Bonarh will bring a glass of water to me and ask for water. But she has forgotten, is that why she's standing in front of me, looking like that? "Plus," I add, "the beef broth with seaweed and fish and rice. I'm sure that made you thirsty too." "Yes," she says. I'm standing in the middle of the room with my arms folded across my chest, I'm waiting. Nothing. Finally, I say to prompt Bonarh, "Bonarh, if you want water, fill the glass and bring it over."

Bonarh fills the glass with water and brings it to me. She hands me the glass full of water, then stands in front of me, like she's waiting for me. I throw the glass of water in Bonarh's face. She's surprised. She seems shocked. But Bonarh we've been through this before. Her shirt is wet and her pants too. I hand her the empty glass.

Bonarh fills the glass again. She brings it to me, hands me the glass and says nothing. Ok, I drink the water. I mean, me too, I've been panting all day too. Bonarh is getting pissed, it seems. She fills the glass again. She comes to where I stand and asks, "Are you going to throw that one at me too?"

"Bonarh, take off your clothes." Bonarh removes her wet shirt and hangs it on one of the hangers in the closet (I might mention here that this motel is so nice it has not only a gas fireplace and a little couch but also actual hangers that can be taken off the closet rod, have clothes put on them and then returned to the rod; no weird unhooking the thing) next to her wet leggings from earlier. I drink the water while I watch.

Now, Bonarh stands in front of me wearing my harness, over her shoulders, meeting in a large ring on her solar plexus, two straps then around her ribs and one down the front to a large ring over her clit and mons and then through her legs meeting with a snap, the long strap that comes down her back, and a pair of socks. Oh, Bonarh you look amazing. She brings another glass of water to me, she hands me the glass and I look at her. She says nothing. I bring the glass to my lips, drink half and then quickly throw the rest at Bonarh. I laugh and hand her the glass again. Here, Bonarh, here's the glass. And again. Finally, Bonarh brings the glass and she comes back again and when she hands me the glass this time I just immediately throw it all over Bonarh. "Right til the end; you're gonna start being defiant now?" I ask. "I'm thirsty!" She cries. And I laugh again. "Bonarh, we have an arrangement. You still have the harness on. Bonarh, you said what you wanted was to please me, huh?" "Yes," she says. "Well," I said, "what has pleased me has been you asking for water when you wanted it."

By the time we are finished, Bonarh is soaking wet, her hair is soaking wet, the harness is soaking wet, the floor where she stands, the carpet in the motel room, is quite wet as well. Some has gone in Bonarh's mouth, I drank some more too. Now, Bonarh is standing like this in front of me wearing wet socks and my harness. I ask if she needs more water. She says no, no more water.

I step toward Bonarh, facing Bonarh and very close. "Ready?" she begins to cry and nods her head yes. "Please Bonarh, I want to hear you say it." "Yes," she says, "I'm ready." I reach for the straps of the harness on her shoulders and I grab them and pull her to me tightly. I wrap my arms around her in a big hug. I kiss the side of her head, I say ok then, c'mon.

Bonarh is shivering as I unsnap first the big ring at her clit. The thick wet strap there falls from her cunt, hangs down behind her, off her ass. My eyes are starting to fill now too. I've knelt in front of Bonarh to unsnap this ring and she's put her hands on my shoulders. I kiss her belly as I do, I feel her crying harder now. Standing up then in front of Bonarh, I unsnap the strap at her solar plexus and ease the harness off her shoulders. We look at each other as I do this and I smile though I'm full of tears. Once it's off her shoulders the harness basically falls to the floor and then there is Bonarh, naked before me. Well, naked but for the socks.

But her socks are wet, and what with the crying and water and wet carpet, Bonarh is shivering. I pull her to me again, hold for a few moments then say, "C'mon, let's get in the bath. I pick up the harness and follow Bonarh to the bathroom door, she turns on the water, plugs in the tub and then gets in. I hang the harness on the bathroom door, on the robe hook there. It hangs next to the tub, a visual reminder. When the tub is full, I begin to undress, pulling off engineer boots, thick wool socks and then t-shirt and a-shirt and toss them in a pile on the floor. I unbuckle my belt and unbutton my levis and take them off as well. Now, I'm naked too. I climb over the side of the tub where Bonarh is laying and I straddle both sides of the tub and I say to Bonarh open your mouth and when she does I let forth a stream of piss. All the glasses of water have paid off and quite quickly Bonarh's mouth is full and overflowing. Swallow it, I say, and as Bonarh kind of chokes I keep pissing and I'm covering her head and shoulders and her whole face. "You're a pig for this, Bonarh, a piss pig." She nods yes.

When I'm empty, I lower myself into the hot water and lay next to Bonarh in the bath. I stroke her body as I look at the harness hanging near our heads. It's beautiful I say. "Yes," Bonarh says, "it's holy." Yes, I agree. This leather object which is literal, not metaphor, not a symbol of submission, but worn, an actual act of submission,

Bonarh wearing this yoke while I hold the space for her; both of us tied with this bond, both of us engaged and working, both of us being reined in to this arrangement of providing pleasure.

In a few moments, I get up from the water, stand dripping in the tub over Bonarh and unleash another torrent of piss in her face, in her mouth, on her head. While I do the stream is unbroken without strain and then I'm done. I lean over to kiss Bonarh on the mouth and I step out of the tub, grabbing a towel and going to the other room in front of the gas fire to dry off. Bonarh stays in the tub.

I towel myself off, stare at the fire and then get up and put on my net a-shirt. By now Bonarh is coming from the bathroom, dry and with her hair combed. I go into the bathroom to hang my towel on the rack and to grab the harness from the hook in there. I bring it to the bed and lay it out in the middle, turning down the sheets as if I'm putting the harness to bed. Bonarh gets into the bed and lays on her side facing it. From my bag I grab the dick and other harness and then I too, turn off the light in the bathroom and get in bed.

Both of us are quiet. Now what, I wonder. And then I lay on my back in the bed. I toss the dick and harness to Bonarh and I say put this on. Bonarh gets excited and sits up. She lays out the harness with the dick on the bed, laying out the straps and then positioning herself over it. I've picked up the big harness and I've laid it out across my body, feeling its weight on me and taking the long strap that was between Bonarh's legs, the strap that crossed her cunt and ass, and I put it in my mouth, kind of licking it, sniffing it, tasting it, wanting it, while I watch Bonarh. She squats over the dick and harness and pulls the straps up in the back, slips them through the d-rings on her hips, tightens and adjusts the dick in front and then, to see if she's ready, grabs the dick in her fist and tugs. Oh, Bonarh you look so good.

Lay on your back, I say. And when she does, I add, jack off for me. Bonarh spits in her hand and begins the slow rubbing and pulling of the dick. I'm on my side now, holding the big harness against myself as I watch Bonarh and the dick. She licks her hand now, pulling spit from the back of her mouth to really wet it and then grabs the dick in her fist and jacks it off. It's sexy. She's rolling her hips as she does this, kind of rolling them side to side. She begins to use both hands as well, spitting on her right hand, grabbing the dick on the shaft and with her left she reaches behind the dick to her cunt and sticks her fingers in, then with this wetness, covers the tip of the dick, just the head, which she's rolling between her fingers. She lifts her hips off the bed as well, as if she's pulling herself up by the dick. A rhythm develops of pushing and pulling and licking and sticking and wow, I'm really into this. I'm watching the dick, her hands, her face and her thighs, all of Bonarh and the big harness is between us.

I get up and kneel over Bonarh's head, straddling her face, open your mouth, I say, and then add, I don't want even one drop to spill on the mattress, do you understand? Yes, she nods and I let go another long stream into Bonarh's mouth. This time she swallows as I fill her and when I'm done, I lean down to kiss her.

Then I climb on the dick.

At first, on it, it hurts. I think this won't even work, I don't even want to get fucked. But quickly with her hips rolling slightly, I'm surprised. I'm just sitting still; the dick feels so uncomfortable inside me and I'm starting to hear all that bullshit in my head. Maybe I'm just the kind of woman who doesn't like to get fucked with a dick, maybe there's something wrong with me, maybe I'm just not good enough, and then, fear this is a big mistake. Fear I don't want Bonarh to fuck me, fear I should just get this over with.

Bonarh grabs my nipples at this point and begins to shake them. She's got them hard, squeezing between her fingers and she's using my nipples like handles to shake my tits. This is through the netted a-shirt and the roughness of the net only adds to the painful pleasure and distraction. Bonarh's rolling her hips and shaking my tits and I'm really into this.

I surprise myself when I find I am moving on the dick. I put my hands on Bonarh's shoulders and lean forward, tilting my hips and really allowing the dick in, taking the dick in. Leaned forward like this, my face is close to Bonarh's. Bonarh isn't thrusting the dick in and out, just rolling her hips and now it's a slow churning of my cunt. Bonarh's got it going around and I'm, I mean there's no other word for it, I'm riding the dick. Bonarh is now flicking my nipples, pulling them between thumb and forefinger bent and pulling them as far as she can until despite her tight pinch my nipples slip from her grip and my breasts fall back to my chest and she begins again. It's sublime.

I sit up right on Bonarh's hips with the dick deep inside my cunt and Bonarh's still rolling her hips. I brace my thighs against Bonarh's sides and I start to rub my clit. My clit is hard and swollen, pulled tight with the dick inside and I'm pressing and rubbing in a circle and looking at Bonarh and Bonarh takes her hands and opens them flat and slaps my bare thighs with her palms. Ooh, yes. She does it again and again. My thighs jump with color and blaze red. I fall forward again, now just left hand on Bonarh's shoulder and she again grabs my tits, pulling shaking pinching being quite rough and hard. Oooh yes. I want this. This is what I want.

The idea of myself is as a woman. It's important for me, politically, to identify as such, as a woman, to be vocal and explicit about my femaleness and woman-ness. But I don't usually feel like a woman. Is that not what it means to be a woman? To not have a knowledge what it feels like to be a woman?

But then suddenly, on the dick on her hips, moving the way I was moving, really riding her and my hips and thighs and tits and cunt in on it, I feel like a sexy woman. I use that word internally not externally, I mean the reason I put on the netted a-shirt was that looking at my physical body, looking at myself, it didn't look sexy, but scrawny and thin and flat. But internally, in myself, I felt like a woman, like I was getting fucked and going for it in my body and that all the uncomfortableness of getting fucked fell away or left and this good feeling was what remained.

I don't come on the dick but rolled off and lay on my back next to Bonarh. I'm still rubbing my clit, hard. Get up on top of me, I say, sit up on my chest. Bonarh straddles me and pins me tight with her thighs and my arms are pinned to my sides. The dick is between my breasts and I'm jacking off. Bonarh puts her hands on my shoulders, leans down and kisses me, filling my mouth with her tongue and I come, shaking and heaving beneath her. She stretches out on top of me and we lay like that.

Later, when we get up, there's blood on the front of my netted shirt. I go into the bathroom and take off the shirt and with cold water and bar soap wash the shirt. Bonarh comes in behind me and we are both in front of the sink in front of the mirror. She says, "25 years." "huh?" I ask. "It took me 25 years," she says, "to come with a dick inside me." I laugh. "Oh, I guess I have a ways to go." I'm thinking I should be able to come after being fucked with a dick 25 times, though if it were that many, I'd be surprised. But I was surprised tonight.

Back in the bed, my netted shirt hung with Bonarh's wet clothes in the closet, I place the big harness at our feet. We roll over together and for the first time I feel Bonarh's belly against my back. It's a good good feeling to feel her actual naked body against mine as we lay together. Rolling over, the feeling of being actually closer to Bonarh as I held her from behind as we slept. No buckles, no rings no leather straps which did make it difficult to sleep with her.

As we turn out the bedside lamps and settle under the sheepskins and blankets, between the sheets, Bonarh says something which I don't catch. Huh? She says, using the format, "I have fear that you were just into the harness being worn by me. I have fear you've never been into me." Did I say I've been into your submission, before I fell asleep. Or I've been into you wanting to please me. Or did I just pull her close, skin to skin.

In the morning we wake early. Too early for me, but we both have to work later this afternoon. We have to drive back to San Francisco. By the time I open my eyes Bonarh's out of bed and has started packing her things and getting the rest of everything ready to go. I do the steps, of course, then Bonarh makes me coffee. I get out of bed soon after and begin to get my things together, to dress, and the rest. But before I get up, I'm watching Bonarh move about the room in her dress.

Even clothed it's obvious Bonarh is un-harnessed. Her body seems completely different, the way she's moving, it's like I don't recognize her at all almost. For these months, at first, the first few times I saw Bonarh wearing the harness, I'd be surprised, it not quite being in my consciousness and so I'd be surprised to feel it when I pulled her close and then surprised again at how I didn't remember she was wearing it. Or I'd meet her and see just the edge of the strap on her shoulder through the neck of a t-shirt and I'd excite.

Then every time, always, seeing Bonarh in my harness, or reading of Bonarh's experience of being in my harness, of being harnessed, notes written to me describing her own adventures and understandings of being in this harness, her own understandings of her submission; seeing Bonarh against trees, on deserted piers, in museums, on the street, was sublime pleasure. Bonarh, your fierce desire and powerful expression of such, not a theory but lived; your careful care of the harness and acceptance of it fully ("It's on me, in my bed with me or in my gold bag being carried by me. I mean, I'm basically with your harness full-time."): all of it, all of it. Watching you and your body move harnessed was always so pleasing; my harness, your body, to please me.

From the bed then, I tell Bonarh to come lay back down so I can fuck her. Pull off your dress. She does and lays down and I pull the tampon from her cunt. I fuck her. We cry and we're naked and then we kiss and she comes. It's sweet.

Then it's time to get dressed and get ready. We set a goal for what time we want to be on the road. I'm sitting on the little couch and I ask Bonarh to make me a final cup of coffee. I'm watching her; she's wearing her dress again, a black wool short dress with short sleeves. It's like a sweater but a tight sweater. She's standing near the counter with the electric kettle. She has her back to me but then looks over her shoulder and when our eyes meet, I say, lift the dress, just the right side. Bonarh does, pulls the dress up her ass to her hip and she kind of cocks her hip to the side when she does.

I don't even know if I can explain what I want here: everything that was amazing about Bonarh in the harness, undone revealed, unharnessed is better. I'm thinking, how could just a few straps, how could the harness have covered up so much of this gorgeous body, a few strips of leather, I mean, it didn't actually go over her ass or waist at all.

Oooh, Bonarh that dress is really sexy, if the result of the harness being taken off is you wearing this dress, well, come over here. I'm on the little couch in front of the gas fire. Bonarh stands in front of me, facing away from me, toward the fire, while I caress her hips and thighs and pet the dress. Then I lift the dress past her waist and she wags her fucking mother fucking ass in my lap. My desire is fierce. Insanely fierce, dangerously fierce. Her ass is rubbing on the front of my unbuttoned levis while I hold her dress up to her waist. "This is how I wanted to dance with you at the club," she says and though I have no idea what she's talking about, what club, I lean in and bite her beautiful waist, so possessive is my desire and especially at this moment when I'm being especially conscious of not expressing ownership or claim over Bonarh. But the idea that she would dance like this with me at a club enflames me like feeding her in public. I'm hot and I'm hard and my head is spinning. And the experience of Bonarh moving unharnessed, unfettered, freely was so beautiful, especially as she was moving, wagging, shaking, posing, in continued desire to please me, for my pleasure. I leaned back, elbows on the bed behind me while Bonarh on my lap, looked over her shoulder at me. Yes.

And then we are carrying our bags to the big truck, loading them in the back. We check the room, double check the room, make sure nothing's forgotten. Bonarh is going to drive and we climb up into the front. I'm mostly at this point trying to figure out what to say, to not cry. We're laughing though, and eating the rest of the snacks, I'm feeding Bonarh crackers and chips and nuts as she drives. We're listening to the radio as we go north through Sunnyvale, with the volume turned up high. I'm singing along to the pop songs I love, smiling. Really, I say, I don't want this ride to end.

The traffic is heavy but moving quickly, Bonarh really has to drive this thing. I piss in a large mason jar, pulling my levis down in the front seat and squatting over the mouth of the jar. Bonarh is wondering what she could ever tell her friends about this whole everything. I hold the jar to her lips while she drives, I pour the piss in her mouth and say, "Tell them 'I drank her piss willingly and also, she spit a mouthful of piss in my face as I drove.'" I leaned over then, drank a mouthful and spit the piss in Bonarh's face. I grabbed her clit in my fist and said, "I want this. This is what I want' and Bonarh pulled the dress up over her hips and sat her naked ass back on the driver's seat. We're going at least 65mph and the music is blaring loud. I pull on Bonarh's clit with my hand and pull her to come. She comes in my hand and then I put my handkerchief over her cunt and do it again, pull her to orgasm again and she comes in my handkerchief and then I slap her pussy with my open palm and turn the volume even louder. The big truck's speakers pound and Bonarh throws her head back, yelling. No harness, she's giving it all to me, full of her own volition and submission to whatever I want, wherever I want it. I want this.

We're near the city now, next exit and we're off, driving to my apartment. As I get out, I say to Bonarh, I'll let go of what I've been holding, no cording, no tying, no trying, no bargaining. I haven't made any claims on you consciously which is why your submission has been so sweet, so generous. "It's been of my own volition," she says. Yes. And as I get out, I don't leave anything behind: no handkerchief, no little piece of driftwood I picked up on Marina Beach the first morning and thought to slip into her bag before I left, no note, nothing.

I drop the holding and walk away.

Canela stays at a friend's house the first night I'm back, to let me get acclimated or just have some space. By the next morning though, I'm missing her here at home. She comes back that night, the next night and I say to her when she comes to bed, thank you for being my friend, Canela. She says, "I've never had a friend like this, consciousness-changing." I turn out the light and we go to sleep.

Telling this story, as you have permitted, has lightened me. And of course, here we are again at the bottom of the page and this letter is also ending where it began: all the trying, all the wanting to convey, the did I say enough, the did I say too much. But also, when this queer object—messy, mistakes, typos, typewritten love sent description of sex magick, tactile and hand-held—is held by you, I'm grateful.

Denise Conca is a writer and cashier living and working in San Francisco, California.

Made in the USA
Monee, IL
20 July 2020